Book design by Dana Bryan

ISBN 978-1-54396-816-3 (Paperback)
ISBN 978-1-54396-817-0 (Ebook)

Published by Bookbaby Publishing
www.bookbaby.com

DANNY SMASHED

Tony Sawicki

Gregory Mantore

Published by BookBaby

PROLOGUE

Los Angeles, CA. Four years ago...

Kenneth Shapiro, Hollywood super agent, looked up at the green and white striped ceiling in the Polo Lounge of the Beverly Hills Hotel. He had his own theory regarding the inspiration behind the color scheme. This was a room where LA powerbrokers, Hollywood hotshots, movie moguls and acclaimed celebrities routinely consummated multi-million, even billion dollar deals. In his mind, the restaurant's green and white design represented the color of money.

Kenneth was alone at the white clothed table, and became aware of the young superstar's arrival when all heads in the dining room turned. Some watched with envy as the spectacularly handsome twenty year old ignored the wait staff and strode confidently through the restaurant. Some watched with lust as the young actor moved with masculine, athletic grace among the tables. Others saw dollar signs, imagining inking a deal with Hollywood's newest red-hot property. A very few, like the aging pop star holding court at center table, were too self absorbed to even notice.

With decidedly un-star like aplomb, Danny plopped into a seat beside Kenneth and grabbed a menu from the table.

"I'm starving," he said, looking directly into Kenneth's ardent eyes. His focus then moved to the menu and he seemed apathetic about his reason for being there.

"I don't know how you can even think about food," Kenneth said.

"We're in a restaurant," Danny answered simply.

"People don't necessarily come here to eat," Kenneth answered. "They come here to make deals. And we're about to make the biggest deal of your career."

"I got it Kenneth. I'm not totally new to this game. I appreciate all the work you did putting this deal together and I'm looking forward to meeting Trent and his agent. But I'm freaking hungry. And people *do* come here to eat because the food is fantastic."

Kenneth was a shark whose emotions rarely on registered on his face, but even the waiters across the room could sense that he was lovestruck.

"I'm gonna have the Kobe burger," Danny decided. "Extra cheese." He tossed his menu back onto the table. Kenneth nodded and stood as Trenton Cash and his agent, John Sparrow, approached. John accepted a handshake from Kenneth while keeping a proprietary eye on his immensely famous young client. With a string of hit songs that each had over five million downloads, Trenton Cash was currently the nation's biggest pop sensation. Danny and Trent exchanged a bro-hug and the four men settled into their chairs.

Trent immediately began examining his menu as the agents launched into the terms of a lucrative deal that had been brokered by super-mogul Amy Price and hammered out over the past few weeks.

"I'm assuming Danny's already aware of the agreed upon terms," John said, smoothing an imaginary wrinkle from his Loro Piana jacket.

"Yes. Main sticking point is that Danny is consenting to second billing under Trent but he gets gross points in the movie," Kenneth answered coolly.

John's smile was predatory. "That works for us. Danny gets the money, Trent gets the billing. My client's main goal right now is to move from music into film."

Kenneth nodded. "*Trust Fund* will be a perfect vehicle for him," he said, sipping from a glass of mineral water. "This movie is a slam dunk guaranteed hit. Hollywood's hottest young actor and the world's biggest pop icon starring in a film adapted from a best selling book. There's a built in audience in the tens of millions."

Trent and Danny looked at each other and exchanged a fist bump over the white clothed table.

"Go us!" Trent said.

"For sure," Danny agreed with a smile that was familiar to millions. "Are we ready to order lunch now?"

The agents both nodded curtly, and perfunctorily tossed their menus on the table. A waiter appeared soundlessly.

"Are you gentlemen ready to order?" The waiter was a middle-aged man with indistinct features and took their orders with professional detachment, but appeared unable to stop himself from sneaking a few glances in Danny's direction.

"I love you in *Mission Bay*," he said sycophantically as he collected the menus. "That is my favorite TV show. I've seen every episode."

Danny grinned. "Thanks, man!"

"Yes, thank you very much," Kenneth said curtly, cueing the waiter that his welcome at the table was already overstayed.

Danny and Trent heartily wolfed down their lunches, ostensibly unaware that their every bite was garnering the attention of watchful and covetous eyes all over the restaurant. The agents nibbled at salads and sipped mineral water.

When lunch was over, John ordered a bottle of Billecart to toast the deal. Danny and Trent guzzled the expensive champagne, washing down their deserts. The agents each took a mere few sips as Kenneth read a text from the screen of his perpetually buzzing phone.

"Paparazzi alert, boys," he announced to the table. "Somehow word got out of a power meeting with Danny Smash and Trenton Cash here at the Polo Lounge. It seems there's not only a crowd of photographers out front, but a big mob of fans as well."

Danny and Trent looked at each other and shrugged conspiratorially as the agents stood from the table, each one already on his phone. The four power players made their way out of the dining room.

"It's a good thing I'm not one of those egomaniac artists," Trent said to Danny as they walked toward the entrance. "Cause I notice that when you're in the room, hardly anybody gives me a second glance."

Danny smiled enigmatically. "C'mon Trent. That's just 'cause we're in a room full of stuffed shirts. If it was teenaged girls, I'm sure the situation would be reversed."

Trent shrugged. "Yeah, I might have the teenaged girls. But you've got the teenaged girls, their boyfriends and their moms."

"Oh jeez," Danny advised him. "Just enjoy your fame. Don't compare yourself to people around you. In this town you could drive yourself crazy that way." A small crowd of industry types and hotel guests loitered at the front door. Danny looked up as a tall, bald youngish dude dressed in the style of a Brooklyn hipster approached with an outstretched hand.

"Casey Spriggs." The young man introduced himself proudly. "I loved your work in *Grunge*."

"Uh, thanks," Danny said.

"You costarred with Kayla Asimov, who I know very well. I directed her in *Acid Wash*."

Realization washed over Danny. Casey Spriggs was a hot young director from New York who made smart, edgy films with top actors like James River and Matt McCrew.

"Oh man, I loved that movie," Danny said with genuine enthusiasm. "Your work is fantastic."

Kenneth had terminated his phone call and was now monitoring Danny's conversation with the intensity of a mother lioness watching over a prized cub.

"Then we're mutual admirers of each other because I find your work to be fantastic as well," Casey said without so much as a glance at Kenneth, who was attempting to wedge himself into the conversation. "The chemistry between you and Kayla onscreen absolutely crackled. I'd love to work with you at some point."

Kenneth inhaled sharply and inserted an outstretched hand in Casey's direction. "I'm Kenneth Shapiro. Danny's agent. I believe we met at the Cohen's party in Malibu."

The director quickly eyed Kenneth up and down. "Yes of course," he lied. Turning back to Danny, he said, "It was nice meeting you. As they say here in Hollywood, let's do lunch sometime." Then, with a wink, Casey ducked through the door and disappeared into the bright California sunshine.

Outside, a long portico whose green and white ceiling echoed the restaurant's interior, led from the front door to the valet, which at the moment was obscured by a relatively well-behaved crowd of fans. The agents hung back as their stars headed out to greet admirers and to start promoting the new film. The appearance of Trenton Cash elicited immediate shrieks, screams, and hysteria. When the crowd saw Danny Smash right behind Trent, they went absolutely wild.

At least one hundred people, mostly young females but of varying ages and genders, waited in the area where the portico met the parking lot. Members of the press corps, no doubt tipped off by Hollywood's non-stop publicity machine, jockeyed with the fans. The golden rays of California sunshine and the enthusiasm of the crowd created the mood of a festive summer event, and Danny and Trent began greeting the crowd in a friendly, upbeat fashion.

"Got to push our new movie, bro," Trent whispered knowingly. "Talk it up."

Cell phones snapped and recorded as the pair of young idols signed autographs, posed for pictures, and answered interview questions, repeatedly mentioning their new movie collaboration. The crowd continued to grow as word spread that Danny and Trent were making themselves accessible to fans.

Two police cars, lights flashing, pulled slowly into the parking lot and stopped at the curb.

"Oh, man. Thank God for the Beverly Hills PD," Trent whispered to Danny. "This crowd is a getting a little crazy." He then smiled charismatically and resumed signing autographs.

Two police officers exited their car and began moving through the crowd, telling people to please step back. Ignoring Trent, the officers walked purposefully toward Danny.

"Daniel Briggs?" The cop addressed Danny aggressively. His tone was not a question, but an accusation.

Danny's jaw dropped. The megawatt smile melted from his face, replaced by an expression of disbelief.

"Uh, yes." He stammered.

"Mr. Briggs, we are placing you under arrest."

The other cop stepped behind Danny and handcuffed him brusquely as the press and dozens of fans silently recorded every second from every angle.

Watching from a distance of a mere few feet, Trent was immobilized. "What the fuck?" He mouthed.

"What are you idiots doing?" Kenneth Shapiro barreled down the portico as if he'd been shot from a canon. "Do you realize who you're dealing with?" Kenneth's tone was at once furious and whiney. "I don't know what's going on here, but you're making a big mistake. Huge."

The officers ignored Kenneth and began escorting Danny to the squad car as the crowd parted to let them pass. Every second was being recorded. Kenneth followed behind and reached for the arresting officer's arm.

The cop stopped instantly and turned with ferocity toward Kenneth. "Sir, I am going to forget you just touched me. Back off right now before I book you for assault and for interfering with a police matter."

Kenneth withered spinelessly and stepped obediently away from the officers. The cop read Danny his Miranda rights and unceremoniously deposited Hollywood's hottest superstar in the back seat of a late model squad care.

BOOK ONE

Bitter Springs, Arizona. Twelve Years Ago ...

Bitter Springs, Arizona, is a dusty, scrubby, sunbaked desert town located about fifty miles from nowhere in the northernmost part of the state. On its outskirts, thirty-plus people live in seclusion on a commune called the Painted Desert Farm. Unbound by the rules, regulations, or taxes afflicting society at large, it was a haven for nonconformists to escape the restrictions imposed by modern civilization.

Lucille Briggs arrived at the commune with her nine year-old son Danny at her side. She and the golden haired, green-eyed boy had emerged from the cab of a dusty blue pickup truck. Lucille, her youthful beauty undiminished by the disheveled clothing or the unruly state of her hair and makeup, carried one large, battered suitcase. As soon as she slammed the door of the truck, it pulled away. Neither she nor the driver looked back or waved.

An unpaved, packed dirt road led to a well-maintained gate made of raw timber and heavy gauge wire. An artisan crafted wooden sign, neatly hung in the center of the gate, warned that trespassers were unwelcome. The farm was encircled by ocotillo cactus, whose bright red flowers attracted hummingbirds and whose sharp spines acted as natural fencing that prevented coyotes, javelina hogs, and other uninvited visitors from breeching the property. Lucille pushed through the heavy gate, dragging one piece of luggage. The suitcase was white, battered, and had Lucille's name written all over it in pencil. Following closely behind, her little boy clung to her hand with a tight grip. This was yet another new environment for the child. He trailed Lucille as she slowly followed a wide, winding path that was bordered by natural stone formations, flowering cacti, and lush Indian paintbrush plants. The air quality here was cleaner and less oppressive than back in Vegas, but the desert heat made breathing more difficult. Dragging the heavy suitcase rendered Lucille short of breath. But her mood was bright. She felt particularly fine, even though she hadn't taken her medication since embarking on this new venture two days ago.

The path emerged onto a flat, open area of cultivated land surrounded by mesquite and silk trees, flowering desert willows, avocado and fig trees. Several men and women with sun browned skin, scant clothing, and wide brimmed hats worked among what appeared to be a thriving fruit and vegetable garden with chickens darting among the plants. A network of irrigation troughs branched from a large, hand powered water pump in the center of the field. Lucille stopped, her shallow breath caught in her throat by the beauty and geometry of what she now beheld. She had heard of this Shangri-La, and now she was here! Her eyes fixated on the water that poured from the pump and through the troughs in the land, vibrant, shimmering shades of silver and gold that seemed to reach out and welcome her.

A woman who had been crouched down, digging in the earth, looked up from her work and stood to face Lucille. The woman approached with an expression of wary suspicion. As she walked to where Danny and Lucille stood, she gruffly pulled off her gloves and eyed Lucille's suitcase.

"Um, I'm Lucille. This is my little son Danny."

The woman's hostile expression shifted to curious bewilderment as she took in Lucille's nearly vacant expression, unruly hair, and unkempt clothing.

"Are you expected?" The woman asked. "Malchus didn't mention anything about any visitors today."

Lucille continued to stare vacantly. Then she cocked her head as a thought seemed to germinate within her mind. "Malchus?" Her head continued to swivel, her eyes moving as if asking the sky for an answer.

"Okay Lucille," the woman said in a measured and careful tone. "I'm going to take you to Malchus now. I have no idea why you're here, but you can sort that out with him."

She led them along a path that bordered the garden and into a simple, unadorned wood planked building with small windows and doors on each side. The interior was filled with round wooden tables, all now empty. Two men were mopping the stone floor.

"Have a seat and I'll find Malchus," she instructed. "In the meantime, if anyone questions you, tell them Ellie told you to stay right here."

Lucille took a chair. Her eyes fixated on the door through which the woman had disappeared. He son sat dutifully beside her, and she patted his head like a puppy.

Very soon, after the woman left, she reappeared with a tall, robust looking man who appeared to be only slightly older than Lucille. His arms were coppery tan and he wore a straw, fedora style hat that shielded a pale, featureless face and cadaverous dull blue eyes. He wore a faded denim button down shirt cut off at the sleeves, cargo shorts, and sandals.

He stalked to the table where Lucille and Danny were seated with an angry gait. His eyes bored into Lucille's.

"Did you not see the 'no trespassing' sign on the front of the gate?" he demanded angrily.

Lucille was unfazed by the man's anger, and stared at him blankly. Finally she said, "I learned about this place at the clinic. A lady in the waiting room told me all about your Painted Desert Farm."

The man exchanged a dubious glance with Ellie. In return, Ellie silently mouthed the words: *she's crazy*.

Lucille continued to stare vacantly. "As soon as I heard about you," she finally continued, "I took my little boy Danny and hitch-hiked up here."

At the mention of his name, Danny squirmed in his seat. The man's eyes turned to the boy as if noticing him for the first time. He took in Danny's unruly nest of golden blonde hair, his healthy complexion, and his bright green eyes. He seemed to stare for a long time as Danny folded his hands in his lap and looked down at them. The man's previously angry countenance appeared to soften.

"Hi Danny," he finally said. "My name is Malchus. Are you hungry?"

The little boy nodded shyly.

"Ellie, go get them some food," he ordered.

The thin, leathery woman scurried away. Five minutes later, Ellie returned with two plastic trays. Each held a generous abundance of food. Fresh fruits, a hunk of homemade bread with jam and butter, and scrambled eggs along with tall glasses of orange juice were placed before Danny and Lucille.

Danny's eyes widened at the sight of the food. He dug right in.

Lucille stared at her plate and then began eating tiny bites of egg. As she as her son ate, Malchus and Ellie stepped out of earshot.

"That woman is crazy," Ellie whispered to Malchus. "And little boys eat a lot of food. We can't keep them here."

Malchus raised an eyebrow. "If I say they stay here, then they stay here," he told her with firm impatience.

Ellie bent her head submissively. "But Malchus," she pleaded. "Everyone here has to carry their own weight. How are we going to take care of that crazy lady and raise a child? I know we don't want to draw attention to ourselves, but we really need to alert the authorities. I think …"

Malchus cut her off sharply. "I don't care what you think, Ellie. I make the decisions here and I do not recall soliciting your advice." Malchus' voice was calm, stern and without empathy. "I own this farm and this property and everyone who lives here exists by my rules. Don't question me again or you will no longer be welcome on this commune."

Ellie bent her head. "I understand, Malchus. My apologies."

"When they're done eating, I want you to take the boy outside," he told her. "Give him a tour of the farm. I'm going to talk to the mother."

In the brief span of their conversation, the little boy had hungrily completed his entire breakfast. He obediently followed Ellie into the sunshine.

Lucille was still slowly eating when Malchus sat opposite her at the table. He addressed her as though speaking with a small and not terribly intelligent child.

"Lucille," he said to her.

She looked up at him and then her focus darted back down at her food. She was unable to maintain eye contact.

"Lucille, does anyone know you are here?" He asked.

She shook her head vehemently. Her unruly, unkempt and straggly hair fell into her face and she did nothing to remove it.

"You said you hitchhiked here, yes?"

Lucille nodded, her head jerking up and down quickly.

"Where did you hitchhike from Lucille?"

Lucille didn't answer but kept nodding.

"Lucille, you need to answer my questions," Malchus's voice was calm and controlled. He sensed that this woman could detonate at any moment. "Unless you answer my questions, I will have no choice but to call the police and have you removed as a trespasser."

Lucille's head shook vehemently. "No. No. No. I will answer. We came from Vegas. Pretty lights but very scary."

"Okay Lucille. So you left Vegas. Did you have any family there?"

Lucille shook her head "No. No family."

"Does Danny have grandparents? Or aunts or uncles or cousins?"

Lucille's head continued to shake. "No. We are alone. Just my boy and me."

"And what about Danny's father? Where is he?"

Lucille stopped shaking her head and stared vacantly across the room, her mouth still chewing. "I don't know," she said vacantly. "Don't know who he is."

Malchus stood. "Okay Lucille," he told her. "If what you say is true, I will consider letting you and Danny stay here. But I will need some proof that you are who and what you say."

Lucille had left her suitcase by the door. She shuffled over to it, then picked it up and carried it to Malchus.

"All the papers are in here," she told him, still unable to establish eye contact. Her voice was a desperate plea. "My cards and identification. The boy's certificate. Have it. Just let us stay."

"Finish your breakfast, Lucille. Take a walk around the farm. Maybe the desert air will clear your head a bit. Later today I will let you know my decision."

* * * * *

Malchus ruffled Danny's hair. His fingers affectionately stroked the sleeping boy's thick yellow-gold locks. "Did you have a good night's sleep?" he asked. Danny nodded sluggishly. "It's you're birthday," Malchus said cheerfully. "Thirteen is a big year!"

"Can I miss out on my lessons today, Malchus?" Danny asked hopefully.

"'Fraid not, buddy," Malchus place a hand on the boy's shoulder. "Even though you're smarter than anyone on this farm, your lessons go on as scheduled. You get off Saturday and Sunday."

Danny groaned. "I sure wish I could go to a real school with other kids." He threw the sheet off himself and swung his legs over the side of the bed, sitting up. His body was filling out with coltish, muscular curves, his skin shone with a healthy glow, and his face grew handsomer each day. None of this was lost on Malchus.

"We've gone through this so many times before," he told Danny with a smile of dramatized exasperation. "Nobody here can enroll you in public school except for your mother. And you know she really isn't able to do that."

Danny's smiling and usually happy-go-lucky expression clouded momentarily. "Um hmm," he nodded. "It would just be nice to have some other kids for friends."

Malchus held out his hands and shrugged in a *what can I do?* expression. "It's true that there have never been any kids for you to play with. But you have so many animals to keep you company here on the farm and you always seem to be having a good time with them. And plus, you're constantly on that laptop I bought for you, watching movies and talking with kids all over the world."

Danny glanced at the floor. "It's not the same though, Malchus," he said sadly.

"We must learn to look at the bright side of things," Malchus exhorted. "You've got run of the entire farm, lots of people here who watch over you, many friends on the internet … and you've got me. I will always take care of you and will always be here for you."

Danny's expression perked up. "I guess so. Thanks, Malchus."

"I have a cake for you," Malchus said. "And birthday presents, of course. That's something to look forward to after your lessons and chores."

Danny smiled. He yawned, stood, peeled off his tee shirt, and padded into down the short hallway toward the bathroom. "How about my mom?" He asked Malchus, almost as an afterthought.

"She's been wandering in the desert since early this morning. She took off almost as soon as the sun was up. If you can find her and convince her come back, she is welcome to join us for your party."

Danny sighed. He had long since given up on trying to convince Malchus to seek medical attention for his mother's mental illness. As he did almost every day, he went through his lessons and farm chores with Lucille weighing heavily in the back of his mind.

She spent her days wandering mindlessly around the farm and in the surrounding desert, where the dangers were myriad. There were poisonous snakes, scorpions, roving packs of coyotes and wild boar, not to mention searing heat, all of which completely failed to register in Lucille's clouded mind.

Just before dinner, Danny headed into the desert to find her. As he left the farm, the path leading into the desert opened up, and the grounds grew wilder and less cultivated. Having spent the past four years on the farm, Danny knew every rocky outcrop, every gully, and every towering cactus within a several mile radius. He ran through the desert, scanning the horizon with his eyes and calling for his mother until there was only place left that she was likely to be. Danny headed toward the Sacred Datura patch in a run, his mind filled with apprehension as he remembered Ellie's lesson, years back, about this place and the plant that grew here.

"This," Ellie had explained to Danny, "is a very dangerous area. These plants are called Sacred Datura. Some people also call it Devil's Weed. All I can advise you is to stay away from here!"

"Why is it dangerous?" Danny had asked shyly, his sharp mind missing nothing, his inquisitiveness knowing no bounds as his eyes examined the round, prickly, porcupine-like fruits of the Sacred Datura.

"Well, this plant is highly poisonous," Ellie had explained. "Eating it is very bad for your brain. It can cause you to see things that aren't there. It can kill you. This is basically a weed that is very common to the area, but it is also famous for being very toxic. Even the animals know to avoid it. We have a doctor here on the farm who uses plants and herbs to cure sickness and who sometimes uses the plant for medications, but even *he* has to be very careful with it."

"Just beyond this area is a ravine," Ellie had explained further. "It's a very steep cliff and a very long drop to the bottom, which is all rocks at the edge of the river. It comes upon you pretty suddenly, so you definitely don't want to be wandering around out here."

Yet this was exactly where Danny now found his mother. From a distance, he could see that she was eating the fruit of the Sacred Datura!

"Mom!" he screamed, his voice filled with panic. He ran as fast as his legs could move. "Put that down! It can kill you!"

As he neared her, he could see that her eyes were wide and bloodshot, her pupils dilated. He reached to grab the fruit from her but tripped on loose rock, landing hard on his knees. Lucille tore away from him.

"Mom, come back!" he screamed in desperation. Lucille stopped suddenly, looking around the sky as if she'd heard a voice cry out from the heavens.

"It's my birthday!" His fear was elevating. Lucille may have consumed a fatal dose of the plant! He had to get her to doctor. "Please come back to the farm and have some cake with me! Please!"

He began stepping slowly toward her.

"What is happening to me?" Lucille mumbled, fear filling her barely audible voice. She grabbed her throat and began stumbling backwards.

"Mom!" Danny screamed. "You ate the poison! We have to get you to the doctor! Come with me, please!" He reached a hand out to her.

Still clutching her throat Lucille stumbled wildly backwards, crashing though a thicket of hopbush. Danny pushed through the thick scrub and noted with horror that Lucille had reached the edge of a ravine. Her body had begun convulsing. She jerked backwards. Spittle drooled from her mouth. Danny watched in shocked panic as Lucille somersaulted into the canyon.

Tears already streaming down his face, Danny ran to the edge of cliff, dropped to his knees, and peered apprehensively over the side. Dread filled every molecule of his being as he watched the unthinkable as if in slow motion. Lucille's body plummeted down the steep, rocky cliff face, bouncing precipitously from rocks and outcroppings and looking more like a falling ragdoll then a real human being. She landed with a solid thud on a massive boulder bordering the river, her legs at odd angles to her body. Suddenly, all was still. Time came to a standstill as Danny stared in shock at his mother's broken, unmoving body.

He was aware of a hand resting on his shoulder, finally pulling him gently backwards.

"She's gone Danny," Malchus said softly. "You tried to save her but your mother was a very ill woman and this is not your fault. There's nothing we can do."

Malchus led him from the edge of the ravine. Danny's sobs became uncontrollable. Malchus held him in a close embrace and tenderly stroked his hair. Finally the convulsive sobs grew muted. Malchus pulled Danny into a standing position and draped his arm protectively over the teenager, who was already almost as tall as an average adult. Together, they returned to the farm.

By the time they reached the residential compound, a cluster of rusty, rundown trailers and small clay houses, Danny was crippled with overwhelming grief. To the concerned residents of the farm, who looked on but said nothing when Malchus put up his palm to warn them away, the stumbling boy appeared dazed, distraught and tearful. Malchus led him to the trailer he used to share with Lucille and sat him on the bed, instructing him to lie down.

"I'll be right back," he promised. "I'm not leaving you alone tonight."

Minutes later Malchus returned, proffering a glass of water and two tiny white pills.

"Take these, Danny," he instructed. "They'll help relax you. Help you feel better."

Malchus led Danny to bed, and as the boy's muscles loosened and became rubbery, removed his shirt and his jeans and gently tucked him under the covers.

"I'll be back to check on you in a little bit," he whispered softly into the boy's ear.

Danny was in a semi-conscious state, a light sleep, when Malchus returned. He was not aware of the rustling of clothes as Malchus disrobed, nor was he initially aware when Malchus slipped into the bed beside him. He became cognizant only when Malchus' body was pressing unwelcomingly against his own.

And before Danny even knew what was happening, on the night of his thirteenth birthday and on the eve of his mother's death, the violation began.

* * * * *

Danny awoke feeling groggy. His first memory was of Malchus pulling off his underwear, and feeling him with his hands and mouth. Danny had never before been touched in that way. Feelings of violation, nausea, and shame washed over him. As his mind cleared, the horrific image of his mother tumbling over the cliff and falling to her death in the ravine came crashing back into his consciousness.

He flung his covers away and jumped from the bed. His mother was still at the bottom of the ravine! Maybe she had somehow survived the fall. He ran to find help.

Malchus was sitting at the tiny table in the trailer's galley kitchen reading his tablet. Danny stopped abruptly upon seeing the man who had debased him the night before.

"Good morning, Danny," Malchus said calmly. He stood from the table, went to the refrigerator, poured a glass of orange juice and proffered it to the boy.

"I remember what you did to me last night, Malchus," Danny said bitterly as hazy images from the night before filled his mind.

Malchus placed the glass of orange juice gently on the table and languidly sat down. He regarded the boy warmly.

Danny rubbed his temples. He had a terrible headache. He wanted the orange juice, but would take nothing from Malchus.

"I was just trying to comfort you last night Danny," the man said calmly. "You were consumed by your grief. We gave each other pleasure."

Danny grimaced. "I want my mother!" He demanded impetuously. Malchus regarded him mournfully. "Your mother is gone, Danny. You saw her fall into the ravine yesterday."

"Maybe she didn't die!" Danny's tone was desperate and pleading. "She could be alive! Call an ambulance! Call the police!"

Malchus leaned casually back in the banquet seat and crossed his arms over his chest. "What would we tell the police, Danny? That you chased your mother into the desert and caused her to fall over the cliff?"

"I did not," Danny screamed. Tears were forming in his eyes. "You said yourself that I tried to save her! You saw it!"

"I saw you reach for her, Danny. She was backing up from you. That's why she fell. Should I tell that to the police?"

"Tell them whatever you want," Danny spat as snot poured from his nose and tears ran down his face. "I'll tell them what you did to me!"

Malchus' smile was patient and knowing. "That will just sound like the ravings of an angry boy, Danny, and no one here will corroborate your story. If they want to stay on this farm, that is."

Danny stood staring as Malchus continued. "Everyone, including you, has it very good here. You have plenty of food, a comfortable place to sleep, and days filled with easy sunshine. I can guarantee that life wouldn't be so easy in a disgusting federal group home, which is exactly where you'll end up if you decide to go to the police."

Danny remained still.

"Nothing terrible has happened to you, Danny. I love you like a son and treat you with gentleness and kindness. I've protected you and cared for you the entire time you've been here. If you want to know what true abuse is, go ahead and call the police. You'll be placed in an institutionalized home and you will really know about cruelty and mistreatment. And if you don't believe me, go on the computer I bought you and look it up. Google 'group homes.'"

Danny hung his head in defeat. He reached for the orange juice and slinked from the kitchen, hopeless with a suffocating despair that he had never before known, and feeling more trapped than one of the farm hogs just before it was brought to slaughter.

*   *   *   *   *

Darlene's slender fingers worked the cash register at the Tuba City Supply Depot. It was Saturday afternoon. A steady flow of customers, many of them Navajo Indians from all over Arizona's Coconino County, were doing business at the large, no frills hardware and farm supply store. Darlene hardly noticed them, even the occasional farm boy who tried to engage her in conversation at the register. Her eyes were focused over their heads, and on the front door, where at any moment the handsomest boy she had ever seen would be passing through. Her heart fluttered with excitement as she giddily rang up and packaged products ranging from packets of vegetable and flower seeds to plastic jugs of water to drill bits.

"Thank you ma'am." A tall, gangly young farmhand wearing a sharp, black cowboy hat nodded and winked at her as she finished his order. He leaned on the counter, tore open a plastic container of beef jerky with his teeth, and tried to keep the conversation going.

"You getting off anytime soon?" he asked, leaning toward her. He was not a bad looking guy, and if she hadn't met Danny, she might be interested in flirting with the cowboy. But when you were in love with the best looking, sexiest guy in the world, all others paled in comparison.

Darlene half smiled while looking past him. "I have a boyfriend," she said absently. A dreamy smile played on her lips, which were liberally coated with iridescent watermelon lip gloss.

"As a matter of fact," she gasped. "Here he is now!" All eyes in the store turned as the young, tall, wholesome, and athletic looking youth entered. His lean, muscled six-foot frame moved with athletic grace and feral confidence. Thick, wavy blonde hair shined with sun-bleached health, flawless skin glowed golden with vitality, and piercing green eyes shone liked emeralds

Darlene threw her smock to the side and called to the store manager, who was busy helping customers. "Herb, I'm going on my break now," she informed him. She stalked from behind the counter, and those who were standing in line were left to wait.

She ran over to Danny as fast as her silver spangled sneakered feet could carry her. "I missed you soooo much," she decreed, throwing her arms around his neck.

He returned her embrace with a magical smile that melted Darlene's heart, and she kissed him full on the lips.

"Today is our six month anniversary," she said wistfully when the intoxicating kiss concluded. The only unfortunate thing about the kiss was that it ended.

He regarded her directly, his green eyes boring straight into her soul. He took her hand, leading her possessively from the store and into the parking lot. "Baby, you know my situation. There's no way I could buy you an anniversary present," he said tenderly. Before he could say more, Darlene put a finger over his lips. "Danny, you are my present. And you're the only present I'll ever need."

Danny removed her finger and kissed it gently. "You are the nicest person I've ever met," he said honestly, pulling her toward a red Toyota hatchback with tinted windows that was parked in the lot. "And I would never ask you for anything unless it was something super important. But this is something we both need if we are going to be able to keep in better contact with each other while we plan for our future together."

Darlene nodded and stared at the beautiful visage that stood before her and had more than once professed his love for her. "When you first walked into the store, I thought that a Hollywood movie actor had somehow landed right here in Tuba City," she proclaimed, not for the very first time. "I can't believe that now we're planning on getting married!" Her voice resonated with joy.

"Shhhh!" Danny whispered playfully, putting a finger to his lips. "That's our little secret until we can make our getaway."

Darlene jumped into the driver's seat of the Toyota, then leaned across and unlocked the passenger door so that Danny could jump in.

Danny allowed Darlene to take his hand in hers. He regarded the face of this sweet, pretty girl who was so very smitten by him. He only pretended that he felt the same for her. He liked her fine, but found her attentions annoying. She could not seem to take her hands off him. The minute he was alone with her, those hands were ever needing, ever touching, ever exploring.

Since the day he'd met her over a year ago at the Supply Depot, he'd known that Darlene could be his ticket out of his trapped and hellish life. She had fawned all over him since the minute she'd laid eyes on him, and he had welcomed her attentions because he knew that she would do anything he asked.

In order to pursue a relationship with Darlene, he had made a deal with Hank, another resident of the Painted Desert Farm with whom he made twice monthly trips into town for supplies. Hank was right now probably on his third beer at Tuba City's local dive bar down the street.

Darlene slid across the seat and was now practically on his lap. Her hand hungrily pawed at his crotch. He pretended to welcome the attention. "You know we don't have a lot of time here, Darlene. Hank is going to come out of that bar any minute. You know my deal with him. He gives me a half hour with you, I give him a half hour at the Thirsty Coyote, and nobody says a word to Malchus."

"This Malchus is a real creep, isn't he?" Darlene breathed into Danny's ear.

Oh he sure is, thought Danny tragically. *If you only knew.*

"He keeps a tight rein on me," Danny told Darlene emotionlessly. "But he can't stop us from running away together and getting married."

Darlene snuggled tighter.

"Darlene, I really have to go," he insisted. "Hank and I have to head back to the farm soon. Do you have the anniversary present?"

"Silly boy, of course I do," Darlene said coquettishly, reaching behind the seat. She presented Danny with a small festively wrapped package.

"It's all set up for you and my number is programmed in," she told him, handing over the gift, which was lovingly decorated with black and white polka dot paper and a red bow. Danny quickly tore into the giftwrap, and opened up a small box that contained a smartphone and charger.

"Now we can talk to each other every day," Darlene cooed. "And when we're not talking, we can text."

Danny's hand was already on the door handle. He felt badly about it, but Darlene's controlling nature and constantly groping hands were almost as offensive to his senses as Malchus' twisted ministrations. He was learning to use his gifted looks to get what he wanted, and the day was coming when no one would ever be able to control him again.

"I'm going to have this phone hidden in a very safe place," he said, stuffing the device into the pocket of his cargo shorts and pulling the car door open. "It's not going to be with me all the time. If you text me, I may not be able to get right back to you. And I will call you when it's safe for me. I cannot let Malchus find out about this phone. He monitors my every move on my computer and blocks a lot of websites. If he finds out about this phone, it will jeopardize everything we've planned together."

He cupped her chin tenderly between his thumb and forefinger, stared tenderly into her eyes, and gently kissed her. "You mean more to me then you'll ever know," he said, his expression filled with young, yearning love. Then he jumped out of the car, slammed the door closed, and jogged across the parking lot, fighting the niggling guilt that played at the back of his mind.

He fingered the device inside his pocket and the guilt disappeared. The phone represented a connection to the outside world that Malchus could not control or monitor. It would be a gateway to freedom that he needed desperately.

A rusty, ancient pickup that was pockmarked with dents and rot holes was parked at the side of the building. Hank had already filled the truck bed with the supplies they'd purchased at the Depot and was waiting in the driver's seat. Danny could smell beer breath through the truck's open windows and was again thankful for the Hank's penchant for booze. The scrawny old dude could down three or four mugs of cheap brew in a matter of minutes, which was all Danny needed to make time with Darlene.

The passenger door of the truck groaned in protest as Danny pried it open. He quickly jumped into the cab's front seat, which was torn and dirty, littered with detritus, and had more exposed foam than upholstery. With practiced stealth, he yanked the door shut as Hank steered the dilapidated jalopy onto the road that would bring them back to the farm.

"We gotta make time gettin' back," Hank said, stating the obvious. "We don't want Malchus getting suspicious. I'm starting to get real attached to these Saturday afternoon beer runs," he snickered conspiratorially and winked at Danny. "And I bet you're real fond of nookie with your pretty little girlfriend."

Danny's shrug was noncommittal. His relationship with the other denizens of the Painted Desert Farm was one of false congeniality. Malchus had been blatantly abusing Danny right under their noses, and all of them turned a blind eye in order to remain safely and snugly on the farm. No one had ever come to his aid. Over the years, his resentment toward them grew but he managed to hold his emotions in check. "Our Saturday afternoon supply runs work for both of us," he told Hank. "And as long as we keep it a secret, we both get what we want."

The pickup had no radio, and the desert landscape passed by in a quiet blur as they navigated the highway. Hank, nursing a beer buzz, became silently lost in the little world of his mind. Relief coursed through Danny as he sank loosely into the seat, tension and worry alleviated by the knowledge that escape was almost assured.

* * * * *

The scrawny, pale little nine year old that had followed shyly behind his mother when the tattered pair first arrived at the farm was now a stunning youth. As he watched Danny and Hank unload the pickup truck after their return from Tuba City, Malchus replayed in his mind the video images he had taken of Danny the night before. Over half a decade of working and playing beneath the desert sun had given the boy's skin a golden brown glow. Three farm fresh meals a day combined with labor-intensive chores, along with caring for the animals, had shaped a young man with a muscular six-foot frame that was sculpted like a Greek statue. Danny's effect on people, even those who had known him for years, was magnetic. His beauty commanded attention, and Malchus was only too happy to shower him with it.

Malchus watched Danny and Hank carefully, but what he *didn't* see was Danny's contraband cell phone, which the boy carefully concealed behind a pile of hay and beneath a loose plank in the barn, alongside a small store of cash that he'd gotten from Darlene. Because Malchus had complete control over even the most intimate aspects of his life, and because there was no part of him that was beyond Malchus's control, Danny had sought and discovered a hiding place that was uniquely his. It was here that he stockpiled whatever cash he could procure. He would keep his cell phone hidden here. He would only be able to charge the phone using the cigarette lighter in the pickup during runs to Tuba City, so the phone's operation would have to be judicious. The cash and the phone were necessary for one thing: escape from this living hell.

Thanks to Darlene, he had nearly enough money to make that plan a reality. But for the moment, he still had to play Malchus' game.

The fifty-eight-year-old leader of the Painted Desert Farm was drumming his fingers on the kitchen table when Danny entered their trailer. Malchus addressed the boy authoritatively.

"How was Tuba City?" His eyes probed intimately. "You and Hank seem to spend more and more time on these runs."

Danny's voice held no emotion. "The store was busy. We had to wait in line. We got all the supplies you wanted and put them in the barn."

Malchus stared into Danny's eyes for a full ten seconds. "And how is your girlfriend?"

A ghost of an expression momentarily clouded the handsome features of Danny's face.

Malchus smirked. "You're my son. It's my job to know everything about you. Tuba City is less than an hour away. Word gets around."

There was an almost imperceptible clenching of Danny's jaw. "I am not your son," he told Malchus, his voice flat.

"That hurts," Malchus said. "I've raised you like my own." His tone was full of endearment.

"No, since my mother died I've been an orphan living at your mercy," Danny stated impassively. "As sick as my mother was she loved me and never did anything to hurt me. You raped me. You still do."

Malchus stood, stepped to the refrigerator, and calmly poured himself a glass of wine. It was cactus wine, made on the farm from the fruit of prickly pear cacti. Malchus was quite fond of it.

"Your mother left you." His voice was at once gentle and accusatory, and his eyes bored into Danny with reptilian coldness. "You scared her off the cliff."

Danny willed himself not to recoil at the evil taunt. He knew that he hadn't been responsible for Lucille's death. "My mother had breaks with reality." His tone was matter of fact. Since his mother's death, he had done a lot of research on mental illness on the computer. Danny leaned forward but his feet remained firmly planted on the floor. He wanted nothing more than to wrap his hands around Malchus' neck and choke the life out of him. But all in good time. Now as always, Danny had to be in complete control of his emotions. "The only thing my mother did wrong was bring me here. She left me in the wrong hands, because her death conveniently put me completely under your control."

Malchus leaned back in his chair and drew a leisurely sip of wine. "If it weren't for me you'd have spent your entire childhood shunted from one hellish foster home to another. I've given you a very comfortable and easy life here. You've been educated, haven't you? I even gave you a computer. Why? Because I care about you, and you were meant to be my son."

"If I were really your son, what you do to me would be considered incest." Again, Danny's voice belied no emotion whatsoever.

"You have a very nice and comfortable life here, Danny. I give you everything you want. You live in a safe and nurturing environment. It's a horrible world out there, Danny."

Malchus paused reflectively and sipped his wine. "You've grown increasingly belligerent lately. Don't think for one minute that your becoming a strapping young man has given you power over me. I can still take you over my knee. But I guess I shouldn't go too hard on you. Teenage boys are known for giving their parents a hard time."

Danny felt his anger and rage reaching a boiling point, but he remained outwardly calm as he stood just outside the doorway to the tiny galley kitchen. "You are not my parent. You will never touch me again. I will never sleep in your bedroom again. You can't videotape me any more."

Malchus finished off his wine, placed the glass gently on the table, and stood to face Danny. "Shower up. We're making a movie in fifteen minutes." There was only the barest hint of menace in Malchus' voice.

Danny folded his arms across his chest. He could smell the cactus wine on Malchus' breath. "I told you. I am not performing in any more of your movies."

Malchus pulled Danny's arms apart and placed them at his side in a swift, strong movement that was not at all gentle.

"You know you like it. God knows you respond," Malchus said salaciously. "And, you are completely, one hundred percent entranced by the camera."

"No. You are wrong." Danny took several steps backwards, retreating.

Malchus came forward menacingly, backing the boy into a wall. "Without me, without this home, you have nothing. You were a little boy out in the desert, hungry and homeless. Thanks to me, you're not homeless or hungry anymore. You have a roof over your head and a warm bed to sleep in."

Danny was trapped. Trapped against the wall by Malchus, and trapped by his dependence on this man who controlled him. Danny had nowhere to turn. Lucille was gone, and the others on the farm were far too dependent upon Malchus, as was he.

"Shower up," Malchus commanded, playfully smacking Danny's backside. "We start rolling in ten minutes."

Danny clenched his fists, bowed his head slightly, and headed for the bathroom.

He had to keep playing Malchus' game. For now. But he had a plan, and he would do whatever he could to escape. Even if it meant hurting some very innocent people. None of them would ever know the hurt, betrayal, humiliation and violation that he experienced on a daily basis.

His trust in people died on the night of his thirteenth birthday. He was now concerned only for his own survival.

* * * * *

Sacred Datura. This fascinating yet extremely dangerous desert plant had been used with great caution by American Indian tribes of the southwest. Its roots, seeds, and leaves could be ground into a pulp or made into tea that was a powerful, mind altering medicine. Ingestion of Sacred Datura induced hallucinations, altered the mental state, and could cause permanent psychosis, coma, or death. Danny had observed this effect with the death of his mother, and again when one of the farm's goats nibbled some of the plant and attempted to walk on its hind legs, resembling a demonic human in the minutes before it convulsed and died.

To the untrained eye, Sacred Datura plants looked like a field of harmless desert greenery. But Danny keenly knew otherwise. The power of the plant had terrified him as a little boy.

"Why don't we destroy all of these plants if they are so dangerous?" he once asked his mother.

Lucille, in a rare moment of lucidity, had somehow sensed the little boy's fear and awe, and had gently taken his hand in hers. "One thing we learn when we live with nature is that everything has a purpose. Even those things that might be dangerous," she explained. "We don't kill the coyotes or the javelinas because they are dangerous. We live with them and admire their majesty and their power."

She then tousled the little boy's hair. Danny would never forget the warm, newly familiar feeling of unconditional love. "Besides," she also explained, "the flower is absolutely beautiful, just like you."

And just as deadly, Danny now thought, reflecting back on an ancient childhood memory. Outside the clay house, the hot August sun was setting over the desert. Danny knew that Malchus was currently off the property, in town at the bank. Danny also knew that his "father" would be returning soon and making a beeline for the cactus wine. In the quiet of the galley kitchen, Danny calmly pulled the bottle from the mini-compact refrigerator. Uncorking the wine, he methodically poured it through a strainer that contained a miniscule amount of Sacred Datura pulp. On his cell phone, he had learned that when ingested, a tiny volume of the juice could cause neurological damage without causing death. Feeling more peace than he had known in years, he then carefully funneled the wine back into its original bottle. He swirled it gently, and stared wistfully at the dangerous potion before returning it to its proper place on the refrigerator shelf.

As he closed refrigerator door, he took a long last look around the confining room that he had come to view as a prison cell. "Drink up, you repulsive monster," he whispered to himself in the quiet emptiness of the kitchen. A sudden fear and apprehension clouded his handsome face. He battled to control his trepidation by focusing on his goals and the outcome of his deed, and ultimately his mind returned to a sense of perfect calm. He actually began to feel a tingle of excitement at the prospect of finally being free.

"You will never touch me again," he whispered to the empty house.

He was lounging like a Cheshire cat in the living room when he heard the wooden front door swing open on its hinges. He pretended to be intensely focused on a television show. From the corner of his eye he watched as Malchus went directly into the galley kitchen. Soon afterward he heard a tinkling of glasses, indicating that Malchus had, in fact, started in on the tainted beverage.

Malchus always gulped his first few glasses very quickly. When he weaved into the living room with glazed eyes, Danny, watching intently, knew that Malchus was already inebriated.

"My beautiful son," said Malchus drunkenly, as his hand fondled Danny's thigh.

Danny brusquely shoved Malchus' hand from his leg and stood. Filling with hatred and rage that had built from years of abuse, he stared down at the inebriated monster with clenched fists.

Malchus began rubbing his temples crazily, an expression of panicked confusion on his face.

A vengeful smile crossed Danny's lips. "Headache, Malchus?"

Malchus' features were contorted, but suddenly he looked at Danny with a countenance that he had never before expressed. Fear. Malchus struggled to stand but Danny shoved him forcibly back into the couch.

"You're no longer in control Malchus," he said calmly. "And you will never have any power over me again. So listen closely, you sick bastard."

Malchus' legs began to spasm involuntarily. He regarded his shaking limbs with terror. Danny grabbed him by the hair and yanked his head upward.

"You will look at me and you will listen to what I have to say while your mind is still working. I gave you enough Sacred Datura to incapacitate you for life, but hopefully not enough to kill you. I want you suffer for a long, long time. Do you understand what that means Malchus?"

The spasms in Malchus' legs worsened. He looked toward the door as if hoping that help would arrive.

Danny followed Malchus' gaze to the door. "It's locked, Malchus," he said, with a cool, calm smile. "Nobody's coming to save you. Just like nobody came to protect me."

Silence passed. Danny watched as a wet spot on Malchus' crotch spread like ink on tissue paper. "It's already too late for you. In minutes your nervous system will be permanently disabled. I'll be long gone. Maybe if you're lucky somebody will come by in a few days and feed you some baby food, or whatever that shit is they feed to people who's brains are fried."

Drool was coming from Malchus' mouth. "I see your mind is still working, because I can see the terror in your eyes," Danny said in a voice devoid of sympathy or remorse. "And you should be terrified, because all of these assholes who live on this farm will keep you alive, just barely, so that they can continue to live here unbothered by the outside world. You'll be at their complete mercy. For the rest of your fucking life. My, how the tables have suddenly turned for you."

"I'm going to be taking all of the videos you made of me," Danny said as he walked from the room. "You better hope nobody comes after me or the footage will be sent directly to the FBI and this place will be torn to pieces in a raid."

Malchus shrunk onto the couch, shaking, drooling, and peeing on himself. He tried to speak, but his voice was nothing but a slur of word salad.

"Two more things, Malchus," Danny said with intensity. "One, you are not and have never been my father. You have been nothing but a monster. And two, I never believed your bullshit about my mother's death being my fault. I was just a little kid. You were there. You could have helped me, but you obviously wanted her to die so you could pursue your own filthy agenda. Wrong choice, Malchus. Look where it's ultimately gotten you."

Danny loomed over Malchus' already shriveling body, staring with intense hatred into the eyes of the man who had destroyed his life. Before he turned and left the house Danny went to Malchus' room. Every movie Malchus had ever made with him was stored on high definition SD video cards, each one only slightly larger than a postage stamp. *And now I'll always have the evidence,* he thought as he pocketed the footage. He turned, left the house, and strode quickly and purposefully along the path that wound among the tiny clay homes and rusty trailers of the Painted Desert Farm.

Ellie was sitting at her dinette table scrolling through Facebook on her tablet when she heard a sudden pounding on the trailer door. She was startled and surprised to find Danny standing outside, a look of steely determination on his face.

"Is something wrong?" She asked with sudden concern. "Would you like to come in?"

"No on both counts," Danny answered resolutely. "Nothing's wrong in my world, and I do not want to come in."

Ellie pulled her tattered silk robe tightly around her neck. The desert was still hot, but a chill ran down her spine.

"You're going to find that your fearless leader Malchus is a bit, um, incapacitated," Danny said coldly. "He's ingested a dangerous dose of Sacred Datura extract. His brain is fried."

Ellie gasped. Something in Danny's tone made her believe him implicitly.

"Where is he?" she asked nervously.

"In his house," Danny answered simply. "Slumped on the couch."

"We need to get him to a hospital," Ellie insisted after a shocked pause.

"Do whatever you want with him, Ellie," Danny told her, ice in his voice. "But let me tell you how it's going to go down."

Ellie nodded and stared at this boy who had lived on the farm for years but who was a stranger to her.

"You, and everyone else on this farm knew what Malchus was doing to me in his house." Danny's tone was angry and accusatory.

Ellie shook her head in denial.

"I have proof, Ellie, of what happened to me here on this farm that's so precious to you and everyone else who lives here. So precious, in fact, that you all turned a blind eye to the fact that I was being molested right under your noses."

Again, Ellie shook her head vehemently. On her face was an expression of revulsion.

"Malchus was making movies of me, Ellie," Danny continued. "And if the authorities ever got wind of the fact that kiddie porn was being produced here on your beloved farm, they would come and arrest every single one of you. And I will tell them you all knew about it."

Danny turned to leave. "I've got all the footage right here in my pocket. If you value your home and your freedom, you and all the rest will forget that I ever lived here, or that you ever knew me."

With that, Danny slung a duffel bag over his shoulder and headed down the path that led to the farm's entrance. It was the same path that he and Lucille had treaded eight years ago when they arrived at the farm. A scrawny, frightened nine year-old boy and his mentally unstable mother. But Danny was no longer a scrawny, frightened boy.

He passed through the gates, walked out to the highway, then hiked a few additional miles to the Marble Canyon Bridge. At the ramp's entrance, on the shoulder of the road, were the headlights of an idling vehicle. Darlene was here to pick him up, as they had planned. The moment he saw her expression through the car's windshield a megawatt smile incandesced on the planes of his sculpted face. He climbed into the vehicle that would provide his escape.

In his mind, he stepped away from the emotions that roiled inside him. He allowed his spirit to fill with joy at the prospect of freedom. Freedom from Malchus and the farm that had become his prison. Freedom, forever, from ever again being controlled by another person.

Darlene's hand reached across and took his.

"Drive," he told her. "Get me out of here."

Darlene hit the gas. The tires squealed as she flew onto the highway.

Danny sunk back into the car seat, a blissful sense of relief and freedom flooding through him.

"I can't believe this is happening!" Darlene exclaimed, reaching for his hand. "Pretty soon we'll be together forever."

Danny gently kissed the back of her hand. "Once I get settled in Vegas, I'll send for you. It should only take a week or two."

"And I'll keep on working double shifts at the Depot so we'll have enough money to get married right away." She squeezed his hand. "Oh my God I can't believe it!" She screamed through the open window and into the desert night. I'm getting married to the man of my dreams!"

"First things first," Danny told her with a wry grin. "We've got to stick with the plan. You've only given me enough money to get us set up in a small apartment on the outskirts of Vegas. It might take me a little while to find a perfect little love nest for us, and by then you'll have graduated high school."

"Oh, wish I was coming with you right now." Darlene's voice took on a whiney quality.

Danny's fingers moved playfully through her hair. "You know we can't. You have to get your diploma. You're going to need it to get a job out there."

"I know, but I'll miss you," she pouted. "And I'll worry about you all alone in the big city."

Danny stroked her cheek. "I'll be okay," he reassured her. "And by the time you get out to Vegas everything will be ready and we'll have the rest of our lives together."

"You take such good care of me, Danny," Darlene sniffed. "You're always putting me first."

"And I always will," Danny professed earnestly. "You're my girl now and forever."

The smile on Darlene's face was brighter than the Arizona moon during the entire ride to Flagstaff. Before they decamped at the Greyhound Bus terminal, the two enjoyed a romantic dinner of burgers, fries, and milkshakes at a Sonic Drive-In. Afterward, as they pulled to the curb of the terminal, Darlene insisted upon waiting inside with Danny until he boarded the bus.

"No way," he told her firmly. "It's already late. You have a two-hour ride back to Tuba City. I don't want you driving alone in the desert in the middle of the night. It's too dangerous and if anything bad happened to you I'd kill myself."

Darlene nodded reluctantly. She got out of the car with him, hugged him fiercely, and insisted on a five-minute make-out session before letting him go.

"C'mon," he said finally. "We're adults now. We're getting married. We need to be able to follow the plan, even if it gets a little tough sometimes."

He gently nudged her back into the car and shut the driver's side door. He kissed his finger and pressed it to her lips. His eyes were filled with love, adoration and yearning as he stared into her face.

"See you in Vegas," he said. "Love you."

Then he turned, entered the bus terminal, and approached the ticket window without ever looking back.

"One way ticket to Phoenix, please."

* * * * *

He placed the contact lenses into his eyes with practiced ease. When Malchus forced him perform for the camera, Danny had often been made to change his appearance using wigs, make-up, hair dyes, contact lenses - and facial hair after he passed puberty.

He was finally free from Malchus, from the farm, and from the suffocating affections of Darlene. And he was determined that the abuses of his prior years would not break him. On the contrary, he would use what he learned in the course of his hellish past to fuel his escape. His naturally blonde hair was now long, scraggly, and mousey brown in color, his distinctive green eyes disguised with pale brown contact lenses. He had grown a scruffy beard and goatee. His lean and muscular body was now thick around the middle with the help of a padded fat suit purchased online, and clothed in an over-sized tee shirt and baggy, ill fitting jeans. He looked in the mirror and smiled with satisfaction. Gone was the handsome teenager who received hungry, attentive stares wherever he went.

He was now Ben Daniels, a featureless, totally forgettable, generic product of the American middle class. It was eight in the morning and, accustomed to rising early, he was fully awake and alert.

The tiny motel was a dump, but it was far safer than where he came from. It was also all that he could afford and as far as his limited funds would take him from Bitter Springs. He pulled back a nicotine stained, ratty curtain and was greeted by bright morning sunshine that obliterated the night and filled the room with the promise of a new day. He was no fan of the dark, where for years unwanted hands would grope him. He was now free from the groping, but in darkness he felt alone with his apprehension and guilt and was chased by demons and filled with remorse about what he had done to Darlene, who was clingy and annoying but decent and good hearted. He had also had remorse about what he next intended to do. His plan that would forever take him from the only life he'd ever known. All of his instincts were firing, urging him to flee further.

Stolen cash would pay for this decrepit motel whose low budget benefit was the absence of security cameras, allowing him to come and go without leaving any electronic proof of his stay. He exited the room, allowing the sun's brightness to fill him with optimism and even hope.

He walked two blocks along Camelback Road and took a bus that was headed a short distance east. In order to avoid suspicion and attention, he exited two miles from his destination. He approached the target on foot. In spite of hot, heavy artificial padding inside his clothing, his gait became jauntier. He was filled with a happy realization that his journey was underway. His plan was a result of meticulous research on his smart phone. It would work. Adrenaline filled his veins. In twenty minutes time he neared a senior apartment complex called Hacienda Ridge. A busy, palm shaded bus stop fronted the main building's entrance. As he neared it, he feigned oblivion to the curious stares of a small, elderly crowd that waited unhurriedly to be shuttled into downtown Scottsdale. He stood back from them, his eyes shaded and concealed by a pair of cheap, dark sunglasses.

He watched two smiling little ladies dressed in bright sundresses and large straw hats. They hobbled slowly to the stop, arm in arm for support, and sat on a bench. One of them pulled a handkerchief from a quilted purse and gently patted the moisture from her companion's forehead. They giggled together as they searched their bags for bus tickets and smiled broadly when they noticed him. His youth brought them back to girlhood, to a time when young men were the most important matters in the world.

He warmly returned their smiles, forcing himself to view them with the compassion of a fox eyeing a warren of baby rabbits. In the course of his young life he had learned, very painfully, the difference between predator and prey. His escape, his very survival, depended on his never again being the prey.

He turned from the little old ladies, adjusted his ear buds, and nonchalantly engaged with the screen of his phone, acting as though he was uninterested in his surroundings. But in fact he'd been here several times before and his senses were fully attuned to every detail.

* * * * *

They stand in a semi-circle against a picturesque backdrop of desert scrub and rocky outcrops. Resembling a row of pearly white dentures, Hacienda Ridge Apartments are a complex of pueblo style buildings situated on a cul-de-sac just beyond the Maricopa Freeway in Arizona. This southwestern retirement village, built in the 1970's, borders a national park famous for its towering Saguaro cacti and immense natural red sandstone formations.

A relaxed outdoor lifestyle, along with the Ridge's very convenient location on a central bus route, make the complex a highly sought after destination for retirees. Potential residents are on the waiting list for so long that a fair percentage of them die before apartments become available. Of those who survive the wait, some subsist from month to month on limited social security payments and sparse pension checks. Just as many, however, have secure bank accounts, generous pensions, and profitable investment portfolios that allow them the luxury of spending their golden years with financial ease under a brilliant desert sun.

Seventy year-old Otto Ehrlinger fell into the latter category of Ridge residents. Otto had owned a successful plumbing and heating supply business in Omaha, and during his working life had managed to amass a comfortable, if not impressive investment portfolio. His wife died of an aneurism when he was fifty, and he never found the strength, or the will, to remarry. Ten years after her death he sold his business, his home, and most connections with his life in Nebraska and moved to the Hacienda Ridge. He had so far enjoyed three idyllic years under the cloudless Arizona sky. He even had family nearby. Soon after he'd arrived here, a messy divorce back in Omaha prompted his daughter Terry and grandson Simon to follow him to the Southwest, and now both were residing in nearby Phoenix. It was, for the most part, a pleasant perk to have them living so close.

He was having a not so pleasant time boarding a bus right now, however. His lazy grandson had failed to show up to drive him to the bank and to run a few other errands, so instead he was waiting at the lushly landscaped stop in front of the Hacienda Ridge's main building. Otto was taking advantage of the Link, a service that ferried residents into downtown Scottsdale for shopping and other daytime excursions. When the bus pulled into the stop, the old man's troubles began.

Due to a recent hip replacement surgery, he was using a four-pronged cane to help him walk. The new assistive device was now proving useless in helping Otto to hoist his body upward from the curb to the first step of the bus. He felt humiliated and ashamed as he struggled futilely while the people in line behind him waited impatiently to board the bus.

"Here, let me help you up sir." An eager young man extended a hand and offered the support of a strong arm, enabling Otto to board the bus, albeit with some difficulty. The kid helped Otto ascend from the curb to the bus's perilously high first step, then assisted the elderly gentlemen to his seat once aboard.

"You're a rarity, young fellow," Otto observed somewhat breathlessly. He was winded, but was now able to appraise the boy. He estimated that the kid was about the same age as his grandson, about nineteen, and while not outright fat like Simon, was certainly a few pounds overweight. Also, like Simon, too lazy to get a haircut, shave, or pay much attention to what he wore. Each generation, Otto mused, got worse and worse. But unlike his grandson, at least this kid was helpful and polite.

"A rarity?" the boy asked, taking the seat opposite Otto. "Is that good or bad?"

Otto couldn't help but chuckle at the boy's innocent, open curiosity. "Most kids your age would have pushed an old man out of the way instead of helping me aboard," Otto said. *Simon certainly would have*, he thought sadly.

"Most kids weren't raised by their grandparents," explained the boy. "I took care of my gramps when he was getting old and having a hard time like you're having right now."

The boy smiled. Dazzling. For a plain looking kid, he had a smile like you could find in toothpaste commercials, the old man thought.

"I'm Ben, by the way," he told Otto, who shook the boy's hand and returned the introduction. Otto noted Ben's grip to be strong and firm, yet not overly so. To a man with more than seven decades of people skills behind him, it was a handshake that conveyed confidence and character.

"Most of the kids your age are racing around in sports cars and would never even consider taking the bus. I haven't noticed you on this one before," Otto said.

"Well, hopefully you'll be seeing me on it a lot more in the future. If I can find a job." Ben's voice was enthusiastic. "I'm on my way to the mall to fill out some applications. I start college in the fall and I'll need to buy my own car. But I'm pretty handy and hard working. I'll find a job doing something, I don't care what it is."

Ben popped on two earphones, pressed a series of keys on one of those high-tech phones which Otto's arthritic fingers could never hope to operate, and sat back to enjoy the music of his generation. Otto unfolded a newspaper that had been tucked into his back pocket, smoothed it on his lap, and began perusing the business page. He couldn't help himself, though, from peering over his reading glasses to steal sidelong glances at the boy. While on the surface he reminded Otto of his grandson, he actually couldn't be more different. This kid struck Otto as someone with a work ethic, quite willing to take a bus, fill out applications, and get a job doing just about anything in order to buy a car so that he could get to college.

Simon, on the other hand, was given a car by Otto but remained too lazy to get off the couch, let alone work a job or even go to college part-time. And the differences between the two teenagers didn't end there. While Ben's features were largely obscured by longish hair, a scruffy beard, and a pair of glasses, Otto could make out angular facial features and clear, healthy looking, blemish-free skin. In contrast, Simon's face was puffy and bloated, his skin pasty and blotched with redness and acne eruptions.

As a grandson, Simon was a massive disappointment. Otto closed his eyes for a nap, regretfully deciding that he already liked this kid Ben a whole lot better than his own flesh and blood progeny.

Thirty minutes later the bus screeched to a halt. At the sunny, palm-lined Scottsdale Mews shopping center, Otto once again found himself the benefactor of young Ben's helping hand. After the pair had exited the bus, Otto opened his wallet and offered the exceptional young man a twenty-dollar bill.

Ben shook his head and held up his hands in protest. "No worries. I was happy to help you out. I had to be on the bus anyway. You don't have to give me any money."

Otto forced the bill into Ben's hand. "You know, if you don't find a job around here today, we could sure use a strong fellow like you back at the Hacienda Ridge," Otto told the boy. "I know plenty of people, including myself, who would pay you to do errands for them."

Ben turned, smiled charismatically, and regarded Otto through dark glasses. "I may have to take you up on that," he earnestly replied.

"What type of jobs are you applying for?" Otto asked.

"Anything and everything."

"Well, if you don't find something regular, just stop by the Ridge and ask for Otto," the old man advised. "Everybody there knows me.

And trust me, the old folks will have you so busy you'll be able to buy yourself a clunker in no time."

Ben's face lit up with genuine appreciation. "Thanks, Otto!" he answered with open gratitude. A wide grin brightened his expression. He turned and trotted off toward the mall.

* * * * *

The courtyard at the Hacienda Ridge was at its busiest immediately after lunch. Poolside patio tables, shaded by large umbrellas, were usually fully occupied at this time of day. Molly Ferguson and Theresa Barry were in their regular seats, where they bragged ceaselessly about their grandchildren. Longtime resident Penny Kent sat with them in her wheelchair and knitted in pleasant confusion while breathing oxygen supplemented by a nasal cannula.

At another table, beneath the fronds of a squat palm tree, sat Otto Ehrlinger with his emaciated-looking daughter Terry and his porcine grandson, Simon. The freeloading nineteen year old refused to get a job, and visited frequently to take advantage of the older man's generous hospitality. Simon was currently attacking a super-sized bag of potato chips. With one hand he stuffed piles of greasy chips into his rapacious mouth. With the other he was manipulating the keys on his phone, where a video game was in progress. He appeared to blatantly ignore his mother and grandfather. "We should encourage him to eat healthier," Otto was arguing. "And he should get a job. When I was nineteen I worked every day after school and on weekends to help out with household expenses." Otto's pleas, as always, were met with a shrug from his daughter.

"The boy's lazy," Otto added. "He never even helps out. He was supposed to give me a lift to the bank the other day and he never showed up. If he stays on this track he won't amount to anything."

Simon looked up as if suddenly possessed. He treated his grandfather to a surly glare, causing Otto to instantly regret his words. Simon slammed the tabletop with a meaty open palm, causing his mother and grandfather to jump in their seats. "I'm sitting right FUCKING here!" He screamed. Potato chip crumbles shot from his mouth. "Don't FUCKING talk about me like I'm some kind of deaf asshole!"

His mother's expression did not register surprise at the outburst. Otto glanced uncomfortably at his watch, a look of disappointment in his glassy eyes. It saddened him that he couldn't wait for his only daughter, and his only grandson, to leave. But they would not be departing anytime soon.

Simon settled his prodigious frame into the patio chair, which creaked in protest. "What time's dinner?" He asked as though his outburst had never taken place. "You promised to take us to Alice's All-You-Can-Eat tonight."

And you'll eat all of it, Otto thought sadly. He nodded in assent, glancing at Terry, who rarely made any effort to rein in her son's explosive tantrums.

Simon swiveled to face away from them and returned to his video game and his chips.

Resignedly, Otto rose from the table and walked to the shuffleboard court. Adjacent to the pool, the Hacienda Ridge's recreation zone was surrounded by a ficus hedge. A group of kyphotic athletes were presently engaged in a rousing match of geriatric sport. The current courtside gossip, already becoming old news around the complex, focused on the recent hospitalization of Alison Kayos.

"They took her away in an ambulance right after breakfast." L.A. Lizzie's puck, or "biscuit," had just slid to a landing inside the "10 off" section of the scoring zone on the shuffleboard court. Lizzie was unfazed by her loss of 10 points, so engrossed was she in telling the story of this morning's drama. She'd been one of the very few to observe it all first hand.

"When they loaded Alison into the ambulance, she was hardly breathing, and her skin was white as a sheet," Lizzie explained melo-dramatically, her sun visor casting a half shadow over the deep wrin-kles in her face.

"The food around here will do that to you," cranky Ed Peals commented as he took a healthy swig from his water bottle. Rumor had it there was more than just water in his bottle.

"Old age will do that to you," Otto, joining his friends, added. His new hip, and the arthritis in his knees, were still slowing him down and were a drag even on his shuffleboard game.

He didn't have the opportunity to join the game, however. He was abruptly tapped on the shoulder by a gentleman named Herbert, whose frayed jacket and oversized name tag announced to the world that he had dutifully attended the Hacienda Ridge front desk for decades.

"There's a kid named Ben out front looking for you," Herbert said.

"Ben?" Confusion clouded Otto's features.

"Yeah. Tall, chubby kid," Herbert explained. "Very polite. Says he met you on the bus."

"Oh, yes, yes," Otto said, suddenly remembering his encounter with the exceptionally courteous and helpful young man on the bus a few days earlier. "You can send him back here."

Ben's arrival in the courtyard a few minutes later caused all poolside chatter to temporarily cease. Grandchildren, and young people in general, had an almost magical effect on the denizens of Hacienda Ridge. The overweight teenager walked with a self conscious slouch but smiled warmly and openly toward each and every inquisitive face. As he scanned the crowd, he found Otto struggling to stand from a low bench near the shuffleboard court.

"No, please, don't get up, sir," Ben said, rushing forward and offering his hand for a shake. "I was in the area and I remembered you told me to stop by if I needed work."

"Is this another grandson, Otto?" Martha Gruber, still spry in her nineties, hustled in from the other side of the pool.

"I'm Ben Daniels," Ben answered amiably, taking her bony hand and shaking it softly. "I met Otto on the bus when I was going into town looking for work the other day. He said if I didn't have any luck, he could give me some odd jobs to do around here." Ben met Otto's eyes. "So I stopped by to take you up on your offer."

A small, inquisitive crowd had formed around them. Charlene Bakersfield stepped forward. "I need my closet painted. Last guy who was supposed to do it never showed up, the jerk!"

"I have some furniture in storage that I want to bring in," said L.A. Lizzie. "I could use the help of a big, brawny fellow like you."

Otto struggled to his feet. "I have a bunch of heavy cartons that need to be carried down and thrown in the back dumpster," he told Ben. "And my grandson Simon can't seem to muster the energy to help me. I can put you to work right now!"

As the elderly man led Ben back into the building, Charlene Bakersfield called after them. "Don't forget my closet needs painting," she reminded them.

The Hacienda Ridge courtyard settled back to its usual activity level. Hattie Maynard thought to ask, "Does anyone know where this young man comes from?"

Her question went ignored.

*   *   *   *   *

Rose McFarland bustled about the kitchen of her one bedroom Hacienda Ridge apartment wearing a KD Lang concert tee shirt and khaki shorts. Her hair, a natural salt and pepper still sprinkled with hints of original brown color, was pulled back in a ponytail.

She had lived at the Hacienda Ridge since retiring from the Los Angeles public school system five years ago, at age sixty-five. Along with many others of her generation, she had long ago flocked to Hollywood with dreams of pursuing a career in the movies. Fortunately, her parents insisted that she attend college in California as a condition of paying her rent and expenses while she chased her dreams. She had never made it as an actress, but managed to make a good living as a high school drama teacher and was now enjoying the fruits of a generous pension in Sunny Scottsdale.

"Why don't you take a break, kid?" she called into the living room, where Ben Daniels was putting up some shelves for her. Rose pulled a tin of easy-bake cookies from the oven. "Have yourself a little snack."

Wiping his hands on his jeans, Ben came into the kitchen. *With a smile that could warm up the North Pole*, Rose thought. In all of her years spent teaching teenagers, she had encountered only a handful of kids that were as polite, as genuine and as hardworking as Ben Daniels. And, while they were all drama students, she would be hard pressed to recall any who were as charismatic and magnetic as Ben. Although he was scruffy and overweight and walked with a slouch, there was something about this boy that filled the room with an electric charge, a palpable energy she had only experienced once or twice in all her years in Los Angeles theatre. His mere presence commanded attention, and if he were so inclined, he could probably consider a career on the stage. Unfortunately, he didn't seem inclined to lose weight, cut his hair, correct his posture, or shave. He didn't even seem to want to remove his omnipresent baseball cap.

Millennials, she thought wryly. *Perfectly content to do nothing more than spend their lives living in their parent's basements*. At least this one seemed to have a work ethic.

"When I was pulling out the couch to put up the shelves, I found a ring," Ben told her. "It looks like it could be an expensive one. I left it on the little table in there."

Rose poured a glass of iced tea, placed a plate of cookies on the table, and motioned for Ben to sit down.

"Oh, that must have fallen behind the cushions when I was cleaning," Rose told him. It isn't worth much at all, but I'm glad you found it all the same. Thanks, kiddo."

Ben wolfed down a cookie. "These are great, Mrs. McFarland. You know, I help Mr. Ehrlinger with his shopping. If you ever want me to pick up anything at the store or run to the pharmacy, I'll be happy to do it."

"Mr. Ehrlinger has become very, very dependent on you. You are everything his grandson Simon is not," Rose observed.

With a mouth full of chocolate chips, Ben nodded affirmatively and swallowed a gulp of iced tea. "That Simon kid pretty much snarls a me whenever he sees me," he told Rose. "He's a mean one, even to Otto, who always just lets him get away with it."

"Simon is a fat, lazy sod," Rose stated flatly. "And as we would say in the education world, he's on the spectrum. He has anger issues like you wouldn't believe. They should have gotten him help long ago. Now it's far too late. They've created a monster."

"Guess you can't really blame Otto," Danny shrugged. "He's just the grandfather. He didn't raise the kid."

"Otto is what we call an enabler," Rose told Ben. "Bought the kid a car, gives him money, takes him to dinner all the time, puts up with his violent outbursts. Lets him behave like a miscreant. Worse than a miscreant. A psycho, to tell you the truth. And I can bet he leaves that worthless piece of shit kid a small fortune."

Ben silently digested the information about Simon's likely inheritance, then stood from the table and made ready to leave. "After I finish putting up your shelves, I have to take care of Boscoe and Bailey. Lot's to do today."

"Who are Boscoe and Bailey," Rose asked.

"Mrs. Neffler's two cats," Ben explained. "She's in San Diego visiting her daughter."

"We old folks can keep you busy from here to eternity," Rose told hm. "But won't your schedule be a little tighter in the fall, when you go back to school?"

"I just graduated from high school in June," Ben explained. "I'm applying to ASU now. I hope to be starting full time, but not until January."

"Where did you go to high school?" Rose inquired.

"I was home schooled," Ben answered without pause. "Up north. Near Tuba City."

"Never heard of it, honey," Rose told him. "Just make sure you get your higher education. In this economy, you need to have a specialty."

She picked up Danny's now empty glass and put it in the sink. Her hands, she noticed for a brief self-conscious moment, were wrinkled and spotted with age. How they contrasted with the vitality of youth! Oh, to be young again.

Ben returned to his task in the living room. "Thanks so much for the cookies, Mrs. McFarland," he hollered back enthusiastically. "They were great!"

After Ben finished the job and had left the apartment, Rose mused that there was something else about this boy, aside from his politeness, his charm, and his charisma. Something beneath the surface that her many years of work with kids had made her acutely sensitive to.

Deep down inside, she concluded, the boy was spooked. Something, somewhere, had scared him shitless.

*　*　*　*　*

"And don't miss a spot!" Charlene Bakersfield demanded. "Even though you aren't a professional painter, I expect the job to be done well. And thoroughly."

Ben smiled, seemingly unfazed by the demands of the cranky, crotchety, and downright mean old lady.

"No problem Mrs. Bakersfield," he said with a composed smile. He was painting her tiny closet in a flat white color that was on sale at Home Depot. He'd gone to the hardware depot, picked up the paint, brushes and other supplies, and had just finished the second coat. The closet looked quite good, and for his efforts he was being paid a princely sum of fifty dollars, a price that had been decided upon after a considerable degree of haggling. Among other things, Charlene Bakersfield was a cheapskate.

"I was really careful, didn't spill a drip on the floor. I'll come back tomorrow after it dries, put up the hanger and shelf." Ben motioned toward the contents of the closet, piles of boxes and clothes that now filled the hallway. "I'll put all these boxes and clothes back once the paint dries."

"You better believe you will come back!" Charlene barked. Gone was the sweet little old lady he'd first met out by the pool. In her place was a grizzled, gnarled old fiend. The geriatric, female version of Ebenezer Scrooge. "I'm not paying a penny until the job is finished. And not a cent more than we agreed upon."

"No, of course not," Ben answered with unruffled clemency. "I can come by tomorrow morning to put everything back for you."

"I'm not here in the morning. I have an appointment with the cardiologist," said Charlene imperiously. "You will have to come after lunch."

"I can't come in the afternoon," Ben told her. "I'm kinda booked the whole rest of the day."

"Booked!" muttered Charlene. "Well, you will have to come by and finish your job at the crack of dawn, before I leave," she demanded.

Ben treated her to an enigmatic, trustworthy smile and an apologetic shrug. "Can't make it here before nine," he answered. "Paper route."

Charlene hesitated. Her stingy brain appeared to be running complex calculations. "Okay," she finally agreed. "Come by at nine.

I'll have to leave you here alone to finish your work while I'm at the doctor. But you won't get your wages until after I get back!"

"That's okay Mrs. Bakersfield I know you're good for it," Ben told her earnestly before dashing out of the apartment. "See you in the morning."

*   *   *   *   *

The following morning, Ben appeared at Charlene Bakersfield's apartment at the agreed-upon time. He re-installed the hanger and shelf in the closet and began slowly, methodically returning shoes, clothing, and boxes of stored bric-a-brac to the refurbished wardrobe as Charlene departed for her doctor's appointment. As soon as the old woman hobbled out, Ben hastily finished filling the closet and set about on an immediate, rapid, and thorough search of the apartment. Local gossip had it that the penny-pinching octogenarian had cash hidden all over her home, and it wasn't long before Ben found an enveloped, stuffed with hundred dollar bills, taped to the bottom of a dresser drawer in the bedroom. He pulled out the bills, stuffed them in his pocket, carefully taped the envelope back in place, and swiftly left the apartment. He had yet another stop to make and he had and a banking errand to run for Otto Ehrlinger.

A small amount of Otto's grandson's inheritance was about to disappear.

*   *   *   *   *

In the fading sun of the cooling desert evening, blue and red strobe lights splashed over the portico of the main building at Hacienda Ridge. Police were in the process of working through the questioning of several elderly residents who had apparently been victimized by a single, serial robbery.

The police activity, coupled with the community's gossip grapevine, created a near mob scene filling the large cul-de-sac in front of the main building.

Officer Gilmore was in the process of separating actual victims from the other residents in order to process the crime scene. From what he could so far decipher, a swindle of monumental depravity had occurred. A squad car was at the scene, and two officers, Gilmore and his partner, were now investigating. Those residents being questioned were consistently mentioning a teenager named Ben Daniels. Clearly this was the perpetrator, but a computer search of the name in police databases yielded no appropriate corresponding hits.

In twelve years on the force, Gilmore thought he had seen every possible type of criminal activity that humankind could commit. He'd investigated offenses that ran the gamut from grisly multiple murders to senseless acts of domestic violence. But in his vast experience within the criminal justice system, this one was unique. These elderly victims hadn't just been robbed of their possessions. They had been victimized by a kind of betrayal that, frankly, filled the veteran cop with disgust.

"Oh fuck," Gilmore muttered as a news van from one of the local TV stations came speeding around the corner. "Now we've got a damned circus on our hands."

The news van screeched to a stop at a curve in the cul-de-sac, only a few yards from the bus stop where Otto Ehrlinger had first met the unassuming yet charismatic Ben Daniels. Katie Cho, a celebrated news reporter from KTVI-TV in Phoenix, hopped to the sidewalk. A diminutive woman, Katie's straight black hair was held tightly in place by a bun, and her porcelain skin looked as though it had never been exposed to a single ray of Arizona sunlight. Closely in tow was her cameraman, who handed her a wireless microphone before she stalked off to get her story.

On the opposite side of the street, Rose McFarland was undergoing questioning by officer Cissy Philmore. Rose had only come outside to see what the commotion was about and that was when she learned of the robberies. Apparently Otto Ehrlinger, Charlene Bakersfield, Molly Ferguson, and a Mrs. Neffler had all been victimized. Because she had known Ben Daniels, and because he'd done work for her, the police were interested in speaking with her.

To Rose, the interrogating policewoman was clearly of the LGBT persuasion. The officer had buzz cut hair and a boxy physique. "I'm surprised," Rose told the officer. Rose's usually animated features were vacant of expression. "I worked with kids all of my professional life, and this one totally duped me. He seemed so . . . pure."

"What do you mean by pure, ma'am?" Philmore's voice was deep and baritone.

Rose stared off at a point somewhere on the horizon. "He just had a very angelic quality about him," she explained after some reflection. "He was sweet, he was helpful, he seemed innocent . . . naive almost. He was scruffy, you might even say unkempt, but if he cleaned up he probably would have been very handsome. Everybody here really liked him. And we all trusted him implicitly."

Cissy jotted notes on her pad as Rose continued.

"I did get the impression that he was spooked. He had a restlessness about him ... he was ... he was on edge. It was very subtle and probably wasn't even noticeable to anyone else, but I worked with kids all my life and I've gotten pretty good at reading them."

Cissy looked up. "Can you provide me with any facts about the boy. Age? Personal history? Family?" She asked impatiently.

"He said he had just graduated from high school and that he was homeschooled up north," Rose recalled. "And that he was starting at the university in the spring semester. Of course this may all have been a lie. At the time I had no reason to doubt him, but now of course ..." Rose's voice trailed off sadly.

Cissy offered a brusque thank you, then moved on to question Otto Ehrlinger.

"I gave him three signed checks this morning," Otto told the officer. "My social security, my IRA, and my stock dividend. He was supposed to deposit them in the bank and be back before lunchtime. When he didn't show up this afternoon, we tried his cell phone but it kept going straight to voice mail."

The cop nodded. Ben's cell phone number had already been checked on the database with no results. It was a burner.

"Disposable phone," she muttered.

"I wasn't the only one who Ben did banking for. Molly Ferguson also gave him signed checks for deposit," Otto continued. "So we called the banks. We found out that the checks had been cashed, but this time the money was never put into our accounts."

"And you believe this Ben Daniels made off with your money?"

"Well you don't see him standing here with it, do you?" Otto asked bitterly.

Across the street, KTVI reporter Katie Cho's news report was shaping up brilliantly. The police vehicle, with red, blue and white strobe lights spinning lazily, served as an ideal crime scene backdrop for a particularly riveting story. Katie was currently asking the residents of Hacienda Ridge some questions of her own. The camera's blinding light was now illuminating Charlene Bakersfield for the report's closing sound byte. Charlene stood, using a cane for support, crying. She was the very picture of a meek and powerless old lady who'd suffered one of life's cruelest and most punishing experiences.

"I'm an elderly woman on a fixed income," she sniffed. "I've scraped together some savings but I don't put it all in the bank. I keep some hidden." Charlene paused and the camera captured a tear trailing down the ancient, frail-looking face. Katie Cho listened with an expression of solemn concern. The reporter nodded solemnly and encouraged the elderly victim with a sympathetic nod. This was good! The soundbyte would definitely make it to broadcast.

"That little hooligan seemed so nice," Charlene continued on cue. She sounded like a brittle and wounded little bird. "But the minute I left my apartment he ransacked every room, found my cash, and robbed me!"

The reporter, wishing to convey objectivity, continued to gently prod her subject.

"So how do you know it was him?" Katie asked. "There must be people coming in and out of this building all the time. Nurses, home health aides, delivery people, visitors . . . what makes you so sure it wasn't any of them?"

"Oh it was Ben all right," Charlene insisted. "He was in my apartment all by himself when I left. I got back home to find that my money was gone and so was he." Charlene pounded her cane on the ground in angry frustration. "That is no coincidence."

Katie turned to the camera to wrap what she was convinced would be a much talked about news report. She stared into the lens with stony sincerity. "It is one of the most coordinated robberies ever to hit Maricopa County," she said with great solemnity. "And perhaps one of the most heartbreaking. These victims were elderly, vulnerable, and taken by complete surprise. They were kind and trustworthy toward someone who preyed upon their fragility. Cash, valuables, and signed social security checks have all but disappeared in the wake of a teenage boy simply known as Ben Daniels."

*　*　*　*　*

Ben Daniels ceased to exist in the front of The OdySea, a massive marine aquarium and popular tourist attraction in Scottsdale, Arizona. In the course of one hour he had left the bank with nearly five thousand dollars in cash, gotten a cheap but acceptable hair cut, and made a final visit to the seedy hotel that had been his home for the past several weeks. He had shaved, and cut up the fat padding, which had made Ben Daniels appear so chubby, into small bits of foam and fabric. He had distributed this, along with clothes, hat, and sunglasses into four plastic shopping bags. He had deposited three of the bags into three separate trash cans at a string of fast food restaurants near the motel and then taken a bus to the aquarium, where he blended in with throngs of tourists and school kids who mobbed the sidewalk at the entranceway. Among a crowd of ten thousand people who visited the aquarium daily, he nonchalantly deposited the final plastic shopping bag, containing the rest of Ben Daniel's remains, deep within a large garbage can.

Lean and tall, clean cut and clean shaven, absent of the hunched gait that he had adopted since his arrival in Scottsdale, the handsome and now hatless Danny Briggs regarded the world through his own emerald green colored eyes, having flushed the brown contact lenses down a public toilet. He walked with a confident stride through the crowd, avoiding eye contact as he moved from one end of the building to the other with purposeful intent. He sincerely regretted not having time to visit the aquarium itself. He wished he could see the fifty exhibits he'd read about on the Odysea website, exhibits that featured over 2 million gallons of water and housed more than five hundred species of sea life. It sucked having to walk right past the building without even a glimpse inside. But Danny's plan left no time for pleasantries.

As he moved among the crowd in front of the aquarium, an even deeper sense of remorse descended upon him. Here were kids his age, or close to it, enjoying one of life's simple pleasures with their mothers and fathers and sisters and brothers who wanted nothing more from them then company and companionship. Even with the intermittent bickering and fighting and complaining, Danny could sense the love and deep bonds that kept these people tied to each other, and in a short span of time he felt progressively alone, isolated, and empty. He experienced an acute onset of anguish at the loss his mother and a deep, abiding sadness at the desperate turns his childhood had taken. The kids here, who likely took their excursion to the aquarium for granted, had no idea how great they had it.

Danny, however, had neither the time nor the luxury for self-pity and instead tried to be grateful for the cover this crowd of people were providing. Here, he was hidden in plain sight.

He tossed his burner phone, wrapped inside a fast food bag filled with the detritus of burger and fry wrappings, into another trash bin. The phone Darlene gave him had been disposed of in a similar fashion upon his arrival in Phoenix. A brand new smartphone, paid for in cash with some of Darlene's money, was tucked into a front pocket. An Uber car pulled to the curb, and Danny jumped into it with his backpack full of stolen cash and jewelry. His movements had been methodical. However, he was painfully distracted by the nearly overwhelming guilt and sadness he was feeling. But he forced himself to shake these emotions. His desperation to escape his past overrode all other considerations.

The Uber took him in a westerly direction, from the aquarium in Scottsdale to the Phoenix bus station. The Greyhound depot was a small, unfussy concrete affair. Buses for Los Angeles left on an almost hourly basis. Danny had timed his arrival at the station to coincide with the 4:20. He would be seated snugly in the back seat with his ear buds in place, the greyhound far into the desert before his actions at Hacienda Ridge would even be discerned.

He was slumped comfortably in his seat, eyes closed, music blaring, when he felt an insistent tap on his shoulder.

He opened his eyes, sat up with a jolt and removed an ear bud.

"Oh I'm so sorry for startling you," said the attractive older woman seated across the aisle from him. "Do you by any chance have any aspirin in your backpack?" She held up an empty bottle of Excedrin by way of explanation. " I have a splitting headache and I've run out."

Danny regarded her blankly. Late thirties, peroxide blonde hair, cleavage on bold display, copious make-up, short skirt, tan legs.

"No," he answered with a shake of his head. He popped the ear bud back in place, slumped back into a position of comfort, and closed his eyes.

Not five minutes later he felt another tap on his shoulder. He tugged the ear bud from his ear and turned once again toward the woman. Her gaze was direct and hungry. It was the stare of a predator. Revulsion welled up inside him.

"Are you a model?" she asked with an attempt at a seductive purr.

His thoughts turned to Malchus, and the saccharine sweetness that came just before the pounce. Thoughts of the Painted Desert farm caused him to shudder inwardly. Not just Malchus, but every resident who turned a blind eye to the man's actions filled him with an almost desperate desire to insulate himself from those who would use him.

The woman pulled a flask of vodka from her pocketbook and poured it into a paper cup. "Would you like a little drinkie?"

"I'm seventeen," he said in a low and clearly disturbed voice. "No, I do not want a drinkie." He looked around and spotted an empty seat a few rows away. He gathered up his jacket and his backpack, stood, and moved.

The lady gulped down her cocktail with a great huff as Danny settled into his new seat. As he escaped back into the reverie of his music he tried to count his blessings. Once again, he was reminded that while his desirability drew all means of unwanted attention, it also gave him great power. Power that he intended to harness.

The bus continued to hurtle closer toward his ultimate destination and further from his past as Danny consulted his smartphone. His first step in Hollywood, he had learned, would be to find himself an agent. He had already bookmarked the website for a low budget talent representative in Los Angeles. He selected the Moyt Agency not because it was the best, or even close, but simply because it was approachable. It was not located in an impenetrable business tower or guarded by a bank of security guards and a fortress of secretaries and assistants. In fact, it was a walk up office located above a cheap furniture store. And while the website indicated that the Moyt Agency did not accept walk-ins, that was exactly what Danny intended to do.

He tucked his phone back into his pocket and attempted to nap. Four hours later, he was in Los Angeles.

He walked out of Greyhound bus terminal on 7th Street in downtown LA. It was after 10 PM. He was hit with a wave of hot, smoggy air as he left the air conditioned building. While he had never been to Los Angeles before, he had done extensive research on his phone and had called up maps and images to orient himself with the city. It was a good thing he wasn't expecting anything glamorous when his sneakers hit the pavement in this part of the city. The neighborhood immediately outside the terminal was industrial and far from exciting. He had read that the area had experienced a renaissance over the past few years, but he could see no signs of it on this particular block. He pushed into the McDonalds on 7th and Alameda and ordered a burger, fries, and some chicken nuggets. When he was done wolfing down his meal, Danny threw his backpack over his shoulder and headed out the door. The Mainstay Hotel was located about a mile away. It was described on Google as a hip boutique Hotel and Hostel, and the pictures looked cool.

He would forego Uber and make the trip on foot. He had already watched a video on YouTube called "7th Street, Downtown Los Angeles", and the area appeared to be safe. He wanted to walk, to get the feel of the city, to be immersed in the L.A. vibe. He could already feel that this was where he belonged!

The street became livelier as he moved north on 7th, in the direction of West Hollywood. There were skyscrapers rising into the night sky, and a hip, gritty urban feel that was decidedly different from Phoenix or Scottsdale prevailed. In fact, it reminded him more of what New York City might be like if it had palm trees. He passed an old fashioned cinema. A Technicolor movie poster in the window promised a "smash hit." On an eye-catching billboard dominating an entire street corner, three attractive actors were touted as the stars of a "smash television series." In the window of a trendy-looking nightclub called "Smash," a hip neon sign promised a lineup of all-star DJ's.

The queue of people at the door checked him out as he passed.

"I think he's a soap star," he overheard one woman tell her friend.

He smiled inwardly at the observation. It was the city of angels, but only a very few came close to looking angelic. And those blessed few, clearly, were revered. He buried his hands in his pockets, continued walking purposefully, and decided upon a new name for himself. Like the smash hit movie, the smash television series, or the hot new club called "Smash," Danny had arrived. And he would call himself Danny Smash.

He located his hotel and quickly checked into his room. Before falling, exhausted, onto his bed, he went online and made an appointment for the following morning at BluFade salon on Sunset Boulevard, where he would treat himself to a short, stylish cut befitting a young LA hipster.

*   *   *   *   *

The office of Phyllis Moyt was located across the street from a Jack in the Box restaurant on Venice Boulevard in downtown Los Angeles. Less than ten miles and light years away from the epicenter of Hollywood's entertainment industry, it was a two-room affair located above a discount furniture store and was the brain center from which Phyllis ran her tiny empire. Here she cultivated clients and managed their careers. Phyllis represented print photography models. She got them jobs and took a cut of their earnings. She was an agent whose roster of talent could be seen gracing daily news-paper advertisements, bus stop posters, nightlife magazines, promo cards, and mail order catalogues throughout southern California and sometimes beyond.

Phyllis was divorced, childless, and on the wrong side of forty. Her short, frizzy red hair was hastily gelled into place. She wore no jewelry on her chubby hands or fingers, far too much makeup on her florid face, and a silky, multi-colored print dress purchased off the discount rack that did little to flatter her flab.

She was a frugal businesswoman who wouldn't hire a secretary or a receptionist even if she could afford one. During busier times she refused to utilize a temp service. She just put in extra hours. Right now she was sitting at her desk in the reception area that fronted her Lilliputian agency. A cigarette dangled from her lips, a pair of non-prescription readers were perched at the tip of her nose, and her right finger manipulated a computer mouse while she intently scrolled down the screen.

She first went through her emails. Phyllis had two types of cli-ents: those who wished to book models, and the models themselves. After deleting dozens of SPAM messages, she first focused on those correspondences that indicated potential bookings. Photographers, editors, art directors, and casting agents who needed models for advertisements, fashion spreads, and catalogues were her bread and butter. Another revenue source were hosts and socialites in the ritzier neighborhoods who booked bevies of alluring young models whose sole job would be to stand around at parties and provide eye candy for the primped and pampered crowd. This was not a main source of income but Phyllis was happy to oblige such requests. It was easy money all around. Each time she sent out a client, she pocketed twenty percent of the earnings.

It was just after 10 AM and already a languid and typical morning at the Moyt Agency. Phyllis responded to the emails from clients looking to book models for a department store fashion flyer, a magazine advertisement for a new restaurant in the Valley, and another magazine ad for a surf shop in Manhattan Beach. In response to requests for modeling talent, Phyllis scrolled through her vast library of electronic comp cards. She had hundreds of these cards digitized in her computer files. Each model had a card, which was a collection of pictures featuring the attractive individual posed in various states of casual and formal dress and in swimwear. Phyllis selected the right faces and bodies for the various job requests and sent those out to the clients. She would follow up on the bookings later in the afternoon.

Next came Phyllis' favorite and most entertaining part of the day, perusing emails from the many, many wannabe models requesting that she sign them up and get them jobs in front of the camera. She got dozens of these on a daily basis, many from the same people over and over again. They came from everywhere in the country, sometimes beyond, and from people of all ages. The email correspondences were poorly written, unprofessionally worded, and badly executed. In a typical letter, the sender would promise that he or she was extremely attractive and had many times been encouraged to pursue a career in modeling. Some were stupid enough to admit that they wanted to be models because it was such an easy job. Most, but surprisingly not all of the would-be models, attached pictures, and this was where things got really entertaining. The pictures were rarely professional and almost never presented in industry standard, comp card format. They were usually photos that had been taken by cell phone in candid situations like weddings, sports events, birthday parties, or just lounging around on the living room couch. Some were selfies that people had taken of themselves in their bathroom mirrors. A few were portraits. Very few of the pictures featured genuinely attractive people. Fewer yet had the quality of looks or bodies to be professional models. And if they did, there was still the question of whether they had enough talent to consistently turn on the charisma when the camera lights flashed. Virtually all who solicited representation by Phyllis Moyt were coolly and perfunctorily rejected.

Phyllis typed a response to a particularly offensive submission from an overweight young woman who attached a picture of herself in an ill fitting bikini in front of what appeared to be a trailer home.

Whoever suggested that YOU should be a model must have been visually impaired, Phyllis wanted to write back. *Give it up, honey!*

She deleted the email as the phone buzzed.

"Moyt Agency," she barked. It was Herb Weinstock from Beverly Boulevard Magazine. Herb was looking for models for an ad campaign for a new nightclub.

"Age, demographic?" Phyllis asked efficiently and then listened intently.

"Ethnic, whitebread ... edgy?" she then asked tartly.

"Bollywood is hot and I have just the guy," she finally said. "Just signed him last week. Very dark, smoldering, and provocative."

A bell rang, signaling that someone had entered the office. "Leave it on the floor," she commanded, assuming it was an expected delivery. She didn't bother looking up.

"Leave what on the floor?" Came the answer.

"The package, nitwit. I'm on the phone."

"Um, I'd like to speak with someone about a modeling job."

Phyllis still didn't bother to look up. The voice had a clear, masculine, innocent quality, but even that wasn't enough to get her attention. Hot on the scent of a signed contract, she was irritated by the interruption. "I don't take walk-ins. Email a comp card," she quipped.

"Sorry," came the reply. "I don't have a comp card."

"Then get one and stop wasting my time," she demanded. Her eyes were on her computer screen. But the boy wasn't leaving, and something about his presence caused her to steal a glance at his face.

"Herb," she said slowly into the receiver, "I'm gonna have to call you back."

Phyllis tossed her phone onto her desk and stared, transfixed, at the visage that had just stepped into the office and interrupted her phone call. Before her stood a flawlessly handsome young man who looked to be just out of his teens and whose wattage filled her dingy office with a nearly tangible electric current. In her business, exceptional looking people were a regular part of life. But very few had that indefinable quality that was a mixture of perfect proportion, feral movement, and casual self-confidence. True sex appeal was in fact a great rarity. Standing before Phyllis was a literal Adonis.

Her crotch tingled to life, and Phyllis recognized the need for composure. She drew in a deep breath.

"Can I help you?" she asked. Her voice was all taffy and cotton candy.

The boy approached her desk and offered his hand. He projected the confidence of a tycoon and the innocence of a puppy. He flashed a disarming smile. Phyllis prayed silently that he was a walk-in seeking representation. This was a young man that Hollywood would bow to, and Phyllis wanted a piece. She realized instantly and instinctively that this kid could put her, and her tiny agency, on the map.

"My name is Danny Smash," he said. "I just got into town, and I need work right away. It says on your website that you'll consider paying for headshots if a person has potential as a model. I'm here to introduce myself and to see if you think I have potential."

As he smiled, an adorable little dimple formed in his cheek while emerald green eyes danced like Gene Kelly at Radio City Music Hall.

Phyllis' normally taciturn demeanor had melted like wax on a candle. "Yes," she answered, attempting to keep the eagerness from her voice. "I do think you might have potential."

Danny looked around the small office. The walls were covered in cheaply framed headshots of Phyllis's clients and print ads from newspapers and magazines advertising nightclubs, clothing stores, gyms, even an LA area plastic surgeon's office. The pictures were carelessly hung, askew, and a fine film of dusk had settled on the tops of the frames.

Danny's eye was caught by one picture in particular that stood out from the rest. It appeared to be a photo shoot featuring a model sprawled suggestively on her back in a four-post bed. Scantily clad in a negligee, she stared suggestively and seductively at a male photographer at the foot of the bed. The photographer was young and beefcake, also barely dressed in leather fetish wear.

"You seem transfixed by that picture," Phyllis said to Danny.

"It's very … suggestive," Danny answered. His attention was now fully back on Phyllis. "Seems different from all rest."

"You're quite observant," she answered, already delivering the sales pitch. "I represent quite a diverse variety of models and have clients from many sectors of advertising and entertainment."

"Do your models do any television commercials?" Danny asked.

"Of course they do!" Phyllis lied. "I send my models to casting calls for TV commercials all the time. Some of my models have even gone on to careers with the soaps. This is LA and the sky's the limit. And I can promise you that if I sign you as one of my models, you will get work immediately. How old are you?"

"I just turned eighteen," he said.

Phyllis nodded. He was still very young. And probably naïve. While he had an innate charm and a clear confidence in his own physicality, he was likely still too young and innocent to fully grasp the utter power of his own appearance. It was a good thing that a walk-in wouldn't get past the guard desks at the big three agencies in town, or this kid would have been scooped up in an instant. She silently thanked God that she had put that lie on her website about paying for headshots. She had never actually done it before but this time she would be delighted to make an exception.

As he stood at her desk, she figured him to be about six foot two. Perfect for just about any kind of modeling assignment. "I can start sending you out right away," she told him. She fought to keep the eagerness from her voice. "Sit down and let me get the contracts together. Then I'll set you up with a photographer for some head shots."

* * * * *

Hollywood Boulevard might have been overwhelming for Danny if it weren't so damned exciting. He walked slowly along the star adorned sidewalk, past giant open air souvenir shops, Madam Tassaud's wax museum with its huge film spool at the door, and the famous Grauman's Chinese Theatre, which was massive and awe inspiring. He had never seen so many people, of so many different sorts, in his life. There was a man carrying a large python. At almost every corner people were fully outfitted as famous film stars and movie characters from the past and present. People drank beer at open-air bars. This stretch of Hollywood Boulevard was tacky, touristy, and chaotic, but Danny never felt so at home in his life.

There was constant police presence on the street, and an officer walking toward him made direct eye contact that left him unsettled. He ducked into a busy Starbucks, ordered a cup of tea and a cake pop, found a seat in a rear corner of the shop, and pulled out his phone. People in the store stared at him with open admiration, and he realized that the cop must've staring at him that way, too. He tried to shake his paranoia. Still, for what seemed like the 100th time, he Googled the words: Scottsdale robbery Hacienda Ridge. Aside from a short online news article, his search revealed no other coverage. Since his arrival in LA he had read the article, carefully, several times, and now he read it again:

TEENAGER ROBS ELDERLY COMPLEX IN SCOTTSDALE

The police are investigating a baffling crime that was reported 5 PM Wednesday afternoon by the residents of a senior apartment complex in in Northern Scottsdale. Officer Cissy Rodriguez responded to a call from a frantic elderly person who claimed to have been victimized by a teenage boy who was known for doing errands around the complex. Officers arrived at the scene to learn that more than one of the residents of this upscale community

were reporting that both jewelry and cash were missing. All of the victims described a plain looking looking, overweight teenager who had been at the complex earlier in the day and who had access to the victims' apartments. The suspect in this crime went by the name of Ben Daniels, however police have so far been unable to find a person of that name matching the description provided by the victims. The suspect is described as being approximately 6' tall. He has light brown hair and brown eyes, and walks with a pronounced slouch. Because he often wore a baseball cap and sunglasses to obscure his features, there are no additional details regarding his appearance. So far, no clear pictures of Mr. Daniels have surfaced, and police remained baffled as to the teen's true identity. Anyone with information concerning this matter is asked to contact the Scottsdale Police Department.

Danny swirled his herbal tea and took a sip. He finished his cake pop and tossed his phone into his backpack. His calm, fluid movement belied inner anxiety and turmoil. When he stepped from the Starbucks and back onto the sidewalk, the frenetic, unconstrained energy of the city, the turbulent commotion of the crowds, and the wailing noise of traffic suddenly became an overload drumming in his head, and left him feeling claustrophobic. He caught a glimpse of himself in the window. With his stylish short hair cut in its natural blonde color, clean-shaven face, green eyes, and trendy new clothing, he bore absolutely no resemblance to Ben Daniels.

Filling with confidence that he had dramatically altered his appearance and relocated to a faraway city, where he was hidden in plain sight among 18 million other people, he slowly relaxed into a sense of safety. The knowledge that he was young, and that his looks made him uniquely desirable, filled him with a serene feeling of satisfaction and power as he headed back to the Youth Hostel.

* * * * *

Phyllis sat at her desk and gazed admiringly at the unequivocal work of art that stared back at her from the computer screen. Danny Smash, her newest client and by far the luckiest break ever to have graced her agency, was equally breathtaking in photographs as he was in the flesh. Years in the business had taught her that even the most beautiful looking person could come across as less than ideal in photographs. It was an intangible quality, but some people were photogenic while others were simply not. Phyllis, ever the businesswoman, had taken some measure of risk in paying a top LA photographer for Danny's headshots.

But boy had the investment been worth it! Danny was not just spectacularly handsome in the picture, but his pose bespoke all American athleticism, his smile was warm and beguiling, and his eyes, those emerald green eyes, radiated a sexual charisma that was purely magnetic. He bore a combination of mystery, seductiveness and congeniality - personality traits that literally emanated from the picture. In fact, the headshot took her breath away, as she was certain it would with casting agents all over town.

Her reverie was interrupted when a porn star known as Thunder Kitten burst through her door in a gust of hectic energy. Thunder, who's real name was Cindy, strode into the office looking like a homeless hooker in baggy sweat pants and a pink halter top that did little to hide her obviously fake double Ds.

Phyllis was unfazed. Porn stars were notoriously ephemeral and did not lead particularly traditional lives. Phyllis reached into a drawer in her desk and pulled out a check.

"Thunder, you really need to get yourself a bank account," she advised the much younger woman, not for the first time. "Everybody else gets direct deposited. This is getting to be a real pain in the ass having to cut checks for you." Phyllis waved the check in the air.

Thunder regarded her agent through glassy eyes. "Yeah, sure, babe. I get it. I'll get around to it."

Yeah, sure, thought Phyllis with disgust, an emotion she hoped was written all over her face. You couldn't even depend on Thunder to show up sober to a shoot, let alone take care of her own responsibilities. It was like trying to manage a little child.

Thunder reached to take the check from Phyllis, glanced at the computer screen, and let out a short gasp. Her eyes were suddenly riveted to the picture of Danny.

"Who's *that*?" She wanted to know.

"That," Phyllis said, hitting a key on the computer that caused Danny's picture to melt from the screen, "is someone who will never work your side of the industry. He's strictly legit, and soon enough everyone in this town will know his name."

Thunder snatched her check from Phyllis and tucked it inside a big leather satchel that served as her both her purse and her suitcase. Her expression turned to a pout. "I'd sure like to co-star with him, whoever he is," she said with longing in her voice.

"That," said Phyllis, turning back to her computer. "Will never happen. Go get yourself a fucking bank account or I won't be booking you for any more shoots."

Phyllis watched as Thunder huffed out of the office. *Goodbye, Thunder*, thought Phyllis. *One day soon I won't have to deal with you or anyone else in the porn industry. I've signed a potential superstar to an exclusive contract, and I finally hold the magic ticket into the big leagues.*

Her phone buzzed to let her know that she had a text. She glanced curiously at the screen. Why was Bryson White asking her to call him? She had already paid the A-list photographer, in full, almost nine hundred dollars for Danny's headshots. Bryson was a veritable icon in Hollywood, and probably had the names of every star in town in his cell phone contacts. Phyllis had to schedule Danny's photo session through a long series of the photographer's assistants, and had to jump through hoops at that. She was shocked that he would be asking her to call him directly. She tentatively picked up her phone, and curiously dialed.

He picked up on three rings. "How do you like the shots of Danny Smash?" his voice was smooth and deep. He spoke with a clipped east coast accent.

"I like them very much," she answered honestly. Her stomach did nervous flip-flops as she tried to maintain her composure. "Very, very much."

"So do I." There was a hint of conceit in the photographer's voice. "In fact, I was very impressed with your client. I've never come across anyone quite like him frankly. I'll say this. I'm straight, but your boy is absolutely gorgeous and the camera loves him. His shots have had my whole studio buzzing ever since I took them. I've already put them on the homepage of my website."

Phyllis was ecstatic and truly flattered. A member of Hollywood's elite was calling to compliment her client! Danny's picture was at the top of a superstar photographer's website. She was headed for the big time!

"Thank you," she worded breathlessly. "He's quite a standout, isn't he?"

"That," announced Bryson, "is the understatement of the year. This kid has charm, personality, and charisma oozing from every pore. He's definitely got what it takes to make it in this town. He's got it with a capital IT. I've already called Becky Dann at Oracle Casting and asked her to call you to set something up. Don't forget that you owe me a favor when this kid gets big."

"Of course," gulped Phyllis finally. Bryson had already hung up.

*   *   *   *   *

The Chaplin Academy of Dramatic Arts was jokingly referred to, by the ubiquitous starving actors and actresses of LA, as *the Charlie Chaplin School for Actin'*. The "Academy" was located on the third floor of a walk-up building on a side street that was two blocks off Hollywood Boulevard. A rickety air conditioner failed to keep out the heat, and soot covered windows failed to let in the sun. Danny climbed the creaky wooden stairs, ignoring the graffiti on the walls, and took a seat in one of the cheap metal folding chairs that surrounded a tiny stage. He was five minutes early for his first scene study class. He surveyed the gritty room with a mixture of excitement and woe. He was thrilled at being part of an acting class in in the epicenter of Hollywood and to be partaking in an experience that was brand new for him. He was disappointed, however, about the fact that Chaplin was rated as one of the worst acting schools -- this in a city where such institutions were abundant. But Danny had been granted hasty admission thanks to his new agent, Phyllis Moyt, who had also paid for the classes here. After a few minutes he sardonically observed that he was likely the most ambitious student in the entire academy, for he was the only one to arrive on time for class.

He folded his 6'2" frame into a front row seat, pulled a packet of pop tarts from his backpack, ripped one open and scarfed it down. It had been a busy week since his arrival in LA. He'd spent the first day here trying to find a bank with an available safe deposit box into which he could stuff all of his cash. Then he'd found a pawnshop on Vine. He hocked all of his expensive stolen jewelry except for the Rolex watch, which was stowed in the bottom of his duffle bag back in his room. He was now staying at the Banana Bungalow, a hip and funky youth hostel in the center of Hollywood where a private room with a kitchen cost less than $95 per night, compliments of his new agent. Phyllis Moyt had also paid for his headshots, which were taken by a prominent photographer at a large, bustling downtown studio two days ago. He had been surrounded by a bevy of assistants who primped and fawned all over him while the photographer fed him endless compliments. It was the kind of attention he could easily get accustomed to. It was not the controlling exploitation he'd gotten from Malchus or the clingy, smothering ministrations of Darlene. It was star treatment and he basked in it.

Tomorrow he was booked for a paid photo shoot, so his agent's investment was already starting to pay off nicely. With each day he was moving further from the thoughts, fears and guilt that had plagued him since leaving Arizona.

The classroom started filling with other students. Most were in their twenties and early thirties, but one man was in his sixties and a few looked young enough to be in high school. A pretty Emma Stone type flounced into the seat beside him and fixed him with a flirtatious smile. A buff California surfer dude sat to his opposite side, checked him out appraisingly, and said, "Hey, dude."

Having grown up entirely among adults, Danny was unused to being surrounded by people of his own age. Aside from Malchus, the residents of the farm tended to give him wide berth and kept the conversations more practical, and less personal, in nature. It was taking time to for Danny to get comfortable among his peers, who were the exact opposite.

Danny returned the attention of each with a polite smile and fixed his eyes on the stage. An older woman, looking like a sixties throwback direct from Laurel Canyon, had climbed onto the platform and now stood staring at the small crowd with a peaceful, almost beatific expression. She wore a loose fitting, flowing, gauzy white dress and was devoid of jewelry. Her brown hair, peppered with gray, was pulled back in a ponytail. Clear and piercing blue eyes stood out from an otherwise unremarkable face. The acting teacher's name was Amanda Beasley.

However tenuous, she was a connection to the world of Hollywood and to the ways of show business. She had Danny's rapt attention.

"Okay everyone." Hers was a commanding presence. "Turn off your cell phones." She surveyed the class, her eyes connecting with each student. Her glance caught for a moment longer when she noticed Danny.

"I'd like for all of you to join me on the stage," she told them.

The students all climbed to the small stage. There was silence such that you could hear a pin drop as they awaited Amanda Beasley's next directive.

"We must train our bodies so that we are in charge of them, not the opposite. Movement is the most important and basic element of acting. In that moment in front of the audience, or in front of the camera, you must be fully within that character, not just in your mind, but in your body and it's language and motion."

The teacher paused and walked among the students, whose attention was engrossed. "You have just learned that you have been betrayed by a trusted ally. I want you to sync your mind with your body. Zero dialogue."

With this, Amanda Beasley folded her arms across her chest and stepped backwards to the very rear of the stage. She said nothing further.

While the rest of the class clenched their fists, crossed their arms, and stormed about the stage angrily with tightened jaws, Danny stood still and his shoulders slumped. He had experienced the ultimate betrayal.

A happy little boy.

Innocence shattered.

Running through the house.

Hoping for his birthday present.

The door shuts. Locks.

The man he trusts like a father demands his silence.

His submission.

Tears stream down his face as he huddles into a tight ball.

Trying to protect himself.

No way out.

Amanda was staring at Danny with a strange expression. "Experience your feelings. Let your emotions control your physical expression," she softly directed.

Danny stood on the stage as thoughts of his mother's failure to protect him, Malchus' abuse, and his own betrayal of good, decent people left him feeling overwrought, overcome, and very, very alone. He was not aware of another person in his universe. Tears streaked his face.

"Okay everyone," Amanda interrupted. She was addressing the crowd but stared directly at Danny. "Now, as I count down from ten, let's release these emotions. Allow peace to flow into your bodies."

Danny stood. Amanda watched intently as a calm demeanor came over him and he returned to his seat.

"Alright," she said once the stage was clear and the students had all returned to their seats. "Before we break, lets do some relaxation exercises that you might want to call upon before an audition. Amanda began slowly raising her arms and breathing deeply, and the class followed her lead. After five minutes of slowly inhaling and exhaling, and gentle movement of the limbs, trunk and neck, she permitted them to break.

"When we resume, I'm going to put you in pairs and assign each pair a short script. We will spend the rest of the afternoon doing cold readings."

The class gasped in unison.

Amanda held up her hands. "I know the cold reading is a nightmare for most actors, but the sooner you get used to it, the better off you'll all be."

When the class began to disperse on their break Danny checked his cell phone. First, he looked up the definition of 'cold reading'. It was, he learned, reading from a script without the benefit of rehearsal. No big deal. There was an email from Phyllis detailing an audition for a TV commercial on Monday!

He then went to the internet and performed his regular Google search, which this time revealed a new article whose headline read: "No Leads in Retirement Village Robbery." He scanned the article. There was nothing there to alarm him. He had grown up totally off the grid; there were no records whatsoever of his existence, so he was untraceable by law enforcement. He felt safe; his crime would go unsolved.

He was interrupted by a gentle tap on his shoulder. He immediately powered down his cell phone and glanced up. It was Amanda Beasley. She was looking at him with an expression of approval.

"I don't know where you came from," she said simply. "But you've got what it takes, kid."

With that she turned and headed toward a group of waiting students, her movements as fluid as a ballerina. When class resumed Danny found himself totally engrossed in the cold readings and he noticed, with great satisfaction, that Amanda Beasley continued to take highly admiring notice of him. Time passed like lightening, and when class was over Danny was invited by some of the other students to join them at the Shake Shack on Hollywood Boulevard.

Danny had never had friends his own age before, and while he wasn't terribly comfortable with the idea of having to trust people he was intrigued with the possibility of having friends. And besides, he decided with a shrug, an actor couldn't spend his life under a rock.

On the way to the restaurant, Brent, the surfer dude, said, "I want to stop at the 7 Eleven on Hollywood and Vine for some ciggies."

Danny stood outside with Carly, the girl who had been seated next to him and who bore a close resemblance to Emma Watson, and Starr, a blonde haired, blued-eyed girl in her twenties.

"I write a blog about being a struggling acting student in LA," Starr boastfully told Danny. "I'm sure you know that Chaplin's School for Actin' is not exactly the Royal Academy, but Amanda Beasley is highly respected. She's one of LA's best-kept secrets."

Carly rolled her eyes. "Starr considers herself quite the authority on Hollywood with that blog of hers," she said with a smile. "But she's relatively new to this town. I've lived here all my life, and my father was in this business since I was a little kid."

Brent exited the 7-Eleven and joined them. The group headed for Shake Shack, a block away, and Carly continued vaingloriously. Her attention was focused on Danny. "My father was a character actor back in the eighties. He was on the Facts of Life, Cheers, Who's the Boss, and the Golden Girls."

Danny nodded, pretending to be impressed. He had only heard of one of these TV shows. Reruns of the Golden Girls were always on the big screen in the lounge back at Hacienda Ridge.

Brent had lit up a cigarette when they left 7-Eleven and snuffed it out as they now entered the Shake Shack. The four of them took their places on a short line at the counter.

"Did your old man ever meet Matt McCrew?" Brent asked Carly. "People tell me I look like him," he said, casting a sidelong glance at Danny. "I saw him jogging in Malibu a couple of times. He's the kind of actor I want to be."

"I doubt my father's ever met him," Carly answered, looking down at the floor. "Dad hasn't worked in a while. He says the business was too competitive. He sells real estate now."

"Real estate! I never knew that!" Starr exclaimed. "Sad, very sad. I'm going to put that in my blog. I'm going to title my entry, *a precautionary tale.*"

Starr was sad, very sad, that she had mentioned it. But it was too late now.

Danny studied them all with great interest. He liked it better when the conversation was not directed at him. He enjoyed listening to the spirited banter.

They all ordered their food. Their trays were soon loaded with thick scrumptious burgers and cheesy crinkle fries, which they carried to one of the wood grain and steel tables that were the restaurant's trademark.

Carly dipped a french fry into her milkshake and started gnawing on it. "So where do you live," she asked Danny.

"Right now I'm staying at the Banana Bungalow down the street," he told her.

"Dude, that place is sweet!" Brent exclaimed. "You either have a job, your parents are loaded, or some old man is taking care of you," he said with a suggestive grin.

Danny felt his back stiffen but kept his expression neutral. "I'll be working," he answered quickly between bites of his cheeseburger.

"Do you have a restaurant job?" Starr asked. "It's a very unfortunate cliché, but most of the actors in LA are waiters. And even good waitering jobs are hard to come by."

Danny wiped a bit of grease from his chin with a napkin. "I have a photo shoot tomorrow for a magazine ad," he said.

"A *paid* photo shoot?" Brent, Carly and Starr gasped in unison.

"Yep," Danny nodded. "And I have a callback for a TV commercial on Monday."

"And you've been in LA for how long?" Carly asked.

"A week," Danny told them.

"Dude, how did you get all this work already?" Brent asked with disbelief. "You're related to somebody in the industry, right?" Starr asked.

"I have never heard of anyone having a call back for anything within a week of getting into town," Carly said. "Did you have this set up before you got here?'

"No," Danny answered. "My agent set it up for me. I had the audition yesterday and I have the call back next week."

"Holy shit!" Starr exclaimed, pulling out her phone. "I'm going to have to take your picture for my blog."

"You lucky fuck!" Brent told him in a voice filled with awe.

"Who's your agent?" Carly asked, dumbfounded.

The table was engrossed. This was epic.

"Phyllis Moyt," Danny answered. "The Moyt Agency."

Brent's expression was blank. "Never heard of that one," he said. He pulled out his phone and consulted with Google.

"Me neither," added Starr. "But if they're taking new clients, pleeaeeesse give her my name."

Carly's previously animated expression became clouded. "Wait a second. Phyllis Moyt? I've heard that name. Doesn't she represent porn stars?"

Danny calmly returned her curious gaze. "Uh huh," he answered honestly. "Quite a few, in fact."

Brent's head snapped up instantly. "Dude!" He exclaimed. "You do porn?"

Danny laughed. "Are you kidding? Just because my agent represents porn stars doesn't mean I do porn."

Starr was riveted. "How did you happen to sign with *this* agency?"

Danny leaned back and sipped his milkshake. "I researched every single agent in LA before I even got here," he answered. "The Moyt Agency struck me as the most approachable, maybe because many legit actors wouldn't want to be associated with the place. My thinking was that, since nobody can even get past the guards at the big talent house, I would have a better chance with a boutique agency with a so-so reputation. I needed an agent I could walk right up to and use my powers of persuasion to get me signed. My goal was to start working immediately," he said with a humble, beguiling smile. "And luckily it worked out for me."

His tablemates sat in silent awe.

"You're a pretty smart cookie," Starr finally said with flirtatious giddiness. "Show me one actor who gets into town and has work in the industry within a week!"

"There's more to me than meets the eye," Danny said with a wink in Starr's direction.

"Dude, you are totally my idol right now!" exclaimed Brett.

"What would you do if this agent of yours tried to get you to do porn?" Carly asked, her eyes grazing Danny's chest and biceps.

Danny returned her gaze with piercing intensity. "That," he answered sharply, "will never, ever happen." Danny's focus then shifted abruptly to his burger, which he devoured in two bites.

Danny's sudden iciness caused Carly to shudder. She lowered her eyes as a hush descended upon the table.

*   *   *   *   *

The Bradbury is an historic building located in downtown Los Angeles. The five-story office complex, built in 1893, is considered a local architectural treasure and has been used as a location for many popular films and TV shows. The legendary rooftop scene in the epic film Blade Runner was shot there, as were some of the movie's interior scenes.

Danny was unaware of the building's storied and legendary history or of its iconic place in movie lore. He had been here just a few days ago for his first audition. He was, though, once again awed when he entered the building's expansive skylit interior for his callback. The atrium had a glass ceiling, subway tiled floors, a cool wrought iron staircase, and the feel of a place from a completely different era.

His callback was on the fifth floor, in the offices of Eros Productions. The elevator in the Bradbury was an ornate, iron cage that looked original to the building. As the ancient car carried Danny to the uppermost floor, he relished the feeling of ascending higher and higher away from the people in the lobby. He was in L.A. for less than two weeks and he was already going on a callback for a television commercial! He could imagine his rise in the elevator mirroring a slow but steady ascent to stardom, to a place high above the world where no one could touch him, harm him or control him. He was walking on air as he exited the elevator and pushed through double glass doors the led the waiting room of Eros Productions. The modern interior he entered was a stark contrast to the building's antiquity. A middle-aged receptionist was seated behind a half moon desk of mahogany, steel, and glass at the far end of the space. A curvy white sectional couch ran the perimeter of the room. Danny approached the desk, noting that the couch was about halfway vacant. It had been packed, with actors shoulder to shoulder, for his first audition.

"My name is Danny Smash," he informed the receptionist with a confident but not too overly friendly smile. "I'm here for the callback on the Tastee Taco commercial."

The receptionist looked like a tired, worn housewife in business attire. She smiled coyly at him and said, "Have a seat, they're actually running on time today."

Danny found a place on the sleek couch and pulled up the copy for the audition on his phone. Since this was a callback, he was already familiar with lines, but this time he carried something a little extra in his backpack to really convince the casting people.

He was focused on his phone and on perfecting his audition when two people on the other side of the reception room caught his eye. His focus was distracted as he noticed a pretty young girl. Sitting beside her was an old lady. As he watched them, it became clear that they were a grandmother and a granddaughter.

The grandmother was fashionably dressed and trendy looking for an older woman. Her fashion sense reminded him of Miss Lizzie back at the Hacienda Ridge. The granddaughter looked to be about 17. The old lady patted her hand. Danny's stomach tightened and a sudden torrent of regret and sadness threatened to overwhelm his buoyant mood.

"You are a very talented actress," the older woman told her granddaughter softly. "And beautiful, too. When you go into that casting session just imagine that your grandfather and I are the only ones in there with you, and that you're talking to us. You're telling us how much you love Tastee Tacos. Which shouldn't be a long stretch … you *do* love tacos!"

At this, they both shared warm laughter and the girl hugged the older woman lovingly.

Danny tore his gaze away from them. He recalled very clearly feeling loved and protected by Malchus at one time. When he was a child, he had idolized Malchus as implicitly as this girl clearly loved and trusted her grandmother. It was Malchus who taught him his ABCs, Malchus who showed him how to add, subtract and multiply, Malchus who read him stories about history, Malchus who uploaded movies for him so that he could learn about the outside world. And later, it was Malchus who betrayed him in the worst possible way. This violation was compounded by a suspicion that others on the compound knew what was going on. This suspicion grew as Danny got older, and it seemed to him that people were willing to turn a blind eye in the interests of their own self-preservation.

He was alone but invulnerable. He had learned early on that people were motivated by their own selfish drives. The grandmother and granddaughter clearly derived benefits from their relationship with each other. But the love seemed genuine, and it left Danny feeling empty and yearning.

He closed his eyes and began some of the visualization exercises he learned at acting school. He had to focus. He studied his copy earnestly. He could not risk another episode of what happened when the camera started rolling the last time he was here …

"Danny Smash," announced the receptionist from her desk. "They're ready for you in the audition room."

Danny stood. He had spent the weekend watching videos on YouTube about the do's and don'ts of commercial auditioning. He had also gotten some tips from Phyllis Moyt. But all the tips in the world wouldn't help him if reacted to the camera as he had on his first audition. When he was last here, he walked into the room feeling supremely confident. He introduced himself and stood on mark about six feet from the camera lens. When the light went on, and the camera started rolling his mind took him back to the very first time he had ever been in front of a camera. He was nearly crippled by that flashback of memories. It was momentary, but it had made him appear camera shy. Not a good impression to make when auditioning for a TV commercial. It was why he'd been so surprised when he'd gotten the callback.

He reached into his backpack and pulled out a neatly folded white bag that was emblazoned with the Tastee Taco logo. He left his backpack with the receptionist and proceeded through the door with the fast-food bag in his hand. He knocked lightly on the door, then opened it and briskly passed through.

The casting room was shoebox sized. On one side of the room was a bare wall painted lime green. On the opposite side of the room, behind a long table, sat at least six people whose faces were obscured behind their laptop computer screens. There was a video camera set up in front of them, and a piece of tape, his "mark," about six feet in front of the camera.

Danny carried a small white paper bag as he walked in and greeted the casting people with an enthusiastic and professional "Hello." He welcomed their stares, knowing that in most casting sessions they barely looked up, if they looked up at all. He knew he had their attention. He took his mark standing straight, shoulders back, a smile on his face. He was excited to be there and highly confident. His expression and body language let them know it.

The camera was turned on. The red light indicated that it was recording, and the light on top illuminated him. This time, he was ready. He didn't freeze. He didn't flash back to Arizona. He made direct eye contact with the lens.

"Hi," he said without pause. His voice was spontaneous and positive, his essence conveyed self-assurance, total comfort in front of the camera likeability. "Thank you for the callback. My name is Danny Smash."

By the silence in the room, he was aware that he had the attention of each and every person sitting behind those laptops.

This session director, who was running the audition, introduced himself as Kirk. "Sides," he said to Danny.

Danny obligingly turned to one side and then the other to show his right and left profiles. There was a murmuring of pleased consent among all of the casting people.

"Are you ready to read?" asked Kirk.

Danny nodded. "I'm ready," he answered authentically.

"We'll do one rehearsal and two takes," Kirk said. "Action!"

Danny looked at the camera and spoke as if he was having a friendly, relaxed conversation with it. He read his lines:

"After a long day of school and sports practice, my buddies and I have worked up an appetite." He shrugged and smiled charmingly at the camera. The lights made his eyes twinkle with youth and vibrancy. "So we head straight for Tastee Taco."

At this, Danny reached into the white bag, pulled out a Taco, and took a bite with an expression of unbridled satisfaction. He swallowed and smiled, again, at the camera.

"Now I've got all the nutrition I need to get me through a night of homework." He winked. "And I'll come back later with my girlfriend, too."

Danny nodded, indicating that he was finished. He began re-wrapping his taco and putting it back in the bag for his next take.

"That was clever, bringing the product with you," Kirk told him.

"And well prepared," said another voice. The man who owned the voice stood up. "My name is Karl Masters and I own the Tastee Taco chain. No need for you to record another take. I want you in my commercial."

"We're shooting on-location in the Valley on the twenty third and twenty fourth," said another voice, this one female. "We'll email the details to your agent."

Danny nodded at them and smiled broadly. "Thank you very much," he answered. He was genuinely appreciative. He left the room with the same brisk efficiency with which he had entered.

He stepped from the Bradbury Building and blinked in the sunshine. He knew how Hercules felt after he'd slayed the dragon. Malchus' camera had been a monster that tried to devour his soul, but the beast had failed to take him down. He had faced the camera today, and he had won.

* * * * *

Phyllis Moyt stood slightly off camera, watching as hair and makeup put the final touches on her red-hot discovery, Danny Smash. At first she thought the name was clearly contrived, even hokey, for a stage name. However, this kid lived up to it. It wouldn't have mattered if he had named himself Danny Shit; Hollywood would still be knocking on the door.

Danny Smash was booked for print ads and television commercials the minute Phyllis mass emailed his picture to casting agents and photographers around Tinseltown. His big break came when he was booked for an advertisement for an unimportant blue jean designer. The photographer on the shoot had been so beguiled that he used Danny as an extra in an already casted photo shoot for Harrington and Stitch, a preppy clothing line favored by the high school and college set and famous for its chiseled, post-adolescent models.

Executives at Harrington saw proofs from the shoot and unanimously insisted that Danny be moved front and center. He had been the top model for H&S for the past six months, and today they were shooting a groundbreaking television commercial that was created to be sensual, provocative, and controversial. Tens of millions in advertising dollars were already committed to a prime-time television campaign that appealed to the teenage and young adult demographic on all the major networks.

When this spot hit television, Danny Smash would be famous, certainly among those in his age group.

Phyllis stiffened slightly as Marc, the director of the television commercial, unfastened the top three buttons of Danny's purposefully torn, form-fitting H&S jeans.

"No more buttons, Marc," she said in a commanding, proprietary tone. "This is a jeans commercial. One more button and it's an underwear ad."

Danny's eyes, as sweet and green as jolly ranchers and hard as gemstones, met Marc's in a lazy, seductive gaze. "Go for it Marc," he told the director, ignoring Phyllis's dictate. "It's my shoot. If I look better showing more underwear, then do it."

Phyllis bristled and turned her attention to her ever-buzzing phone.

Danny, already shirtless, the muscles in his tight torso gleaming with spray oil, worked the moment and bathed in the attention of the cameraman and crew. Lights had been strategically placed and pointed to enhance every contour of his body and to illuminate his most amazing asset: his looks. Wavy blonde hair shined in the light and framed a face that was ruggedly handsome yet beautiful in the same moment. His smile, which could disarm a terrorist, had already sold countless tubes of toothpaste and bottles of mouthwash by way of print ads and TV commercials.

Phyllis, standing just beyond the backdrop and outside the tight band of production assistants, held her tongue as the director's fingers adjusted the lining of Danny's H&S underwear, lingering longer than necessary on the boy's washboard stomach. She was aware that she needed to build a good relationship with Marc, who was one of the fashion world's top video directors. If it were a lesser in the industry, she would have told him to get his fucking hands off her boy.

Danny's smile was all for the director and his camera. Phyllis knew that Marc, like most at the top echelon of fashion, was gay. Danny didn't have a gay bone in his body, at least he had never displayed such tendencies, but she still resented the much older man's fondling of her client. Danny didn't appear to mind. In fact, he seemed to be egging the director on, encouraging him, flirting. *Smart boy*, she thought. *Kiss up to the people who can help you.*

Danny continued to ignore her, and when the shoot wrapped he walked off the set without a second glance in her direction.

Phyllis followed him to the dressing room and gently pushed aside a rack of clothing. A production assistant was toweling moisture from Danny's torso. She finished off and scurried away when she saw Phyllis.

Danny's expression flashed anger when their eyes met. "I'm the boss when I'm on set, Phyllis. And the only one who is ever in control of my body is me."

Phyllis blew a wisp of hair from her face and appeared to be deeply considering his words. She ignored the constant pinging of her cell phone.

"The more I get to know you, the more I realize that you have very strict boundaries," she explained. "I'm sorry if I offended you. I wasn't trying to imply that I'm in control over your body. I'm your agent, I'm just looking out for you and your best interests."

Danny stood from his dressing room stool and leaned toward Phyllis.

"You're my agent, not my babysitter," he said coolly. "You're supposed to be in your office making deals for me, not overseeing me at work. More and more you are inserting yourself into parts of my business where you don't belong. It's a problem."

Phyllis inhaled a sharp, deep breath and stepped back. Her face reddened with the embarrassment of knowing that she had clearly trespassed into territory where stars belonged and agents did not.

"You're young," she stammered. "I'm just trying to protect you from the harsh realities of a very exploitive business."

"I may not know everything about this business but I'm a fast learner, Phyllis." His eyes were thunderous but his expression was unruffled. "No one will be exploiting me."

Danny's phone buzzed. He glanced at the screen and back up at Phyllis. "I need to take this," he said by way of dismissal.

* * * * *

Powerful Hollywood super agent Kenneth Shapiro had been visiting at another table across the pool patio at the Terrace on Sunset Boulevard when he saw Danny enter the restaurant. This was a place where industry elite lunched al fresco on a sunny patio with fabulous views of the City of Angels. Tourists often flocked to the restaurant, located in the iconic Sunset Tower, in the hopes of seeing a movie star, as this was one of many Hollywood eateries that was a known celebrity hangout. But, like Kenneth, most industry types dining here were behind the scenes people, and, while powerfully connected to the stars, were largely unknown to anyone outside the entertainment industry. The man whose table Kenneth was visiting was an example of a Hollywood behemoth that the average tourist would never even notice. The man was in his fifties and dressed impeccably yet casually in a tailored blue jacket, jeans, and expensive loafers. He was tanned, overly botoxed, bald, and sported a perfectly trimmed beard. He was the president of TTC, an acronym for The Teenage Channel, or as it was affectionately known in the business, the Tween channel.

All heads turned as Danny loped onto the patio with the grace of a panther. The charge that went across the outdoor dining area when he arrived was almost palpable. *Certainly*, thought the tourists, *this was a bonafide star.* Kenneth knew otherwise. The kid might not be a star yet, but he had the rare magnetic quality of a Brad or a Matthew; one day he would certainly top the A-list. Kenneth had every intention of putting him there. It was more than Danny's potential as a moneymaker, however, that first enticed Kenneth to pitch himself as his agent. Kenneth wanted to nurture Danny's career, and perhaps much, much more.

Kenneth waved as Danny scanned the poolside tables. This was the first time they would meet in person. Kenneth was one of several of the town's top talent agents who desperately wanted Danny in their stable. The kid was, up until now, only a print and television model, but the handful of commercials that he'd already starred in had sent the much coveted demographic of 18 to 30 year olds into a frenzy of tweets, likes, and adulatory comments. Danny's commercials had all gone viral on YouTube, and the products being advertised all saw massive spikes in sales. Hollywood was all about the dollar, and Danny had become, overnight and from out of nowhere, the latest golden boy.

Kenneth's handshake was firm, effusive, and enthusiastic. His expression was warm and open. He led Danny to their table, and, Danny noticed, seemed to enjoy the covetous looks Danny received from other tables.

"You smirked," Kenneth observed with a flirtatious smile. They reached their table, which was positioned poolside and shaded by a large umbrella. Kenneth pulled a chair out for Danny and then sat opposite him at the table. "What are you thinking?"

Danny shrugged and returned the smile. "I can't believe I'm sitting across the table from you." Danny leaned forward in his chair, making the space between he and Kenneth more intimate. The playful smile on his face was devoid of the usual Hollywood guile and deceit. "You represent the biggest stars in the business. And I'm wondering why you asked me to lunch."

Kenneth stared for a moment more than was prudent into Danny's eyes. "You get right to the point," he said, fighting breathlessness. "And so will I. You've been in this town for less than a year, and everything you've touched since you've gotten here has turned to gold. Trust me, Hollywood has taken notice."

Kenneth paused, permitting his words to settle, then added, "and so have I."

Danny leaned back a fraction but maintained intensive eye contact with Kenneth.

Waiters hovered around the table's perimeter but knew better than to interrupt the conversation.

"As you know," Kenneth continued. "I represent some of the biggest names in the film industry."

Danny nodded, encouraging Kenneth to continue. He knew exactly where this was going.

Kenneth reached into the inner pocket of his jacket and extracted a tablet computer. "I'm prepared to offer you my services. I've been in this business long enough to recognize raw star power when I see it. I believe that you will have a huge and long lasting career, ultimately in films." Kenneth held up the tablet so Danny could see the screen, on which was a lengthy written document. "I have a contract right here for you and I'm ready to hit send. Would you consider signing with me?"

Danny was filled with elation. But one detail niggled his conscience.

"I'm going to have to fire my current agent," he told Kenneth. "And she won't go down without a fight."

Kenneth let out a laugh. "I know all about Phyllis Moyt and her illustrious agency. I can make the call and terminate her services for you."

Danny held up a palm. "You go ahead and hit the send button," he told Kenneth. Give me some time to read over the contract and I'll call Phyllis and let her know my decision. I owe her that much."

Danny exhaled, leaned back in his chair, and picked up the menu that was in front of him on the table. Kenneth followed suit. Then the waiter came and took their orders. Danny ordered a burger, Kenneth a salad.

"Take a look across the patio, Danny," Kenneth suggested, glancing at a table placed in the shade of a large potted ficus tree. Danny followed Kenneth's gaze and shrugged slightly.

"The guy in the blue suit is Michael Harmon. He's the president of TTC. They're casting for a romantic male lead a new series called *Mission Bay*. It's supposed to be one hot property. Everybody in town wants a piece of it, and if you sign with me I can get you in the door."

Danny didn't take a second glance at Michael Harmon's table. Best to appear ambivalent. These Hollywood sharks could smell hunger in the water from a hundred miles away. Danny's focus remained steadfastly and deferentially fixed on Kenneth.

"Tell me about this new series."

"Okay, get this," Kenneth pitched enthusiastically. "The story takes place at a hotel on Lake George in upstate New York called *Mission Bay*. A lot of students from the exclusive private college nearby, a bunch of preppy rich kids, do internships at the hotel. The lead role is for a handsome, all American prep who is manipulated and controlled by his grandfather, a meddling patriarch who owns all of *Mission Bay*."

Danny nodded, a shy smile creeping up on the corner of his lips.

Kenneth returned his deep gaze. "Who better to play a red-hot, sexy, all American college kid than Harrington and Stitch's red hot poster boy?"

Danny leaned in across the table. "Who better?" He picked up Kenneth's computer tablet, activated the screen, and put his finger to it. "I just hit the send button," he announced. "When do I audition?"

Kenneth pulled a card from the breast pocket of his richly tailored silk shirt. "Here's the address in Century City. Be there at ten, tomorrow morning. Frankly, I think the audition will be just a formality. I've heard whispers all over town that they want the Harrington and Stitch kid for this part."

Danny pocketed the card. "I'll be there."

Their waiter brought their food. He fawned all over Danny, proclaiming his undying dedication to the Harrington and Stitch clothing line. Danny calmly took a bite from his burger after the waiter left. He needed something in his stomach to settle his nerves. While he was the picture of cool confidence on the surface, in his mind he was conflicted. He felt guilty at betraying Phyllis, and this guilt was compounded by his remorse for his actions against the elderly people in Scottsdale. But Phyllis was needy, controlling, and simply didn't have the clout or the connections to make him a true star. It was time to move on from her.

"Your metabolism is both astounding and enviable," Kenneth observed wryly, breaking into Danny's thoughts. "You wolfed down that whole burger and you're as lean and fit as a thoroughbred athlete."

Danny could read a measure of adulation in Kenneth's voice. In the months that followed the launch of his Harrington and Stitch commercials, not to mention billboards all across the country, from Hollywood Boulevard to a massive electronic neon screen that flashed to millions of observers daily in Time Square, Danny had become accustomed to recognition, even reverence. But it was pleasantly surprising to experience this reaction with someone as powerful and elite as Kenneth Shapiro.

Danny's flirty smile at Kenneth was as genuine as it ever got. Inwardly, the turmoil he'd been feeling moments ago melted like warm toffee.

* * * * *

"I discovered you. You owe me some loyalty!" Phyllis Moyt struggled to keep her voice even. Her phone shook in her hand.

Danny kept his breath slow and even.

"You had *NOTHING* when you got to LA." Phyllis' voice escalated several octaves. "You had just stepped off a bus. I paid for your headshots. I paid your first month's rent here. I got you your first job. I got you your first television commercial. Where would you be if it wasn't for me?"

"You should be happy for me Phyllis," Danny said earnestly. "If the shoe was on the other foot, I'd be happy for you."

"Happy for you?" Phyllis almost screamed the words. "After all I've done for you, you turn around and betray me?"

"It's not betrayal, Phyllis," Danny's voice held steady to the point of detachment. "It's business. Ken Shapiro will open doors for me that you never could."

"I took a major risk for you," Phyllis' voice was laced with vitriol. "And then you step on me to get to the next level."

"You took a risk on me because you knew I'd make money for you. Which I did," Danny said confidently. "On top of which, thanks to me, the Moyt Agency now has a nice healthy roster of bankable talents who are all working, making you more money. Your visibility in this industry has skyrocketed. We both benefitted from what you did for me, but now it's time to move on."

Phyllis took a sharp intake of breath as Danny continued. "My contract period ends this month. Obviously I'm not renewing. Let's make this amicable."

"You little bastard," Phyllis spat. "I made you a star."

"You didn't make me a star," Danny answered, voice wavering slightly. A flashback to Malchus entered his mind. "I made myself a star so that nobody, including you, will ever be able to control me."

Phyllis paused as realization descended upon her. "You think because you're a big star no one can control you? Think again," she hissed knowingly. "Your new agent Kenneth Shapiro is going to expect favors. Everyone's got a reputation in this town and I happen to know his. He will try to control you in ways you can't imagine."

"I know all about Kenneth's reputation," Danny tranquilly told her. "It doesn't worry me."

Phyllis had no further argument. It was over. She felt like a balloon that had once been bouncing against the ceiling and was now deflated on the floor.

"Well hey, kid," she said finally in a resigned voice. "We had a good run. It was fun while it lasted.

Danny's smile came right through the phone. "Yes we did Phyllis, and I'll always appreciate what you did for me. Good luck to you."

"Good luck to you, too, kid," Phyllis answered. But the line was already dead.

Phyllis reached into her desk, pulled out a joint, and lit it. Since the day Danny had miraculously appeared in her office, she knew this day would come. She just didn't realize it would be so soon.

She took a deep draw on the joint and reached for her phone.

* * * * *

As he did almost daily, Danny Googled the words: *Hacienda Ridge*, *robbery*, and *crime*. Until today, nothing new had popped up. However, this time his search revealed a disturbing article that had been posted in MaricopaCountyNews.com:

Robbery Victim Dead at age 70

Otto Ehrlinger, a resident of Scottsdale's affluent Hacienda Ridge retirement community, was pronounced dead at Thompson Creek Medical Center on Thursday. Mr. Ehrlinger was survived by his daughter Terry LeFloeur and grandson Simon LaFloeur. While the cause of death is officially listed as complications due to stroke, the deceased's grandson has made pleas to the media and local police to investigate this as a homicide.

Mr. Ehrlinger was the victim of a yet unsolved robbery that took place at his Hacienda Ridge residence in the year preceding his death. His grandson Simon has vociferously petitioned for the Scottsdale police department to consider the death a direct result of the robbery, which was perpetrated by a teenager who endeared himself to several Hacienda Ridge residents, gained their trust, and then quite literally disappeared with over five thousand dollars in cash and valuables.

"I want this (expletive) caught and charged with the murder of my gramps!" Mr. LaFloeur stated. "My gramps was in perfect health until that little (expletive) robbed him and gave him a stroke. He was in and out of rehab ever since. He got depressed because he couldn't hardly walk, and finally he died."

As Danny read, waves of despair, bereavement, and terror threatened to cripple him. With shaking hands, he forced himself to continue scrolling through the article.

Scottsdale Police, however, are ruling Mr. Ehrlinger's passing as death by natural cause. "This case absolutely will not be investigated as a homicide," Scottsdale detective Michael Cohen told the Maricopa County News. "We understand that the family is grieving, and perhaps looking for someone to blame. But our justice system doesn't work like that. The robbery in question occurred over a year ago. Mr. Ehrlinger was neither attacked, assaulted, nor even touched by the perpetrator, who remains guilty of robbery but certainly not murder."

Danny's pulse slowed and his hands stopped shaking. At least he wasn't a murderer. A feeling of profound guilt and sadness at the passing of Otto, a kindly old man who had never done anything but tried to help him and who was now dead, overcame him. He might not have murdered Otto, but he certainly felt profound guilt over the man's passing.

Hours later, Danny's mind was still reeling at the news of Otto's death. He was slumped in a chair, nursing a glass of whiskey on the brick patio of his tiny cottage apartment in Santa Monica. The night sky was dark and empty, the stars obscured by an omnipresent haze of LA smog. Usually, the seclusion of his tiny, private yard reminded him of the calmness in the desert where he grew up; a place that had provided escape and solace throughout his childhood. The familiar sound of cicadas buzzing in the night, the occasional hoot of an owl and the subtle fragrance of flowers all conspired to provide soothing comfort. The still evening air usually acted as a calming balm, but right now he sat nursing a glass of whiskey and was tormented by his past. Thoughts of his mother's death, of Malchus' abuse, of his deceitfulness toward Darlene, of the unexpected kindness shown to him from total strangers at the Hacienda Ridge, of his escape to LA, and finally his ascendency as a model, actor, and now possibly a superstar. But even his rapid rise in Hollywood was not enough, right now, to keep his thoughts from returning to darkness, to the day he met Otto Ehrlinger on the bus in Scottsdale. Had Otto not trusted him, the old man might be alive right now. The idea filled Danny with an inescapable grief and overwhelming sense of guilt and gloom.

Finally he roused from his physical inertia. He knew that, ultimately, he had to deal with the facts. He couldn't turn himself in. That would be sacrificing all he had built and all that he stood to gain. Besides it wouldn't change anything. He decided that he would somehow have to bury his guilt, but that he could assuage his remorse by making amends to Otto's family and the people he had robbed.

He reached for his cell phone, and, after a moment of ambivalence, picked up his cell phone and dialed Kenneth. His agent had made it eminently clear that he would do anything for Danny. Danny knew there would always be a price to pay. He wasn't sure exactly what that price might be, but he had a pretty good idea.

With a shrug, he dialed the agent. The busy dealmaker picked up on the second ring.

"Hey. Is everything okay?" Kenneth asked. "It's kind of late for you to be calling me."

"I'm sorry," Danny apologized. "I lost track of time. Should I call you back in the morning?"

"No, no, no, no!" Kenneth's response was instant, his voice placating. "I'm here for you whenever you need me. What's up?"

" I need twenty thousand cash out of my account, all in hundred dollar bills. I'd like to have by morning."

A brief pause ensued.

"It's your money," Kenneth answered finally. "And I'm guessing I don't want to know the details."

"Affirmative," Danny nodded. "And if it ever comes up ..."

"No loose ends," Kenneth interjected. "I'll take of it for you."

"Thanks," Danny answered, grateful for Kenneth's uncanny ability to read between the lines. "You're awesome."

"Like I said, I'm here for you." There was a protective note to Kenneth's tone.

Phyllis would have asked me a million freaking questions, Danny thought as he hung up with Kenneth.

He woke up at 6 AM after a restless night's sleep. His mouth was dry, and his head throbbed from the whiskey. He washed up, hydrated, popped some aspirin, and filled himself with a greasy, salty breakfast (which his acting school friends touted as the perfect hangover cure). Shortly after 9, as promised, a courier delivered an envelope thick with hundred dollar bills. A sense of relief overcame him as he handled the weighty package. He would make amends for the wrongs he had committed. He grabbed his keys, jumped in his car, and headed for LAX.

His plane landed in Las Vegas shortly after noon. He was dressed inconspicuously in baggy clothes with a gray slouchy beanie on his head. A backpack was slung over his shoulder. A pair of aviator glasses covered his now somewhat famous green eyes. He stepped out of the airport and caught the 212 bus to the nearby town of Henderson, exited at a stop on Green Valley Parkway, walked until he found a public mailbox.

Last night he had purchased padded envelopes at a nearby dollar store, addressed them to every single person he had stolen from, as well as Otto's daughter, whose address he found via a simple search of the white pages. He had filled the envelopes with at least double the amount that he had taken. He now pulled the envelopes from his backpack and quickly deposited them into the mailbox. He purposely avoided glancing around at his surroundings in order not to draw any attention, and walked quickly past the mailbox once his task was complete. He continued walking until he found another bus stop, then made his way back to the Las Vegas airport.

He was back on his patio in LA by nightfall, calmly sipping a bottle of mineral water.

* * * * *

Mission Bay was in its final week of production. Danny Smash, playing heartthrob Trey Godfrey, was on-set. Trey stared forlornly through the window of his grandfather's hotel, his eyes teary from a recent confrontation with the family patriarch.

"CUT. Nice take," said Cal, the director. A makeup artist materialized and blotted Danny's nose, cheeks, and forehead.

"You are absolutely flawless. Perfect skin. Great lips. And those cheekbones! You are a makeup artist's dream."

Danny smiled the smile that would be breaking hearts around the world once the series began its debut in the fall. "Thanks, Marissa."

Cal's voice sounded from hidden speakers. "Quiet on the set." Marissa scurried off behind a prop wall. "We're following through on this scene with the lover's intro. Danny, this is the first time Trey sees Cassie. You've just been belittled by your grandfather, and you turn to see this girl who fills you with a passion you've never known. The minute you see her, you know that she is the one. The emotion on your face goes from devastation to hope."

"Got it." Danny told the director confidently. "I've got the motivation. I think the scene might work better if Trey sees Cassie from behind, first, and doesn't' think anything of it. Maybe she could be dusting or hanging drapes or something. My character is barely paying attention, he's so wrapped up in his own misery. And then she turns and suddenly he notices her."

"I like it," Cal agreed. "Get her a dust rag."

Danny turned to the "window" and the forlorn expression returned instantly to his face.

"ACTION," called Cal after the necessary adjustments had been made and direction modified.

Kayla Asimov, the actress playing Cassie, came through a door, quietly crying. She was wearing a maid's uniform. After taking a moment to collect herself and smooth out her skirt, she began dusting. Danny, as Trey, turned from the window and regarded her with the same detachment as the furniture. Cassie still upset, knocked a vase off the table that was is dusting and it landed on the floor with a crash. Startled, Trey's attention focused on her. Her eyes filled with dread, darting back and forth between the shattered vase and the grandson of Willard Godfrey, the owner of Mission Bay Hotel, her employer. Trey's eyes locked on Cassie's, and his expression turned to awe. His features brightened as his face filled with the wonder of discovery.

"Sorry. So sorry," muttered Cassie, wiping tears from her eyes with trembling hands. "I swear! I've never broken anything before!"

Trey continued to stare in enraptured amazement at this beatific girl, his face filled with awe and joy.

Cassie brushed past him and disappeared down the hall. He turned and followed her with his gaze.

"CUT! Take! That was amazing!" Cal rose from his seat and treated Danny to a hearty back slap. "Let's break."

Danny walked off set. So inured was he to the admiring gazes of the cast and crew that he didn't notice his movement being carefully followed by the cunning eyes of the marvelously famous Kayla Asimov, who did not like to be ignored. The twenty year-old actress grew up as the teenage queen of TTC, the teen channel. She starred for over six seasons in the network's biggest hit, *Manhattan Sleuth*, which had spawned two movies, also hits, and also starring Kayla. She followed this by playing the title role in the very successful sit-com, *Kayla*. There were more movies, all blockbusters, magazine covers, and a wild group of teenage celebrity friends, who came to be known as the "Mean Tweens" by an increasingly hostile media. Then came the widely publicized family disputes over custody and control of millions of dollars that were pouring in to her bank account every year. Ultimately, the fame began to take its inevitable toll. At seventeen, Kayla was in and out of rehab. At eighteen she was busted three times for drunk driving and once for possession of cocaine, narrowly escaping jail time. She had a string of hot, sexy, wannabe actor-slash-boyfriends and a much older girlfriend who was also a well-known pop star and with whom she appeared on the cover of every tabloid. Stories, most of them true, ranged from allegations of wild Hollywood orgies, lesbianism, drug addiction, and finally, a very public breakdown on national television.

This job on *Mission Bay* was her first time working after nearly a year in rehab and represented a significant fall from grace for an actress who would never had deigned to do television again.

Danny made the fall totally worthwhile, however. Kayla's new co-star on this series was the sexiest man-boy she had ever laid eyes on. When they were first introduced at a script meeting three weeks before, she was utterly entranced. She had been with every white-hot Hollywood bad boy, and then some, but no one in her experience had ever thrown off the aura of pure magnetism, smoldering sex appeal, and captivating charm of this Danny Smash.

But he was, after all, the ex-underwear model for Harrington and Stitch, a relative unknown, and, therefore, a peasant to her royalty. She remained aloof, believing that any smart actor would give his left nut to be seen with her, even for one night. Thanks to an aggressive publicity campaign, they would soon be on the front page of every tabloid, the lead story on every entertainment news network, and blowing up the blogosphere. She had already started fantasizing about how she and Danny would appear in pictures that would be flashed around world.

The problem was that this "peasant" of the entertainment industry had hardly even seemed to notice her. He walked off the set, his eyes never so much as grazing hers. Most novice actors would have gushed all over the great Kayla Asimov immediately after the scene was in the can. Not this one. But it was time for things to change.

Danny took meals in his trailer, away from the rest of the cast and crew. He was currently reclined on a black leather club chair, feet up on the designer coffee table, with a script open on his lap and a Reuben sandwich in his hand. He studied his script but, as usual, could not help being distracted by his surroundings. The trailer that had been assigned to him for the duration of the *Mission Bay* shoot had a sleek kitchen with deep espresso Euro style cabinets, white quartz countertops, and stainless steel appliances. The floors were bamboo hardwood. A large screen television was recessed into the wall. The bedroom, though small, was like a luxury hotel room.

And again, he couldn't help but to compare the beaten up, rusty trailers of Hacienda Ridge to this one, and muse that, as far as he'd come, he was still in a trailer. His thoughts inevitably went to Malchus. He shuddered involuntarily. It had been over a year since he'd left the Painted Desert Farm and he wondered how Malchus had fared after being poisoned. Once again, he put those thoughts away and focused on his script.

There was an incessant knock on his door. "It's Marcos, Danny."

The assistant director. Nice kid, he thought. Danny put the script aside, wolfed down the rest of his sandwich, and stood to open the trailer door.

"What's up, Marcos?"

Marcos was Venezuelan and a film school graduate from New York. This was basically all Danny knew about him. They had been working together for three months.

"Um …" Marcos, usually quite self possessed, stammered nervously. "Cal wondered if you could come to the production office at 1:30."

"Okay." Danny's demeanor was calm, his smile warm. "Is something wrong?"

"Um, don't kill the messenger but apparently there's a teenage girl who's dying to meet you. We know it's a pain in the ass, and Cal really didn't want to bother you, but his girl's father is Peter Grubich."

"The name sounds familiar, but who is Peter Grubich?" Danny asked.

"He's an executive producer with the Tween channel," Marcos answered. "A big, important suit. Apparently he was screening some footage from the show this weekend and his daughter was in the screening room. Now she won't leave him alone until she gets an introduction. Basically Peter would be thrilled if you would just go in and say hello to her."

Danny smiled. "If that's the worst thing I have to do today, I really can't complain Marcos."

Marcos visibly relaxed. "We'll send someone for you when she gets to the set."

Danny gave Marcos a little salute with his two fingers, smiled, and disappeared back inside his trailer.

He dialed craft services and ordered two cheeseburgers. The Reuben hadn't filled him up. Seconds later, there was a knock on the trailer door. *Wow, those cheeseburgers got here fast!* He thought.

It wasn't his cheeseburgers that came breezing into the trailer door, though.

"They gave you a nice trailer." Kayla Asimov, wrapped in a white silk kimono, quickly took in the clean, organized interior. "Looks like they're already treating you like an established star." Her eyes looked him up and down, savoring his body like it was a rare delicacy.

Danny smiled broadly as Kayla helped herself to a seat on his plush leather couch. He sat down on the chair opposite her, his demeanor neutral.

Kayla wriggled in her seat, her fantastic body rippling beneath the sheer silk that wrapped tightly around it. She crossed long, tanned legs. A blood red Manolo Blahnik spiked heel dangled from her foot. She leaned in toward Danny, revealing copious cleavage.

"It usually doesn't take me three months to get inside my co-star's trailer," she purred. "Usually the invite comes pretty quickly."

Danny calmly appraised her, a smile playing on the corners of his lips.

Kayla met his eyes and attempted to hold his gaze. Danny leaned easily back in his chair and glanced to the ceiling.

"I've seen you on TV since I was a kid," he told her in a voice that combined charm and detachment. "I think you're a great actress and certainly you could have stopped by at any time. Were you waiting for an invitation?"

Kayla stiffened slightly, then slunk back into the plush seat and began running her fingertip along her lip. "Well of course I was waiting for an invitation," she said in a sex kittenish, pouty voice. "You're a gorgeous man, I'm a gorgeous woman. This is a movie set. Its what we do in this business."

Danny smiled knowingly. "The key word is business. This is a job. I'm really flattered by your interest, but I'm here to work."

Kayla sat up abruptly and tightened her kimono. Gone was the cleavage. In its place was a girl who was suddenly unsure of herself. She chose her next words carefully.

"You know," she began. "When we're on set, the chemistry between us sizzles. And when you kiss me, I feel it down to my toes. I feel an intense connection with you."

She implored him with her eyes, waiting hopefully for some type of affirmation. He regarded her impassively. This was a manipulative girl who'd had a long list of lovers, one-night stands, and flings. She was a black widow spider whose web he had no intention of falling into.

"Don't you feel anything when you kiss me?" Her voice held a mixture of curiosity, disbelief, and entitlement.

Danny shrugged. "I'm in character when I kiss you. My character feels something, but *I* don't. No offense, but I'm a professional. I'm not stepping over any lines here."

Danny stared as Kayla stood, moved toward him, and sat on the arm of his chair and leaned in provocatively. He could smell the peppermint scent of her breath. "Okay, I get it," she told him, still purring like a sex kitten. "You're all business. But I've been in the business a lot longer than you have, and there's one thing I know. We make one hot couple on screen. The paparazzi would go crazy for us. I guarantee they would even give us a moniker, like KayDan. We should be seen around town together, get our pictures taken, get into all the tabloids. You can keep your dick in your pants, but if you want to be a star, you've got to play the publicity game. And I guarantee that all the top tabloid photographers will be wherever I tell them to be."

"I'm in for that," Danny said matter-of-factly. He stood from his seat. "That's a game I'll play, but remember, I play by my own rules."

Kayla stood and reached to touch him, but Danny took a step away from her.

Kayla shrugged. "Okay, we follow your rules. But let's get the game in play. Justin's having a party tonight at Poppy on La Cienga. Patrick and the whole young Hollywood gang will be there."

"Then so will we," Danny replied jubilantly.

* * * * *

Principal photography on *Mission Bay* wrapped three weeks later, by which time Danny and Kayla had been seen and photographed all over Hollywood and had graced the pages of every major celebrity gossip rag. Danny found splashy pictures of himself inside WE Magazine, Famous Faces, Persons Magazine, and Celebrity Insider. He was even on the cover of TV Today, where the main image featured pop star Trenton Cash and his record selling world tour. On the top corner of the magazine cover, inside a heart shaped puff, was a shot of Danny and Kayla leaving a party in Beverly Hills. The coverline read, "Kayla's Mystery Man." Danny was prominently displayed in the foreground, a detail that did not escape Kenneth.

"You're all over the tabloids!" Kenneth's voice was so excited that Danny could almost picture the agent doing handsprings down Rodeo Drive. And you're in every single important blog. Pop Bitch, Holy Moly, and Go Fug Yourself! This level of publicity is pretty much unheard for a name that isn't even established yet. I can't even fathom what's going to happen once *Mission Bay* starts airing in the fall. Major players all over town are already calling me, wanting to take meetings about you. Clarence Hunter, who runs the biggest television production company in the world, called me to ask, and I quote, *so who the hell is this Danny Smash?*"

Now it was Danny who felt like doing handsprings. He nearly jumped out of his seat, spilling the script he'd been reading onto the floor. "That's great! Awesome! But ... any word back on the test yet?"

In a typical test for a network series, a sample audience watches several episodes of a new show and then rate it. In some cases, random individuals are paid a small sum of cash to be monitored for their emotional responses as they watch. These tests can make or break a show before it even makes it to the small screen. Everyone involved in the series, from the executives down to the production assistants, wait anxiously for the test results to come in.

"That's another reason for my call, Danny," Kenneth said warmly. "Test audiences for the show's demographic loved it. I told you not to worry about the damned tests anyway. The Tween Channel is one hundred percent committed to this series. Apparently Michael Harmon has been creaming himself over the dailies for weeks. He's already committed a fortune to promoting it."

Danny walked into his bedroom and fell backwards onto his bed with a grin as big as the Grand Canyon spread across his face. "Dude, I'm speechless," he finally said to Kenneth."

"But there's more, Danny," Kenneth breathed, a definitive fondness in his voice. "Word is that you are carrying the show. This was supposed to be Kayla's vehicle, but industry gossip has you emerging as the big star. Apparently, you've managed to out-talent and upstage a seasoned pro."

Danny was silent as he joyfully absorbed all of this information.

"I'm proud of you, Danny," Kenneth finally said. "I know how hard you worked on this series, and it really shows."

Danny's expression melted and he sat up slowly on the bed as Kenneth's words resonated with him. It was the first time anyone had ever said they were proud of him.

"This is amazing, Kenneth," Danny said softly. "I don't even know what to say."

"Say you'll join me for a bottle of celebratory champagne," Kenneth suggested.

Danny shrugged and a broad smile returned to his face. "Sure. That' be great."

"I'm sending a car now," Kenneth announced. And even though the agent generally played his cards close to his vest, Danny sensed a distinct lilt in Kenneth's voice.

Ten minutes later, a red Tesla Roadster was idling at the curb in front of Danny's apartment building in Santa Monica. Also waiting at the curb, disturbingly, was a gaggle of fans, mostly young and female. Danny watched them through the window. The group seemed to multiply daily. There were about fifteen people out there, which didn't pose a threat right now. But a multiplying crowd could easily turn into a mob, which wouldn't only disturb the neighbors but could pose a very real danger. He would have to talk to Kenneth about finding a less accessible place to live. And soon.

For now, he put on a baseball cap and shades and started walking toward the Tesla. Girls screamed and shrieked as he approached, photographing him with their cameras and beseeching him to stop and engage in conversation. He smiled politely and moved quickly for the car. He briskly pulled the door open, and then froze in his tracks. A young woman with a toddler held tight in her arms stepped forward from the crowd and blocked his path. Time suddenly ground to a horrifying standstill.

"Hi Danny," Darlene said, holding up the child. "It took us a while to find you. But here we are."

Quickly and deftly, Danny guided Darlene and the infant into the backseat of the Tesla, jumped in behind them and slammed the door shut.

"Take us the hell out of here," he told the driver. "Now!"

The car pulled away from the curb. Danny kept as much physical distance between himself, Darlene, and their baby as possible within the small confines of the car. Darlene leaned toward him, opened her mouth and began to speak. Danny angrily put his finger to his lips and shushed her.

"Not here," he growled. He pulled out his phone and hammered out a quick text to Kenneth: Ran into a problem. Will be late. Explain later.

"Take us to Palisades Park," he instructed the driver. During the ten-minute ride to the beachfront park, Darlene extracted a bottle from her baby bag and fed the baby. A million emotions swirled wildly in Danny's mind as he watched the surreal and unbelievable happen before his eyes.

The Tesla glided to a curb. Danny got out of the car and motioned for Darlene to follow. They walked in silence along a gently curving dirt path that bordered the blue waters of the Pacific on one side and an expanse of emerald lawn and lush greenery on the other. They sat down on the first available empty bench, facing a magnificent ocean view. Darlene bounced the baby on her lap and turned to Danny, her face scrawled in righteous indignation.

"When you left me I was a stupid, love-struck teenage girl." Her voice was steady and measured. "I'm not that girl any more. I've had plenty of time to think and to heal. I've had a baby. I've had my heart broken and I've been abandoned. I don't love you anymore, Danny. I don't know why you did what you did but I don't trust you. You are mean and cold hearted. I definitely don't want you anymore, so you can stop worrying about that."

Danny stared down at this lap. He couldn't face Darlene. He couldn't look at the baby. "I'm not cold hearted," he said weakly.

"What you did to me was as cold hearted as it gets," she said, her voice a mixture of anger and disgust. She held the baby tightly to her. "Do you know what it feels like to be lied to, abandoned, and discarded? To love someone with all your heart and to finally realize they have taken your money, broken your trust, and left you alone like you were a bag of garbage?"

Danny was shrunken. He certainly did know what it was like to be used and abandoned. His handsome, tanned face turned a ghastly pale. He could feel nausea rising in his belly.

"Do you know what it's like to work two jobs to feed a baby and keep a roof over his little head?" Darlene was now crying. She stared out over the gorgeous vista of Pacific Ocean.

"I once heard it said that selfish people sleep the best at night. How do you sleep at night, Danny?"

"I didn't know, Darlene," he said. "I didn't know you were pregnant. And I sent you more than enough money to make up what I took from you."

She turned and regarded him directly. "Well, even though you obviously don't give a shit how badly you hurt me, it's a good thing you're bringing up money, Danny. I don't care if I ever see you again and I have no interest in you and your greedy, flashy Hollywood life. But you ARE going to support your child. Starting immediately."

The baby was staring at him adoringly. There was no question in his mind that the child was his. He tentatively leaned forward to touch the little one's tiny, perfect hand. Darlene quickly pulled the baby away from him.

"Here's the deal," she told him. "I don't want you in our lives. I don't want our son to be influenced by your horrible values and selfish nature. I don't want him to grow up with you as an influence of any kind. You are going to support me and the baby, stay out of our lives. In return, I will never go public with what you did to us."

Danny, who had never before experienced rejection of any kind, stood unsteadily from the bench. His fists were balled at his side. Raw emotions pinged through his mind.

Darlene reached into the baby's carry-all bag, pulled out a slip of paper, and brusquely handed it to him. This is where to send the money. I'll sign any papers you want."

She turned to walk away. "I'll be ubering back to Arizona, and you'll be paying for it," she told him.

"What's my son's name," he asked, his voice a croak.

"You have no need to know that," Darlene didn't even turn back. "It sure as hell isn't Danny Junior."

Danny stared for a long, long time after Darlene and his baby disappeared from sight. Golden California sunshine warmed his neck and his bare arms, and he felt a cold chill into his heart. Hands buried deep in his pockets, head bent, Danny walked slowly back to the waiting Tesla and instructed the driver to take him to Kenneth's.

The expensive sports car piloted slowly through traffic on San Vicente Boulevard, through Brentwood, and into the foothills of the Santa Monica Mountains. Danny's mind was haunted by the visage of Darlene and his baby. There was no doubt in his mind that the baby was his, and that knowledge flooded him with longing. Darlene had changed dramatically since he'd seen her last. He had stolen her innocence in every way. He could not imagine the difficult journey that had been forced upon her. It had caused her to transform overnight from a giggly, sweet teenager to a strong, confident woman and, seemingly, a nurturing parent to his son. She had become a mother, and it seemed like she was a very good one. Thoughts of his own mother filled his mind and threatened to overwhelm him. As mentally unhinged as Lucille had been, she had loved him unconditionally and cared for him without demanding anything in return. His memories of his mother were of happiness and safety, two things that had been stolen from him by Malchus after his mother had died.

He was pulled from the depths of his thoughts as the car turned from Sunset Boulevard and glided through the West Gate of Bel Air at Belaggio Road.

The Tesla driver piloted slowly along a narrow street bordered on both sides by tall hedges, thick shrubbery, palm trees, and evergreen spires. The dense growth and hilly topography occasionally gave way to glimpses of huge mansions that stood like fortresses behind ornate fountains, imposing gates, and long private driveways that seemingly disappeared into landscaped havens. Danny stared from the window, magnetized. Inside the luxurious cocoons of these homes lived people who had reached a pinnacle where they were unassailable, untouchable and elite. They were internationally famous actors and actresses, movie moguls, sports stars, and media celebrities, and inside the dense protection of their rarified neighborhood they were safe and protected. They were also in complete control.

It was a world that Danny was becoming increasingly familiar with, and the idea of living here, safe and untouchable in the stratosphere, filled him with peace, contentment, and hunger. His mind cleared, and for the first time he realized the incredible comfort of the Tesla's back seat. He allowed himself to sink into the plush, supple leather.

The car glided smoothly and adeptly through the winding neighborhood. Danny lowered the window and was enjoying the sweet scent of jasmine, primrose and sage from the surrounding gardens. When they reached Kenneth's home, a massive steel gait swung open on their approach and the car purred to a stop in the driveway. Comprised of three cubic rectangles, the house was constructed of steel, exotic wood, polished concrete and massive plates of glass that were cantilevered together and topped by pagoda style roofs. The building seemed to float in a long rectangular fountain that ran the length of its entire front. Tropical flowers formed a carpet around the trunks of tall, gently arching palm trees.

The front door was monstrous, made of steel and teak, and accessed by rectangles of rough granite that formed elegant stepping-stones across the fountain. Kenneth, dressed in a crisp white linen shirt with a casual pair of khaki shorts and loafers, came immediately through the front door and jogged down the steps, across the stepping stones, and eagerly approached the car.

"You had me a little worried," he said with a hint of anxiety as Danny stepped from the car. "Is everything okay?"

Danny stretched in the sunlight and regarded Kenneth with a beguiling smile. "Everything's fine," he said truthfully. "Let's go have a glass of champagne."

*   *   *   *   *

Beverly Pop couldn't sit still. The twenty two year old singer/songwriter's first single had recently gone to number 5 on the Billboard chart, and her music video had over twenty million hits on You Tube, landing her a guest spot on the hugely popular "Greta Show." Beverly nervously paced the green room, awaiting her appearance on Greta's nationally syndicated afternoon talk show that garnered high ratings and millions upon millions of viewers. Beverly had been invited on the show to perform her song, called Love+Music+Memories, and to sit down for an interview with Greta, who was a famous and well-loved TV star and comedienne. Her talk show was widely viewed, partly due to the funny pranks she did with celebrities and because of the prizes and giveaways she tended to lavish on her studio audience. Beverly knew that everyone back in West Orange, New Jersey would be watching her on Greta, and she was scared shitless.

Also in the green room awaiting an appearance on the show was teen heartthrob Danny Smash. Seated on a dove gray couch with one leg crossed casually over the other and an arm draped easily over the back of the seat, Danny watched with rested disinterest as Beverly paced.

One of the show's copious production assistants, a plain looking young woman who appeared to be barely out of high school, popped her head inside the door and addressed Danny. "Mr. Smash," she said in friendly tone, "You're on in five. I'll be right back to bring you out."

Danny nodded and smiled. "And I'll be ready," he told her. His voice was smooth and his tone unwavering.

Beverly Pop started doing Yoga poses and deep breathing exercises. She was also stealing admiring glances at Danny, who pretended to ignore the attention. He calmly reached for a bottle of water on the coffee table and took a relaxed sip. On the TV in the green room, Greta was announcing him.

My next guest is an overnight Hollywood success story. Only a year ago he was a virtually unknown model for the Carrington and Stitch clothing line. He's since shot to national acclaim for his role as Trey Godfrey on the hit series, *Mission Bay*, and is slated to co-star with Kayla Asimov on the upcoming romantic comedy, *Starlight Café*. This TV hunk has managed to amass more followers on Twitter than the president of the United States and more Instagram followers than world famous soccer star, Riccardo. Ladies and gentlemen, I'll be joined by Danny Smash right after this commercial break.

The studio audience erupted with the screams of post adolescent females, and the monitor in the green room cut to a commercial. Danny stood, anticipating his cue from the production assistant. Moments later, she popped her head back inside the door. "Okay, Mr. Smash, you're on," the PA told him. Danny followed her down a short hallway that was lined with hundreds of pictures of Greta and her celebrity guests.

"The audience is really, totally stoked that you're on today," the PA, who had introduced herself as Miriam, said. She, however, appeared ambivalent toward him. She had led everyone from Hollywood's top leading actors and actresses to television's cheesiest reality TV stars down this very hall. "A lot of *Mission Bay* fans out there in the world, I guess."

Miriam's headset crackled and she listened intently. "You're on," she said as they reached the end of the hall. "SET" was stenciled in bold black letters on a white door, above which a red light blinked. "Go straight through this door, walk to the front of the stage, acknowledge the audience, then go and greet Greta on the couch. In five, four, three, two, one, GO!"

She gave Danny a gentle nudge. As he passed through the door, his world did a 360° turn. Suddenly bright lights, screaming girls, and the loud pulsating beat of music enveloped his senses. A self-satisfied smile filled his face as he approached the stage, stopped, and waved warmly into the audience. The screaming got louder and reached a crescendo as Danny walked to the couch, where he was greeted with a hug and a peck on the cheek from Greta.

The pair got comfortable in their respective seats and Greta leaned in toward

Danny, elbows on her knees.

"I'm a huge fan of *Mission Bay*," she said gushingly. The audience squealed in delight.

"And I'm a big fan of yours," he told her. "You know I was an army brat," Danny explained. "And I spent most of my time growing up on bases overseas. But I lived for American TV shows like yours." Danny looked at the audience and treated them to a wink and a smile. More screams erupted.

"But I never dreamed I'd actually be on your show one day," he said. "It's a huge honor to be sitting here with you."

"Did you ever dream that starring on one television series, for one season, would bring you so much attention?" Greta's smile was encouraging.

Danny looked contemplative for a moment. "Honestly it was not something I ever would have even thought about. I came here, took some acting classes, and hoped to break into TV commercials.

So no, I guess I never dreamed that all of this would happen. Certainly not so soon."

"Well it did happen for you," Greta told Danny. Then she addressed the audience. "And we're about to find out why. We have a clip from *Mission Bay*. Danny would you like to introduce it?"

Danny smiled and nodded. "My character Trey Godfrey is the grandson of the owner of *Mission Bay* Hotel and Resort. He's a strict and steely businessman played by the incredible Herbert Pyle. In this scene, Trey gets caught by his grandfather in one of the hotel rooms with a chambermaid, who of course is the beautiful Kayla Asimov."

The screen cut to a clip from the show. The video ran for roughly sixty seconds, during which Kayla and Danny were discovered in bed together by the tyrannical scion of *Mission Bay*.

The screen cut back to close up on Greta, who appeared to be shocked and scandalized by the clip.

"Wow! Let's get down to the nitty gritty here," she playfully exclaimed. "This is not the only steamy scene with you and Kayla. As the season went on, you two seemed to lock lips more and more."

Frenzied female screams erupted again.

"Of course I'd never ask," Greta said after the discord subsided. "But is it strictly professional between you two?" She winked conspiratorially at the audience who once again went berserk.

Danny fell back into his seat, put his face in his hands, and shook his head, feigning embarrassment.

Just then, a huge black and white picture of him, shirtless, lounging poolside with Kayla at the Polo Lounge, appeared on the screen behind the couch. Danny turned to look at it.

The howling audience was nearly deafening.

"Oh my God," Danny said, laughing. "Is nothing sacred? Greta, were you hiding in the bushes?"

Greta laughed along with him. "That was me! I've crawled through a lot of bushes, gotten a lot of spider bites," she joked.

"However, you didn't answer my question," she continued when the laughter died down. "My spies tell me you and Kayla have been seen canoodling all over town."

"Oh, I can canoodle with the best of them," Danny told her, winking again at the audience and re-inciting the frenzy. "That doesn't mean I'm dating them. Honestly and truly, our cast gets along amazingly. They're one big family to me. Basically, here in the US, they're the only family I have and I'm grateful for that."

Greta smiled, nodded, and let him off the hook. "Well," she said, changing the subject entirely. "You recently finished shooting an indie film which is loosely based on the life of legendary rocker Kurt Cobain."

Danny nodded. "The movie is called *Grunge*. The editors must be miracle workers because it's already due to hit indy theatres next week."

"You must be a miracle worker, too. You sure have been busy," Greta acknowledged. "You're also scheduled to co-star with Kayla Asimov in Jonathon Key's new rom-com, *Starlight Café*."

Danny exhaled dramatically and looked to the ceiling in mock despair. "We started shooting the day after *Grunge* wrapped," he told Greta. There was exasperation in his voice but a bit of a grin on his face.

Greta once again changed the subject, moving the interview forward.

"Having grown up outside the US, how do you like it here in LA?"

"Aside from the traffic, what's not to like?" he returned the question with a question, then answered it. "Palm trees, sunshine, movie stars, and the people here are fantastic!"

Another glance at the audience, another smile, another wink. Again, the crowd went wild.

"We have time for one last question," Greta announced. A picture of Danny, shirtless filled the screen behind them. Danny was wearing red jogging shorts and running shoes and was sweating. The picture was taken in Santa Monica, and in it he was standing at a burger joint on the beach, holding a cheeseburger in one hand and an order of fries in the other. It was a picture one of his fans had posted to his Instagram account.

The crowd went absolutely bat shit wild over the shirtless pic, and Danny smiled and slid down shyly in his seat.

"If you wanted the audience to see me without my shirt so much, you could have asked me to come on without a shirt," he laughed. "I'm not shy. I would have obliged."

It was Greta's turn to laugh.

"It seems like you're channeling Mat McCrew in this shot," she told Danny. "Yet I've never known Matt to touch carbohydrates, let alone burgers. How do you eat like you do and keep that flawless body?"

Danny shrugged. "Just lucky, I guess," he answered humbly. "Genetics."

Well, how 'bout if before you go, we let the audience get lucky," Greta asked with a devilish grin.

Danny turned his head and regarded her curiously.

"You said you weren't shy," she told him. "And if you're so inclined I'll make you a deal. You take your shirt off for my audience, and the Greta show will donate five thousand dollars to the charity of your choice."

Danny smiled and nodded as the crowds' screams became deafening.

Striptease music blared from the speakers. Blinking laser lights danced from the ceiling. If the audience had been going nuts before, now they were absolutely off the rails insane, standing, stomping, and wildly cat calling.

Danny smiled and stood, excitement filling his mind and adrenaline pumping in his veins. He began gyrating slowly and sensually to the music, slowly lifting his shirt to reveal his abs and making eye contact with individual members of the audience.

The television cameras followed his every move, their recording indicator lights jolting him back to the red-eyed monster in Malchus' bedroom. He had done this striptease before. But now he was in control and the world was in the palm of his hand. Malchus could never hurt him again, he thought, as he pulled the shirt over his head to the deafening beat of music, the pulsating strobe lights, and screams of his fans. He held the shirt in his hand, twirling in like a lasso before tossing it into the frenzied audience.

Back in the Greta's green room, Beverly Pop watched with growing despair as the cameras followed a shirtless Danny Smash off stage and the image on the monitor cut to a commercial. In her mounting anxiety, she considered running out the door. How she wondered, was she ever, ever going to follow an act like that?

* * * * *

"Is there any reason you failed to mention that you were being courted by Amy Price without my knowledge?" Kenneth demanded of Danny.

Kenneth was floating in his infinity pool, which had a commanding view of Stone Canyon and the deep blue reservoir at its basin. The morning sun glinted off his crystal champagne flute as he polished off his second Bloody Mary.

Danny kicked off his sneakers, took his time stripping off his clothes, and dove into the pool. Water droplets clung to his tanned body and sparkled in the bright sunlight as he emerged beside Kenneth's float.

Danny crossed his arms over the edge of the float. "Could I get a sip of that?"

Kenneth tentatively handed over the cocktail. His eyes covetously explored Danny's bare skin. "It's almost 10 AM. Where were you last night?"

Danny took a sip of the cocktail and handed it back to Kenneth, allowing Kenneth's fingers to graze his for longer than necessary. Their eyes met and held.

"We've been through this," Danny said with a sigh. "Just because I live here with you doesn't mean you have any right to keep tabs on me. I like what we have together, but I'm not cool with anyone trying to control me."

Kenneth's eyes yearningly explored Danny's face. "I'm not exactly sure what it is we have together here," he said finally. "I'm still trying to figure out our relationship, if you could call it that. But either way, I'm still your agent, and it's kind of a slap in the face to learn that you were seen having dinner last night at Viale dei Romani with one of the most powerful women in the industry."

Danny rolled his eyes and treated Kenneth to an impish smile. "I ran into Amy coming out of the studio yesterday and she invited me for dinner. There was nothing sneaky about it. If I was trying to go behind your back I wouldn't have shown up at Viale."

Kenneth relaxed into the float, and then his face clouded. "Obviously you slept with her." Upset, disappointment, and sadness filled his voice. "I know everyone in this town and I know how the machine operates."

Danny pushed away from the float, swam to the pool's edge, and pulled himself up from the water. A combination of lust, love, and ache filled Kenneth as he watched Danny slowly toweling his naked body in the sunlight.

"I have no interest in Amy Price," Danny told him honestly. "And we didn't cut you out. She'll be calling you tomorrow to package the biggest deal of my career."

Kenneth finished the last of his Bloody Mary, his eyes never leaving Danny's naked body.

"I've had my share of heartthrobs." Kenneth appeared to choose his words carefully. "And I've never really cared what they did or who they did it with once they got out of my bed in the morning. After all this is the land of musical beds. But I gotta tell you." Kenneth paused. "When I found out that you were sleeping with Amy Price last night, I cared."

Danny sat on one of the Balencia lounge chairs surrounding the pool and relaxed into a supine position. Still naked, he kept his legs partially spread, offering a tantalizing visual distraction to Kenneth. "Truthfully, you are the most decent person I've met in this business." His eyes were serious, intense. "You've always been honest with me and put my best interests first. You don't try to control me and you show me respect. You don't come on to me, and I'm never fearful that you will."

Kenneth smiled. "Sitting there like that, maybe you should be a little fearful," he said half-jokingly. He paddled his raft to the edge of the pool and began playfully splashing Danny with water. Danny rose from his position on the lounge, walked to the edge of the pool, and began splashing back. They were so busy laughing and horsing around that they didn't notice they had a visitor.

Kayla Asimov, looking every bit the Hollywood trendsetter that she was, had thrown open the massive French doors that led from the house to the patio. She wore a short, tight denim jacket over a white halter top, micro-dot Alexander Wang shorts, and a pair of white Coralia velcro strap boots. Trailing closely in her wake was Marta, Kenneth's maid. Kayla stopped when she reached the pool and stood glaring at Danny and Kenneth with her hands on her hips and mouth agape.

"Oh, isn't this cozy and sickeningly cliché?" she hissed. "I feel like I just stepped back in time to find Rock Hudson or Tab Hunter playing splashy splash in the nude with a Hollywood mogul. It would be downright nostalgic if it weren't so sickening."

"Meester Chapeero, Meester Chapeero!" Marta beseeched Kenneth. "I no let her in! She climb dee fence and pushed through dee door when I answer. You want me call policia?"

Kenneth climbed slowly from the pool and held a calming hand up to Marta. "It's okay, Marta. You can go back inside now."

The maid nodded her head, turned tail, and retreated quickly into the house. Danny wrapped a towel around his waist as Kayla unleashed her full fury in Kenneth's direction.

"There's a few things you might want to know about your darling boy-toy here," she told him. "He's good at fucking his way to the top and fucking over anybody else. Including you."

Danny toweled his hair dry and appeared unfazed, but his eyes regarded Kayla warily. Even though her hair was perfect, thick, shiny, and gorgeously styled, and her skin fresh and dewy, her words were slightly slurred and Danny could tell that she had been drinking. She continued rambling angrily at Kenneth.

"You're not the only stop on your boyfriend's bed hop this weekend. Seems your little fuck toy who you're so in love with spent last night getting his brains screwed out by Amy Price."

Kayla waited for this bombshell to hit, but Kenneth merely nodded in acknowledgement, which seemed to fuel her fury. She turned to face Danny.

"And you, you backstabbing Hollywood whore!" She screamed, her anger reaching a crescendo. "You cozied up with Amy Price and screwed me out of my role in *Trust Fund* with Trenton Cash. I was advised this morning that the part was no longer mine."

Kenneth shot a quizzical glance at Danny.

"Oh that's right, Kenneth," Kayla continued. Hatred dripped from her voice. "After all the publicity I got for your little sex doll, he tells Amy Price to drop me from the picture. Apparently I'm not a big enough name to share the credits with gay boy here and Trenton Cash."

Kenneth walked to the outside bar and poured himself another Bloody Mary, already pre-mixed in a crystal pitcher. Leaning coolly against the bar, he faced Kayla directly.

"This is Hollywood," he told her matter-of-factly. "Deals get made and broken, roles get lost and won, and people sleep around to get what they want. I happen to know you've done it yourself on more than one occasion. You're a big girl Kayla and you're not new to this game. It's always disappointing to lose a role, but again, this is Hollywood."

"It's not just that I lost the role, Kenneth," she spat furiously. She turned and glared venomously at Danny. "It's because I was totally backstabbed and screwed by somebody I thought was a friend. A co-star and a colleague who I *liked*."

Silence hung like a dark, heavy curtain in the jasmine scented, rarefied air.

"Amy Price didn't want you," Danny finally told Kayla softly. "She didn't want to package a deal that had you in it."

"Liar!" Kayla screamed, but her rigid stance was already going limp.

"Kayla," Danny said softly. "We were never really friends and I made it very clear to you that I had no romantic interest. But I didn't screw you over. A lot of people lost a lot of money on you when you were doing drugs. Amy was one of the people who got burned. I'm pretty sure you know that."

Kayla walked unsteadily to the bar, grabbed a two thousand dollar bottle of Alize vodka, and took an outsized swig directly from it. Slamming the bottle back on the bar, she sloppily wiped her mouth with the back of her hand and once again regarded Danny with an expression of clarity and sudden, sober focus.

"You just lie, lie, lie to people and nobody knows the real you," she said with firm conviction. "Like, I'm sure you told Kenneth here all about your little baby and your white trash girlfriend living in a trailer park back in Arizona."

The words hit both Danny and Kenneth like a freight train. Kenneth's head swung in Danny's direction. Danny stared at Kayla with dumbfounded disbelief. He erased his facial expression to one of calm neutrality an instant later, but not soon enough for Kenneth to miss his reaction.

Kayla smiled sweetly. "Oh, so you didn't know that your boy-friend here was secretly harboring an illegitimate baby," she said in a sing-song voice. "Well, I guess he lies to you, too. I guess you're not as special to him as you thought, Kenneth."

With that, Kayla treated herself to another, hearty swig of vodka and retreated back through the house. The only sound that could be heard was the song of a mockingbird as Danny and Kenneth stared each other down from across the pool.

*　*　*　*　*

The Sugar Mountain Awards are held at the Hollywood Arena in West Lost Angeles. Named after a song by legendary rocker Neil Young about the lament of lost youth, the awards honor the biggest stars under the age of twenty in television, music, and film.

The red carpet for this event spans two full blocks and gen-erally requires more than an hour to traverse. Young stars are led, usually by their publicists, from the highly guarded and protected red carpet entrance outside the swanky Hotel Z to the private laby-rinthine hall of the Hollywood Arena's backstage. Along the way, the young celebrities are photographed, videotaped, and interviewed on the red carpet. A wide range of journalists and pseudo-journalists await them on the sidelines, from the charming Marcus Cardillo of the "H" Hollywood Channel, to the preening Cutter of the Tattletale

Network, to bloggers as popular as Poppy Pissante and as obscure as ValleyGirlGossip.com.

Danny Smash and Kayla Asimov were two of the biggest stars on the red carpet this year due in part to the tremendous success of their series, *Mission Bay*. They were now a red-hot Hollywood couple that the tabloid media had already dubbed "DannyKay." The public was unaware that the two had never truly been a couple, or that they were now barely on speaking terms. This was, after all, Hollywood, the land nothing was as it seemed.

The pair opted to forgo escorts by their respective publicists on the red carpet, instead embarking along the press bordered walkway with each other. Their publicists, however, would still be hovering a few steps behind. A pair of glossy, scheming vultures hungry to live vicariously on the backs of their clients.

The publicists always paled beside the stars themselves, of course. Kayla wore a Lucius Mark gown that looked like a gold lame scarf that had been wrapped tightly, and seductively, around her flawless body. Her endless legs, full breasts, and gym-toned abs were on sinful display, with only the most intimate areas concealed by a swath of shiny gold fabric. A chunky bronze necklace and matching bracelets covered more skin than the entire dress.

The paparazzi went berserk the instant Kayla and Danny stepped onto the red carpet. Hollywood's sexiest bad girl paired with television's newest and hottest hunk provided the chemistry and the kind of provocative imagery that the entertainment press lived for.

"Kayla!" They called to her as though they personally knew her. "You are a knockout! Gives us a smile … look this way!"

"Danny, Danny, look over here," the photographers screamed. Light bulbs flashed furiously. Behind the steel police barricade fence, there was fierce competition to get the perfect shot or to record the most compelling sound bite before television's hottest young couple continued down the carpet.

Kayla smiled and twirled before the cameras and chatted amiably with microphone wielding reporters. She held tight onto Danny's arm, giggling at the appropriate moments, occasionally throwing her head back as if she were being photographed for a magazine cover, which in fact was always a possibility. The red carpet was her runway.

Preceding them on the carpet were the members of Triplets, three drop-dead gorgeous brothers whose edgy dance music was currently topping the charts.

Kayla whispered in Danny's ear as if she were sharing sweet nothings with him.

"Look, it's the triplets," she said, nodding at the rock star brothers. "Riddle me this, Mr. .Pansexual. Would you rather have a foursome with them and Amy, or with them and Kenneth?" She cocked her head flirtatiously toward the paparazzi and smiled effusively as the cameras clicked.

Danny nodded and laughed as though he had just been told a funny joke. He said nothing in response. She meant nothing to him. He had already left her far behind. Besides, his attention was focused on the myriad cameras pointing in his direction. His smile was megawatt. He didn't need splashy designer clothing or props to rule the carpet. Unlike The Triplets, who were dressed head to toe in grunge that looked like it fell from a truck but had, in fact, been arranged by a Beverly Hills stylist and probably cost a small fortune. Danny didn't need the gimmick. He wore a pair of Harrington and Stitch jeans, black loafers, and a simple black button down shirt. The clothes draped his long, lean, muscular frame and conveyed casual urban masculinity.

Under the hot lights and flashbulbs, he glowed like a superstar. Many of the kids who shared the carpet with him had been nervous and anxious before going out. Not Danny. He felt calm, confident, and perfectly at ease. This was where he belonged, his zone at the center of the white-hot spotlight.

Under the glare of the media's attention, Kayla barely registered in his mind until her publicist gently corralled them further down the carpet. "You guys are wanted in the Tattletale Network kiosk," said the plain looking woman. "Cutter is evidently going ape shit on his field producer. He's throwing a big bad temper tantrum until he gets an interview with you two."

Kayla smiled broadly and waved at the endless wall of cameras, blowing tiny kisses into the air. "Ready to kiss the ass of the biggest and best connected reporter in Hollywood?" She whispered in Danny's ear. "Let's hope Cutter doesn't ask about the little baby that you have locked away in a trailer in the dusty desert of Arizona. *That* would be embarrassing for you."

Danny smiled effusively and nodded carelessly, but the words stung on many levels. On a professional level, he didn't know how Kayla knew about Darlene and the baby, and he worried about whether she would mention it during the interview with Cutter, who was in fact the most influential journalist in town. Cutter himself might already know, as he had access to many of the town's most deeply held secrets. Fortunately, his interviews on the red carpet tended to be upbeat and cordial.

Danny focused on the positive. An interview by Cutter in the Tattletale Network kiosk was huge. Especially since this was Danny's first nationally televised red-carpet event. And Cutter was perhaps the most important member of the assembled press right now.

Currently, he was shouting into his headset. "This light is too harsh. Do I have to be the one to tell you that? Do your jobs, please!"

Assistants scurried to and fro.

The bigger entertainment networks had entire kiosks erected beside the red carpet at events like these. Their crews didn't have to mingle with the common media folk. The Tattletale kiosk was large and bright with nearly blinding television lights. It had its own carpet with its own trademarked shade of red, and it was filled to capacity with production assistants whose job it was to perform as Cutter's royal subjects.

Cutter's voice became saccharine the instant that Kayla and Danny stepped into the kiosk. His expression changed to one of nearly angelic benevolence.

An assistant dabbed moisture from his face. As lights were adjusted, he appraised himself critically in one of the multitude of monitors and then pulled Kayla and Danny alongside him in front of the cameras.

He smiled brightly as he spoke. A sixty thousand dollar boom microphone was above his head, just out of camera range. "I'm here now with Kayla Asimov and Danny Smash. Hey guys, great to see you. Congratulations on your incredible success with *Mission Bay*. Kayla . . . what a comeback! Even though it is on the small screen, it's gotta feel great for you to be back in the public eye in such a big way."

Kayla's eyes flashed steel at the jibe. She prided herself on being a quick-witted interview, but before she could formulate an answer, Cutter had already turned his attention to Danny.

Kayla interjected quickly. "As you know, Cutter," she said, sweetly touching the reporter's arm. "I'm on my way back to the big screen. You of all people should know that."

Cutter smiled, nodded and displayed little interest.

"You know that Danny and I are starring together in *Starlight Café*. I'd really like you to have a front seat at the premiere so you can witness my triumphant return to the big screen. I'll even give you the first interview, because you know how much I adore you and the Tattletale Network."

Cutter responded with a friendly nod. He turned to Danny.

"And you, my friend, are on a rocket to the stratosphere. Since your arrival in Hollywood two years ago, you shot from obscurity as a jeans model to the star of a hit television show. You've got one movie out, another in the pipeline, and it is whispered that you and Trenton Cash might both be casted in *Trust Fund*. That script isn't even finished and it's already the hottest property in Tinseltown. Dude, where did you come from?"

Kayla recoiled at having been snubbed in favor of Danny, but recovered instantly and gazed beatifically at her "boyfriend." For the cameras, she was his loving, supporting friend and co-star. Inwardly she seethed.

"Look," Danny answered, flashing the trademark smile that was plastered on posters and magazine cutouts in the bedrooms of teenage girls across America. "It's true I got to LA as a total stranger, but I lucked out by meeting some amazing people who got me on the path I'm currently following. I'm really lucky, I guess, and really grateful to be where I'm at."

Kayla noticed that Cutter was staring with adulation into Danny's god-like face while she was being blatantly ignored.

"Very quickly," Cutter said. "Can you tell us a little about what's going on with *Trust Fund*?"

"The deal hasn't even been inked, yet," Danny laughed. "At this point it's just in the pipeline. Amy Price at Mammoth has optioned the book. I'm certainly interested in the role of Nick and I've heard that Trent wants to play Major. The truth is I haven't seen the script and I haven't even met Trent, but he's super talented and I definitely hope that we can work together."

Kayla stood beside Danny, smiling and nodding approvingly at his words. Inside, hatred, jealousy and bitterness threatened to consume her.

*   *   *   *   *

The Riverview Country Club is affectionately known as "the Riv" by its roster of Hollywood A-List golf playing members. The clubhouse, an imposing Spanish style mansion nestled on a gentle hill overlooking the green, was currently hosting the Kara Lash Cosmetics "Women in the Film Industry" awards banquet. Kayla Asimov sat at the bar in the clubroom, nursing her third straight vodka on the rocks. She was oblivious to the star-studded event unfolding in the adjacent room, and instead sat staring morosely at black and white pictures of silent movie stars that lined the bar's dark paneled walls.

Where was London? Damn, she needed another bump.

She'd been on a binge since leaving the Sugar Mountain Awards, alone, in a limo whose bar she had plundered all the way to her empty, palatial home in Laurel Canyon. There, her dealer delivered to her door a bottle of fifty delicious pills. *No big deal, I know how to handle this*, she thought, swallowing two of the pills. She'd been handling them ever since, along with vodka and bumps of coke, for the past two days.

London Wyatt, a socialite famous for simply being famous, plopped her hundred thousand dollar crocodile bag on the bar and then plopped herself down on a stool beside Kayla. "Get this shit," she said tendentiously. "Your sexy boyfriend Danny Smash was just named one of the top ten celebrity Tweeters. As you know, this means he'll be making bank from social media alone. Not to mention major exposure."

Kayla felt the angry knot in her stomach tighten and her fist clenched tightly around her cocktail glass. The public, and all of her friends for that matter, still believed that she and Danny were something of an item. She'd been forced to play the dutiful girlfriend to that backstabbing bastard at the Sugar Mountain Awards, only to find herself reduced to arm candy, another prop in his ruthless climb. Her hatred was savage, yet she was powerless to do anything but watch idly as he smoothly scaled to greater heights of fame.

"Let's go do a bump, Biatch," she said playfully. No way would anyone know what he had done to her. Kayla would continue to exploit her connection with Danny for her own gain. She had learned to capitalize on connections, however tenuous, and to painstakingly hide any weakness. In this town fragilities were exploited and powerlessness, like blood in the water, attracted a frenzy of Armani clad, unforgiving sharks.

All well and good, but right now she needed to be wasted and London Wyatt always had the best blow in town.

"Come, girlfriend." London beckoned with a perfectly manicured finger and Kayla followed her into the powder room, where the two ensconced themselves in a luxurious stall and proceeded to snort huge lines. London, of course, came prepared with a sterling silver straw and a diamond studded compact mirror with which to imbibe the drug.

"Let's follow this down with a little X," London said, proffering a tiny bottle and digging out two pills. Each girl swallowed one down and they headed back to the bar.

"Let's get back to the main event," London suggested, still looking great for a girl who had a dangerous mix of drugs and alcohol running through her veins. "It's pretty freaking boring here in the bar."

"Having just been in there, I can tell you that the main event is pretty freaking boring, too," Kayla said, slurring her words. "Lots of endless speeches and platitudes. And that bitch Amy Price taking center stage. Barf!"

"Let's just leave, then," London said with a shrug of her elegant shoulder. "Justin's having a party up at the house."

Balancing themselves on impossibly high heels, the girls tottered out through the front doors of the club. Kayla was starting to feel much too good to worry about Danny anymore, and suddenly everything London said was hysterical. The two girls exited the Riv laughing and giggling like a bunch of valley girls at the mall.

"Oh my God, I always wanted to drive in one of those!" Kayla announced, pointing to a queue of golf carts that were lined up at the curb.

"Oh shit they are soooo cute!" London declared as if she'd never seen a golf cart before. "We should totally take one for a spin!"

"Let's get in!" Agreed Kayla.

The girls climbed aboard the first golf cart, Kayla taking the driver's seat. "Oh shit, the key is right here!" She happily exclaimed. She turned the key, and the golf cart started with a lurch.

"Careful, biatch!" London laughed uproariously as Kayla steered the golf cart onto the macadam and headed toward the green.

The golf cart bounced over the curb. Kayla had her foot pressed firmly on the gas pedal, and the cart reached its maximum speed of fifteen MPH. The girls sped around sand traps, through bushes, and nearly plowed down groups of highly irate golfers, who were making frantic calls to club security.

For their part, the girls were oblivious to the havoc they were causing on the course. They continued to speed forward until a wrong turn took them over the edge of a steep hill. Kayla lost control of the cart and within seconds the vehicle went from a slide to a full on roll down the hill. Over and over it went as the screams of the terrified girls filled the air. The cart finally came to a stop, landing with a crunching thud and coming to rest on the inert body of Kayla Asimov.

* * * * *

After nine straight hours of playing the video game Grand Theft Auto, Simon LaFleour put his computer to sleep, waddled out of his room and decided to relax his mind by channel surfing on the TV set. Mostly uninterested in any form of entertainment except for video games, Simon flopped lazily onto the couch, tore into a bag of potato chips, popped open a can of soda, and began absently flipping through the channels with the remote.

The Tattletale Network was covering some red carpet event and Simon stopped surfing as the image of a gorgeously slutty looking movie star filled the forty-six inch television screen. Simon dropped the remote onto the coffee table and settled back into the couch to focus on her smokin', barely dressed and perfect body. The names Danny Smash and Kayla Asimov flashed on the screen. Simon watched Kayla, who was standing beside a freakishly handsome actor. The pretty boy movie star was being interviewed by some ass-hole reporter while Kayla stood there with her gorgeous body and long legs on full steaming display.

As he watched, his eyes widened as he noticed that pretty boy stroked his chin in a way that was instantly familiar to him. A slow drag of the middle finger across the chin, followed by a blindingly white smile. Suddenly something in Simon's brain clicked, followed by instant anger that quickly escalated to rage. With a sudden, violent motion, Simon picked up a table lamp, ripped it out of the socket, and smashed it into the television, which continued to play even as a spider web crack moved across the plasma display.

He stormed into his bedroom. The door slammed shut with a force that shook the dusty pictures on the adjacent wall. The ensuing stillness was finally broken by a sudden screech from his mother, who had previously been resting in her room.

Simon tapped furiously at the keys to his computer, attempting to find footage of Ben Briggs, aka Danny Smash, at the Sugar Hill Awards. He ignored his mother's rants outside his locked door, hop-ing that she would finally just give up. But she didn't. Finally, after finding the footage and downloading it onto a flash drive, Simon climbed over piles of dirty laundry and crunched past half-con-sumed bags of corn chips to open his bedroom door, whereupon his mother stood, her nostrils were assaulted by a combination of marijuana smoke, dank laundry, and pungent body odor.

"What the fuck happened to the television set?" The birdlike Terry LaFleour demanded.

Simon pursed his lips like a petulant child. "I threw a lamp at the screen," he told her sluggishly.

"Why did you have an outburst, Simon?" Her voice was crazed. "I thought the doctors and the medicines were helping you. Why did you lose control and throw my beautiful lamp at the TV screen?" Her eyes never left his. "This is scaring me, Simon. This ... this violence and destructiveness. I can't have it in my house. When is it going to stop?"

Simon moved imperceptibly toward his mother. His lids were heavy, eyes glassy and stoned. "Don't forget I paid for that TV with my disability check. And I will buy us another one and it won't happen again. I won't ruin the TV again."

His mother was not totally appeased, but, sensing his drug induced sedation, felt comfortable pushing him. "Why did you do it, Simon? What happened?"

He responded with another question. "Guess who was on TV tonight, Mom?"

His mother's arms were folded tightly against her chest, but they relaxed as her curiosity was roused. She shrugged.

"I don't know, who?"

Simon responded with yet another question. "Do you remember that jerkoff con artist who robbed the place where Grandpa lived?"

She nodded. "Of course I remember, Simon."

Simon stepped in closer to his mother. "That little fucker was on TV tonight. He's a big movie star now. His girlfriend is *Kayla Asimov*."

Her expression turned from hardness to one of quizzical disbelief and shock. "That doesn't seem likely. Are you sure it was him, or someone who just resembled him, Simon. What was the kid's name? Benny Briggs?"

"Oh it was him all right," Simon answered through a haze of marijuana intoxication. "He's going under a different name, and he looks totally different, but I'll never forget the way he rubs his finger slowly across his chin right before he smiles cunningly. And I will never forget that smile, either. Now he cleverly calls himself Danny Smash. Go ahead . . . have a look at my computer. I downloaded a video of him."

Simon's mother picked her way through the garbage and debris of the bedroom. She kicked a pile of video packages out of her way bent forward to the computer screen while Simon called up the video clip. She had only seen the boy a few times, and he'd been wearing a baseball cap and had several days of beard growth, but there was no mistaking the mannerisms and gestures, which she viewed with mixed emotions. She strongly suspected that three thousand dollars in cash that she had received anonymously shortly after her father's death had been sent by this very kid. She was positively stunned.

"Simon, this is an extremely bizarre coincidence," she mused. "Maybe it's the same kid, but what are the chances?"

"I know it's the same fucking dude," Simon spat. "And he has to pay for what he did. He killed my Gramps!"

Terry pondered the likelihood that a teenage handyman could somehow turn into a famous star. But this kind of thing, she knew, could happen. Her intuition was telling her that Simon was right. "I guess we should notify the authorities," she said finally.

Simon held up a flash drive. "All of the video footage is on this stick. I'm taking it to the cops right now."

She looked at the memory stick and then into Simon's glassy, bloodshot eyes.

"I don't think you are in any shape to walk into a police precinct," she told him.

Before he could argue she took the flash drive from his hand. "I will take this directly to the detective who was investigating the robbery. We'll let the authorities take it from there."

When she left the apartment, Simon sat glowering in fury. *I don't trust the fucking authorities*, he thought. *That mother fucker killed my gramps.*

*　*　*　*　*

ONE YEAR LATER ...

The Regal Palm Resort and Spa in Scottsdale Arizona is touted as an "oasis in the valley of the sun." Phyllis Moyt had just treated herself to a ninety-minute deep tissue massage on the secluded balcony of her expansive suite. The luxe accommodations boasted a stunning desert mountain view. She didn't mind the $2,600 per night price tag, especially since the bill was going to be paid by *Persons Magazine*, which was also forking over six figures for transcripts from the meeting that she had cleared and scheduled for later today.

Despite the early hour of 11 AM, Phyllis sipped a Dom Perignon and fresh squeezed orange juice mimosa and enjoyed a breakfast of raspberries topped with rich, savory whipped cream.

The intercom to her suite buzzed. She rose from her luxurious settee and practically skipped to answer the call.

"Yes, hello!" She said, pressing the button.

The voice on the speaker was a rich timbre of youthful male subservience. "Miss Moyt, your car is ready."

"Thank you concierge. I shall be down in just a moment!"

Phyllis checked herself in the mirror one last time. Her red hair had been stylishly coiffed in the resort salon just a day ago. Her dress, a Paloma cotton print, was a gift to herself from a boutique in West Hollywood. She looked like a professional, confident, high-class talent agent.

And she was off to close a big deal with the man who had become her unlikely golden goose.

The catastrophic fall of Danny Smash was a major windfall for Phyllis Moyt. Danny Smash had been on the cusp of young Hollywood superstardom when he was arrested for bilking the elderly residents of a senior citizens community, one of whom had subsequently died of a stroke.

When Danny was exposed as a felon, the media went ape shit, dubbing Danny Smash "Granny Smasher." The entertainment news machine shifted immediately into overdrive, ferreting out anyone who had had any involvement in Danny's rapid ascent to stardom. Danny's supremely uptight agent at the time of the arrest, Kenneth Shapiro, had closed ranks and refused to even provide a sound-byte to the press. But Phyllis, as his first agent and manager in the business, had been only to happy to oblige, and found herself besieged by media attention. Always a shrewd operator, Phyllis was quick to capitalize on the fact that the Hollywood gossip sharks were now swimming right outsider her door, bloodthirsty for the information that she alone could provide on Danny. And, barracuda that she was, Phyllis did provide. At a cost.

She made money just selling Danny's first Hollywood head-shots (which she originally bankrolled with her own cash, thank you very much). For an intoxicating price, she gave interviews to all of the entertainment news programs, wherein she divulged the story of Danny Smash, from his humble arrival at her office, to her careful guidance of his early career, to his ascent to stardom, to his cold termination of their business partnership. She was paid handsomely for an hour-long interview with entertainment reporter Cutter, the king of Hollywood gossip whose words had the power to either advance or derail a star's career. As a result of all of this media attention, the talent agency of Phyllis Moyt was a hot commodity in the industry. She had signed a number of promising, legitimate actors and actresses. Talent behemoth Creative Heads even called with the prospect of an acquisition deal.

She still couldn't quite believe her luck at this highly unlikely and unexpected turn of events. Practically walking on air as she made her way through the luxuriant interior of the Regal Palm, her mind was swirling with plans to once again take control of the star that she herself had discovered and created.

Phyllis glanced at her reflection in the floor to ceiling mirrors of the hotel lobby and pushed from her mind the insecurity that always haunted her regarding her appearance. She reminded herself that she was a hard working, comfortable woman and had built a busy and lucrative business, and boarded a town car that was waiting for her beneath the sun kissed portico of the Regal Palms. The car's air-conditioned cool starkly contrasted the 100 plus degree outside desert temperature. Phyllis lounged on the deep leather seats as the driver piloted her south of the city and into the sun baked desert en route to the Arizona State Prison Complex, a minimum-security penitentiary in Florence. The prison was a complex of concrete structures surrounded by a tall chain link fence topped with rolls of barbed wire. Phyllis was filled with ambivalence at the sight. A lump formed in her throat that a fate like this should befall such a talented promising young man, but there was also a sense that justice had been done. The sight of barbed wire and imposing buildings sent a shiver up her spine. The car turned into the prison. The surroundings were dusty, bland, and depressing.

Phyllis permitted the chauffer to open her door, and then, like the visiting royalty she considered herself to be, emerged and confidently entered the prison complex, whereupon she was met with a blast of chilled air. The antechamber she entered was bleak and the front desk was aseptic. A motley crew of visitors looked as if they just crawled in from the seediest of rat holes.

Phyllis signed an OV, which, she learned, is an official visitor book. She filled out a request form to see Danny, and was suddenly filled with a sense of unease. This was the first time she had seen Danny since he fired her as his agent, and she had no idea how he would react to her now. He had agreed to see her, but she couldn't imagine what prison life may have done to him. She was directed to a locker, where she hesitantly deposited her Hermes Bag and her cell phone.

She was then led through a dreary corridor and into a large, cafeteria-like room. Security guards paced the perimeter of the space and walked among plastic topped tables. It was a sea of shaved heads, orange jumpsuits, and gang tattoos. What may have looked sexy and alluring in a print ad was nothing short of dreadful in real life, thought Phyllis.

Orange is certainly not the new black ...

Choosing an empty table that was as far away as possible from the others, Phyllis slid in to a drab green plastic seat. She waited with a combination of excitement and fear, avoiding all eye contact and focusing on the door. A scrawny kid who looked like a heroin addict wandered to the table. There was a hideous scar on his arm and a tattoo of a snake wrapped around his neck. The head and tail of the snake crossed at his throat.

"You do pro bono?" He asked through cigarette stained teeth.

"No," Phyllis answered, regarding the scraggy delinquent dead in the eye. "I do not." Phyllis then returned her gaze to the door as the jailbird wandered away mumbling something about stuck up lady lawyers.

Phyllis nearly gasped aloud when Danny entered the room. She had expected him to look defeated, hollowed, and depressed by his incarceration. On the contrary, however, he looked every bit the movie star that he had nearly become. He walked with a grace that bordered cocky, his head was held high, his eyes were clear, his hair as shiny as any shampoo model, his body tan and buff. He was led into the room by a female guard who had that sexy/tough lady cop thing going on. Phyllis noticed that a smile passed between Danny and his guard, and she realized that the little charmer had already gotten himself all set up and protected within the prison system.

It was so easy to get lost in the young man's beauty and appeal. But Phyllis wasn't permitting herself to get distracted.

Danny casually kicked out a chair and sat facing her, his demeanor as calm and confident as an A-Lister at a star studded soiree. Every eye in the room darted curiously his way, and while Phyllis took all of this in; Danny appeared oblivious.

"I'm glad you decided to see me," Phyllis told him. " "Do I call you Danny or do I call you Ben."

"I'm still Danny," he answered. A smile played on the edges of his lips. He was lounged back casually in the chair, his arms draped over the sides, legs spread wide and feet planted on the floor.

Phyllis knew the posturing well. Danny always used seductive body language. She also knew that this was how he controlled and manipulated people.

"Were you surprised to hear from me?" she asked him.

His wickedly sensual, emerald green eyes bored into hers. "Nothing surprises me."

Phyllis crossed her arms over her chest. "So you weren't surprised when the cops showed up at the Beverly Hills Hotel and arrested you? Because everyone else in Hollywood were sure as hell shocked."

Danny settled more comfortably into his chair as a silence ensued between the two.

"You're out in ten months," Phyllis said finally. "What are your plans?"

"Eight months," Danny corrected her. "Good behavior." A knowing wink.

"Okay, eight months then."

Phyllis worked hard not to squirm. Or stammer. His unbridled self-confidence, even under these circumstances, was disarming to her.

"What are you doing in eight months?"

"By then I'll have done the time and paid for my crime," Danny returned. "I will go back to Hollywood and pick up the pieces of my career."

Phyllis leaned back in her chair and fixed him with a calm, direct stare.

"You cannot be serious," she told him. "Do you think your agent Kenneth Shapiro would take you back? Has he even been here to visit?"

Danny said nothing.

"I didn't think so," she answered knowingly. "In fact, he's been squiring a James Dean lookalike all over town for the past couple of weeks. Sorry kid, but he's moved on. That's how Hollywood works."

"I know how it works, Phyllis," he answered with a shrug. "I may have to sign a new agent. I've got contacts now. I've still got a name. In fact I'm more famous now than ever before."

She leaned in and continued to regard him with a stare that bordered on compassionate. "You are infamous, Danny, not famous. There is a huge difference."

"Aside from tabloid reporters, has anyone from the legitimate industry been here to offer you a deal?"

Danny's expression was non-committal.

"Again, I didn't think so," Phyllis told him. "Aside from the heartless nature of the crime you committed, which is unforgive-able on its own, you have your so called ex-girlfriend Kayla Asimov blaming you for a horrific accident that left her nearly crippled."

"Oh, come on," Danny said. "I was nowhere near her when she had that accident."

"Well, she publicly blamed you for her relapse. And the inter-view she gave from her hospital bed made her look like a very believable victim. She said she had loved and trusted you only to learn that you had a girlfriend with a baby in another state. She said you knew that she was fragile, fighting her addictions, and that you led her on to build your own career."

Danny's face reddened slightly but his voice remained steady. "I never led her on. She was just pissed because she didn't get the role in *Trust Fund* and she blamed it on me."

"Doesn't matter," Phyllis answered candidly. "You've already been tried and convicted in the court of public opinion. A well-known actress was in a horrific accident and the public blames you. An old man died of a stroke and the public blames you. You robbed elderly people who trusted you. You are one of many celebrities whose bad behavior is unforgivable. In the mind of the people, you are no better than the sexually abusive morning show host, the perverted movie producer, the esteemed actor who molested a sixteen year-old boy, or the lovable female comedian who sent out a racist tweet. Their careers are over. Do you think you're any different?"

Danny's spine stiffened but he said nothing. Fearing that he would get up and leave, Phyllis decided to put the brakes on. She had made her point.

"I'm in prison paying the price for what I've done," he finally said. "I was desperate. I was scared. I was running from my past. I did what I had to do. For your information, I paid those old people back as soon as I had the money. And you don't need to know any more than that."

Danny looked away and exhaled a deep breath.

What the hell did this kid live through? Phyllis wondered sadly. In retrospect, Danny always seemed like he was running from something. On his way to anywhere else, and fast. She hadn't paid close enough attention because this was the story with half of Hollywood.

He turned and faced her with a hardened expression.

"Why are you here, Phyllis?"

"I get it now," she told him. There was genuine warmth in her voice. "You were trying to escape something horrible in Arizona, so you came to Hollywood to become a big star, to put yourself in a place where no one could ever hurt you again."

Danny swallowed hard. "Again. Why are you here, Phyllis?"

She pulled a slip of paper from her pocket and handed it to him. He regarded it curiously and unfolded it. There were three vaguely familiar names on the paper, two were women and one was a man. Beside each name was a multi-million dollar figure. He looked up at Phyllis, perplexed.

"Those are the three highest grossing stars in the erotic entertainment industry," she told him. "You'll note that each one is worth a minimum of ten million dollars."

Danny's jaw clenched and he exhaled quickly. "You are kidding me, right?"

"Hear me out," Phyllis said. "Porn stars can make millions of dollars. They have legions of fans. And they've become pretty mainstream, especially since one of them got caught having a tryst with the president."

Danny crossed his arms over his chest. "That is so sleazy and crude, Phyllis. I'm a freaking Hollywood star."

"You *were* an *up and coming* Hollywood star," she said softly. "But you fucked up. Your chances of a comeback are virtually non-existent. And how much money could you possible have left after paying off all of your legal fees?"

Danny slid his chair back and made ready to end the visit. He handed back the slip of paper.

"Remember those names," Phyllis said, pocketing the paper and standing. "And those figures. Any and all of the top grossing erotic performers would co-star with you in a minute. You're a smart boy. You could learn this business with ease. I will bankroll a studio with your name on the deed. You will get a back end percentage on everything you touch. Your movies would make millions, tens of millions even. You would have a built-in audience. Gay men, who have created many stars, would be rabid for you. You *could* be a star again. Plus you could produce, direct, and have total control."

Phyllis turned to walk away. "Total control," she repeated. You've got nothing but time, so you really should think about it."

"Thanks for coming, Phyllis," he called as she retreated from the room. "But forget it."

Philadelphia, PA. 3 years later ...

Dr. David Bachman fastened the Kippah to the top of his head and began slowly ascending the steep walkway that led to the front door of his childhood home. The large English Tudor was in in Bala Cynwyd, an affluent suburb of Philadelphia. The hedges were trimmed, the landscape was wooded, and the grounds were sloped. Mature trees bordering the walkway dropped multicolored leaves in his path. The chill air and the scent of autumn brought him back to his childhood, and memories that were deeply bittersweet. His steps were measured, his pace stalled by trepidation. This place was intimately familiar to him, yet he was a stranger here. He was almost certain that he wouldn't be welcome. But his family still lived inside, and there was a need that drove him, step by anxious step, toward the front door.

His finger lingered on the doorbell as he stood momentarily paralyzed that this could be his very last visit home, the last time he might lay eyes on his parents, possibly even his seven siblings. Finally, breathing deeply, he pressed the doorbell. After what seemed an eternity but was in fact less than a minute, the door opened several inches and his father peered out at him. His father hadn't changed since he'd last seen him 10 years ago. An overweight, bald man with a full dark beard who even seemed to be wearing the exact same clothes from a decade ago: black pants and jacket with a white tieless shirt.

"Tati," David said tenuously.

"What are you doing here, David?" His father demanded in a voice laced with ice.

David looked into the face of the patriarch he hadn't seen in forever. If he'd been expecting an open arms greeting after a protracted absence, he would have been disappointed. Still, he was crushed by the stony expression fixed upon him by the ultra orthodox Mordechai Bachman. It was a look of undisguised disgust. Hatred, even. But David pushed on.

"I am your son. Did you not wonder what became of me? Did you not care at all? Aren't you at least a little happy to see your own flesh and blood?" David stared into the eyes of his father.

"You were once my son," his father told him with perfectly controlled anger. "And I briefly mourned your death, even though you jeopardized this family. You shamed us in the eyes of the community. You imperiled my livelihood. Your brother's and sisters were punished because of your sinning and your selfishness."

David's eyes bored into his father's. "There are gay orthodox people everywhere, father. We have support groups all over the world, including Israel. Until very recently, gay people in our community have chosen to live their lives as a lie, but that can't happen anymore. Spirituality and sexuality are equally strong components of the personality. You cannot expect one to cancel out the other. More and more orthodox families are willing to accept that. Why can't you?"

David's father bristled and began to close the door. "Your kind are menaces to our society and are cancers upon orthodoxy. You have failed yourself and this family."

Before the door slammed in his face, David caught a glimpse of his mother and his youngest sister, Miryam, peering at him from inside the house.

"I am not a failure!" David screamed, his fist pounding angrily on the closed door. "I am a doctor of psychology. I am a published author. I am in Philadelphia to give a lecture about my book. I am successful! I am not a failure simply because I don't adhere to your antiquated laws. You might be an observant Jew, father, but your beliefs and your rituals have made you a cold and inhuman. You speak of God, but only a devil would turn his back on his own son just because he wishes to live a different life."

David's fist fell away from the door, sore and exhausted from pounding on it. He stared at the door and then he turned from the deathly stillness of the house, shoved clenched fists into his pockets and walked angrily toward the street. He opened the door to his rental car and dropped into the driver's seat. His anger gave way and he buried his face in his hands and wept.

* * * * *

The Unity is the oldest gay and lesbian bookshop in the United States. The store enjoys a prominent location on a quaint corner of Pine Street, in Philadelphia's Center City district. This neighborhood, often affectionately called "the gayborhood," is an enclave where same-sex couples live, work and play.

Steeped in neighborhood history and lore, the Unity Bookshop is housed in a two-story brick building that had been a carriage house during pre-revolutionary times. The shop serves the Lesbian, Gay, Bisexual and Transgender community, selling fiction and non-fiction books, magazines, DVDs, calendars, greeting cards, rainbow flags, pins, and sundry gay themed collectibles. During the course of its own storied past, the venue played host to a roster of legendary gay authors and was frequented by the likes of Truman Capote, Quentin Crisp, and Allen Ginsberg. When in town, Crisp would hold court in one cramped corner. He sat in an overstuffed chair surrounded by a gaggle of admirers.

In later decades, the store nearly succumbed to competition from mega book selling chains, but concerted community effort, clever financing, and the launch of a successful online business saved it from oblivion. Now more than just a bookshop, the Unity embodies survival, tenacity, and longevity, and as such has been considered a metaphor for the gay community itself. The landmark institution continues to serve as a neighborhood crossroad where books are perused, men and women are cruised, and dirt is heartily dished.

The window fronting the bookshop serves as something of a community bulletin board. Taped to the inside surface of plate glass are promotional notices heralding everything from girl band performances to edgy independent film festivals. These free ads are the best marketing deal in town, offering artists and performers tremendous exposure to an endless stream of foot traffic. The ads are regularly scanned and meet with varying degrees of fanfare by area residents. The newest had been taped up just yesterday and was already garnering a great degree of attention. It was glossy and provocative and stood out boldly because of its raw, erotic content.

The ad featured a nearly naked photo of a tanned, chiseled young man whose sheer physicality was mesmerizing. Daniel Smash, porn star and mogul, was arguably the most renowned icon in the history of gay erotica, a medium that had created its fair share of gods and princes. As the poster indicated, Daniel was scheduled for a personal appearance right here at the Unity Bookshop. He would be here to promote the latest in a long line of products launched by his erotic empire - this time a coffee table book entitled *BEHIND the Scenes*. The book, according to the ad copy, featured intimate photos of Daniel at home and backstage on various porn sets in the picturesque city of Prague, Czechoslovakia. Those who purchased the tome on the day of Daniels's visit would be able to meet him, get their books autographed, and take photos with the star.

Directly above this ad was another poster. It announced a free lecture by a renowned pair of psychologists, doctors David Bachman and Zahara Shelby. The two had recently published a book titled *Marriage with a Q!* Their self-help manual focused on gay monogamy. The authors would be speaking about the book, and about building strong, fulfilling, and committed relationships. Their eye catching-poster, with its bold colors and modern graphics, went largely ignored.

Three men in their late twenties stood in front of the bookstore and were peering through the window.

"I might go to this Daniel Smash thing," said the first man, who was dangerously thin and heavily tattooed. He wore a tight black tee shirt, ripped jeans, and high top sneakers emblazoned with decorative skulls and crossbones.

The second man lit a cigarette and waved it in the air. He was quite chubby. Long bangs hung over his forehead and into his eyes. A smattering of pimples dotted his complexion. He exhaled a plume of smoke.

"I'm definitely going," he declared.

"I'm really interested in seeing him in person," added the third man, who wore a long black coat, and was carrying several plastic grocery bags. "He truly is something to look at."

The tattooed man nodded in agreement. "This event is going to be a shit show. I'm going to get here early."

"Yes, me too," said the man with the groceries.

"If I went to the gym every day and didn't eat a gram of carbohydrates for a year, I could still never hope to have a body like that," Chubby observed with a shrug. ""I'll probably just be torturing myself, but I'm still dying to feast my eyes on this guy."

All three men failed to notice a darkly dressed older man, who'd been quietly observing them. Bachman was standing with a slouch at the edge of the curb.

Brian Rowe and Steve Hytower were approaching the bookstore from the opposite direction. Brian was stocky, solidly built, and in his early thirties. Steve was tall, lean, and lanky with a light complexion and fine features. He and Brian eyed the three men who'd been huddled at the bookstore window.

"I'm pretty sure the one with the blonde hair went to our high school. His name is Gene, I think. Graduated a few years after us," Brian recalled.

"He looks a little familiar. Are you sure he graduated *after* we did?" Steve's voice was smooth and baritone. Each word he enunciated was clear and succinct. His was the voice of a professional announcer. "We seem a lot younger, I think."

Brian smiled. "Of course *you* look younger," he chided his best friend. "But then again your face is practically paralyzed by toxic levels of botox and restyline."

Steve laughed as the two approached the window of the Unity Bookstore.

"Hmm, this is interesting," Brian said.

Steve was busy checking out his reflection in the window. "Don't you think my hair looks thicker since I started taking the keratin supplements?" he asked.

"Can you pull yourself away from your self for a second," Brian said, ignoring Steve's hair entirely and reading from the poster instead. ""Remember Danny Smash, the dude from *Mission Bay*? Apparently he'll be here signing some book during Rainbow Ball Weekend."

This got Steve's attention and he began studying the poster intently. "Daniel, or whatever he calls himself now, is a still a big name," he said finally. "People are really going to show up for this." Steve pulled an iPhone from his pocket and punched a number into the touch screen.

Brian winced. "Shouldn't you sanitize that thing? You've made four calls already without wiping it down once! I have disinfectant towelettes if you need one."

Steve paid no attention to his germ phobic friend's offer. "Stacey." He spoke into his phone and left a voice mail message while reading details from the poster. "There's going to be a celebrity book signing at the Unity Bookstore on Twelfth Street. Four P.M. two weeks from today. Daniel Smash, aka Danny Smash. See if you can get in touch with his publicist and schedule an interview. Also call the bookstore and get clearance to send a crew in."

Steve pressed the touch screen and ended the call.

Brian's mouth hung open, incredulous. "Your station is going to let you cover a book signing by a *porn star*? A *gay* porn star?"

"Come on, we both know he's more than just a porn star," Steve replied. "He's fucking Danny Smash, crash and burn superstar. His reinvention makes a former pop star look like an amateur."

"If you're covering this I'm coming," Brian said. "This guy really fascinates me."

"He fascinates me, too!" Steve exclaimed. "Look at that body. Look at that face.

"I agree, but that's not what I find so fascinating," Brian answered. "You've got to wonder what makes a guy like him tick. Because for such a good looking, intelligent guy, he sure has made some unexpected decisions in his life."

"Agreed" Steve nodded. "You can come here with me when we shoot the interview. You can carry batteries for Frankie the cameraman or something. This could make a pretty awesome story. Hot and wholesome Hollywood leading man falls from grace and re-emerges as an erotic mogul and porn icon."

"I don't know that your boss will go for that story," Brian told him. "The gay porn angle may not sit well with Brenda, that uptight old bitch."

Brenda Silverman was Steve's piranha of a boss. She was the News Director at PHILY-TV, which was where Steve worked as a reporter. As Steve's best friend, Brian sometimes tagged along on celebrity television shoots, was a frequent guest at newsroom parties, and had had the pleasure of meeting the ferocious television executive on more than one occasion. The two actually got along famously because Brian had a wicked sense of humor and was basically afraid of no one. Once Brenda realized that her fear factor didn't work with him and that, in fact, he found her amusing, the two became fast friends.

As for Brian and Steve, they had been best friends since attending high school together in Philadelphia's far northern suburbs. Now in their mid thirties, they were single, professional, and largely happy. Each, however, had individual neurotic tics and fluctuating degrees of existential angst.

"I'm not going to emphasize the porn angle when I pitch this to Brenda," Steve insisted. "There isn't a straight woman or gay man in the civilized world that didn't watch *Mission Bay* and drool over Danny Smash. And nobody could forget that steamy scene with him and Kayla Asimov on the beach in *Starlight Café*. Then came the scandal. Three years later he's in Philly, emerging from the ashes. That's the story I'll pitch to Brenda."

Brian shrugged. "Well, when you put it that way it may even sound palatable to your buttoned up network bosses," he agreed. "But I'm hungry. Let's go to that new brick oven pizza place."

They turned and continued to walk in the direction of Broad Street, never once noticing the quiet, somber man who was standing at the curb with his head bent and his hands buried deeply in his pockets.

When the sidewalk was clear, Dr. David Bachman approached the window, his body moving with slow, leaden steps, his focus riveted on the provocative poster featuring a scantily dressed, spectacular porn star. He reached the window and closely inspected the ad, realizing despairingly that the porn star's book signing coincided with the date and time of his own lecture. After staring hypnotically at the sexually charged image, he glanced above it, at the poster in which he and his co-writer were featured prominently. With sad eyes he inspected his own photo, which had been blatantly and repeatedly ignored in favor of the porn star. As he studied the image of his own face, he felt as though he were looking at a stranger. A stranger whose expression bore a feeling of hope that he no longer felt.

*   *   *   *   *

There was a post-summer chill in the air that carried a scent of dried leaves through Philadelphia's City Park. Ancient trees were autumnal in shades of red and yellow. At the base of a particularly tall and gnarled oak sat Zahara Shelby. Cross-legged, she lounged against its substantial trunk, watching skateboarders race by a fountain as they attempted to outdo each other with their stunts. Another kid skated past as his dog ran along beside him on a leash.

Dr. Zahara Shelby, PhD, known to her friends and family as "Zee,"

was in town as part of a multi-city lecture series whose purpose was both promotional and educational. She and her colleague, Dr.

David Bachman, had collaborated on what was essentially a self-help book written for the gay and lesbian population. The book was titled *Marriage with a Q!* and had been published several months ago. She and David wrote it to help people of alternative lifestyles to achieve satisfying, successful, long-term relationships. Relationships that, for many, were evasive. But because of the book's unbiased evaluation of gay marriage and its objective exploration of both monogamy and promiscuity, it had been greeted with an unfair share of negative attention and controversy.

Zee believed this publicity proved to be a double-edged sword. A saddening and unexpected result of the book's publication was vitriolic backlash from powerful LGBT pro-marriage organizations. These groups lambasted Zahara and David, accusing them of sabotaging public attitudes about gay marriage ... simply because their book argued that same sex matrimony was fundamentally different from traditional "straight" marriage.

Fortunately, however, the outcry from these organizations, whose influence ultimately proved limited, provided a tipping point. It gave the book enough attention and created sufficient curiosity to generate initial sales. After that, reviews in the LGBT media and subsequent word of mouth helped to further increase sales. *Marriage with a Q!* had already been downloaded onto tens of thousands of writing tablets, both in the US and the UK, and hard copy sales had been strong and steady in cities with robust gay populations.

In fact, the modest success of the book was the reason Zee was sitting here right now, in this charmingly historic city. Philadelphia was the second stop on a lecture that Zee and David designed to raise awareness about *Marriage with a Q!* The lecture was also intended to share some of the suggestions and methods found in the book.

She and her co-author genuinely wished to help people of alternative lifestyles achieve fulfilling, long-term relationships.

By profession Zee was a professor, counselor, and social psychologist. A woman of color with an educational pedigree that included multiple graduate and post-graduate degrees, Zee's work focused on the gay subculture. Zee always had an attraction for women and had come out of the closet and embraced herself as lesbian after a badly fated love affair with a heroin-addicted sleazebag who had been a massive disappointment both physically and emotionally. After months of lies, deceit, and heartbreak, she left him. With her she took a horrible, nefarious souvenir from the relationship that she would carry with her forever. She was nineteen years old at the time and was never again intimate with a man.

At the time she was an undergrad at U.C. Berkeley. In permissive, liberal San Francisco she met her first girlfriend, who introduced her to the city's ubiquitous lesbian and gay community. Here Zee immediately found a home, an anchor, and an outlet for passions she didn't know she had.

Even during her earliest forays into the LGBT lifestyle, however, she sensed an underlying discontent, a lack of fulfillment, and a sense of unrest and ennui that was prevalent among many gay men and women. The thesis for her Masters degree in social psychology further analyzed and objectified what had originally been a casual observation. Now considered to be a specialist in the area of gay and lesbian culture, Zee was professionally committed to her people.

She took a deep breath and filled her lungs with fragrant fall air. She was still typing lecture notes into her notebook when she noted that the sun was slowly disappearing behind the tall buildings to the

West of the city. She stood slowly, dusted herself off, and headed back to the hotel.

Back in her room, watching the traffic three stories below, she wondered why she hadn't heard from David. It was dinnertime, and they usually ate together in the hotel dining room or sampled a local restaurant.

A half an hour later and there was still no word from her co-author. Zee walked across the hall to his room and knocked lightly on his door. When she got no response, she knocked harder and called his name. She had already begun to contemplate dining alone when the door opened with a slow click.

She could tell by the forlorn expression on David's face that something was very wrong.

"I won't be coming to dinner tonight," he told her, his voice little more than a whisper. "I'm not feeling well."

"Is everything all right?" she asked with genuine concern.

He was staring over her shoulder and deep into space. A grim, hopeless expression clouded on his face.

"David," Zee asked him. "What's the matter? What is going on?"

"I went to see my family earlier today," he intoned. His voice was trance-like, and very distant.

"May I come in for a minute," she asked with a sympathetic tone.

He shrugged weakly, turned, and held open the door so that she could follow him into the room. The room was dim, with only one lamp burning, and a chair was turned to face the window.

David sat down on the bed and buried his face in his hands. Zee sat beside him and resisted the urge to put an arm over his shoulders. He was not a demonstrative person and generally eschewed physical contact with others.

He lifted his head and stared out the window.

"Coming here was a big mistake for me," he said, hopelessness flooding his voice.

Zee nodded but said nothing, her silence encouraging him to continue.

"As you know, I grew up here in Philadelphia," David said softly after a protracted silence. "What you don't know is that I come from an extremely strict orthodox Jewish family. Orthodox Jews are slavish adherents to tradition, to the very, very extreme. Courtships in the community are fast, marriages occur at a very young age, and lots of children follow immediately after the wedding day. Homosexuality is not only taboo, it is considered a violation against God, against family, and against the entire orthodox community."

David choked back tears. "Unfortunately," he continued, fighting to control his voice. "I learned today that the influence of that community is powerful enough to extinguish a parent's love for his own child."

Thoughtful silence passed before Zee responded. "David, this is one of the cold realities of being an LGBT person," she said softly. "Gay kids get thrown out on the street in the name of religion, and intolerance, all the time. But that doesn't make it any less painful for you or any less personal. Did your family reject you when you came out?"

"I never came out to them," he told her. "It was actually much worse than that. I met a boy at my Yeshiva. His name was Levi, and we fell in love. We were very young and very physical and we couldn't keep our hands off each other. We became careless and ultimately were caught in a very compromising situation. I cannot emphasize how dire this was. In the orthodox world, it was nearly as serious as being caught committing murder."

Zee sighed. "I can imagine how devastating this must have been for you, because it's clear you've buried it deep down inside. In the entire time we've been working on *Marriage with a Q*, a book that's all about relationships, you've never once mentioned this to me."

David harrumphed. "Oh I buried it all right," he said bitterly. "Because it got uglier and uglier. Levi, who I loved and trusted, turned it around and blamed everything on me. He said he was going through an emotionally challenging period, that he was weak and vulnerable and that I took advantage of him. I was thrown out of Yeshiva. Levi stayed. He never spoke to me again. I'm sure that he is married with many children now."

"Can you tell me what happened when you went to see your family today?" Zee asked him in a soothing voice.

David hung his head. "My father answered the door but wouldn't even open it all the way. He looked at me with pure hatred in his eyes. He told me that I was dead to him, and that I had shamed the family. I said a few words in my own defense, but he slammed the door in my face." David's voice was filled with anguish. "It's clear to me that I will never see my family again."

Zee was silent. She knew that putting words to this awful experience was making it even more real for him.

"I can't imagine the pain you are feeling now, David," she said finally. "I'm so sorry this happened to you."

He lifted his head, and turned to look forlornly though the window. The lights in the nearby buildings illuminated the gray cityscape as darkness descended upon Philadelphia. "For years I dreamed about reconnecting with my family," he intoned sadly. I believed that the passage of time would heal some of the wounds I had caused. That my absence would make their hearts grow fonder, as they say. But now I have to face a very cold and devastating reality. I am totally, utterly alone in the world."

"David you are not alone," Zee said with quiet conviction. "You have me. You have your friends and colleagues. And you have your work. You are here in Philadelphia because you are helping an entire community with our book."

David snorted derisively. "I left my family to be a part of the gay community. Now I learn that the gay community could care less about me."

Zee's expression clouded in puzzlement. While she had been working with David for over a year now, sometimes he still seemed like a stranger to her. He was generally shy, quiet, and reticent, and was not type of person that she would ordinarily have become friends with. However, they had met and subsequently become close colleagues because of his groundbreaking doctoral thesis, titled: "Homosexual Pair Bonding in Urban Centers."

In the thesis, Bachman theorized that gay people have a more difficult time finding and forming lasting pair bonds. He used statistical findings to postulate two main reasons for this. One was the dynamics of same-sex romance. The other was the fact that gay and lesbian adolescents generally don't have the opportunity to engage in same-sex courtships but, in fact, spend their teenage years hiding their identities as opposed to celebrating them.

Bachman's many supporters encouraged him to expand his thesis into a book. But even the most ardent of his adherents agreed that for a book of this nature to be successful, Bachman would need to pair up with a co-author who presented a more humanistic approach. To this end, David had been introduced to Social Psychologist Zahara Shelby. Zee was a published specialist in LGBT counseling, a highly respected clinician, and a writer well known for compassionate, incisive observations of gay and lesbian culture.

"David, I know you're feeling vulnerable right now," she said. "But you've already been so well received by the LGBT community in the last two cities we visited. Our book and our lectures have been tremendously successful so far. I can't imagine why you would say that the gay community doesn't care about you."

David guffawed. "The gay community might listen to my lectures on monogamy if they have nothing better to do," he said bitterly. "But compared to something as base as a porn star, I cease to exist. I am as dead to them as I am to my parents."

Zee stared at him with exasperation. He'd just been abandoned by his parents and now he was worried about a porn star. The trauma of losing his family had clearly left him hypersensitive and irrational. But she realized that it was clearly threatening to David. Enough to push him over the edge.

"This X-rated star is like a God to the gay community," he continued. "He's like a human shrine. He's physically perfect, so everything he touches turns to gold. He has a coffee table book that's nothing more than soft porn, yet the entire neighborhood is agog over it. And he'll be right down the street from our lecture, at the exact same time!"

His voice sounded so pained and hopeless that Zee wanted to hug or physically comfort him in some way, an impulse she resisted. She realized that this latest turn of events truly served as a perfect storm upon his psyche.

"A famous porn star will definitely get people revved up." Zee kept her tone relaxed, kind, and patient. "Sex always sells, and prurient material always excites. We have no control over who else is appearing in town as a part of Philadelphia's LGBT celebration. What if a big movie star was here? People would go crazy about that, too. So what?"

"You didn't witness what I saw down at the bookstore window earlier," he answered in a defeat-filled voice. "Men think sexually. Do you really believe that many of these guys are going to sit through a discourse on monogamy when there's a big pheromone cloud hovering right across the street?"

"David, we just finished an extremely successful lecture in DC," Zee calmly reminded him. "The ever percolating gay marriage storm has made our book tremendously controversial." She became animated and increasingly passionate as she spoke about the book. "*Marriage with a Q!* is a lightening rod in arguments both for and against gay marriage. Homophobic religious bigots are using findings as evidence that gay marriage was doomed and unnatural. Gay friendly liberals are touting it as a means by which to make gay marriage a working, mainstream institution. We are at the center of a culture firestorm. We are shaking the very foundation upon which traditional society operates. You cannot compare us to a porn star."

David's face was in his hands. Zee continued in her attempts to reason with him.

"Our book is doing brilliantly. Almost every gay person I've spoken with in Philly has heard of *Marriage with a Q!* You are freaking out over nothing."

"I've been abandoned by my family, and I was just first person witness to the fact that my work in the gay community, and by extension myself, are fully insignificant. Meaningless and inconsequential."

"David," she said firmly. "You are certainly, totally overreacting. Pornography is a diversion and an escape tactic. Nothing more. Some people will choose a diversion and go to see the porn star. Others will choose a learning experience and attend our lecture."

David remained unresponsive, sitting slumped on the side of the bed with his face buried in the palms of his hands. Understanding that there was nothing more she could say, Zee turned and quietly left the room.

*　*　*　*　*

The corner of 12th and Pine Streets in Philadelphia is the crossroad of the city's "gayborhood." Early on Saturday morning the streets were already bustling with people as diverse as the colors of the rainbow. All were stepping out to greet the day and begin their weekend.

Inside the Safari Spray Tans, every booth was full.

"Daniel Smash, I'm sick of hearing the name," Darryl cried as one bejeweled hand worked the cash register and the other manned the phone. "Booth four is ready. Go, honey."

Business was brisk. The waiting area was standing room only. Men flipped absently through back issues of Ebony Magazine, which had been thoughtfully left out by Darryl. The more observant of them noted that all pictures of pop star Candace Coco had been excised with near surgical precision.

Darryl addressed the clientele who crowded the waiting room. "I can't believe that all my gay sisters want to be blacker than me. You go right ahead girls, you just get dye sprayed all over your body. Get yourselves all nice and dark for that big porn star, who's just gonna sign your book and take your money away."

One of the customers looked up from his magazine. "I'm not a girl."

The man was in his late forties and wore a tight denim shirt. His gym buffed body and inelastic skin reflected an ongoing battle with the aging process. "I'm not here because of the stupid porn star. Rainbow Ball is Saturday night. It's the biggest party of the year. That's why this place is so damned busy. So just swish on over and get my booth ready. I'm sick of listening to your judgmental bullshit."

Darryl's head snapped up as if driven by an electric jolt. "Excuse *you*, Miss thing. I'm not being judgmental. I'm just telling it like it T-I is. And besides, don't you think you're a little bit old for circuit parties??? Porn stars or Rainbow Balls, it is all the same thing. Personally, I think you would be a lot better off if you embraced your true self. When you're in your forties, you really don't belong dancing under the disco balls with twenty year olds. And you probably won't be catching one, anyway. You're better off staying home with a good book."

Denim shirt threw his magazine to the side. The wrinkles in his tan, handsome face tightened. "Who the hell do you think you're talking to? You're nothing but a minimum wage worker at a spray tanning salon. I'm not about to sit here and take attitude from some femmy little queen with girly fingernails!"

"Then don't," Darryl shot back. "Your tanning appointment just got cancelled." With flourish, Darryl's hands went to the keyboard of his computer. Long, well-manicured nails, expertly maintained with clear lacquer varnish, moved gracefully over the keys. "Watch closely, baby. I'm deleting your name from my book right now."

The man's mouth dropped open at the prospect of not being able to tan. "Oh, fuck you. Get me the manager right now"

The rest of the waiting room watched the exchange with rapt attention.

"I *am* the manager!" Darryl told him, reaching for the phone. "And I do not put up with profanity in my shop. Now get out or I'm calling the police."

One of the other men in the waiting room, a regular named Curtis, looked up as denim stormed out the door. "He *was* talking about seeing that porn star," Curtis told the quiet room. "And I was actually thinking about going to meet Daniel Smash myself."

"That's all well and good," Darryl replied. "But as for me, I have big plans for that day. I won't be wasting my time chasing some magical fantasy like all the rest of you. And I don't go to bars. I'm going home tonight, do my nails, and watch the oldies channel. They're playing a re-run of *Lady Sings the Blues*."

"I love that movie!" Curtis said. "I'm going to watch it, too."

"Well then we'd better get moving," Darryl replied with palpable excitement. "Booth six is ready. Get moving Bobby J!"

Bobby J stood and hustled toward his tanning cubicle. Curtis, familiar with Darryl's idiosyncrasies, chuckled and went back to his magazine.

"Now, if you girls would kindly act like ladies and allow me to share my plans for Rainbow Ball Weekend."

No one in the waiting room spoke. There was only the hard beat of disco music coming in from recessed wall speakers and the hiss of spray tanners in the background. Darryl continued.

"Next Saturday, while you're all chasing rainbows like you always do, I will be at a very important lecture. I'm going to listen to two very educated, important people who teach gay people how to live better. Nails aren't everything, you know. And neither is the Rainbow Ball or that corrupt porn star. While you're all confusing your fantasy with your reality, this girl's gonna be enriching her life!"

*   *   *   *   *

He'd been driving almost eleven hours and was now in the Texas panhandle on the outskirts of the city of Amarillo. He had made few stops along route I-40 East, all of them brief, either to fill his gas tank, empty his bladder, or to gorge himself on drive-through, dollar-menu food. Although his focus was intense, and he possessed an all-encompassing ambition to reach his destination, Simon LeFlouer was spent. His legs were torturously stiff, his eyelids were heavy, and he was finding it more and more difficult to focus or to stay awake. He followed the GPS on his phone to a truck stop where he planned to find cheap eats, a bathroom, and a dark, out of the way spot to park his car and sleep for the night.

He exited interstate 40 and drove less than a mile to the rest stop. In spite of the late hour, oppressive heat, and desolate location, the place was buzzing, and the dusty parking lot was nearly full. A sign directed trucks to the left and cars to the right. Simon entered the lot and drove around, finally locating an empty, isolated spot under the shade of a large pine tree. It was a perfect place to park for the night. He wasn't, however, the only one to covet the location. A mini-van had stopped, turned its blinker on, and begun backing toward the spot. Seizing a millisecond of opportunity, Simon hit the gas, gunned his engine so that his car jetted into the opening between the van and the parking space, narrowly filching the spot.

Turning off the ignition, he ignored the stream of curses and loud horn blasts emanating from the mini-van. When it finally pulled away in search of another spot, Simon opened the door of his own car, walked a few paces to a grassy patch, and proceeded to take a satisfying piss. There were bathrooms inside the rest stop, but this was of no concern to Simon. He zipped up, climbed into his back seat, locked the doors, opened the car windows a few inches each, and made a pillow from a ball of clothes. He lit a short roach with a cheap butane lighter and savored the remaining hits of his Arizona grown Cannabis. Simon only had five joints to last him the entire trip and was now finishing his second.

He had held the delectable smoke deep in his lungs for as long as possible. While he slowly exhaled, his cell phone blared a heavy metal ring tone that indicated an incoming call. Lifting his substantial buttocks from the seat, he fingered the phone from his front pants pocket just in time to answer a call from his mother. She'd been pestering him all day, and he'd been letting the calls go to voice mail. He decided to hit the answer button and put an end to her annoying attempts to reach him.

"Simon, Simon," she breathed frantically when she realized that he had actually picked up. "Where are you? Why didn't you answer the phone?"

Simon was stoned. His brain, mellowed by the ingestion of marijuana, was now as clear as a bell. Pot served this purpose for him.

"You sound really, really stressed, Ma," he said lazily.

She barked back, "Where are you, Simon?"

Simon relaxed in the back seat of his car, refusing to let his mother kill his buzz. "I'm at the campgrounds at the canyon. I needed to get away for a couple of days."

"Are you driving around with pot?" she demanded in an inquisitor's tone. "The last time you disappeared like this you got yourself arrested! It cost your grandfather and me a lot of money in legal fees!"

Simon refused to take the bait. He was enjoying his high. "Ma," he drawled. "That was over a year ago. I'll be home in a couple of days. You don't need to call me every five minutes. I'm not a baby. I will call you to check in."

Simon then hit a button that ended the call. He did not feel like dealing with his pesky mother any further. As the pot took effect, his eyelids became heavy and he promptly fell asleep in the backseat of his car, a tire iron wrapped tightly in his fist for protection during the night.

Early the next morning, Simon was rudely awakened by the blaring of a car alarm that sliced across the parking lot at the break of dawn. The noise subsided and he had slowly fallen back to sleep when an SUV loaded with a large, noisy family parked next to his, waking him once again. Simon squeezed his eyes tightly, angrily willing the disturbances to stop. But they kept right on coming. Finally he emerged from the back seat with a headache and a foul mood. Before leaving the car, he unlocked the glove compartment and withdrew a small glass vial that was carefully nestled in a crumpled towel. He gently placed the vial back into its nest and then grabbed his backpack, which contained his toiletries and a few items of clothing. Slamming the car door and locking it behind him, Simon ambled his way across the parking lot toward a building that housed bathrooms, shops, and restaurants.

The bathroom was a beehive of travelers coming and going. Simon leisurely relieved himself, not at all concerned with the hygiene of his surroundings or the flatulence emanating from his body. He washed his hands and splashed soapy water on his face, also getting it all over the floor and mirror, where he checked his reflection and was satisfied with what he saw. Three days of beard growth had already begun to mask his appearance.

Next, he took a booth in a restaurant that was part of a chain that had locations all along the interstate. In the window was a sign advertising an "endless stack" pancake special, and Simon was a huge fan of all-you-can-eat deals. The waitress brought him his first three stacks of pancakes in quick succession. Each time she passed the table, Simon asked for more butter, more jelly, more syrup, more milk. But as the restaurant got busier, the waitress's trips past the table became less frequent and more hurried. Simon kept checking the time on his phone. He needed to get back on the road soon.

"Where is this bitch?" he said under his breath, scraping at the tiny amount of syrup that remained on his plate. Growing more impatient by the second, he leaned from the booth and craned his neck in both directions, scanning up and down the restaurant floor. Finally, he flagged a scrawny busboy that was hurrying past the table.

"I need my waitress," he told the kid. "I'm in a fucking rush here and need to get back on the road."

The busboy stared wide-eyed and nodded his head. Simon's voice was demanding and authoritative. "She hasn't been here in ten minutes. I want her at this table now."

The busboy hurried off. Simon watched as he pushed quickly through swinging doors that led into the kitchen. Minutes later the waitress appeared at his table with his check, and Simon held his hand up to stop her.

"I want another stack." His expression was stony, and he looked straight into her face.

"I was told you wanted the check," the waitress said. She was a bony woman on the wrong side of fifty whose face showed the deep etchings of a difficult life. There was a hint of impatience in her voice and expression as she regarded Simon, who continued staring directly at her.

"I didn't say I wanted the check. I said I wanted my *waitress*," Simon said slowly, enunciating each word through a clenched jaw. "This is supposed to be an all-you-can-eat deal, and you haven't been past this table in fifteen minutes. Your service really sucks." His voice rose as he spoke.

"Sir, we've gotten very busy," she said, handing him the check.

Simon looked at the check but didn't take it. He slammed his hand on the table, causing glasses and ceramic plates to create an explosive clatter that momentarily silenced all other tables in the vicinity.

"I want another stack! And more milk!"

The waitress jumped back from the table. "I'll get them," she said, and fled toward the kitchen.

Simon ate three more stacks of pancakes. They were delivered by the busboy. Leaving no tip on the table, he paid at the counter and continued toward Philadelphia, where his attack would be swift, vicious, and without mercy.

✳   ✳   ✳   ✳   ✳

The building housing the LGBTQ Civic Center was erected during the late 1930's. From then until the early 1970's it served as home to the Grover Cleveland elementary school. During its later years, the school became a crumbling fortress of soot-blackened brick, its windows covered by heavy mesh wire. The surrounding neighborhood disintegrated into a blighted, low rent district as middle class families relocated to the outlying suburbs over the course of many decades. Ultimately, the Grover Cleveland School finally closed its doors on a dwindling student population.

It stood for many years, unused and largely ignored, as the neighborhood once again began changing. Revitalization encroached. Decaying town houses and run-down apartments surrounding the old school were settled by artists and young Bohemians. Many of these early residents were gay men and women who had fled the stifling intolerance of the suburbs in exchange for the less conservative lifestyle of the city. They cleaned-up, refurbished and renovated, ultimately gentrifying the neighborhood into a high-rent "Gay Ghetto."

By the late eighties, the Grover Cleveland building no longer fit in with the aesthetic landscape of the neighborhood. It had, in fact, become a flagrant eyesore. A white elephant, it was viewed as a behemoth of urban blight over its neighbors, trendy boutiques and posh town homes whose window boxes, brass door knobs, and sandblasted brick facades stood in sharp contrast to its Dickensian gloom.

A fashion designer from New York who had already successfully restored a crumbling hotel on Miami's South Beach purchased the Grover Cleveland building from the city of Philadelphia. Before he could fulfill his plan of turning the building into part of his swank hotel chain, the designer was brutally murdered by a male prostitute. The designer's sole heir was his mother, an aging widow who, having no idea what to do with a blighted school building, bequeathed it to the Philadelphia Gay and Lesbian Coalition with the proviso that, in memory of her son, it be turned into a center for supporting the LGBT Community. However, there were insufficient funds ear-marked for the extensive renovations required to return the building to its original historic greatness. A neighborhood Coalition formed. They spent nearly a decade fundraising, and their tireless efforts were rewarded when the building was triumphantly unveiled as the LGBTQ Community Center.

The building's exterior masonry was refurbished, the windows were replaced, and the front entrance received a grand facelift. In the interior original historic details were revitalized as the layout was rearranged to accommodate the needs of the community that would be calling the building home. The Philadelphia LGBTQ Community Center now mends modern demands and historic character. To those who now frequent the gentrified and re-purposed high school, it is known simply as "The Center".

Darryl Gilmore turned the corner and approached the build-ing. His arms were thrown wide into the air and he sashayed along the sidewalk, imitating the on-stage theatrics of Candace Coco, one of his few idols.

He sang loudly to the music in his headphones, oblivious to the stares of other people. Those who lived in the neighborhood were familiar with the colorful, highly animated figure that was Darryl. He paid them no mind as he swept along, singing and swaying. A silk scarf trailed in his wake and the sleeves of his blouse billowed as the autumn wind lifted his shirt like a sail. Not one for neutral colors, Darryl was like an alien streak of purple, red, and orange.

He turned when he reached the entrance to The Center, climbed its five cement steps, and pushed though the heavy front doors. He passed a large community bulletin board on his way through the vestibule. Affixed by a multitude of constantly recycled thumbtacks were an assortment of flyers announcing everything from casting calls for local actors to apartments for rent. Darryl was pleased to see that his own flyer was still up. Half the time it was ripped down and replaced by somebody else's stuff, and Darryl would hastily respond by tearing down the offensive sheet of paper and replacing the original in its rightful place. His flyer was simple, and featured a professional, albeit older, picture of himself, hands crossed against his chest, sublimely displaying his perfect manicure. His advertising copy read:

GLA-MORE NAILS

By Darryl, Nail Stylist Extraordinaire

TIPS, WRAPS, AIRBRUSHING, ACRYLIC ART WORK

Baby, in today's world, it's all about nails. Your nails. Hi! I'm Darryl, and baby, nobody loves your nails like I do! Nails for night, day, work, or play. For hands as beautiful as you are, visit my website.

www.gla-morenails.biz

(You'll also get free tips on your tips when you visit my site!!!)

I'm gonna have to update that flyer, he thought to himself. *Now that I've got an Instagram account and some new pictures to show folks*!

Proceeding past the bulletin board, Darryl also noticed the glossy poster announcing porn star Daniel Smash's planned visit to the city for a book signing. He grimaced. He smiled, however, when his eyes alighted on the picture of renowned psychologist David Bachman, who would be lecturing in this very building later in the week.

"I have a date with *you*, Dr. Bachman," Darryl declared in the empty vestibule before climbing the stairs to the Center's third floor computer room.

Access to the computers was on a first come, first serve basis. Darryl came on a weekday afternoon, hoping that the place wouldn't be too crowded. He was in luck. A technical administrator sat behind a desk in the center of the room.

Just one other person was in residence; a heavy set, middle-aged black man with cornrows and badly plucked eyebrows was tapping busily on his computer keyboard. The man's shirt read: *Wink, Wink. My Husband is Out of Town!*

The man's name was Roger. "Hey Girl!" Darryl stopped at his terminal. He took Roger's hand and examined it carefully. "Don't tell me you go on stage with this kind of manicure."

Roger was better known by his drag name, Cinnamon Spice. He was a performer in the gay bars of Philadelphia, Atlantic City, New Hope, and Rehoboth Beach.

"Girl, you think these bitches are looking at my fingernails?" Roger replied bawdily.

Darryl's hand flew to his heart. He gasped. "Honey, you are in a glamour profession. It's all in the details!"

Roger leaned back in his chair and eyed Darryl curiously. He couldn't help but smile as the passionate young man dug into his shoulder bag and extracted a colorful brochure.

"Honey, I will give you three inch metallic silver nails that will reflect every disco light in the club. Let me do your hands and you'll be the Drag-arella of the ball."

Roger examined the brochure for Darryl's service, Glamour Nails. "I'm going to be starring in a comedy at the Teeny Weeny

Playhouse," he told Darryl. Maybe you could come backstage and do nails and makeup. We need somebody."

"Call me anytime, sugar. I'm a patron of the arts and I'll do your hair and makeup for free if you let me put my brochures into the playbills."

Roger nodded. "We could do that. And a lot of people will see your ad. We're a guaranteed sellout."

The butch lady at the Tech Support desk looked up from her magazine. "Not hard to sell out thirty seats," she said dryly.

"How would you know?" Roger snapped. "I never see you supporting any of our shows." He turned to Darryl and spoke loudly so that his comment could be heard across the room. "Miss Butch here is notoriously cheap."

Darryl waved a bejeweled hand in the air. "I will be at your play. And I will give you nails that will make you the envy of all drag queens."

"I could go for some long metallic silver nails," Roger said, pocketing Daryl's brochure. "I will definitely call you with the deets. Cinnamon Spice has to dazzle."

"Yes she does, girl," Darryl sang as he sashayed to the Technical Administrator's desk. "Yes she does!"

The Tech Support woman wore an ID badge that identified her as Miranda. She sat behind the desk, looking utterly bored and flipping through a copy of a movie magazine.

"Miranda. That's a pretty name," Darryl told her. He tried to focus on her lovely blue eyes and to ignore the muscular, tattooed arms, the big, bony hands, and, especially, the stubby finger nails that were bitten to the quick.

Miranda threw her magazine aside in disgust. "Agnes Anne is of course on the cover. She's an openly gay movie star and I love her! Her girlfriend is a skinny blonde nobody actress. What does Agnes see in her? I'd like to spend a night with that honey pot and make her forget her little blondie."

It starts with the nails, baby. Agnes isn't going to be spending any nights with you if your fingers look like elephant toes," Darryl thought.

"Not everybody is within reach baby, 'specially not those Hollywood types," he told Miranda, examining her short, spiky, jet-black hair and copious piercings of the nose, ears and eyebrows. "But a pretty girl like you must have plenty of opportunities for love right here in Philadelphia."

Miranda shrugged.

"Anyway baby," Darryl told her, reaching into his shoulder bag and extracting an envelope containing a thumb drive. "I have this thingy with some pictures on it that I need for my website, glamour-nails dot biz."

Miranda looked bored.

"I need to upload these new pictures for my website, but I've been having trouble getting them onto my computer. Can you help me?"

Miranda roused herself from behind her desk, took Darryl's drive, and popped it into her computer. "The files are pretty big for a download. I'm going to shrink the sizes of the pictures for you and they should be easier for you to use online." Her stubby fingers expertly tapped the keyboard. "Give me your email address and I'll send the smaller pictures to your personal account as attachments. Then, when you get home you can open your email and save the pictures to your hard drive. From there, you can upload them to your website.

Darryl was having a hard time focusing on Miranda's advice. He recited his email address and tried to think clearly while ten badly chewed nails danced menacingly before his eyes. They were screaming for rescue, and yet there was no way he could help.

"Oh hell," Miranda said, interpreting Darryl's look of consternation as a misunderstanding of her instructions. "So many people just don't know a thing about computers. I'll just put the pictures up on your website for you. While I'm at it I'll put them up on your Facebook page, too."

An hour later a gleeful Darryl left the computer room, his various social media accounts completely updated with the new pictures, compliments of Miranda, who watched him sail out of the door.

"I'm gonna tell all the lipstick lezzies about ya," she called after him. "They're into all the makeup and fashion and that kind of shit. Maybe they could throw you some business."

"Thank you, baby."

Darryl sailed through the building's foyer and headed toward the exit doors. He was so ecstatic about his updated website that he didn't notice the dangerously handsome black man who was standing there, intently studying his flyer. Darryl swept past the man, who looked up from the flyer with an admiring gaze that carefully followed Darryl's oblivious countenance as he exited the Center.

* * * * *

David Bachman stood in the small hotel bathroom and stared at himself in the brightly lit mirror. He was a plain man. There was nothing memorable or striking about his features. To compound this issue, the ravages of age were becoming progressively visible. His hairline had receded to a point that the frontal half of his head was barely covered. The few dark wisps that remained only served to make his scalp appear pale and anemic in contrast. His skin hung bag-like around his eyes, which were too small for his face, and created jowls at his cheeks. Thick glasses roosted atop a beaklike nose. All in all, he admitted grimly, a face that was very easy to overlook.

He felt ignored and inconsequential. His family had rejected him, and he'd experienced a deeply lonely sense of irrelevance when he stood among his contemporaries on the sidewalk of the bookstore. He just wanted to fit in somewhere.

Growing up, he had never felt as though he belonged within the orthodox Jewish community. Now, he was feeling detached from the gay men who constituted his community and his adopted culture. He had never felt that he truly belonged anywhere, or with anyone, and yet he loved people and longed to understand them. They fascinated him. They were, in so many ways, unfamiliar, and as an observer he was deeply interested in what motivated them, what drove their behaviors. Unable to learn this through genuine human contact, David immersed himself in reams of psychological research and data. Statistically, he understood people intimately. In real time, he couldn't figure them out at all. He was more comfortable in the controlled and quiet world of academia then in the fervid chaos of real life.

Restless, David left the hotel room. He took the elevator three short flights to the lobby, sharing it with a young couple. A twinge of sadness, mixed with an unsettling envy, gripped him as he watched the handsome man place a protective hand on the woman's back. She whispered something to him, and the man laughed with comfortable mirth. Bachman was reduced to feeling like a speck of protoplasm, standing alone in the elevator chamber as the contented pair breezed past him and into the lobby.

Hands deep inside the pockets of his corduroy trousers, head hanging limply, David walked through the lobby and into the crisp night. Wandering with subconscious purpose, he found himself once again approaching the Unity Book Shop. There, standing at the window, gazing inside, was a strikingly handsome African American man dressed in jeans and an expensive bomber jacket. The man lingered for a few moments, then proceeded quietly on his way.

David continued to walk until he was standing directly in front of the bookstore window. He closely examined the image of porn star Daniel Smash. He took in the exceptionally handsome face and chiseled body and wondered what it must be like to be so physically beautiful. But more than beautiful, this very young man had also achieved a pinnacle of fortune and fame. Obviously, the porn star wasn't just another pretty face. There had to be some cunning, some level of intelligence, to parlay one's physical features into iconic status. Daniel Smash was selling fantasy, Bachman concluded, while he, with his book, was selling a way to deal with reality. Fantasy and reality would be competing on opposite sides of the street on the day of his lecture, and Bachman had no doubt that fantasy would rule the day.

He turned slowly from the window, feeling deflated and more defeated than ever.

* * * * *

Bobby Brennigan and Nonstick Pam stepped through the giant revolving door that led inside Indigo Red. The high-end Southern

BBQ and Soul Food restaurant on Chestnut Street was housed in a building that had originally been a bank. Like many such establishments in the city, Indigo Red had recently been repurposed from an historic business edifice into a chic and stylish eatery. Upon entering, Bobby and Pam were met by the skeptically raised eyebrow of a tightly dressed, tall and slender woman who wore a buttoned up designer blouse that strained mightily to contain a massive pair of breasts. The twenty-something lady had the skin of a corn fed mid-westerner and yellow-blonde shoulder length hair to match. Her eye makeup was copious.

"We'd like to speak to the manager, please," said Bobby politely.

Bobby was wearing an ill-fitted business suit that had thrift shop written all over it. Standing beside him was Pam, a petit drag queen of a certain age, who wore a sensible pair of wedge shoes and a pantsuit that likely came from the same thrift shop.

The woman, seated behind a teak hostess stand engraved with the restaurant's logo, stood and appraised them as if they'd just crawled up from the sewer.

"I'm the manager," she stated imperially.

"We're here from the Teeny Weeny Theatre Company on Pine Street," Bobby told her, offering his hand for a shake.

She examined Bobby's hand and after a moment's hesitation returned a weak and very quick shake. She then looked Pam up and down as if she were shopping in Tiffany's and had just discovered a piece of tawdry costume jewelry. Pam bristled, and withered, under the royal scrutiny.

"Our theatre company is presenting a play during the Rainbow Ball weekend, and we're offering advertisements in our playbill to businesses in the neighborhood. We hoped you might be interested in buying one of our ads."

The manager, who hadn't yet bothered to tell them her name, checked her watch then crossed her arms over her chest.

"Our play is called Drag's Happening," Pam explained in earnest. "It's a spoof on a seventies sitcom about three friends who lived in the ghetto. Our version will have drag queens playing the principal female roles of Shirley, Dee, and Mama. The script is hysterical!"

The manager looked as though she had just swallowed spoiled caviar. "Teeny Weeny? Drag? The ghetto? *Mama*?" she repeated, her voice dripping in condescension and disgust. "Who in God's name would pay to see something like that? I wouldn't."

"Gulp," said Pam.

"This play is for the Rainbow Ball weekend," Bobby said after recovering from the sting of the manager's proclamation. The woman's animosity was of a nature that might be expected in the Bible belt, but not here in the gayborhood. "This is a celebration of queer culture, it's a culture we're very proud of and so are many others. Our productions at the Teeny Weeny theatre are always popular, and local businesses are usually happy to support us."

"This is an upscale restaurant," huffed the manager. We don't really want to be associated with that kind of an element."

"What kind of an element?" Pam had been biting her tongue in order to present a businesslike demeanor but finally let her drag come out. "You mean you don't have gay people in your snooty restaurant? Let me tell you something, Miss uptight homophobic backwoods bitch: In this neighborhood, half of your customers are gay. Or as *you* would probably refer to us, faggots. But after they learn about the hater who manages this place, your job is going to get a whole lot easier because you won't have anybody walking through your door."

The manager stepped back and glared at them. "We don't allow profanity here," she huffed with finality. "And we do not need your perverted friends in this restaurant. She pointed angrily toward the door. "You can leave right now!"

"Gladly," said Pam, turning on her heel.

At that moment, a very handsome man with skin the color of toffee came from behind a decorative steel wall that separated the vestibule from the dining room. He was wearing a soiled white chef's shirt and black and white checkered pants. He wiped a smudge of grease from his forehead with a towel as he came forward to meet them.

"Good afternoon, gentlemen," he greeted them with an apologetic smile and firm handshakes. "I overheard part of your conversation. I'm Jamar Lucious and I own this restaurant. I see you've met my new manager."

"Oh, it was an unforgettable treat," Pam told him as she theatrically gagged herself.

"I don't think you can actually say we met her," Bobby said. "She never really introduced herself."

"Please meet Madison," Jamar told them. "Who has been here for a week and who is no longer employed by my restaurant. As of this minute."

Madison's mouth dropped open and her eyes widened.

"Madison, you are fired," Jamar told her. "I know that you're a new graduate and recently relocated to Philadelphia from a much smaller city. Evidently you are not sophisticated enough to work in a restaurant of this caliber."

The manager pointed a lacquered fingernail at Pam and Bobby. "Those drag things called me a bitch!"

"And yet you were so warm toward them," Jamar replied. "I do not abide intolerance of any kind, in my personal *or* my business life. And it just so happens that the guy who signs your paycheck, meaning me, is part of the community that you just insulted. I don't think you need a degree in hospitality services to figure out that I'm gay."

Madison gasped in surprise as this realization fell upon her.

"What did these two people do to you to make you treat them so poorly?" Jamar asked her.

Her eyes were on Non Stick Pam. "This person is a freak," she said. "It isn't natural for a man to walk the streets looking like that. And God did not intend for two men to be together. It's a perversion of nature."

Jamar scowled. "If you are so worried about God, why don't you let him be the judge while you treat all people kindly like Jesus asked us to do?"

Madison had no quick reply.

"I cannot fix ignorance," Jamar told her. "But I won't have it in my restaurant. Go get your things, punch out, and leave. And I would advise you to stay out of the restaurant business because it's filled with perverts like me."

"And stay out of churches, too, Miss Right Wing Christian," Pam added. "The choirs are also filled with perverts like us!"

Madison slinked to the back of the restaurant to collect her things.

Bobby and Pam were now staring with awe at Jamar. This was *Jamar Lucious* a renowned member of the upper echelon of Philadelphia's business and social worlds. His famous parents filled the seats and barstools of Indigo Red with their celebrity pals, and glamorous pictures from the restaurant continuously graced the pages of the local papers.

Nonstick Pam eyed Jamar's chef outfit, which had clearly been in the trenches of a busy lunch hour.

"I didn't know you cooked, too, Mr. Lucious," she offered timidly.

"Well, I *did* go to culinary school," Jamar explained, examining the smudges of grease and sauce stains on his own outfit. "But I don't usually cook. You caught me on a day when my head chef was out sick. It's a good thing I happened to be passing through the dining room when I overheard your conversation with Madison. And by the way, my apologies once again."

Bobby and Pam nodded mutely.

"Now why don't you guys tell me again about what you need from Indigo Red."

"Well," Bobby began, "we are putting on a play at the Teeny Weeny Theatre Company over on 13th Street. It's called Drag's Happenin'. It's a spoof on an old TV series from the 70's and it has drag queens playing all of the female roles. It will be running through the week of Rainbow Ball, and we came in looking for advertisers for our playbill."

"It's a great way to support your local arts scene," Pan added. "And people sure do like going to dinner after the theatre."

"Indeed they do." Jamar nodded and smiled.

Just then, a colorfully dressed young man floated past the restaurant's front window. He wore pointy blue leather shoes, a gold lamé fedora hat, a paisley matador jacket of cobalt and gold, and a turquoise cape that billowed out behind him as he strode vibrantly past.

This caught Jamar's attention, and he watched wistfully and intently as the bright visage continued down the street.

"Oh that's Darryl!" Pam explained. "He's doing the makeup and nails for our show."

"Darryl," Jamar whispered to himself. "So he's working for the show, too, huh?" Jamar returned his attention to Bobby and Pam. "Well guys, not only am I going to take an ad in your playbill, you can put me down for a full page and I'll take the best spot you have available."

"The back page is still open," Bobby said. "And that's the main sponsor."

"Then I guess I'm the main sponsor now," Jamar told them. "Why don't you guys come by tomorrow afternoon and I'll have the artwork and a check ready for you. Oh, and by way of apology for Madison's behavior, Indigo Red will cater food for the cast and crew on opening night."

Bobby and Pam could hardly believe their great luck and high-fived each other ardently. "Thank you so very much, Mr. Lucius," they chorused in a panegyric tone. "This is more than any other sponsor has ever done for us."

"Why does everyone my own age insist on calling me Mr. Lucius?" Jamar wondered aloud. "Please just call me Jamar. Mr. Lucius is my dad!"

"Okay, Jamar, we'll be by tomorrow afternoon," Pam said, smiling broadly as they all shook hands.

Jamar watched as Pam and Bobby left the restaurant with a new bounce in their steps, thinking that he now had two things to do.

One, he had to find a new manager. And two, he had to figure out a way to meet Darryl.

*   *   *   *   *

For as long as either of them could remember, Steve and Brian met for happy hour at Woodpeckers every Friday after work. Located on a busy stretch of 13th Street, the club had been the social hub of the gayborhood for decades. Downstairs sported a collection of comfortable, dimly lit bar areas and a small bistro. Upstairs was a lounge that overlooked the street, and, behind it, a huge dance floor that was surrounded by several more bars.

It was happy hour and the disco wouldn't open until later, but the upstairs lounge was buzzing with a mix of people running the gamut from pinstripe to torn denim, all enjoying early evening cocktails. There was an easy, relaxed vibe, without the cruising frenzy that would develop much later in the night. By ten thirty, the dance club would be filled to overflow, and in the lounge it would be difficult to navigate.

Right now, dwindling sunlight streamed in through the large front windows, and an old RuPaul video was playing on monitors that were visible from every vantage point in the room.

"This weekend is turning into one fucking huge event for me." Steve took a gulp of ultra lite beer direct from the bottle.

"It's turning into a huge event for the whole freaking city," said Brian as he sipped tentatively on his Sambuca. "Between the Rainbow Ball and Daniel Smash making his personal appearance, this neighborhood is going to be one big cluster fuck of traffic and out-of-towners."

They were seated on barstools at a ledge that ran the length of a large window with a view of the pizza parlor one story down and across the street.

"Yeah, and we'll be right in the epicenter of that cluster fuck, my friend, while my cameraman captures every single money shot." Steve was exuberant. "Believe it or not, I'm the only reporter of the three affiliates that's covering this book signing."

"It's the gay porn angle," Brian offered. "He's here to promote an erotic book. Not exactly family fare for the five o'clock news."

"Yeah, but this isn't any ordinary porn star." Steve took another swig of beer. "This guy was huge. He had a top TV series, two award-winning movies, and a successful modeling career all before he was nineteen years old. He's slipping in under the radar here in Philly because now he's a porn star, but there is no mitigating his cultural significance. My biggest fear is that the Tattletale Network or one of those other nationals will show up and steal my scoop."

"Oh, I doubt they'll come to Philly," Brian said. "They'll just wait for Daniel to come to New York. But don't you think I'll just be in the way if I tag along on your shoot?"

"No, you won't be in the way. Don't even try it. You're coming."

"I don't know. Maybe I won't be in the mood," Brian said. "What happens if I get in really late? My cats expect me home at a certain time or they get anxious."

"*You* are the one who gets anxious if you're not tucked into bed by nine," Steve argued. "Haven't your series of doctors prescribed you Xanax and Lorazepam for that very reason? Take your pick and bring along backup. You're coming."

Brian stared out the window. People were standing outside the pizza parlor, enjoying slices in the waning sunlight. "I don't know."

Steve's expression turned incredulous. "Do you know how many people would kill to tag along on this shoot? You're always talking about celebrities all the time, now you have a chance to meet one of the most mysterious and controversial of them all. You said yourself that you are very curious about him. And then, after the shoot, we'll have all points access to the freaking Rainbow Ball, which for everybody else is ninety bucks a ticket."

Brian shrugged. "Well, I am your friend and if you want me to be there I'll go. How late will we be out?"

"Who cares?" Steve asked him. "You don't have to be anywhere the next day. Let your hair down a little. I know you hate crowds and late nights, but just this once it won't kill you. Besides, once we pry open those lips of yours and pour a couple of cocktails inside, you'll transform into one of the funniest people in Philly. You always do."

Brian shrugged in acquiescence. "It will be interesting to see Daniel Smash in person," he admitted. "To see how he acts, what he's like. I mean, who goes from being a successful actor to being a porn star? I'm really curious to see how this guy behaves in real life."

"What really makes him enigmatic," Steve said, leaning in toward Brian, "Is that there is absolutely no evidence of his existence before he arrived in Scottsdale and robbed those old people. No school records, no high school yearbooks, no social media posts, no evidence of any past acting endeavors, no living relatives, no past addresses. Nothing. He says he was raised abroad in an army family, but there is no evidence of that either."

"He's quite mystifying" Brian nodded. "Which only makes him that much more alluring to people."

"Plus the fact that he's drop dead gorgeous." Steve smiled wickedly.

"And there's that," Brian agreed.

"I'm thirsty," said Steve. "Let's get another round."

* * * * *

Simon motored along interstate I-44 East, mercilessly pushing his twelve year old car at 80 MPH. In just over an hour he passed the state line into Oklahoma. After three and a half hours without stopping, he hit Oklahoma City, where he exited onto route 44 toward Springfield, Missouri. His bladder at near bursting point, Simon turned off the highway in the town of Chandler. He vaguely recalled that this town was once home to a famous baseball camp, but at the moment he didn't recall the name and couldn't care less anyway. He still had seven more hours of driving to do today. After filling his car at a gas station that was a relic from the 1950's, he turned into McDonald's, where he used the men's room and then filled a bag with ten bucks worth of dollar menu items.

Once back on the highway, Simon used his phone to find a cheap hotel in Springfield. Tonight he needed a shower and a bed, and it seemed as if the cheapest rate available was thirty-eight dollars a night, in a hotel whose online reviews included descriptions of smelly rooms and dried fluids on the bed sheets. It seemed like a lot for the price, but Simon realized that it was necessary for him to be well rested and on top of his game if the next few days were to play out as he planned. A link on the phone's screen allowed him to call the hotel. In his attempt to switch to speakerphone mode, he was so distracted that he nearly careened into a working road crew. His hands tightened on the wheel, his foot reflexively hit the break, and he swerved just in time to miss one of the orange jump-suited men in the shoulder of the highway.

He slowed down his speed considerably as he passed the prison bus, a dismal gray vehicle with the letters "DOC" stenciled on the side and heavy gauge mesh covering the windows. The prisoners, indistinguishable in their identical threads, were collecting roadside debris under the scrutiny of several armed guards. As Simon passed, he reflexively scanned the faces of the individual inmates.

His mind flashed back fifteen years, to when he was a terribly shy six-year old boy standing outside the prison gates where his father was incarcerated. The memory was burned into his mind. He held his mom's hand tightly as both stared up at what would be his father's home for the next fifteen years: the state pen. A steely chain link fence surrounded a dangerous-looking edifice and was topped with loops of barbed wire. The walls of the building itself seemed tall enough to touch the dismal gray sky. Simon felt a foreboding sense of not belonging, which heightened his fear. The tension in his mother's body told him that she, too, was terribly uncomfortable. But he wanted very badly to meet his daddy who'd been in and out of jail since Simon had been born and whom Simon only knew through stories his mother told him. Never letting go of his mother's hand, he dutifully followed her through a metal detector and past the prison gates. At a pitiless guard booth, his mother had to show identification for the both of them. Then they proceeded into Nebraska's maximum-security state penitentiary.

Armed guards stood at the doors of the communal visiting room. Simon's mother gasped when his father was led into the room. His father had scary looking tattoos of snakes and devils and monsters on his arms, which were covered in little scars. Jimmy sneered at little Simon as he approached the table and regarded Simon's mother with a shifty smile. Body contact of any kind, including hugs and handshakes, were not permitted in this prison. Simon's father sat down at the table and proceeded to ignore his little boy, focusing only on the mother.

"You looking good, Terry," he said. There was both lust and sincerity in his voice.

"Don't you want to say hello to your son, Jimmy?" she asked him. "I came here because this little boy has never met his father. He's been crying for his daddy. He has nightmares."

Jimmy did not take his eyes from Terry. "I don't even know for a fact this fucking kid is mine," he snarled.

"Look at him, Jimmy," Terry said. Her voice took on a note of pleading, of desperation, and of regret for having made the trip here. "He's got your eyes. He's your son and you know it."

Jimmy Laflour leaned back in his chair, his arm draped over the empty chair next to him. "Do me a favor Terry. I need you to put some money in my account. I ain't got nothing and I'm in this shit hole for lotsa years. Help me out so I can get cigs and stuff at the commissary."

Terry pulled back from him and put a protective arm around Simon. "Is that why you sent those letters begging me to visit? Because you wanted money from me?"

"Well yeah, baby, what did you think?" Jimmy appraised Terry with a combination of fury and hunger, never once looking at Simon.

"I thought you'd want to see us." Terry was now speaking through a clenched jaw. "I thought maybe you did some thinking in prison and decided you maybe wanted to see your family. Your son."

"We ain't married and I ain't got no family," he spat through crooked yellow teeth. "You can't even throw me a little cash. What the hell did you ever do for me? Give me some fat kid that I never wanted? I told you straight up to get rid of that baby, remember? I told you to get an abortion."

Recognizing that she had made a terrible mistake, Terry wrapped her arms around Simon and covered his ears. But it was too late. The damage had been done.

Simon never saw his father again and had long ago pushed all paternal memories into the back of his mind. Miles after he'd passed the road crew on I-44 his fists still held a vise-like grip on the steering wheel, and the muscles of his jaw were tightened in anger. *I hope you're dead by now, you good for nothing mother-fucker*, he spat into the rear view mirror. He pulled a roach from the ash try, lit it, and inhaled deeply. Slowly, as the miles rolled by, Simon's thoughts of Jimmy Laflour faded back into distant memory. He still had about seven hours of driving before he would be in Indianapolis. His mind focused back on his mission.

He allowed his mind to fill with pride and satisfaction at his success in procuring a vial of hydrofluoric acid, one of the most dangerous and corrosive substances on the planet. All it would take was a drop. The moment the acid made contact with the skin it would begin to disintegrate the tissue and would continue burning through flesh all the way to the bone.

Simon envisioned himself splashing the acid into pretty boy's face, where it would eat its way through his eyes and maybe even into his brain, severely disfiguring him in an agonizing fashion. Simon pressed on the gas pedal and sped further along the highway, every mile taking him closer to Philadelphia.

*   *   *   *   *

"So now your *Daniel* Smash," Kenneth said softly into the phone. Danny could still sense a yearning in his ex-agent's voice. He hadn't spoken to Kenneth since his arrest. It was time to reconnect.

"It's more adult. More in keeping with my current persona," Danny said, a bit of playfulness in his voice. "You can still call me Danny."

There was silence on Kenneth's end of the line. It was 9 AM in Los Angeles and 6 PM in Prague, Czech Republic. Danny was on the terrace of his apartment in Old Town, sipping a glass of mineral water and watching one of the ubiquitous riverboats lazily carrying tourists along the Charles River.

"This call comes from out of the blue," Kenneth said finally. His voice was guarded and his words were measured. "I didn't think I'd ever hear from you again."

"It's only been two years," Danny said. "Did you think I forgot you?"

"Two years is a long time in this business," Kenneth said warily.

Danny exhaled. "I'm not calling to talk business, Kenneth. I've got all the business I can handle right now and I'm six thousand miles from LA."

"Fair enough," Kenneth said. "I'd heard you relocated to Prague. A universe away from LA. So why *are* you calling?"

Danny stood and slowly paced the patio. The picturesque view of the ancient city of Prague seemed to fade away. In his mind's eye, he yearned for the palm trees and sunshine of Los Angeles. He even missed the things he'd grown to eschew there, like the overcrowded Santa Monica pier and the seediness of downtown Hollywood. "For one thing, I feel that I owe you an explanation, Kenneth," he said honestly. "You never returned any of my calls when I was in prison, and I think the reason runs deeper than the fact that I was poison in Hollywood at the time."

"At the time?" Kenneth's response was instantaneous. "Do you think that's changed?"

Danny's hand tightened on his cell phone. "I don't know Kenneth. I do know that with time *everything* changes."

Kenneth exhaled a troubled breath. "Well, in terms of your standing in Hollywood, it's gotten worse. Instead of just disappearing and laying low, you became a porn star. And not just any porn star, but a prolific, world recognized porn star. *That* doesn't play well in legitimate Hollywood."

"Maybe we can save that conversation for another time, Kenneth," Danny said guilelessly.

"So what did you call to talk about?"

Danny brought his mind back from images of LA and stared without focus at the rooftops of Prague. "Before the shit hit the fan, we were more than just agent and client," he said carefully. "I disrespected that dynamic. Maybe I even took advantage of it. And I know I let you down."

Kenneth was silent. "The past is the past, Danny," he said without conviction. "I've let it go."

Danny answered him sincerely. "If I've learned anything about the past, it's that it's hard to let go of. You can try to bury it, but it follows you."

"Very philosophical," Kenneth observed wryly. "Prague is a beautiful city. Wandering around those quaint little streets must have given you plenty of time for introspection."

"That, and sitting around in jail," Danny jested. "I've definitely had a lot of time to think."

Kenneth chuckled. "You haven't lost your charm, that's for sure."

Danny grinned. "You always brought out the best in me."

"Alright, you've got me intrigued," Kenneth admitted after a beat. "I'm interested in hearing the pitch, though I can't imagine what it might be."

"I just finished up a book tour in Europe and I leave for a junket in the US tomorrow. I'll primarily be on the East Coast, but I'm coming to LA first 'cause, believe it or not, I really miss it there. It's home. Think we can meet at some point in the next two weeks and maybe spend some time together?"

A slight pause, then Kenneth's smile came though six thousand miles of fiber optic phone line. "Let me see what I can do."

* * * * *

Darryl limped toward the door of his apartment building feeling both weary and euphoric. He had spent the better part of the day traversing the city, from Northern Liberties to South Philly, visiting every neighborhood grocery store he knew of and affixing his flyer upon the community bulletin boards. He carried a backpack filled with thumbtacks, tape, a staple gun, pens and pencils, business cards, and what remained of his flyers for "Gla-More Nails." Darryl carried the detritus of an earlier era, when flyers and posters, not the internet, were the primary vehicle for cheap advertising. He sincerely believed that the world-wide-web had its limits, especially in terms of making connections with folks.

His difficulty climbing the stairs to his third floor walk-up in the western part of the city, twelve blocks and worlds removed from the University of Pennsylvania, was due to the fact that his left shoe was missing a heel. The heel had gotten torn from his shoe when he'd gotten it stuck in a grate somewhere between the Organic Grocers in Society Hill and Shopwell in Olde City.

Darryl's clothes had fared no better than his shoe. His sleeve, which got caught in a turnstile while he was racing to catch a departing train, was torn wide open from shoulder to elbow. And his pants were soaking wet, compliments of a city bus that had plowed into a huge, water-filled pothole, saturating him with a near tidal wave of grimy, muddy liquid. Streaks of mascara ran down his face, and makeup stained his collar.

Darryl found his keys after fumbling hastily through his backpack, unlocked an assortment of bolts and latches on the door, and stumbled tiredly, yet excitedly, into his apartment.

"Miss Coco!" he cried as opened the door. "Miss Coco." A little French poodle barked excitedly and ran to greet him.

"Mama's home, baby!" Darryl greeted the overindulged canine with a weary pat on the top if its coiffured head. The black poodle was meticulously groomed right down to its Lilliputian toenails, which were painted a bright lipstick red.

"Look at ya mama, baby. She's a mess," Darryl sighed, miserably examining his tattered reflection in the mirror. "It ain't easy being a career girl. But your mama got her business *done*. I hung up fifty-seven signs today. "

The dog lovingly licked some of the makeup from Darryl's cheek.

Darryl held up a pink cell phone, which had been pre-programmed with a ring tone from Candace Coco's song, "*Dance Happy*."

"Soon this phone will be ringing with nail work for your mama."

Darryl cradled the dog and admired her little collar, which was last year's Christmas present. The collar was studded with multi-colored rhinestones. Dangling beside the rabies vaccination tag was a silver locket, fashioned in the shape of a dog bone. Inside the locket were two photographs. One was of pop star Candace Coco. The other was the very same picture of Darryl that was now posted at fifty-seven locations across town.

Darryl allowed Miss Coco to lick his face for a few more seconds and then gently settled the poodle on the floor.

"Mama's gotta shower and put on a *new* face, baby. Then you and I are gonna sit down and watch *Celebrity Profiles*. They're doing a special on your namesake Candace Coco tonight."

A half hour later, Darryl was snugly wrapped in a thick pink terrycloth robe. He was setting up his portable nail salon in front of the TV when the phone rang.

"That's an unknown caller, baby. Maybe a new customer!" The dog looked up from her pink satin pillow-bed and yawned regally.

"Hello," Darryl said briskly into the receiver.

"Is this Glamour Nails?" said a female voice.

Darryl's sat up a little straighter on the couch. "Oh, yes baby," he answered briskly, heart pumping an adrenaline dose through his veins. "What can I do for you?"

Cradling the phone in his ear, he ecstatically grabbed his purple backpack. It was on the hallway floor, where he had unceremoniously dumped it when he first staggered in.

"Do you make house calls?" the woman asked.

"Baby, I go anywhere for nails," Darryl exclaimed, digging for his new, never before used appointment book from the backpack.

"Oh, that's great," the woman told him. "I'm getting married next week, and we're having a hair stylist come to the hotel and do all the bridesmaids' hair. I saw your advertisement, and I thought it would be a nice treat to have you come and do the girls' nails."

"What's your name, princess?" Darryl asked warmly.

"Cheryl. Cheryl Jackson."

"Cheryl, honey, if those girls don't love my nail work, the job's free. And I am going to do your nails for free anyway because it's your weddin', baby."

They discussed price and other relevant details as Darryl jauntily recorded date, time, and place in his new appointment book.

His head was in the clouds after that phone call. His day of slogging through the city, hanging flyers and talking up his business, had paid off. His business prospects already looked bright.

Within an hour Darryl was snuggled up on his couch with Miss Coco and a cup of herbal tea, watching his beautiful, talented and kind idol Candace Coco on TV.

* * * * *

David Bachman, sitting on a barstool at the circular main-floor bar of Woodpecker's, was completely out of his element. According to David's research on the city's gay life, he knew that Woodpecker's was primarily for the guys, while Dolls, the predominantly lesbian bar, was right around the corner.

It was cocktail hour on Friday night and Woodpecker's was bustling. The circular shape of the bar gave Bachman a bird's eye view of the activity, and since the only available seat was directly beside the bus station, he was also privy to the exchanges between the cocktail waiters and the bartenders, whose comments and quips were fascinating to him. Glimpses, as they were, into the inner work-ings of the gay bar scene.

Bachman had spent his whole professional life researching gay, lesbian, bisexual, and transgender people, but had always felt intimi-dated by the prospect of entering a gay bar alone. He was, by nature, introverted, shy, and uncomfortable in crowded places.

He obliquely observed the clusters of high-spirited men. He wished he could be more like them. In his own mind, he was a social geek, terrified of entering a room full of strangers. But that was exactly what he did when he walked into Woodpeckers.

What was I so afraid of?

Rejection.

Ridicule.

Inadequacy.

Invisibility.

The list went on, rooted, he knew, in his own insecurities. However, sitting here in a gay bar facing the prospect of rejection was nothing compared with the rejection he had just suffered at the hands of his father. Perhaps, it dawned on him, his father's very rejection of him had pushed him to seek acceptance elsewhere.

David's eyes scanned the club. Most of the people were a decade or two younger than he. They stood or sat around the bar in small groups, and a very few, he noted, were there alone. He was forty-seven years old, but sadly realized that even in his early twen-ties he did not possess the self confidence of youth or the ability to successfully navigate unfamiliar social situations.

Almost directly across the bar was a tall, incredibly handsome Asian man. He was in his mid–twenties and had beautiful thick, shiny black hair. He wore a tight black tee shirt that looked as if it had been painted on the torso of David. Clearly, to the group of men encircling him, this man was an object of worship.

His admirers were attractive themselves, and perhaps in the same age range as the handsome Asian. They were not in the same league as far as appearance, but they had enough going for them to embolden their approach to this fellow. Like kids to a new Christmas toy, they were flirtatiously rubbing his chest, squeezing his arms and overtly ogling him. He was smiling broadly and nodding enthusiastically at their attentions, which he was clearly enjoying. The guy's body language, however, a backward leaning posture with hands folded at crotch level, indicated that he had no interest in a sexual dalliance with any of these men.

I *won't be seeing any of them at my seminar,* Bachman mused.

At another section of the bar, observing the Asian and his sycophants with total indifference, were two other handsome men who appeared to be in their early-thirties. On closer inspection Bachman recognized one of them to be Steve Hytower, the openly gay television news reporter from channel 6. Prior to coming to Philadelphia, Bachman had found Hytower via a Google search, and sent him a press release about his upcoming seminar. Follow-up phone calls to Hytower at the television station had gone unreturned.

Promoting oneself required an inordinate amount of social aggressiveness. Bachman knew that a good self-promoter would approach Hytower and try to convince the reporter to do a story about his seminar. But the psychologist remained glued to his bar chair, unable to muster the courage to approach the television personality, who appeared sleek, sophisticated, and completely at ease in his surroundings.

Then, the unthinkable happened. Bachman was caught staring at the reporter. Steve Hytower and his friend stared back at him quizzically. They exchanged words, clearly discussing Bachman because they kept glancing in his direction. Seconds later, Hytower made his way around the bar and directly addressed the psychologist, who froze in fear of being publicly chastised for staring.

Hytower held out his hand in a friendly manner, throwing Bachman completely off guard. It took him precious seconds to regain his composure and offer his own hand to return the shake.

"You're that author, aren't you? You've got a seminar coming up. I got your press release." Hytower was open, self-assured, and without pretense.

Bachman stammered, attempting to articulate a request for the reporter to do a news story on his and Zee's seminar and book.

"Hey, I'm sorry I can't cover your event, " Hytower told him in a friendly voice. But I wanted to wish you good luck with it."

"You can't cover it?" Bachman heard himself say in a voice that sounded much like a whimper.

Steve took a hearty sip of his cocktail. His left palm was open. Bachman recognized this as body language that indicated the speaker had nothing to hide.

"No. We're on another story. I'd love to give you some publicity, but we're really limited as to how many events we can cover."

Bachman's frame slumped slightly on his bar seat.

"If I was a print reporter, I'd be all over it," Steve added enthusiastically. "Did you contact Ted McPherson over at DishMiss?"

"I sent him a press release, yes," Bachman said with a sigh. "But I haven't heard back from him, either."

"I'll shoot him a text," Steve said encouragingly. "He probably gets dozens of press releases every day, so it may have been overlooked." Hytower gave Bachman another handshake. "Good luck, though, and it was nice to have met you."

With that, Hytower returned to his friend, leaving Bachman feeling alone and disappointed.

"Can I refill that Merlot?" the bartender asked. Bachman slid his empty glass across the bar and nodded solemnly.

* * * * *

Simon made it to Indianapolis without incident and found a convenient rest stop on the highway. This one wasn't as populated as the place in Amarillo, nor was it as brightly lit. He easily found a secluded parking spot far from the building. After checking to make sure that his vial was safely locked away and undisturbed in the glove compartment, he climbed into the back seat and promptly fell asleep. A pool of drool had just started forming on the corner of his mouth when the heavy metal ring tone of his cell phone roused him from a comatose slumber. He had to dig through a pile of empty soda cans, candy wrappers, fast food bags, cartons, and clothes before he finally found the phone, which had by now stopped ringing and gone to voice mail. Through blurry eyes, he read the caller ID, which said, "mom." He sluggishly hit the call back button and mentally prepared himself for the interrogation that would surely follow.

"Simon, where are you?" She was on him instantly. "You have been gone for three solid days. You've never been away for this long. What is going on?"

Simon didn't immediately answer.

"Are you there, Simon? Are you there?" She wailed frantically.

Simon inhaled deeply. He was still half asleep. "Yes mom, I'm here."

"You sound like you were sleeping, Simon. Where are you staying?"

Simon's head was resting on his knap sack, his body jammed into the narrow back seat, his legs bent uncomfortably against the opposite door. He shifted to redistribute his bulk to a more comfortable position. His back ached.

"Why are you asking me all these questions? I told you where I was. Why are you badgering me? I'm all grown up, Ma. I can take care of myself for a few days."

"Simon this is the first time in your life you've been away from home for more than a weekend. And you left without telling me where you were going. You just up and disappeared. Are you all right, Simon?"

"Yes. I am all right," he answered, annoyance creeping into his tone. "I told you I needed to get away. I'll be home in a few days."

"A few days?" she shrieked. "Do you have your medicine with you? You can't go all this time without your medication, Simon."

"I have my medication. I'm taking it!"

His mother, detecting the agitation in his tone, backed off. "Okay honey, well, please keep taking your meds. What day will you be home?"

Simon was getting angrier. He was tired and wanted to go back to sleep. "I should be home by next Friday. A week from tomorrow."

"A week from tomorrow?" Her voice was barely controlled hysteria. "Simon, you have never been gone this long before!"

Simon sat up from his supine position in the back seat. "So fucking what?" he demanded. "I'm twenty one years old. There's gonna be a lot of firsts in my life. Get used to it! Stop your pestering because it's pissing me off and I'm trying to sleep. I will see you next week."

With that, Simon hit the "end" button, threw his phone onto the front seat, returned to a semi-comfortable resting position, and drifted back to sleep.

Early Friday morning, after a perfunctory use of the restaurant's bathroom facilities, Simon headed West on I 70 toward Harrisburg, PA. The first five hours went smoothly. Using cash only, Simon had filled his tank outside of Columbus Ohio and stopped at a Mexican fast food place in Wheeling, West Virginia. He filled a bag with dollar menu tacos and burritos at a drive through and continued on his journey.

Simon noticed that the scenery had become increasingly colorful. The change of seasons went barely unnoticed in Arizona, but as he traveled east he couldn't help but appreciate the foliage. He entered the Pennsylvania Turnpike, where, for the first time in his trip, Simon encountered real traffic. He didn't have EZ Pass, and certainly wouldn't use it on this particular trip even if he did. When planning the trip he budgeted enough cash for gas, tolls, and a few nights in cheap hotels. His tolls were paid in the cash-only lane, and just outside of Harrisburg, this lane was clotted with vehicles that stretched almost a mile.

Simon entered the EZ Pass lane, knowing full well that he would not be passing through the EZ pass entrance. But he had no patience for waiting in a long line, either. He quickly passed most of the cars that were moving at a snail's pace through the cash only line. Then, when he was just a few car's distance from the tollbooth, cut quickly toward the cash only lane, attempting to force his way into a small space that had opened between two cars. But the car that he was attempting to cut off moved aggressively forward, blocking him from the lane and causing him to slam on his brakes to avoid a collision. The vehicle, a BMW SUV, was driven by a portly looking woman wearing sunglasses who continued edging forward to prevent Simon from getting in the lane, while simultaneously blaring her horn at him. In an instant, Simon was filled with blinding hatred for this woman. His car was angled toward hers but he was out of the EZ Pass lane. Other drivers were now honking impatiently, and Simon's rage built. He reached across to the passenger side window and with furious jerks of his arm, rolled it down.

"You fucking cunt!" he screamed. The woman responded by giving him the finger and then turning to dismiss him. She moved forward, out of his line of vision. The driver directly behind the BMW was a younger woman with a car full of kids. She timidly waved Simon into the cash only lane and for her efforts was treated to a blaring of horns from other drivers behind her. Without acknowledging any of this, Simon pulled behind the BMW and stayed close on its bumper. The woman in the BMW passed through the tollbooth, grabbed her ticket, and sped onto the turnpike. Simon barely stopped on his way through the booth, ripped his ticket from the dispenser, and raced toward her. When he reached the BMW it was pushing 80 in the fast lane. Simon floored his car, passed it on the left, and quickly cut the wheel, nearly side swiping the BMW as he cut in front of it in the fast lane. Then he tapped his breaks, causing the SUV to lurch. It began weaving almost uncontrollably in the lane. In the rear view mirror he could read both the fury and the fear in the bitch's face as she brought her vehicle to a crawl.

Simon stayed directly in front of her. He screamed at her in his rear view mirror. He wanted her dead. He wanted her mangled on the side of the road. "You want to fuck with me, bitch!" He was now in front of her, and in control, and his rage began to diminish. The woman slowed her vehicle, moved out of the fast lane, and receded into the background as she permitted other speeding vehicles to put distance between herself and Simon.

Then, as Simon slowed to get back in front of her, he noticed the sirens. Red and blue strobe lights were flashing in his rear view mirror. A state trooper was approaching rapidly and cars were moving out of the fast lane to let it pass.

Mother Fucker! Simon thought to himself. *I have illegal shit in this car. I am so fucked*! He moved slowly into the right lane as the trooper approached. He wondered how he would explain this to his mother when he called her from the police station.

* * * * *

The offices of PHILY-TV were located in the Liberty Media Building at the corner of 5th and Market Streets in Center City, Philadelphia. Steve Hytower was in one of the edit bays on the 23rd floor, adding voice-overs to his report for tonight's broadcast. Steve was the entertainment and human-interest reporter for the local newscast, PHILLY 2-Nite. He not only wrote the copy but also physically edited his raw footage. He was alone in the edit bay.

An intern, likely from Temple University, stuck her head in the door.

"Brenda wants to see you," said the chirpy, eager to please intern.

Shit, he thought, right when I'm in the middle of a freaking pain in the ass cut. Editing video required an incredible attention to detail in a medium where units were measured in frames, which were 1/30th of a second in length.

"I'll be right in," he told the intern, not bothering to look up. He wasn't trailing after some freaking college kid into his boss's office. He finished the cut, reviewed it, hit the save button, and headed to the corner office of Brenda Silverman, executive producer of the local news at PHILY-TV.

Brenda's was a high-pressure job, one that Steve would never, ever aspire to. Brenda did not appear on camera, while Steve got a rush from seeing himself on television.

Brenda, he knew, got her reward from the power that came with putting together a brand new, hour-long episode of the news every night. An episode that had to be smarter, sexier, and wittier than all the rest and that had to deliver the ratings to prove it. To that end, Brenda worked with one eye on the flat screens that lined her wall, another eye on the computer screen, and a third eye on everything that was going on around the city, the world, and the newsroom.

Steve knocked lightly on Brenda's open door and walked into her office. "Hey . . . You wanted to see me?"

Brenda pushed a swiveling computer monitor out of her way and motioned for Steve to sit in a stiff, chic, leather couch near her desk.

"Steve, you know I'm your biggest fan," her voice was husky from a thirty year, pack a day, cigarette habit. "But a five fucking minute report on a gay porn star? Are you shitting me?"

Steve was not intimated by Brenda. He loved her Joan Crawford bitchiness and her big, bold personality. He could see through her steely fortress and appreciate that at her core Brenda was one of the biggest fag hags in Philadelphia.

"Bren," he leaned forward toward her. "He's not just a gay male porn star and you know it. His past is totally mainstream. His story is compelling. And I've got all kinds of footage and images from five years ago when his legit career was going ballistic. I've even gotten some good soundbytes from people who knew him when. At the center of all of this is an exclusive interview with the star himself, who is totally controversial. You know the story will get big ratings."

"But this is also a man who committed a deplorable crime." Brenda argued.

"Don't we have people on the news every night who commit deplorable crimes?" Steve argued. "And besides, he's making amends now. He's giving back. He's donating money from this appearance to charity."

"Oh that warms my fucking heart. I'll give you two minutes for the report."

"Three," Steve shot back.

"Two thirty and not a second more," Brenda told him. "Now get the fuck out of my office. I gotta run downstairs and have a smoke."

Steve tried to keep the smirk off his face. When he first pitched the four-minute segment he figured she'd give him two minutes, tops.

And two thirty was enough to turn this segment into an Emmy-worthy report. Well, maybe . . . a guy could dream.

* * * * *

Drag's Happenin' was an unqualified hit at the Teeny Weeny Theatre Company. The sixty seats in the cozy little Center City playhouse were sold out for the entire weekend. It was common for play producers to give away tickets to make the theatre appear to be full and to give the illusion that the show was a success. But this play was already a genuine hit. A preview show which had been presented for the press the previous weekend had by now received rave reviews by both *City Paper* and the *Philadelphia Gay News*, along with mainstream media from the African American Community. It was heralded as a brilliant satire, a parody of the nineteen seventies television hit *What's Happening*? In the play, all of the female roles were being portrayed by drag queens. The character Mama was played by a famous New York performer by the name of Splendora. Little Dee was brought back to comic life by a brand new female impersonator named Mocchiatto Supreme. The pivotal role of Shirley, the wise-cracking and opinionated waitress, was played to incredible reviews by Roger Washington, aka Cinnamon Spice.

The atmosphere in the cramped backstage area was heady and filled with the intoxicating energy of early theatrical success. Nerves ran high as the cast prepared for their first public performance. Because of the early reviews and the hype, tonight's audience would be expecting a lot. Backstage was a beehive of activity, with members of the cast and technical crew jostling to make ready for the show.

"Don't be nervous, baby," Darryl told Roger. "You own the stage. Girl, when you come on the audience goes crazy! The papers all said so." Darryl had already neatly clipped all of the reviews and pasted them around his makeup mirror. His little station, tucked away in a small corner, was something of a respite from the frenetic craziness of the backstage. Somehow he had managed to create a nook for himself and his clients, where he could work his beauty magic.

"Guuurrllll," Roger exclaimed, "you know how it is in show biz. They love you today, they crucify you tomorrow. But we queens can handle the haters. We been livin' with it all our lives."

Darryl delicately painted Roger's giant thumbnail, which was festooned with a glittering gemstone on the tip. "There's hate in the world and there's love girl. I gotta focus on the love," said Darryl.

"Oh, Amen to that sister!" Roger's sizable frame was squeezed into a girdle. His corn rowed hair was pulled back by a tight, nylon net. Darryl took a short Afro styled wig from the head of a styrofoam mannequin and placed it gingerly on Roger's head.

"Now don't touch this hair, baby. Your nails are still wet," he instructed Roger. "Girl, you look just like that Shirley from the TV series!"

Roger examined his highly polished, purple nails, each of which glistened with a gemstone. "Girl, I don't know how I ever survived without you!"

"Well honey you had nails like a pterodactyl, but otherwise you would have survived just fine!"

The two burst out laughing. "Bitch, you are too much fun. You my mulatta mama! I'm gonna go run and put on my waitress mumu and become home girl Shirley." Roger lifted his considerable bulk from the tiny folding chair. "But don't you forget you gonna be stylin' me all up for the Rainbow Cotillion. I'm hosting the party so I gotta look my best. I hear they're having some scouts from that *Drag Race* TV show gonna be there."

"Okay, baby, but I'm gonna be running late," Darryl said thoughtfully. "I have a serious lecture to attend at the LGBT Center and I'm not gonna miss it. A girl always has to nurture her mind. Besides, I'm lookin' to find me a solid, kind man someday, honey. A man who loves his mama, loves Jesus, and loves me. And this lecture's gonna teach me how to find him."

"Well, you go to your lecture, baby. Then come round the corner and meet me at Woodpecker's. I need you girl."

As Roger turned to leave, he smashed into, and nearly knocked over, a man who had been standing silently by. It was anyone's guess how long the man had been standing there, but Roger recognized him instantly and let out an audible gasp. It was Jamar Lucius. Jamar was not only drop dead gorgeous chocolately heat, but he was also the owner of a very popular restaurant in Center City called Indigo Red. The restaurant had become the main sponsor of *Drag's Happenin'*. The ad for Indigo Red was prominent in the playbill and in all promotional material for the play. Mr. Lucius had proven to be a true patron of the arts and had certainly helped to make this little production possible.

Roger's eyes widened in his fleshy, open face. It was as though he were witnessing a vision. And many would say he was. Jamar Lucius was perhaps one of he best looking and eligible gay males in the city of Philadelphia. Actually, not just Philadelphia. He also had a restaurant on Miami's trendy art deco Ocean Drive called Lucius. His father was Lucky Lucius, the lead singer of a top R&B band in the 80's who had gone on to become a top music producer linked with Grammy award winning artists and his mother was a gorgeous Portuguese soap opera star from the eighties named Dores Santos. In the gay vernacular, Jamar Lucius was a household word. He was often listed among the hottest one hundred gay men in the world by the widely read LGBT magazine, DishMiss. But rarely, if ever, was he seen outside his places of business. Though he was A-Listed all over Philly and New York, he was not generally present at high profile events and was definitely not a nightlife denizen.

Roger's hand clasped his chest and for a moment he resembled a heart attack victim. "Mr. . . . Mr. Lucius," Roger stammered.

Jamar Lucius smiled warmly and his response was without an ounce of pretension. "So it's mister, is it? Kind of makes me feel old, but okay."

"Oh, no insult intended, Mr. Jamar," Roger said, his voice both giddy and awestruck. "We're all so grateful to you for supporting our show."

Jamar glanced at Darryl, who was busily tidying up his makeup and nail station in preparation for his next client. "Well thank you for making this show a profitable success." Jamar laughed genuinely. "This is the first show I've ever bankrolled that didn't lose money."

"Well there goes your tax write-off," Darryl joked, paying greater attention to his nail kit.

Roger gasped, fearful that the omnipotent Jamar might take offense.

"Very true," Jamar said with a broad smile. "I see we have a businessman here."

"Oh honey, this businessman is losing all kinds of money tonight. This is my pro bono time. A girl's gotta support the arts, you know."

Lucius cocked his head. The sudden gleam in his eye was that of child who had just unexpectedly happened upon something wondrous. "And you would be?"

Darryl turned and finally gave Lucius his full attention. His eyes immediately went to the hand that was now being extended for a shake. The hand was strong, with a hint of muscularity, masculine yet clean and well maintained, with long, well formed fingers and perfect cuticles. Darryl nearly gasped in delight.

"It is a pleasure to shake your hand, mister. My name is Darryl, and my company is called Glamour Nails."

Lucius' grin was captivating. "And you can call me Jamar. Not mister, please! Why does everyone my own age call me mister?"

"Well okay, Jamar," Darryl responded in a brisk, respectful tone. "It was very nice to meet you. And now I have to get back to work. We got to pack this house and get you back all your money!"

With that, Darryl motioned to Splendora, who was next in his makeup chair.

Jamar Lucius watched as Darryl tenderly applied base to the drag performer's skin. Splendora could not take her eyes from Jamar, but Darryl was transfixed by his work. Jamar's stare lingered on Darryl, who was simply too absorbed to notice. Then the enigmatic businessman and patron of the arts slipped surreptitiously behind a heavy black stage curtain and was gone.

* * * * *

Prague, Czech Republic

The offices of Temple One Productions, the movie company formed by Danny and Phyllis to produce and distribute their erotic content, was located in the Florenc neighborhood of Prague. The company, on the top floor of an ancient warehouse, was a rambling warren, a maze-like hallway of small offices and editing suites ending in a huge, fully equipped sound stage where hi-def pornographic video was produced on a daily basis.

In the hall adjacent to the sound stage, Danny sat in his office, feet up on his desk, scrolling through his phone when Phyllis came bustling in.

"Every time I come here it gets harder to return to LA," she announced breathlessly. "This city is the most magical place on the planet."

Danny threw his phone on the desk and stood to greet her. "I wasn't expecting you until tomorrow."

"Well, I just landed and it *was* a long flight, but I have so much good news. I couldn't help myself. I came right over."

Danny nodded. His expression remained neutral. "What's the news?"

Phyllis took a seat, dug through her Birkin bag, extracted a tablet, powered it up, and began scrolling.

"Our profits from premium content were two million last month alone. That doesn't include revenue from pop-ups on the free tube sites, income from banner ads, linkage commissions from the live camera sites, or the money we're making from our new line of sex toys." Phyllis sat back and smiled like the Cheshire cat. She looked around the office. "We've built a cash cow empire here and the money doesn't stop pouring in. What's the most expensive restaurant in town? Because I'm taking us to it tonight."

Danny's shrug was indifferent. "How 'bout V Zatisi?" He suggested. "I don't know if it's the most expensive but the food is incredible, and it's not too far from your hotel in Prague 1."

Several hours later, Danny was disinterestedly stirring his spiced pumpkin soup while Phyllis eagerly attacked the venison pate with smoked almonds at their table at the elegant and sophisticated V Zatisi restaurant in Old City, Prague.

"I feel like a princess in a magical medieval city whenever I'm in Prague," Phyllis crooned while sipping a glass of house pinot noir. "You are so lucky to be able to live here full time."

Danny inhaled a deep and uncomfortable breath. "Funny you should say that Phyllis, because actually I won't be living here full time for much longer."

Phyllis stopped chewing mid-bite, and gulped down her mouthful of food. "What do you mean?"

"There's no easy way to tell you this, Phyllis," he said, his eyes boring into hers. "I'm leaving Prague. And after my book tour in America, I'm leaving the business."

Phyllis's expression went slack. "What do you mean leaving the business? We're making millions here. You're at the height of your career. Look what you've created. Look what you've done."

"I'm not proud of what I've done Phyllis. I did this out of desperation and because of hopeless circumstances."

Phyllis's expression softened as Danny continued.

"My whole life, it seems, I've made decisions due to desperation. I never wanted to be a porn star. I never wanted to run an erotic empire. The one thing I did really enjoy was being a famous actor in Hollywood. I want it back."

Phyllis's posture became upright and rigid. "Hollywood fucked you over," she said flatly. "As soon as they smelled your blood in the water, they attacked like a school of hungry sharks. Your friend Kayla Asimov butchered you to the press, and your former agent Kenneth Shapiro turned around on you and never looked back. The director of that movie you were working on replaced you without a second thought."

"That was all karma, Phyllis," Danny said evenly. "I fucked people over, too. I fucked you over, as I'm sure you recall. And for that I am truly sorry, by the way."

Phyllis shrugged and shrunk in her seat. "I thought you were happy. You're at the top of a 15 billion a year industry."

"Money is important, Phyllis," he told her. "But it's not everything. At least not to me. In my heart I'm an actor and an artist, not a porn star or a mogul. Prague is a beautiful city and it's been a great place to heal from everything that's happened to me, but I'm going back to LA."

Phyllis looked down at the white tablecloth, then lifted her wine glass and took a long sip. "Don't expect to be welcomed back with open arms," she said finally.

"I don't," Danny answered firmly. "But I will claw my way back into the business. I did it as an unknown, I can certainly do it now."

"Your reputation, your history, will work very strongly against you in this case," she said honestly and without a hint of rancor.

"I'm aware of that," Danny countered. "But I've got millions in the bank, and if I have to I will finance my own independent films. One thing about Hollywood, it's a town where bullshit walks and money talks. Fortunately, I've got enough money to talk pretty loudly."

Phyllis summoned a waiter, who refilled her wine glass. She raised it in a toast to Danny. "I've got millions, too," she said with a wry smile. "And if you need any help financing your movies, this girl will be here for you."

* * * * *

David Bachman was seated at a tiny table in the rear corner of Pine Street Bean. At 10 AM on a Friday, the place was relatively empty. Plenty of larger tables were available, but the PhD had opted for the smallest. His hands were wrapped around a ceramic mug of French vanilla coffee, but even the physical warmth of the cup and the gentle scent of vanilla failed to calm his nerves. His was a mixture of anxiety and excitement. Bachman found media interviews to be nerve wracking. One had to be interesting, colorful, have the ability to hype and to sell, and be able to verbally parry with potentially skeptical reporters. A very tall order for a private and largely introverted man such as himself.

Bachman was waiting for Ted McPherson. Ted was the Entertainment Editor at DishMiss, an online magazine of LGBT arts and culture, and was meeting with David for a sit down about his upcoming seminar.

David recognized Ted, who was also a well-known commentator on the public television series, *Under the Pink Carpet*. The on-air personalities on the program were highly visible members of the LGBT community, and essentially, Bachman was about to be interviewed by a gay celebrity. Ted wore a nicely fitting black leather biker jacket over a graphic tee shirt, dark jeans and leather boots. The journalist scanned the room and smiled in acknowledgement when his eyes settled on David. Ted approached the table with an easy, open manner as Bachman stood to shake his hand.

After formal introductions were made, Ted put his backpack over the chair, pulled out a tablet and placed it on the table. He also extracted a copy of Bachman's book, whose pages were dog eared and marked with copious post-its, and tossed it casually on the table. "I'm just gonna grab a coffee and then we can get started," he said with a friendly wink.

Bachman settled back into his chair and felt some of the stiffness leave his body as he sipped his French vanilla. He was very pleased. It appeared that this reporter had done the research and taken the material seriously.

"Sorry your writing partner couldn't be here too," Ted said as he returned to the table with an espresso.

"Yes, it is either feast or famine," David answered. "It seems we were both scheduled for interviews at the same time today. Zee's over at the radio station at Drexel University. She's got a whole hour on a talk show that's celebrating lesbian authors."

Ted smiled and nodded eagerly. "A whole hour. That should be amazing publicity for your book. And for your lecture tomorrow."

"Yes, Zee will be able to plug the book and the lecture," David agreed. "She's an excellent speaker and I'm sure the interview will go well for her."

A moment of silence passed between the two men. "You've written a book about monogamy," Ted said finally. It's about successful gay pair bonding, but in my research I couldn't find any mention of you having a partner."

"I'm single," Bachman said, staring down at the tabletop. "I'm basically quite shy, and I come from a repressive culture which has made it hard for me to come to terms with my own sexuality."

Bachman stopped himself. He realized that he was revealing too much, and being too personal. There was something about this Ted McPherson that made him want to open up. But that was likely reflective of Ted's skill as a reporter. Bachman decided to stick to the facts.

"The book is based on research, not personal experience, in the area of monogamous behavior in gay populations."

Ted chuckled warmly. "Hey, I'm the opposite of painfully shy and I can't seem to meet anyone either. This is not an easy lifestyle." Ted motioned toward a poster that hung on the wall to advertise Daniel Smash, who would be doing a book signing as part of the

Rainbow Ball's weekend-long festivities. "Correction. This is not an easy life unless you look like *him*."

Bachman nodded in sad agreement. "I'm sorry that I have to concur. Especially with men, youth and beauty are of utmost importance. In the gay male equation, you've got a dynamic which magnifies the importance of looks."

"That's an interesting observation," Ted acknowledged. "In fact I never thought of it that way until I read your book. If you've got two people who are primarily interested in each other's looks, there definitely is going to be less emphasis on the other things."

'Yes, David nodded. We gay men tend to be attracted to the superficial facets of our partners, and jump quickly into intimacy. Very often we then move on."

"We?" Ted asked.

Bachman toyed with his coffee cup. "Well, I use the term collectively. We as gay men."

Ted pecked away at his tablet, then looked up. "That kind of makes the notion of monogamy a bit evasive, wouldn't you say?"

Bachman nodded earnestly. "Infidelity is a definite component in gay relationships, especially with men," he said. "Men are very visual, so when they see something that attracts them, they find it hard to resist. Very often they don't resist. It makes monogamy very . . . evasive as you say."

"So, in writing the book, are you trying to sell monogamy to the gay community?" Ted asked.

Bachman shook his head vehemently. "No, we are not trying to sell anything," he answered. "But whether we are gay, straight, bi, whatever, from the moment we are born we have an instinctive drive to find a mate. Homo sapiens evolved to be monogamous. It's in our hard wiring. Our culture is built around it, and we are trained to aspire to it."

Ted nodded in agreement. Bachman's button down oxford shirt was open at the collar, and Ted's eyes lingered briefly on David's neck. "You make clear, insightful observations," Ted said, "but what message do you want the reader to come away with after they finish the book?"

"First, that gay people have as much of a right to pursue monogamy and marriage as straight people," Bachman answered. "And two, that the dynamics between same sex couples are different than those between heterosexual couples. We would like for the reader to come away with a better understanding of those dynamics, thereby possibly having a better chance of creating a healthy relationship with a partner of the same sex."

The journalist did not respond to Bachman's answer with a follow-up question. The pair's eyes locked for a fleeting moment, but the silence had no time frame. The doctor felt a strange uncertainty, coupled with a distantly repressed emotion . . . desire.

He sipped at his coffee, which had turned from lukewarm to downright cold.

The researcher and so-called expert on gay relationships suddenly found himself in new, uncharted territory. *Perhaps*, he thought, *this reporter is attracted to me*. Despite years of research into same sex dynamics, he was utterly clueless as to how to proceed.

"In your book, you talked about the gay ideal and how we can't meet its expectations."

Ted had blue eyes that sparkled with life. His clean smile, macho goatee, and eagerness for new information were all exciting to the normally reticent scientist, who was suddenly having a hard time concentrating on the interview.

"Can you expand upon what you have coined as 'the gay ideal,' and discuss how we can learn to rise above it?" Ted asked.

Bachman forced himself to focus. "When I refer to the gay ideal in the book," he explained, "I'm talking about the expectations that many gay men have when searching for a partner. We have found that many are, into adulthood, still trying to recapture that guy they lusted after in high school. The classic hunky young stud or the super-jock football star. They are looking for qualities that they themselves do not possess, often to achieve a greater sense of self worth."

Bachman drew a small sip of his cold coffee and continued, his demeanor becoming animated. "We even try to impose those ideals upon ourselves. We become bulimic or we use steroids, we have surgeries or we spend thousands on skincare and beauty products. All to look as perfect as we can. Our focus becomes very superficial, not on the real core of ourselves, or our potential partners. And in that way the gay ideal, as I call it, sabotages our very attempts at achieving a relationship."

Ted regarded Bachman with an expression of fascination. "I'm not proud to admit it, but I can see some of those characteristics in myself and in many of the gay men I know."

The doctor nodded. A silence ensued between the two men, who each beheld the other with open interest.

"There are many," Ted finally continued, "who would argue that there is an entire sub-community of gay men who reject that whole male model look. They are called "bears," and they eschew pretty boys and, basically, everything that the classic gay guy stands for."

Bachman nodded knowingly. "I know about it. The bears, the otters, the silver foxes. As I said, we all have a different concept of what is ideal. The bear community embraces a concept of appearance as much as the male models do. Their unique perspective is on being macho as opposed to being buffed and primped. They are overweight, bearded, hairy, and not conscious of the trendiest fashions though they have their own very specific dress codes. They are no different in trying to create a gay ideal. Just their own version of it."

Ted nodded, transfixed.

"Let's face it. If the bears weren't attached to an ideal, there wouldn't be so many bear beauty contests and titles. Mr. Grizzly, Mr. Metro Cub, Mr. Folsom . . . the list goes on and on," Bachman continued.

Ted tapped furiously on the keyboard of his tablet, nodding eagerly at intervals but not stopping for several minutes. "I think I've got it all now," he told Bachman. "You've given me so much to write about and some terrific quotes, too. That was a great interview. Thanks very much for your time."

Bachman, taking this as his cue to leave, stood clumsily wishing he had the nerve to ask Ted for a date. But he was terrified of rejection.

"How long are you in town?" Ted asked him.

"We're leaving on Sunday," Bachman stammered.

"Have you been to any of the restaurants in Old City?"

"No, I haven't ventured too far from the hotel."

"Oh boy, you don't know what you're missing!" Ted's voice held youthful enthusiasm. "This town has some of the best food going."

"That sounds good. Can you recommend something?"

"I can do better than just recommend," Ted said with a quirky grin. "I can personally take you to my favorite place. Are you free for dinner tonight?"

Bachman stammered, pleasantly thrown off by the unexpected. " Uh, um, yeah, I guess I'm free."

"Good. It's a date. And I hope you'll be nice and hungry because you're in for a real treat."

* * * * *

The soulful sound of Nina Simone's song *Don't' Smoke in Bed* gave Philadelphia's best known French bakery, Le Petit Pastry, the timeless, languid vibe of a lazy Sunday morning. It was actually early evening, but the unfilled seating area and comfy, sophisticated Parisian décor still gave the place a wonderfully relaxed atmosphere.

Darryl, immersed in a book, breathed deeply though his nose. He always made a conscious effort to appreciate every good thing around him, and the tantalizing aroma of French vanilla coffee and of fresh baked delicacies wafted through the air. Nibbling on a red velvet cupcake and sipping from an oversized mug of chocolate latte, he was unaware when Jamar Lucius passed by the window and stopped to peer inside. Darryl was similarly unaware when the incredibly handsome and very sought after restaurateur came inside, ordered a cappuccino, and sat down at the table beside him.

Jamar spilled a packet of stevia into his drink and stirred. His eyes were riveted on Darryl, who was oblivious to his presence. Finally, Jamar rapped on Darryl's table as if he were knocking on a door.

"Hey, there. We meet again," he said when Darryl looked up from his book.

"Oh, hi, Mister," Darryl said, extending a perfectly manicured hand. "You're the play producer! You were backstage at Drag's Happening! You do great things for the arts."

"You know, we're probably around the same age," Jamal said with a friendly smile. "You don't have to call me mister."

Darryl took a delicate sip of his latte. "Well, you're wearing such an expensive suit and you look very important, so you just seem like a 'Mister' to me."

Jamar leaned back lazily in his chair. His arm was draped over the back, his hand hanging in the air between himself and Darryl. Darryl once again noticed it was strong, clean, masculine, and well manicured.

"Let me reintroduce myself to you. My name is Jamar. I'm actually a pretty informal guy and I do like to support the arts."

Darryl also noticed that Jamar's skin was smooth, flawless, and almost the exact same color as the cappuccino in his cup.

"Very nice to meet you again, Jamar. And my name is Darryl."

Jamar's warm brown eyes bored into Darryl's. "I remember your name."

From behind the bakery counter came the shriek of steam blowing from a cappuccino maker. The Nina Simone compilation gave way to soulful French crooning from Edith Piaf.

Jamar's eyes never left Darryl's. "You have a good memory, Jamar."

Jamar smiled. "I guess I'm blessed that way. Where do you live, Darryl?"

"West Philly," Darryl answered calmly. "Cobbs Creek."

"I lived in West Philly when I went to school at Penn. Some of those old West Philly neighborhoods have a lot of charm."

Darryl nodded. He nibbled daintily on his red velvet cupcake. He liked this Jamar, who was friendly, modest, and seemed to be generally interested in supporting the arts. "I grew up in an old house with a flower garden on the side and a big tall oak tree out front," he said wistfully.

"Those old houses can be very charming in a southern country kind of way," Jamar smiled. "But that neighborhood can also be pretty tough."

Darryl nodded and looked Jamar straight in the eye. "It's tough all right," he said. "There was a crack house two blocks over. Drug deals going on everywhere you looked and drive by shootings happened a couple times a year. But up there, nobody bothers you if they know you're from the hood. Everybody knows everybody else who belongs there."

Three rowdy college kids, two boys and a girl, all with multiple piercings and tats, bustled noisily into the bakery, placed orders at the counter, and took a table across the room. Neither Jamar nor Darryl paid attention.

"I'm hungry," Jamar said. "I've had a busy day. This place is famous for their chicken salad sandwiches. How 'bout I get a couple for us?"

"That's awfully nice of you," Darryl said.

Jamar went to the counter and returned with the sandwiches, along with coleslaw, pickles, and sweet-potato chips. He held up two exotic looking bottles of soda. "This is called Lorina. It's French lemonade. It's one of my favorites, but if you don't like it, I can get you something else."

Darryl cleared a place on the table for Jamar to put all of the food. "Oh I'm sure this Lorina drink will be fine," he answered happily. "I love trying new things!"

"What were you reading there?" Jamar asked.

Darryl daintily cleaned his fingers with a napkin and held up the book, which had been positioned prominently on the table. "This is the real deal, here," Darryl explained with seriousness. "It's called *Marriage with a Q*." It was written by two very smart, famous doctors who really care about gay people and want us to be happy. They did a lot of research about gay relationships so that they could teach us how to meet someone and have a nice, happy partnership."

Jamar took the book and examined it. "Are you looking for a happy partnership?"

Darryl shrugged. "I'm always looking to improve myself," he told Jamar. "These two doctors are giving a free lecture at the LGBTQ Center on Saturday. They wrote this book and I bought it because I am going. I like to put myself among intelligent, positive people whenever I have the chance. And I like to learn new things."

Jamar leaned back in his chair and regarded Darryl anew. He smiled. "So, is your objective for reading the book and attending the lecture simply to expand your mind, or are you looking to establish a partnership yourself?"

"Both," Darryl answered simply. "I am single right now, and I'm happy and satisfied with just me. But I think if I met the right person one day, it might really make my life more complete. Which is one of things they teach you in this book. You have to be happy in your own life before you can share it with someone else."

Jamar smiled. "That much is certainly true. I've dated men who were basically very unhappy inside. They had low self-esteem and very little true confidence. They were attracted to me because I'm self-assured, which was something they were lacking. Of course, some of them just want to get their hands on my sexy bod," he added with a disarming smile and a wink.

Darryl waved his hand dismissively. "Oh I see it all the time at the tanning salon where I work," he said. "These men come in so full of themselves, but you know it's all an act. If they really had inner peace, they wouldn't have to try to make themselves look so good and to try to impress other people so much."

"What impresses *you*, Darryl?" Jamar asked seriously.

"I'm impressed by what's inside folk's hearts," came the prompt answer. "I'm not impressed by fancy wrapping. There's a lot of mean people out there who are very pretty to look at."

"People are very visual, though," Jamar said. "And appearances can be very important." He looked purposefully at Darryl's hands. The nails were long and expertly lacquered, each festooned with a tiny, perfectly centered diamond. He gently took one of them between his own fingers and continued to examine it. "And you, quite obviously, work on your nails."

"I consider myself an artist," Darryl answered. "Nails are my art. And my life."

Jamar continued to hold Darryl's hand, massaging it gently. "You seem so much more complex than that. If you're so focused on nails, how are you different from the men at the tanning salon who are obsessed with their looks and their bodies?"

Darryl pulled his hand defensively from Jamar's grasp. His sitting posture became entirely erect.

"I am not flaunting myself, trying to look good for my night out and for my next pickup, like those men at the tanning salon,"

Darryl said tightly. " I have a skill. I have a talent. I am an artist. I make people's hands beautiful. I make my own hands beautiful. My art is sacred to me. It's an insult for you to compare me to a bunch of vain, promiscuous men."

Jamar felt a jab of instant regret.

Darryl, quickly packing his book into a purple backpack as though he had just received an emergency call, didn't notice Jamar's expression of pure regret.

Jamar jumped up from his seat. "Look, I didn't mean to offend you. It was just an academic question. A challenging topic. Not a personal attack." A pleading, dismayed countenance stormed across his handsome features.

"This is a coffee shop, not an academy," Darryl said, standing. "And I'm not an intellectual, I'm a manicurist. Thank you very much for the sandwich."

Jamar stood staring at the door for many minutes after Darryl's hasty exit.

"Damn hell," Jamar muttered. "Damn, damn, damn! I am so stupid." He absently bussed the table and with a slumped, defeated gait, left the cozy bakery for the cold street.

*   *   *   *   *

From his small office on the 12th floor of the PHLY Media building, Steve Hytower stared through a small sliver of a window. His was a minimal view of the highly trafficked, heavily traversed corner of 5th and Market Streets in Philadelphia's most historic yet highly urbanized old city neighborhood. He stared, daydream-like, at the rain drizzled cityscape, his mind absently visualizing how tomorrow's news segment would play out. To Steve, this particular report had to be meticulously scripted and conceptualized in detail before the camera rolled, the light blazed, and the microphone went live.

Steve stopped staring through the window and his attention returned to his computer screen. He had finished writing the draft for the script for his big scoop and began looking it over, editing, considering all angles and possible outcomes. This one required far more attention to detail and planning than most of his others. His gut told him that his upcoming interview with Daniel Smash, and the report that he would create, would bring big ratings and make him an ever more prominent newsman.

Steve's position as entertainment and human-interest reporter for the top independent television station in the third largest broadcast market in the country was enviable. It was a job that many, many people would gladly give an appendage for. He routinely interviewed the coterie of celebrities, among them supremely famous stars, who regularly passed through the City of Brotherly Love. As the mainstay of his beat, Steve covered film festivals and movie premieres, concerts, plays, book signings, glitzy over-the-top parties, and interesting special events. When a movie was shooting in Philly, as many did, Steve was on-set interviewing the stars. A local celebrity in the huge, sprawling, exciting metropolis that was his hometown, Steve was frequently recognized on the streets and in shops and restaurants as "that reporter from TV."

Most of those who recognized him, however, could not specifically recall his name. Or even what station he worked for. He was simply one of the many ubiquitous television reporters that the public recognized from the small screen but quickly dismissed as largely interchangeable talking heads. At this point in his career, Steve certainly had not managed to stand out from the pack. There were people in his field who commanded seven figure salaries, those whose names and faces were instantly recognizable on a national scale and who were sometimes more famous than the stars they interviewed. This was the level of success that Steve aspired to. He wanted to work in New York or LA for one of the big entertainment news networks, like Tattletale, and to have a name that was as recognizable as that of the hugely successful entertainment reporter, Cutter, and the commensurate multi-million dollar net worth that went with it. This was Steve's dream, his burning ambition.

He believed that his interview tomorrow with Daniel Smash and the report that he wrapped around it would bring him one step closer to this dream. He could not know or imagine that the events of tomorrow would shape a report that would catapult him more swiftly toward his goal than he could ever possibly dream.

Steve worked the keyboard of his computer. He typed a few more keys and read over his stand up for tomorrow's report again and again:

"This is Steve Hytower, reporting today from Center City's historic Unity Bookshop, one of the oldest retailers in the country. Today, this store's historic relevance will be further cemented by a visit from a former Hollywood A-lister. The G-rated golden boy once known worldwide as Danny Smash has transformed himself into a star and mogul in the world of erotic entertainment. Now known worldwide as "Daniel Smash," the icon himself is scheduled to appear here today to sign copies of his first book, an erotic tome entitled "Behind the Scenes."

"Today, I'll be taking you behind the scenes of this unprecedented book signing to meet Daniel Smash, to learn about his book, and to check out today's event."

Steve kept at memorizing his stand-up, saying it out loud again and again so that it rolled from his tongue in news-speak. Once satisfied that he had it roughly down, he reached for the phone and punched the key that direct dialed his best friend.

"What are you bothering me for?" Brian answered on the third ring. "Don't you know I take a nap at this hour?"

Steve laughed. "Are you getting excited to meet your first porn star tomorrow?"

"Are you kidding?" Brian asked acerbically. "Someone who has contributed so profoundly to the well-being of mankind? I absolutely cannot sleep." There was a pause, and for a moment Steve thought the connection had been lost. Then Brian said, "Oh, I'm sorry. I must have nodded off."

"Actually, porn stars really do have a positive function within society," Steve argued.

"Of course. They're money makers," Brian answered. "Sex sells."

"It sells because a lot of people out there have fantasies that go unrequited," Steve said. "I've done quite a bit of research about porn stars for this report. And overall they do provide an escape and a sexual outlet for a lot of men. Many women, too."

"So what are you going to ask him in the interview?" Brian asked.

Steve checked himself out in the mirror that hung beside his desk, running a finger over a forehead crinkle that had been filled with restyline.

"Daniel's publicist set very narrow boundaries for the interview before granting it. I am not allowed to ask him about his Hollywood past, about his crime or imprisonment, or about his performance in porn movies. I am only allowed to ask questions that pertain specifically to the book and to his signing."

"Are you serious?" Brian asked incredulously. "What the hell are you going to ask him then?"

Steve was still looking at himself in the mirror. Taped to its lower corner was an article about a plastic surgeon in LA who had pioneered a breakthrough in facelifts for men.

"I'll ask him benign questions about his book signing," Steve said matter-of-factly. "I can add all the juicy, scintillating details about his life when I edit the report together. We will shoot a lot of footage of him signing books and interacting with his fans. I'll use this with a voice over talking about his porn career and postulating why he went into porn in the first place. I can address his Hollywood past with archival footage. I may not be able to ask him about it, but I can damn well use it."

Brian was scrolling through a particularly informative blog on the subject of sinus health. He remained partially focused on the conversation while gently touching his forehead, sinuses and lymph nodes, checking for tenderness or increased temperature that might indicate a medical condition far worse than sinusitis.

"It would be interesting to know how he went from being a vilified Hollywood outcast to a being a porn icon in such a short time," Brian mused.

Steve was now scrolling through his computer, viewing before and after images of men who had undergone facelifts. "I've done the research, and I can answer that now," Steve said. "Remember I told you that Daniel's manager when he first got to Hollywood represented a lot of porn stars?"

This got Brian's full attention. "Um hmm," he nodded.

"Apparently," Steve continued. "When Smash got out of prison he didn't have a friend in the world. No family to speak of. In fact, the only person from Hollywood said to have visited him in the prison was his first manager, whose name was Phyllis Moyt. From all accounts, it is believed that Moyt convinced Smash that his only way of making a comeback was as a porn star."

"Was it?" Brian asked.

"Certainly in America," Steve said, "where he had absolutely no chance of getting back into the legitimate entertainment industry. And apparently he needed money. He spent a fortune on legal fees and is rumored to have also given a lot of his money to the mother of his son."

"I guess it makes *some* sense," Brian said. "He sure wasn't going to pick up a job at Target."

"No," Steve joked. "That surely wouldn't have supported him in the lifestyle he was accustomed to. He went to Prague, the porn capital of the world, and along with his ex-manager built an erotic empire worth tens of millions of dollars?"

"Wow! But a bit surprising," Brian said. "With free porn all over the internet, you have to wonder how anyone's making that kind of money from it."

"That's what I originally thought," Steve explained. "But I did the research, and it turns out that free porn actually represents a very small piece of the pie. Pornography is still a huge revenue generator. To the tune of 97 billion dollars a year worldwide."

"Sex will always sell I guess," Brian said.

"Would you believe that porn sites get more traffic each month than Netflix, Amazon, and Twitter combined, that about 35 percent of all internet downloads are porn related, and that a third of all of the data moving across the internet is porn?"

"But aren't most of the big porn stars women?" Brian asked.

"Absolutely," Steve answered. "But every once in a while you get a guy who comes along who has universal appeal, and he can make a shit ton of money. One of the biggest porn legends to ever live was John Holmes. Back in the seventies, he was making three grand a day. He was known as the king of porn and was famous well beyond the industry he worked in."

"I've heard of John Holmes," Brian said. "But didn't he do straight porn?"

"Primarily, yes," Steve answered. "Though I think he did a scene or two with another guy."

"So why gay porn for Daniel Smash?" Brian asked. " Why not straight porn? I thought he was straight. Wasn't he shacking up with Kayla Asimov back in the day?"

"The tabloids said they were an item," Steve answered. "But his actual sexuality is another gray area. Some say he is gay for pay. He allegedly just got seven figures to star in a straight porn movie with Savannah Minx, the world's most renowned female adult star. But with that said, after choosing a career in porn it's pretty clear why he would choose to do gay. Straight porn is primarily made for straight male viewers. And straight men aren't buying their porn to watch the guy."

"I agree," Brian said, "That makes sense. And by the way, did you get us on the guest list for the Rainbow Ball party tomorrow night? Because I am *not* spending money to get in!"

Steve laughed. "Yes, you little tightwad. I got us on the guest list and I also got us a handful of free drink tickets. We are going to party hearty! I for one will be celebrating getting that Daniel Smash footage shot and safely downloaded into my editing system. And boy, will I be in a mood to celebrate if everything goes smoothly on that shoot!"

"Oh, nothing's going to go wrong with your shoot tomorrow," Brian answered dismissively. "What could possibly happen?"

"Anything," Steve replied, all too knowingly. "From equipment failure, to sloppy camera work, to a testy publicist who suddenly changes her mind about the interview, to a celebrity who simply fails to show, to any other totally unforeseen circumstance. That is why I will party like a rock star when that footage is in-the-can. Because theoretically, *anything* could go wrong tomorrow."

* * * * *

Simon drove carefully through the busy, confusing streets of Center City. It was Saturday, almost noon. It had taken him two hours to drive to Philadelphia from Harrisburg, where he spent the night in a budget hotel after getting the scare of his life on the Pennsylvania Turnpike. Thanks to the bitch who had royally pissed him off on the highway, and his justified attempt to run her off the road, he thought he was about to be pulled over by a state trooper. He had believed that the asshole cop was after him but he'd lucked out in the end. The troopers were on their way somewhere else. After Simon had pulled over with his car, the speeding police vehicle with its flashing lights went racing right past him.

Now he drove with care through the streets of downtown Philadelphia, using anger management techniques his therapist had taught him, especially for moments like when someone cut him off or when he missed a green light. Moving through the city streets was slow, confusing, and daunting, but Simon was very, very close to his mark. Everything was going perfectly according to plan. No way he was going to fuck it up now.

He was moving west on Walnut Street. The GPS on his Smart Phone indicated that a parking garage was a few blocks up on his right. He located the garage, passed it by mistake, and after circling the block found its entrance on a narrow, alley like street that also housed an adult bookstore and a few cheap looking bars. Passing into the garage, he took a ticket from the machine and entered as a gate lifted. A spiral driveway took him to the rooftop level of the garage, which afforded a bird's eye view of the immediate surroundings. He parked, got out of the car, and peered over the wall into the neighborhood. A cityscape of rooftops, alleyways, and skyscrapers loomed before his eyes. It was a crowded, sooty, cold metropolis.

His anger simmered inside of him. A cold dedication to avenging his grandfather's death grew even stronger. He would deface and destroy his grandfather's murderer. His rage fueled his hunger for justice. But his rage was tempered by a feeling of fear at being in a place that was bigger and more foreign than anyplace he'd ever been in his life. In fact, before this, Simon had never traveled beyond Omaha, Nebraska.

He lit a roach and inhaled deeply, allowing the cannabis to calm his nerves and help him think clearly. The sheer size of Philadelphia, and its dense population, would help to camouflage him. He could blend in with the crowds, unnoticed and ignored. He took another hit and then stubbed out his roach. According to the GPS on his phone, the Unity bookstore was a few short blocks away.

*   *   *   *   *

When the building that had originally been home to the Grover Cleveland Elementary School was renovated in 1985, the old gymnasium was configured to serve mixed purposes. Today, rows of metal folding chairs were arranged in front of the auditorium stage in preparation for a lecture.

Dr. Bachman stood on the stage, staring with trepidation at the sea of empty seats and at the cartons of books in the front row. The sound of his footsteps echoed across the empty room as he walked, once again, to the windows of the old gymnasium. Flamboyantly swathed in dramatic chintz drapery, the windows afforded an indirect view of the Unity Bookstore.

It was a half a block away, but the line that had begun forming at its door shortly after noon now stretched well past the LGBTQ Center. David stepped from the stage and stared through the window. Deep in his own thoughts, his expression was both somber and pensive. He had been back and forth from this post all morning, observing worriedly as the line took on its own life, stretching like a tentacle past his window and around the block.

Zee entered the lecture hall carrying yet another carton of books. David turned to her, his eyes on the box.

"Do you really think we need all these books?," he asked her, turning once again to the window. "How many people do you believe are actually going to show up today?"

Zee placed the carton on a table that she had set up on the stage, and began stacking books. "I think we are going to have a very successful turnout today, David. There are tons of people in town for Rainbow Ball weekend. We pretty much have a built in audience here."

David continued staring out the window. "I'm sure we'll get a handful of people, but the big event is across the street," he answered. "The porn star has a television crew, a police patrol, and a line around the block for *his* book."

Zee continued arranging their books on the table. "David, I just spoke to our publisher and our unit sales keep increasing. Downloads on reading tablets are also way up every week. Clearly there are people out there who are interested in what we have to say."

Zee stopped stacking the books, descended the stairs, and approached David at the window. She gave his arm a gentle squeeze. "You're comparing apples to oranges here," she told him soothingly, her voice like a warm balm. "You are a doctor of psychology. You know that life is full of competition and that we have to deal with it. So let's get the show on the road, here. We have a lecture to give."

David turned from the window. "You're right. I've got to get my shit together."

Zee pulled back with an expression of surprise that gave way to an amused smile. It was the first time she'd ever heard David curse.

"Damned straight," she agreed, tearing open a large, flat, box. "Let's get these promo posters up! Marketing, marketing, marketing! It's clearly working. Sales of the book on every major e-reader have exceeded all expectations, and we got amazing publicity from the Washington DC lecture."

Zee unrolled a poster that featured an impressive image of David looking every bit the academic and the scholar. "David, just look at yourself," she told him. "You have made a profound contribution to this entire subculture. Many, many people have read your words and taken your message to heart. You have already touched so many lives, and the book hasn't even hit its stride in terms of sales.

You look outside and you see these crowds clamoring to another event, but what you're not seeing is that you are still a vital part this community. And a vital part of this Rainbow Ball weekend here in Philly."

The observation drew a mixture of emotions from David. Zee's words resonated. He *was* a vital part of the LGBT community. Of that, there could be no doubt. Unfortunately, it was at the banishment of the community that he had been born to and raised in. As proud as he was of his present accomplishments, he felt a deep, underlying sadness that his family could not share in, or even appreciate, his success. In fact, his success in one realm granted upon him status as a pariah in another.

"I've always been torn," he confessed to Zee with a sigh. "There's always been this feeling inside me that I've got one foot in the gay community and the other foot in the Jewish orthodox community. Ever since I've been an adolescent, I've felt like I don't really belong to either one. And standing here, like an outsider observing a community of gay men from behind a pane of glass, I feel it even more acutely. It's a very lonely, unsettling feeling."

It was Zee's turn to sigh. She understood that David felt disenfranchised and torn.

"David, for someone who feels like an outsider, you've certainly managed to get into the heart of this community."

David's eyes watered as he turned to face her. "When I was young, I always considered myself to be an outsider, like I didn't fit in. I was always so alone. It took me a long time to admit that I was different. I finally became conscious of the fact that I was gay and I realized that there were others like me. Finally I felt as though I belonged to something. That there were people I could fit in with. I tried to fit in with the gay community. I tried to find my place. But the gay community had no place for me. I was always ignored and overlooked in favor of those who were much better looking." David paused introspectively. "I so badly wanted to fit into the gay community by making myself an important part of it. But in the process, I've lost my family and the community that raised me."

Zee rested her hand on David's back and gently guided him away from the window and toward the stage. "We wrote the book about gay marriage," she said encouragingly. "You more than anyone know that it's possible to start your *own* family, and to nurture your family in a community that will accept and embrace you for who you are."

David shrugged, and Zee winked conspiratorially at him.

What about that handsome guy you had dinner with last night? You came back to the hotel on cloud nine. Doesn't he hold some possibility for the future?"

David's face clouded anew. "Actually, I haven't heard from him since dinner last night," he admitted. "He told me he would text me in the morning about coming to the lecture tonight. But it looks like I'm up for another disappointment."

Oh shit, Zee thought. *This guy can't get a break.* She began to seriously worry that David's dark mood could undermine the entire lecture.

*   *   *   *   *

The excitement on Pine Street was palpable. A long procession of ebullient men formed a queue that stretched around the block and took on an animated life of its own. The crowd had become a veritable sea of black leather jackets, tight jeans, hip sunglasses, funky hats, and work boots. In addition to this colorful collage were a surprising number of women. Philadelphia's copious drag queens and androgynous gender benders were also accounted for. Against this kaleidoscopic backdrop, PHILY-TV reporter Steve Hytower was shooting the opening for his report. He stood on the sidewalk with the colorful crowd setting the tone behind him. He walked toward the camera as he delivered his introduction:

"This is Steve Hytower, reporting today from Center City's historic Unity Bookshop, one of the oldest bookstalls in the country. FUCK!"

His first take was interrupted when a handsome Asian guy dressed in a jeans and a stylish jacket staggered drunkenly in front of the camera, ruining the shot.

Brian was standing beside Frankie the cameraman, holding a clipboard. He took his voluntary job as Steve's assistant very seriously. "Are you blind?" he yelled at the inebriated man. "Did you miss the camera? We're shooting here!"

Steve stepped back a few steps as his cameraman re-adjusted the shot.

"No worries," Brian told Steve in an unruffled tone. "We've got plenty of time to get this right. Apparently Daniel is running late. Not a big surprise."

The next take went well, but Steve wasn't happy with the way he'd delivered some of the lines, so they shot another. And another. Finally, after the sixth take, Steve was satisfied.

"That was definitely your best," Brian told him.

Steve toyed with his microphone, which was flagged with the bold logo of PHILY-TV news. "Good. Now let's get some sound bites."

Followed closely by his cameraman, Steve approached a man standing about ten people from the front of the line. Something about the man was different and he looked completely out of his element. He was disheveled; he wore a hoodie, baseball cap, and oversized sunglasses. He had a scruffy, unkempt beard, which made his presence here intriguing. But most importantly for Steve, he was alone. Not only could someone like this provide an unexpected, ironic sound bite, he would be easier to engage because he was solo. It didn't matter that he was not particularly telegenic. The important thing was to get the first decent sound bite in the can. Somehow, in Steve's experience, the rest always followed smoothly after the first.

Steve faced the camera as he approached the man. "Many of the people here today have been in this line for hours. Especially those up at the front. Sir, how long have you been waiting here to see Daniel Smash?"

Steve moved the microphone toward the man's mouth. The man was semi-turned away and had not been paying attention to the video crew. When the microphone was placed in front of him, he covered his face and turned away.

Steve promptly moved on. "Thank you, sir," he said, and turned to the next person on line, who was standing with a friend. Both were eager to grab a moment in the spotlight. The pair were dressed almost identically and appeared to be on the kind side of forty.

Once again, Steve faced the camera before turning to the men. "Many of the people here have been in this line for hours. Especially those up front."

He then turned to the men. "Gentlemen," he said, leaning toward them, "how long have you been waiting to see Daniel Smash?"

As he directed his microphone in their direction, the closest man eagerly grabbed it and launched into a response.

"We still can't believe we're going to meet him in person!" the man exclaimed. "We used to salivate over him when he starred on television in *Mission Bay*."

Steve gently removed the microphone from the man's hand. "So you're a big fan of Mr. Smash?"

"You better believe it! We've been fans since he was a Harrington and Stitch model and we remain fans to this day."

The other man nodded eagerly.

"What is it about Daniel Smash that clearly magnetizes you?" Steve asked them.

"This is a man that had everyone fooled. Nobody, nobody could have seen it coming that this guy would end up doing gay porn. But wow, once we heard he was doing it, we definitely wanted to see it."

"And we weren't disappointed!" joked the other.

Steve maintained a serious composure. "We all know that Daniel has a criminal past. Does that taint your image of him?"

Now it was the other man's turn to make a grab for the microphone. Steve let him speak but did not relinquish control of the mike.

"He did his crime and paid his time," the man answered. "The prison thing doesn't bother us because, really, what's sexier than a bad boy?"

His friend chimed in. "Lot's of celebrities commit crimes and make comebacks. We the public can forgive and forget!"

"How do you think the public feels about someone who makes a comeback doing porn?" Steve asked. "That's never happened before."

"Well," the man answered intelligently. "Think of the celebrities who either started their careers with sex tapes or had their careers derailed from sex tapes. I can think of several cases where the public forgave and forgot."

"And didn't an ex-stripper just get a Grammy Award?"

"Those are excellent points. Thank you, gentlemen," Steve said, and then turned to the camera. "It seems that Daniel's criminal past may be part of his appeal, at least to some of the people here today. Let's go see what others have to say."

He turned from the men and began moving down the line.

Brian joined him. "That was great! You've now got some quotes that are salient and hysterical at the same time."

Steve smiled in agreement. "Yep," he said, scanning the crowd. He spotted a few women among the men and decided to also get a female's point of view. "We'll keep shooting sound bites until Daniel arrives. Better that we get too much than too little."

Many people were already waving to him, eager for their own moment in the camera's lights.

* * * * *

Darryl was all business as he marched purposefully toward the LGBTQ Community Center.

Up ahead, he could see a line at the bookstore, which ran for two blocks and then wrapped around a corner. Darryl's only concern was getting a good seat in the lecture hall, where his mind would be treated to important, valuable information that could enrich his life. Briefly, he worried that there might be a similar line at the Civic Center, but his concerns disappeared after he performed a mental reality check.

The proof is in the pudding, he thought as he passed the bookstore. Several men in the line were now fawning over an extremely good looking, well built young man who was quite obviously very drunk. Darryl's eyes scanned the scene with great distaste. A clot of admirers had formed around the drunken man. They were oblivious to the presence of pedestrians and left no room on the sidewalk for Darryl to pass."Excuse me," Darryl said politely, wishing simply to proceed down the sidewalk. He did not care to step into the gutter. He was wearing a brand new pair of shoes from Sassy Footwear on Market Street.

"Excuse me," he said again after his first entreaty went ignored. The circle of men tightened as they inched closer to the handsome drunk. To Darryl, they were a pack of hyenas that smelled weakened prey, around which they hungrily circled. As they inched closer to their quarry, a space opened and allowed Darryl to squeeze past. But as he did, one of the men suddenly took a small step backwards, stepping on his new shoe but not bothering to notice.

Darryl checked the shoe for damage before forcing his way into the circle of men.

He turned and addressed them en masse.

"Could you people be any more rude?" He stood glaring at the men.

"Could you be any more tacky?" one of them said. "Who do you think you are, Dorothy with your ruby red slippers?"

"I'm tacky?" Darryl huffed, nodding his head at the handsome, intoxicated man who was clearly the center of everyone's attention. "You drool all over the Philadelphia town drunk here, and you're standing in line to see a pornographer. You call *me* tacky?"

Darryl's perfectly tweezed eyebrow was raised in disgust. Tightly clutching the strap of his backpack, he tried to push past the men. "I won't let you dull my sparkle," he told them.

"Listen to the undernourished drag queen with shoulder pads," said one of the men. He had slightly pockmarked skin, thinning reddish blonde hair, and wore tight blue jeans rolled up primly at the cuffs.

Darryl stopped dead in his tracks. A hush fell among the group of men.

"No, you did not!" one of them said with a measure of shock and surprise in his voice.

"I don't care about your poisonous words and I don't care what you think about me." Darryl's voice was steady. He fought against the hurt and humiliation that threatened to make him tremble. "But at least I *know* who I am. You're very one-dimensional. You don't know anything about me yet you judge me cruelly. But the *porn star* who stole from good people and has sex for money is someone you are standing in line to see. Something's wrong with this picture, baby."

A brief silence ensued.

"All right for you, little dude!" the handsome but wasted guy, upon whom the others had been fawning, clapped his hands haphazardly. His words were slurred. Alone, he turned from the group and stumbled further down the line. "That is one feisty little black dude," he told the crowd.

The men's faces clouded with disappointment as the handsome drunkard receded from their sightline. Darryl stood a little taller, held his shoulders a little straighter, and a smile played on the corners of his mouth.

"I've wasted enough time," he addressed the now subdued men. "I have an important lecture to attend."

With that, Darryl turned on his considerable heels and sailed toward the Community Center.

* * * * *

It was pure pandemonium inside the little Unity Bookstore. An obtrusive television crew was making reality of the expression, "Lights, Camera, Action!" at the front door. A police officer stood post nearby, looking at her cell phone. In the rear of the store, a half dozen VIPs, who had secured back door access via connections with the store's owners, waited with impatience and a sense of entitlement. In response to the huge crowd outside, store employees were feverishly tearing open additional cartons of books. The books were being stacked nearly to the ceiling on three tables. Daniel would be sitting behind the fourth table, which was immediately accessible to the back door entrance. Three chairs, currently empty, were set at Daniel's table. The star was to be, per specific instructions, closely flanked by his publicist. Red velvet stanchions, rented for the occasion, were now being positioned to create a walkway that would lead from the front door, past the book displays, to Daniel's table and then to the cash register.

Daniel himself was scheduled to appear at 3:00 and it was already half past the hour. A chauffeur who had been sent to the airport to fetch the porn star was somehow not reachable on his cell phone. As could be expected, the manager of the book shop, was completely beside himself with nerves and anxiety.

"Please, please, be patient," he beseeched the swelling crowd, who surged contentiously outside the doors of his shop, where a second police officer was posted. The manager's voice was nearly drowned by the impatient group who formed a teeming mass on the sidewalk.

The store's assistant manager burst through the rear door, which led to the alley. "He just got into Center City!" came the breathless announcement. "I finally reached the limo driver on his cell phone. They are on the I-95 ramp. *Daniel Smash has arrived in Philadelphia!*"

The television crew stopped what they were doing and moved hurriedly toward the back door.

Those standing just outside the front door were notified that the star had arrived and would be ready to sign autographs any minute.

The first in line would soon be granted entrance, and the rest would be corralled, somewhat like cattle, through the velvet roped passage that led to the table where their idol would hold court.

*   *   *   *   *

Simon felt his pulse quicken when the man from the bookstore came outside and announced that Daniel Smash was now on the premises and that the line would begin moving shortly. Simon pulled his baseball cap further down over his forehead and tightened the hood of his sweatshirt down over the cap. He hiked his backpack up so it was tighter against his shoulder blades. He wore blue tinted glasses and his face was covered with five days of beard growth. He was fully incognito but still he glanced uneasily behind him. He did not want that annoying reporter, or anybody else, pointing a camera at him.

Fortunately, the reporter was the only person in the crowd who had so much as glanced at him. The rest had been much too preoccupied with themselves, their friends, and their silly conversations to pay him any mind. They were all now anxiously craning their necks to watch the door for a sign that the event was underway. Most of them had been speaking in loud tones and acting with exaggerated gestures the entire time they stood in line. Since the announcement came that Daniel arrived, their theatrics were almost manic.

Simon had avoided crowds all his life and had little experience being among large groups of people. One of his favorite teachers in high school had been gay, but that was the extent of Simon's connection with these people. They shrieked, they bounced and bobbed on their feet, they talked about nonsense, and some of them dressed completely over the top. Simon felt as if he had been transported to an alien world where adult men and women stood in line to idolize and worship a degenerate.

He tried to ignore their conversations.

"I can't believe he's actually right here, right now, right inside that building!"

"This will definitely be the best $29.95 I have ever spent. Worth every penny to be right next to Daniel Smash!"

"OMG I would totally spend three times as much to be face to face with perfection. That man truly is a god."

"A Greek god and an ex con. Could it get any hotter?"

These people were stupid and blind. Simon could feel cold rage percolating within him. He began fingering the acid filled vial in his pocket, rubbing it angrily between his fingers. Simon wished he could throw some acid at these idiots who were shameless enough to idolize a man who had stolen from a bunch of nice old people and destroyed their lives. *And killed my grandfather*, he thought.

Simon's anger at the men in line was instantly diverted when the door to the bookstore opened and the first people were ushered in. Simon hiked his backpack tighter against his body and prepared to move.

"I am never going to forget this day," someone shrieked behind him.

That's right, motherfucker, Simon thought. *You can't even imagine how unforgettable this day is going to be . . .*

* * * * *

Danny had arrived in Philadelphia from the West Coast on Kenneth's private jet. The two were now sitting snugly with Danny's publicist in the back seat of a chauffer driven Escalade that was now turning off Interstate 95 and entering the ramp that led into Philadelphia's Center City district. The powder blue Benjamin Franklin Bridge was magnificent on the SUV's right side, but Danny hardly noticed. He was already forty-five minutes late for the book signing, but he hardly noticed that either. His fans would wait for him. They knew he wouldn't disappoint.

Kenneth had cracked open a window, and the unfamiliar crispness of the Northeast air cascaded bracingly into the car's luxuriant interior. Danny was sitting closely beside Kenneth. His hand rested possessively on Kenneth's knee. Cassidy, Danny's publicist, was seated across from them, staring wordlessly and without expression through the window. As the vehicle pulled to a stop at a light, a young woman entered the crosswalk. A little blond haired boy held tightly onto her hand, trailing behind the woman as they crossed the street.

Danny was overwhelmed by a sudden feeling of loss and grief that threatened to incapacitate him. He thought of his mother, of the Painted Desert Farm, of Malchus, and about the trajectory his life had taken. The little boy in the street reminded him of the innocent little boy he had once been, before he was defiled and robbed of a childhood. Then he thought of his own son, an innocent child who deserved far more from him.

"Are you having second thoughts?" Kenneth interrupted his reverie and snapped him back to the present.

"About what?" Danny asked, shaking his head vigorously.

"About this whole book signing? Is it really necessary?"

"It's necessary, Kenneth, because of the media presence. I'm using the opportunity to publicize my retirement from the porn business. We talked about this, remember."

Kenneth's eyes bored into Danny's. "We discussed the fact that you want to get out of porn and try to make a move back into the mainstream. You didn't go into the details."

Danny squeezed Kenneth's leg. "Well, we got busy with something else up in that jet of yours."

Kenneth smiled at the memory. Cassidy looked out the window and pretended not to hear.

"I heard you optioned Megan Flanagan's script, Celebrity Culture," Danny said, steering the conversation back to business.

Kenneth's eyes widened and his mouth opened slightly. He smirked inwardly. The Hollywood super agent turned mega-producer momentarily lost his poker face.

"How did you know about that deal?" he asked with open surprise. "It hasn't even been leaked to the trades yet. Nothing's been announced."

Danny's body moved tighter against Kenneth's, distracting the man's intensity. "Before we left LA I had an interesting lunch with Caleb Cross," Danny said. "Apparently you're already in discussions with him about casting."

Kenneth's body tightened. He was silent as their car glided past the brownstones and shops of Philadelphia's Center City neighborhood on its approach to the Unity Bookshop.

"You lunched with Caleb?" Kenneth asked with an accusatory, possessive tone.

Danny looked Kenneth straight in the eyes. "Why would I not?"

"That queen is the biggest degenerate in Hollywood. His casting couch is notorious. Please tell me you didn't go there."

Danny allowed himself to sink into the leather seat. "Are you kidding me?" he demanded. "Caleb Cross?"

Kenneth said nothing but was clearly rebuked. An expression of regret clouded his face.

"I am perfect for the lead role in that movie, Ken," Danny said, inching closer. "The controversial crash and burn Hollywood tabloid star. Cast me. You can't go wrong."

"It would be a hard sell to the investors," Kenneth said after a moment's consideration. "A known porn star is box office poison. That kind of casting has never even been considered. I'm surprised Caleb didn't tell you that."

"It actually happened with a porn star in the seventies," Danny said. "And times were a lot more puritanical then. Today, porn queens and prostitutes are having sex with the president and the biggest reality star on the planet got her start from a sex tape. For me, the important thing is that I've got a following, I'm controversial, and *I can act. That's* what Caleb Cross told me. And don't worry, I didn't have to sleep with him to get his support."

Their limousine was now turning into a small, alley-sized street that would take them to the rear entrance of the Unity Bookstore. As they rounded the corner, they were afforded a view of the crowd of people in line.

"Look at the mass of people who are here for me," Danny said to Kenneth. "At the risk of sounding arrogant, I am an icon. An idol. I can sell books, I can sell porn, I can sell movies . . . I can sell *anything*. Get me that role in *Celebrity Culture*. Your investors don't have one damned thing to worry about. They will make money."

Kenneth swallowed hard. "I'm sorry. I should be more supportive, too. You *can* sell anything. I can pitch you," he nodded earnestly. "That's all I can promise. Ultimately, though, it won't be my decision."

Danny's eyes burned into Kenneth's. "Please make it happen," he implored. "I'm done with porn and I want to get back to Hollywood where I belong. I know how hard it is to go from porn to mainstream, but this is the new millennial generation. We are quick to forget and don't exactly hold our celebrities up to a high standard."

Kenneth gave a snort of laughter in agreement. Cassidy, a product of the millennial generation herself, sunk back in her seat

The wheels of the limousine bumped gently along a narrow alleyway that led to the back entrance of the Unity Bookstore. A television camera was pointed at the limo as it slid to a stop.

The moment the camera lights came into view, Danny's attention abandoned Kenneth. He moved to separate himself and sat up straight in the car's plush leather seat.

"Stardom suits you," Kenneth observed, staring through the window. He'd escorted any number of A-list celebrities to red carpet events, but there was something unique about Danny's star power that always shined brightly and magnetized attention. " Go meet the masses. I'll be here waiting when you're done."

Danny nodded and turned to Cassidy, whose hand was on the door handle. "Remember what we talked about," he told her. "Don't open the door yourself." His emerald eyes were serious and intent. "Let the driver open the door for us. The cameras are rolling and they're looking for glamour and the visuals that come with it."

Cassidy lifted her fingers from the door handle. She worked for the prestigious Obelisk Agency, a public relations firm that specialized in bringing media attention to books and their authors. She had worked with many celebrities in her short tenure. Her job was to service the public relations tour of Daniel Smash. In her tenure with the company she had never before experienced anyone like him. He was so delicious to look at, yet behind the gorgeous façade there clearly lurked a brilliant and instinctive mind. He knew exactly how to be a star and when to turn on the magic, and his aura shined more brightly than any celebrity she had ever experienced.

Steve Hytower watched as Daniel emerged from the limousine. The camera was rolling and had captured the car's arrival. Steve could feel his heart pounding in his chest. While he had enough footage to edit the report without an interview attached, a one on one with Daniel Smash, even if very short, would turn the report from average to engrossing.

Steve had met his fair share of film and television stars. In real life, these people rarely looked as good as they did on screen. The men were usually shorter and their physical flaws were more apparent. Daniel, however, was tall, athletically proportioned, and so magnificently handsome that Steve's breath nearly caught in his throat when their eyes met. Steve fought to focus his mind on his pending interview. Daniel's publicist Cassidy made introductions and the two men shook hands.

The cameraman moved in front of them and framed them in a two shot. Steve tapped his mike for a sound check. "We're rolling," he told Daniel. "We'll do this quickly so you can get to your signing."

Daniel's smile was dazzling and charismatic. He nodded at Steve as though the pair were best friends and they were the only two people on the planet.

Steve turned to the camera and spoke. "I'm here with Daniel Smash, a Hollywood star whose evolution has taken him to the zenith of the adult entertainment world. Daniel is here at the Unity Bookstore in Center City Philadelphia to sign his book, *Behind the Scenes.*"

Steve then turned seamlessly to Daniel. "What inspired the creation of this book?" He turned the microphone toward Daniel.

Daniel smiled effusively and placed his hand warmly on Steve's shoulder. "First of all, Steve, thanks for the interview and for giving coverage to this venture of mine, which is all about giving back."

Steve nodded and encouraged Daniel to continue. "My book is a nod of thanks to my fans. It comes with a link to a complimentary download from my latest movie, so the book itself is pretty much free. And I did it because I get letters and emails all the time from fans that wonder what my life is like behind the scenes. Since I always have a still photographer on the movie sets, I actually had a nice chronicle of my life off-camera. So I put together over one hundred candid pictures that give my fans a nice, clear understanding of what I'm like when the camera's not rolling."

Steve listened intently while formulating his next question. He was only permitted to ask questions that pertained to Daniel's book and today's event.

"Obviously you will be meeting a lot of your fans face to face today," Steve said to Daniel. "Is there anything that you'd like to say to your more global audience who could not make today's signing?"

"Buy my book!" Danny joshed, smiling broadly at the camera and then winking at Steve. The spontaneity and suddenness of his answer had the intended comical effect, and both men laughed before Daniel continued. "No, seriously. I'm not making a cent from this venture. It's very important for me at this stage to be able to give back. I've been very blessed and lucky, but like everyone, I've made mistakes. I've learned from my mistakes and I've used those lessons for growth and for the good of others. Every penny from my book goes to two charities that I have established, the Lucille Foundation, which provides shelter for homeless gay youth, and Danny's Fund, which aids struggling senior citizens." Daniel's eyes were full of sincerity as they stared deeply into Steve's eyes.

"So I'm guessing we can expect more philanthropic work from you in the future," Steve said.

"Yes, absolutely," Daniel answered with a broad smile and a nod. "And I have a big surprise announcement for you." Daniel's eyes briefly met Kenneth's, who was standing just beyond the camera crew.

For his part, Steve tried not to drool. A surprise announcement? This could be the get of the century. He nodded eagerly at Daniel, encouraging him to continue.

"This book tour marks the end of my involvement in adult entertainment. I've already sold off my share of my company, Temple One Productions. I've made my last erotic film."

Steve didn't miss a beat. "I'm sure your fans will be disappointed. What are your plans moving forward, then?"

Daniel flashed a spellbinding smile. "I can't divulge any details about it right now," he told Steve. "But I will advise that everyone pay close attention, because there are some big things coming."

Steve shook Daniels's hand and thanked him for his valuable time. The interview lasted a full five minutes and could not have gone better. Now he just needed to get some gravy shots of Daniel signing books and his report was in the can.

Nothing could possibly go wrong at this point.

* * * * *

"Look David," Zee said in a calm but enthusiastic tone. Her demeanor belied her true feelings of concern, which started in earnest when David demonstrated what she had recognized as an expression of extreme anxiety. "There are plenty of people here. The lecture starts in half an hour, and the seats are almost all full."

They were standing in the front of the auditorium, which had been slowly filling. Zee was nodding warmly at people in the first few rows of seats. David was staring forlornly into the crowd.

"It's a shame my family couldn't share this with me or even appreciate it," he sadly intoned. "Their community, their precious culture and their traditions are more important to them than their own flesh and blood."

"But look at the people in *this* community," Zee gently contradicted him. "*This* community is embracing you. Men, women, young, old, religious people, non-religious people . . . it doesn't matter. *This* is your community, not those people who rejected you without ever embracing your talents or your gifts." Zee motioned toward individuals in the audience. "Look," she said. "There's a couple here with their little boy, and there's even a guy in a wheelchair. And if you're interested in having young, good looking gay men in the audience, just take a look at that gorgeous black guy in the front row. We already have a very diverse crowd. It's a full house. Doesn't that make you feel good?"

David shrugged. "I wish I could enjoy this success," he said. "But I just can't. I keep thinking about my own father slamming a door in my face. Accomplishment doesn't feel like much if there's no one to share it with and if it makes the people you love feel ashamed of you."

"David, we can't pick our families. And it's not just Orthodox Jewish families that reject their gay kids. People do very strange and even cruel things in the name of God and religion. I'm sure that there are people in this very crowd who have experienced familial abandonment. But here they are, trying to better themselves. Why? Because the human spirit is indomitable. *Your* spirit is indomitable. This whole thing was just very bad timing for you."

"That's for sure," David nodded solemnly. "The pain is very raw."

Zee could see the back rows of the auditorium filling up. She glanced at her watch. In another five minutes they would have to start the lecture. She turned back to David.

"It pains me to see you like this. But let me ask you a question. Did you write this book to impress your family, or to make a mark on the gay community?"

"That is actually a very good question," he finally answered Zee. "And to work through it I need to try to answer you honestly."

Zee nodded, encouraging him to do so.

"I wrote the book for the community, certainly," Bachman explained. "But if I have to be brutally honest with myself, I'm coming to realize that I wrote the book to somehow become a part of the gay male culture. I wanted to connect with men because men use sex for validation, while women use it for emotional bonding. I thought that if I could teach men to look at sex with a different perspective and to take emotional risks, that I would be truly changing their lives, and connecting with them."

"Well here they are," she said, waving her arm in the direction of the audience. "And they are all just waiting for us to connect with them." Zee gently placed her hand on his shoulder. "When you see these people, all waiting to hear what you have to say, you should realize that you have achieved your goal. You have done it without the help of your family and you don't need their approval or their blessing to get out there and enjoy your success."

The lights dimmed as Zee and David looked out upon the crowd, each absorbed in their own deep thoughts.

From his seat in the front row of the lecture hall, Philadelphia's most eligible bachelor, Jamar Lucius, anxiously scanned the crowd. He had arrived early enough to secure two excellent seats. He was beginning to feel his own despair when the steel doors of the auditorium flung open. In sailed the eccentric, otherworldly individual that Jamar had been waiting for. Darryl's theatrical presence caused most heads in the room to turn. He was waif-like and delicate, yet he radiated energy and light. Jamar found him irresistible. Thoughts of Darryl had been running rampant through his mind ever since they'd shared dinner at Le Petit Pastry and Jamar had inserted his foot in his mouth and managed to offend the one man in Philadelphia whom he looked upon as both an enigma and a genuine prize.

Darryl was strikingly clad in a scarlet jacket with dramatic shoulder pads, tailored black pants and high heeled, red, faux alligator boots. His eyes held an expression of lofty focus. Under one arm he carried a note pad and jacket. A purple backpack was slung over the opposite shoulder. A silk rainbow scarf trailed in his wake.

Darryl stopped, surveyed the crowd, and scanned the auditorium. Jamar had thrown jackets over his two front row seats to reserve them. He walked rapidly to where Darryl was standing and looking for a vacant seat.

"Hey Darryl, it's Jamar." He held out a hand for Darryl to shake.

"I'm really sorry that I offended you the other night," Jamar said quickly. "It wasn't my intent to minimize who you are or what you do." He paused as Darryl considered his words. "I have two seats in the front and I reserved one with you in mind. I hope you'll sit with me."

A huge smile spread over Darryl's face and his expression became one of delight. Suddenly he felt like a kid who had just found a perfect seashell at the beach or seen his first shooting star.

"A front row seat with you sounds just perfect Jamar," Darryl answered with enthusiasm. "Thank you for thinking of me. And for remembering that I would be here."

Jamar took Darryl's arm and proudly led him to their front row seats. An attractive, light skinned African American woman emerged from behind the curtain and stepped to the podium. Darryl sat, his attention immediately riveted.

"Good afternoon, everyone. My name is Zahara Shelby," Zee stepped closer to the microphone and warmly regarded the entire audience. "Thank you all for coming, and I can tell you from the bottom of my heart that my colleague Dr. Bachman and I are delighted that you've taken the time to join us. He and I worked very hard to bring our book, *Marriage with a Q!* to the lesbian, gay, bisexual, transgender and questioning community. Dr. Bachman's positive influence is both refreshing and noteworthy, and is clearly evidenced by the fact that the lecture hall is now filled to near capacity even though our competition is tough. I understand that Daniel Smash, the porn star, is right now signing autographs just across the street."

Polite laughter followed. Zee continued. "We're expecting Daniel to come here and buy *our* book right after his signing. We understand he's looking for a meaningful relationship."

The audience roared with laughter. Zee waited for it to die down before continuing. "And now, I would like to introduce my colleague, co-author, and friend, Dr. David Bachman."

Enthusiastic applause followed. Zee turned to the curtain, expecting David to emerge. The audience watched with eager anticipation. As the seconds ticked past, the room slowly became silent. No one appeared from behind the curtain.

*   *   *   *   *

The door of the Unity Bookstore had been open for five minutes and the first people in line were granted entrance. Simon was just inside the door, where he had been standing in a line that was once again unmoving.

Simon watched with growing rage as Danny came into view, every bit the self-satisfied media king. Sitting beside him was a well-dressed and conceited looking businesswoman. Simon breathed to control his fury as Danny, decked out in very expensive clothes and looking like a spoiled super rich kid, greeted fans with charm that oozed from every pore. Simon couldn't wait until his acid burned its way through that handsome face and straight into Danny's brain. The acid was that powerful, and nobody deserved it more than this primped-up fucker who had robbed and killed Simon's gramps in order to climb to the top.

Simon forced his mind back to the task at hand. It dawned on him that he could have done a more thorough job of planning this attack. A better mastermind would have given himself time to case the joint so that he'd know exactly what he was up against. Now that he was inside the store he had a little time to study the interior and perfect his plan. He decided exactly how and where to place his bomb. Midway between the table and the front door was a bookshelf. There were a good five inches of space between the floor and the first shelf. He would easily be able to slip the bomb underneath without detection. The store did not appear to have a fire exit, but there was a relatively unhindered path of escape.

Simon watched the first two men in line, who were fawning all over Danny as he signed their books. There was a television camera recording the exchange. The TV reporter was standing off to the side, watching his cameraman work. The line inched slowly forward as Danny chatted up the small groups of people who purchased his book. As Simon advanced toward the signing table, he could once again observe at close range Danny's devilishly deceitful charm. Soon he would be melting that movie star smile right off the asshole's face.

He moved a few more steps, and was now near the bookshelf under which he would be slipping the bomb.

Then he caught a lucky break. The camera crew moved to the front of the store to interview the people who had gotten their books signed.

With the crowd's attention focused on either the camera crew or on Danny, Simon crouched to the floor with his backpack, opened it, took out his small, home made bomb, and slid it neatly under the bookshelf. The self-absorbed jerkoffs in line were too preoccupied to have noticed that a bomb had been placed in their midst.

It dawned on Simon that he had passed the point of no return. There was no going back. He felt fully relaxed and focused. He knew for an absolute fact that his plan would be a success and that he would finally avenge his grandfather's death.

There were three people in front of Simon in the line. He had a clear, close-up view of Danny's face. His target.

Simon's gloved hands were both in his pockets. In his left hand he held the detonator. In his right hand, he carefully uncapped the vial. There were now two people in front of him in the line. The guy with the bouffant hair and skater boy. Simon stood patiently.

Skater boy handed his book to Danny. With a smile that would melt glass, Danny opened the book's cover and, pen in hand, prepared to sign.

"What's your name?" he asked skater boy.

"Connor," skater boy said, his voice giddy. "I've downloaded every movie you've ever made. I never, ever missed an episode of *Mission Bay*. I am your biggest fan!"

Daniel's smile never faltered. "To my biggest fan, Connor," he said as he wrote. "Thanks for your support."

Danny then signed his name with a flourish. He closed the book cover and handed it back. "I can't tell you guys how much I appreciate your standing in line and coming out to see me and buying my book. I would never be where I am without the gay community. That's why whatever money I make from this book goes to help homeless gay kids."

Danny obligingly offered to take individual pictures with the two young men. He leaned forward on the table to pose with skater boy as bouffant held up the camera to snap. Simon, with a clear, direct, close path to Danny, sprang into action.

Simon pressed the bomb's remote detonator button. Within seconds a thick, nearly suffocating cloud of smoke began hissing loudly from beneath the bookshelf, quickly engulfing the immediate area. Everyone turned to look as those closest to the bookshelf began to shriek in terror.

In the next instant, with all attention focused on the smoke bomb, Simon took two steps forward. He was now mere inches from Daniel, who was obscured by smoke. Simon pulled the vial of acid from his pocket and splashed it in the direction of Danny's face. He knew he'd scored pay dirt when he heard an agonized scream. Simon turned and was already halfway out the door as the alarms sounded and someone screamed, "FIRE."

Simon did not have time to watch Danny's face sizzle away. But even over the cacophony, he had the satisfaction of hearing agonized screams as he made his final retreat from the store. He and the panicked crowd poured through the door and onto the street, which had suddenly become a melee of chaos and confusion. The police officers stationed outside, completely disoriented by the sudden onset of pure calamity, didn't even notice as Simon walked nonchalantly past them, head down and hooded by his sweatshirt, backpack over his shoulder. Simon crossed the street, calmly traversed the several blocks to the garage where his car was parked, and entered it as though nothing had happened. He didn't even bother to take in a final glance of Philly from the elevated parking lot. Filled with serenity and a sense of profound accomplishment, he calmly drove out of the lot and crossed Center City to Interstate 95. In his mind he continuously replayed Danny's screams of agony. The memory was music to his ears.

* * * * *

The ambulance screamed past Ted McPherson as he climbed the steps of the LGBTQ Center. Since his interview with David Bachman, Ted had been infatuated with the nerdy yet somehow very sexy psychologist. Enough so that he had foregone attending the Daniel Smash signing, planning to attend Bachman's seminar instead. He'd sent a friend to get pictures with Daniel Smash and planned to write a story about the event without actually going to it. Now it was obvious that an even bigger story was brewing as smoke billowed into the street from the Unity Bookstore and people ran in all directions while emergency vehicles came screeching to the curb. Screams mingled with the sounds of sirens, and Ted's first thought was: *terrorist attack.*

He stood immobilized at the door of the Community Center, shocked into indecision by the melee assaulting his eyes and ears. He watched as the cops secured the sidewalk, and his instincts as a reporter kicked in. Ted ran, got as close as he could to the scene, and started taking video with his phone.

Inside the Community Center, thick walls and dense curtains rendered the crowd in the third floor auditorium oblivious to the chaos just across the street. The audience was now watching with a mixture of curiosity and confusion as Zahara Shelby stood alone on the stage waiting for her co-author to appear. Dr. Shelby wore an uncertain and solicitous expression as she moved apprehensively toward the side of the stage. The entire auditorium was fixated on her. After a few seconds, whispers began circulating among the audience.

Outside, Ted McPherson continued videotaping the astonishing scene at the Unity Bookstore. The smoke had already started to dissipate when firemen first entered the building. Police from the bomb squad unit followed. Finally, paramedics were called in. Minutes later a stretcher was hastily carried from the building and swiftly loaded into the ambulance, which sped away in a blaze of strobe lights. From his vantage point in the crowd, Ted could not see the body on the stretcher. Getting any closer to the crime scene would have been impossible. The details would emerge soon enough.

Inside the Community Center's auditorium, behind the curtain and out of view of the audience, David Bachman pulled himself together. He had an audience full of people who were here because they respected what he had to say and a colleague who clearly cared about him. He took a deep breath and took his place on the stage.

He was met with enthusiastic applause as he emerged from behind the curtain. Zee noted with pleasure that David's expression no longer conveyed signs of worry or anxiety.

On the stage, David gave his co-author a warm embrace. "Thank you Dr. Zahara for that more than generous introduction. You are a brilliant psychologist and counselor whose work has not only impacted me on a professional level, but on a personal level as well."

Zee smiled warmly and Bachman addressed the audience. "My, we certainly seem to have a wonderful mix of people here today!" he told them. "It's so enlightening to see diversity within our own community, and I sincerely want to thank each and every one of you for coming." His focus turned back to Zee. "Because we both wrote the book for *everyone* in this community. We wrote *Marriage with a Q!* to help each and every one of you to achieve a healthy same sex relationship. Because *all* people deserve the experience of being loved and enjoying a committed partnership."

Enthusiastic applause and cheering filled the auditorium. Darryl was furiously scribbling down every word in his notebook, unaware that Jamar had surreptitiously draped an arm over the back of his chair.

Zee picked up after the applause had died down. "For those of you who have not read the book, the central theme is personal for me. As an HIV positive woman who has been in a ten-year relationship, I have personally overcome profound obstacles and challenges. I felt the need to write this book because there is a difference between a strong, functional relationship and a perfect relationship. The perfect relationship doesn't exist, and a strong, functional relationship can be challenging to achieve, especially so when the same sex dynamic comes into play. That said, we wrote the book because every person in this audience has the potential, and the ability, to find true satisfaction with another human being. And, aside from the incredible Philadelphia cheese steak sandwiches, this is why Dr. Bachman and I are here today."

The auditorium was filled with laughter and more applause.

Dr. Bachman joined in the applause, now smiling broadly. Then something happened that made his heart flutter. He spotted Ted McPherson! He hadn't heard from Ted since their dinner together, and the sight of the cool, hip writer filled him with joy. He enthusiastically picked up the lecture where his colleague left off.

"My esteemed co-author has brought many of her passions into the writing of this book. And so the emotions of our community are beautifully reflected in the pages of *Marriage with a Q!* But our work is not based on emotion alone. Much of our book, and what we discuss in it, is based on years of research into LGBT relationships, marriages, and yes, divorces. From our research we have gleaned a tremendous amount of insight into what makes gay relationships work and what leads to their failure. We have been highly criticized for broaching the subject of gay divorce in our book. But all of us in this room know that a certain percentage of marriages are going to end in divorce, and the gay population is not immune to this statistic. However, our research into the entirety of gay behavior, relationships, and the termination of those relationships has yielded information that we feel is crucial in helping *you* to better navigate the pitfalls of potential connections with another person."

On the word *you*, Bachman's eyes scanned the audience in the auditorium. He noted with pleasure that the vast majority of attendees were transfixed. Zahara once again picked up where David left off and from that point the two went back and forth, discussing personal, psychological, and sociological aspects of gay relationships. They spoke about being single in the LGBT community, the search for appropriate partners, dating and courtship, committed long-term relationships, gay marriage, and divorce. Audience attention to the subject matter never wavered. Darryl scribbled furiously in his notebook.

Sixty minutes later, the lecture concluded. "And now," the writers culminated, "we will be taking questions."

Multiple hands shot up in the audience. David pointed to a middle aged blonde woman in the rear of the auditorium. She stood after having been selected.

"Hello, Dr. Bachman, Dr. Shelby. My name is Dana and I first want to say that both my partner and I love your book. It actually inspired us to commit to marriage."

There was applause in the audience. Broadly smiling from the stage, David and Zee nodded in appreciation and encouraged Dana to continue.

"But for those in the audience who are single, do you believe that people are fulfilled only when they have a partner?"

"Not at all," Zee answered. "A lot of people are happy being single, but just as many are looking for a relationship. Our book is a tool to help them create a good one."

Bachman interjected. "One of the things we emphasize in the book is that, first, you have to be comfortable in your own skin," he explained. "Your self esteem is very important in a relationship. If you project negative energy, you are going to attract the wrong person."

"So it is really, really important to like yourself and to be happy with you and you alone," Zee continued. "To embrace your life, your friends, your interests, your goals, your sexuality. One of the most important lessons in this book is that when you truly learn to love and accept yourself, it doesn't matter whether or not you have a partner. The ironic thing is that when you *do* have a sense of your own self-worth, people will be magnetically drawn to you, and you will attract someone who will love you for all the right reasons."

Oblivious to the chaos that was taking place just across the street, doctors Bachman and Shelby continued their Q&A with their very enthusiastic audience.

Darryl's well-manicured, bejeweled hand, which was fatigued from furiously scribbling pages and pages of notes, shot into the air waving his pink plume feathered pen. Dr. Shelby pointed to him and invited his query.

"Thank you for that nice speech, baby," Darryl said with genuine gratitude. "I just want to say that I think it's so wonderful that there are people like you and Dr. Bachman in this world. Honey, you are so right-on-target with that book of yours. You just keep preaching your message, because at this very minute there's a lot of people out there who need to hear it. Our people need teachers like you and Dr. Shelby."

Jamar smiled warmly at Darryl, spellbound by his authenticity. Darryl continued to speak. "So you go on doing your great research work and keep telling it like it is. I'm right in your corner, baby. Thank you again."

Zahara was pleasantly surprised by this unique individual and by his refreshing point of view. So too, apparently, was the audience, who began clapping enthusiastically. As the applause subsided, Zahara regained her composure and leaned toward the microphone to thank Darryl for his words of encouragement. Before she could respond, David gently took the microphone from her. His expression was one of pure beatific joy and gratitude.

"Thank you, young man," he told Darryl. "Sometimes I wonder if our message is getting across, if anyone really cares about what we have to say. It is certainly refreshing to hear affirmation from someone like yourself. Again, I really need to thank you for your monumental support."

The giant room was silent as Darryl, the manicurist, shook a glistening fingernail at Dr. David Bachman, the educated and revered doctor of psychology. "You don't need to thank me, baby. We all owe you a lot. You're trying to *teach* us something. You're trying to teach us the truth. Sometimes the truth hurts, but we all need to hear it. So you just go on telling it, baby."

* * * * *

The ambulance carrying Danny Smash screeched to a halt at the entrance to Temple University Hospital emergency room, whereupon he was immediately transferred to the fourth floor burn unit. He had never experienced pain this unendurably excruciating. A young doctor had immediately flushed his burn with several syringes of fluid. He was hooked up to an IV.

"We're giving you morphine," a nurse explained. "You are very lucky that you just got a splash on your arm. Whatever burned you was extremely caustic and very strong. I know you're in a lot of pain right now but trust me it could be so much worse. You will heal from this."

They were in a curtained-off cubicle. Kenneth stood nervously beside Danny's bed. He had a terrified look on his face, and watched anxiously as Danny received medical treatment. As he closely observed the unfolding scene, he saw things in Danny's expression that he had never witnessed before: fear and vulnerability.

Their eyes met. "Somebody really hates me," Danny said. "In a million years I would have never expected that something like this could happen."

"This is one of the hazards of being a public figure," Kenneth said morosely. "This is what they call the dark side of fame."

"You can't be a Mister Nice Guy and claw your way to the top," Danny mused in agreement. "You're bound to make enemies along the way. If that poor kid getting his book signed didn't stumble in front of me when that smoke bomb went off, we wouldn't even be talking right now because my face would have been burned off. I can't even imagine what I've done for someone to hate me that much."

Kenneth nodded solemnly. "Danny, whoever did this to you likely didn't even know you. It was probably someone who hated you on principal. It could have been some crazed fundamental Christian who was trying to punish you for your sins, or a lunatic who was jealous of your looks or your success. The list of possibilities is actually endless."

"That's comforting," Danny answered, sinking deeper into the hospital bed.

Kenneth looked at the floor. "Sorry," he said in a near whisper. "I think you'll feel better once whoever did this is behind bars."

Danny sat up suddenly in the bed. "Kenneth, you've got to find out if they caught the guy."

* * * * *

THE AFTERMATH ...

Simon had been driving for almost ten hours and had reached the outskirts of Columbus Ohio. It was now after midnight. He turned in to a desolate truck stop and pulled slowly into a parking spot.

The ride from Philadelphia had been a mixture of elation and exhaustion. He had escaped without detection and his attack had gone perfectly as planned. He dug out his phone and began a Google search for any information about his attack. The internet was already buzzing with the news! He linked to an article that he found on Tattletale.com:

FORMER TELEVISION AND MOVIE STAR
TARGETED IN TERRORISTIC ATTACK

Actor Danny Smash, best known to mainstream audiences for his role as Trey Godfrey on the once popular television series _Mission Bay_, is believed to have been the intended victim of vicious attack in Philadelphia on Saturday afternoon. Smash, who was once one of Hollywood's most promising actors, was in the City of Brotherly Love to promote a book detailing his more recent exploits in the porn industry.

Convicted and imprisoned three years ago for robbing the residents of a retirement community in Arizona, the handsome actor left Hollywood in disgrace and launched a highly successful

and lucrative career in the erotic film industry, where he built a worldwide empire. He now calls himself Daniel Smash, and was greeting fans inside the Unity Bookshop when the attack occurred. Witnesses to the incident describe an orderly event that quickly escalated to pandemonium and terror when the room suddenly began to fill with smoke and the sound of agonized screams pierced the air.

The assailant used a highly corrosive acid, which caused severe burns to the victim, a 28 year-old unidentified man who was standing near Smash when the attack took place. Police believe that the probable target was actually Smash himself, who received a small splash of the caustic acid when the smoke, from a remotely detonated bomb, caused diversion and panic in the crowd. Smash was rushed to the Temple University Hospital burn unit. He was treated for relatively minor injuries and released within a few hours.

"This was definitely a planned attack," said an officer on the scene. "It was clever, diabolical, and personal." When asked if the attack could be defined as an assault on the gay community, the officer replied that the strike was "probably less about any specific community and more about the intended victim."

"Fuck, fuck, fuck!" Simon screamed. "Minor fucking injuries!" Simon bashed his phone repeatedly into the car's dashboard and steering wheel. Finally he tossed the now broken phone into the back seat and furiously lit a joint. "All this for fucking nothing," he fumed.

And now he would have to drive from Ohio to Arizona with a busted fucking phone.

*　*　*　*　*

Danny was still trembling as the gulfstream lifted from the runway and the lights of Philadelphia glittered beneath the plane. He accepted a neat glass of bourbon from the flight attendant and sunk into a deep leather seat. Kenneth studied him closely.

"I have never seen you this shaken up," the agent observed. "In fact, I've never even seen you get flustered. Even though we're on our way back to LA, you still don't feel safe, do you?"

Danny swirled his cocktail and stared contemplatively into the glass. "I grew up not feeling safe, Kenneth. I haven't felt entirely safe since I was thirteen years old."

Kenneth's expression was one of sudden astonishment. He continued to study Danny carefully.

"I never told you the truth about my past." Danny continued staring hypnotically into the glass. "I never told anyone. I never trusted anyone, and besides it wasn't something I ever wanted to think about. But now I realize that I'm not going to escape it, so I'm going to have to face it. And I'm going to have to own it."

Kenneth sat back in his chair and folded his hands on his lap. "I'm listening."

Danny took a long pull of his bourbon, put down the glass, and told Kenneth the story of his life, beginning with his arrival at the Painted Desert farm and ending with his arrival in Hollywood. He left out no details.

Kenneth listened without comment and sat in silence for minutes after Danny finished his story.

"First of all, I'm very sorry for what you went through," he said finally. "It actually explains a lot."

Danny nodded. He no longer looked frightened. He looked exhausted.

"I look back at my life and I realize that what happened to me as a kid drove me to do many wrong things as an adult. I hurt a lot of people. I robbed, I cheated, and I was ruthless. I seemed to act without any moral compass or conscience. But I had nowhere to turn, no one to trust. I was alone, afraid, and trying desperately to put myself in a place where no one could ever hurt me again. "

Kenneth nodded, an expression of sad understanding on his normally impassive face.

"I'm coming clean publicly with all of this," he said. "I was robbed of my innocence. I don't want anyone to go through that. I want people to know what happened to me, and that it can happen with others. And I want kids to know that they can go straight to the police if anything like this happens to them."

Kenneth's shrewd mind processed Danny's words.

"I would keep what you did to Malchus to yourself. I wouldn't publicize the fact that you committed a crime of that magnitude," he finally advised. "But I have a strategy for you. We can tell your story in a way that ensures public forgiveness. In fact, you will probably be perceived as a hero. Because after what you've told me, I believe that you truly are."

*   *   *   *   *

Charlene Bakersfield sat at a poolside table on the patio at Hacienda Ridge. It was morning. The desert sky was clear, birds were singing, hibiscus and other tropical flowers were blooming. Rose McFarland was casually flipping through the paper. Her reading glasses were perched on her nose and she was sipping a glass of orange juice. She turned the page and nearly choked on it.

"You okay Rose?" asked cranky Ed Peals, who was sitting across the table. "You look like you might be having a heart attack. Not much a long shot at our age." Rose leaned across and showed Ed and Charlene an item that she had found in the paper. "Look who's re-surfaced."

"Spunky little bastard," Ed said after perusing the article. "He really must have pissed off the wrong person. But he got lucky."

Rose stared sadly at a fixed point on the horizon and then slowly shook her head. "My heart goes out to that kid. I really don't believe he was out to hurt anybody. He paid back all the money before he was ever arrested, which means he gave back the money because he wanted to, not because he was forced to. Sure, some of us lost sentimental things that cannot be replaced. Every single person here, even those who weren't directly robbed, had our trust violated. If somebody's teenage grandson walks in here now, half of us are afraid he might steal from us. A sense of kindness and goodwill has been lost. Nobody wins here and believe it or not I actually feel very sorry for young Ben. Or Danny, or whatever he calls himself now. He was clearly a very troubled boy."

Cranky Ed, normally cantankerous and salty by nature, nodded in agreement. "He was a likeable little con man. I know that Otto's grandson blames him for the stroke, but Otto had a bad heart condition to begin with. And quite frankly, that Simon could just as easily caused the stroke, he was such a holy terror toward Otto. I sure liked that little Ben kid a lot more. And you have to give Ben credit. The little charmer pulled off a pretty clever caper. He paid his dues in prison, and now he's paid it back again in that attack in Philadelphia. I just hope he's learned something from all this."

Rose shrugged, an expression of sadness shadowing her geriatric features. "He always seemed like he was hiding something, or covering something up. Something very dark," she commented. "I worked with kids his age all my life, and even though he hid it well, I always got the impression that he was running from something."

LA Lizzie was sitting quietly at the next table, observing. "We were all taken in by that kid," she added. "And each one of us made the individual decision to trust him. It's very sad and hurtful that our trust was betrayed, but this is the world we live in. This generation is a mess. They have no morals. No decorum. No shame. They do anything for attention, including pornography in Benny's case. But I see it with my own grandkids. Their parents over indulge them. They are given no boundaries and no limits."

Ed took a gulp of lukewarm coffee. "They call this generation the Millennials. And from what I hear on the news, they are on more medication than we are." A round of hearty laughter went around the table.

Rose let out a deep breath and felt her shoulders relax. Her heart was warm. She was lucky to be in a place where she was surrounded by a group of trusted friends. She realized that they all had each other's backs, and that was something no one could ever steal from any of them.

"How 'bout some shuffleboard, guys?" Cranky Ed suggested.

*　*　*　*　*

Kayla Asimov, in her role as the National Spokesperson for the LA Animal League, attended as many pet rescue, adoption, and fundraising events as her busy schedule permitted. The biggest of these was held in the auditorium of the Laurel Canyon Dog Park just outside of West Hollywood and Beverly Hills. Because of its location, and because celebrities are generally an animal loving lot, the yearly event had become a star studded affair.

Actors, actresses, media and sports personalities, and political VIPs approached by way of a red carpet entryway, and stopped to be photographed, videotaped, and interviewed in front of a step and repeat that featured logos from the LA Animal League and big money organizations that were supporting the event. The queen of the red carpet step and repeat was Kayla Asimov. She was accompanied by her rescued cockapoo, Dumplin', and by Hollywood's current boy toy actor du jour, TJ Colton.

Nothing makes for a better picture than a rugged, handsome man and a cuddly, adorable puppy. Flashbulbs were popping wildly as paparazzi and other members of the press stood behind a red stanchion, begging the stars to look in their directions and peppering them with questions. Kayla, hanging onto TJ's arm, moved closer to the press corps.

"Don't be taking *our* pictures," she said, holding up little Dumplin' for the multitude of cameras. "Take *his* picture. Today isn't about the people, it's about the animals. Little Dumplin' here lost his family in the fires and was found wandering the streets. If I hadn't adopted him, this lovable little mush might still be homeless. Or worse. Every year, over two and a half million dogs and cats are euthanized because the shelters are too full. There are over thirty shelters right here in LA filled with animals that need forever homes."

"How did you get involved in this organization?" A reporter shouted.

Kayla smiled and gave adoring glances at Dumpin' and TJ before answering. "I've always loved animals and I've had pets my whole life. They are one true source of unconditional love." Kayla then looked directly at the camera. "So if you want a friend and a companion who will love you no matter what, please consider adopting a rescue pet."

Kayla turned to field another question but froze mid-movement as something caught her eye. The smile melted from her beautiful face and her expression turned to one of shock and disbelief. In an instant the flashbulbs began popping more furiously and the paparazzi went crazy with a barrage of questions about this new nugget of gossip: Danny Smash and Kayla Asimov, long known as bitter enemies, were once again sharing a red carpet.

"Kayla, are you reuniting with Danny Smash?" A reporter hollered.

"Can we get a picture of you guys together?" Another yelled.

Danny was carrying a small terrier mix, which he held up for the photographers. "How 'bout taking a picture of this little guy. These dogs are the main reason we're here. This is Harry. His elderly owner was put in a nursing home, and now he needs a new home for himself. I'm here trying to get him adopted."

Maintaining a distance of several feet from the press corps, Danny held the dog's face close to his own face, and the photographers snapped away happily.

A woman stuck a microphone in his direction. "Are you an animal lover, Danny?"

"Of course," he grinned as Harry licked his cheek. "I grew up on a farm and the animals were always my favorite part. I named every single chicken, and there were dozens of them!"

Kayla finished traversing the red carpet and, without looking back, demurely exited to the adoption booth. The booth was the center of the rescue activity. It was filled with dogs, cats, and a wide range of celebrities, from social media stars to radio and television personalities to bona fide movie actors. Because of the nature of the event, and because everyone was lavishing their attention on the cuteness of the animals, there was less pretense, and more of a feeling of goodwill, than was typically on display at a large gathering of celebs in LA.

Kayla was on her knees as two pit bull puppies ran circles around her, entangling her in their leashes.

"Can I help you out here?" Danny bent down, unclipped one of the puppies from its leash, and unwrapped it around Kayla.

Kayla wiped her pants and stood up. "Um, thanks, I guess," she said. "What are you doing here?"

"Kenneth got me in," Danny answered as the puppies jumped and played at their feet and people in the crowd took pictures with their phones.

"Oh, you two again," Kayla said with a roll of her eyes. "Again, why did you come here? Don't expect me to believe you really named all of the chickens on some mythical farm."

"It's all true, Kayla." There was raw sincerity in his voice, and his tone got her complete attention. "There are a lot of things about me, and my life, and my past, that are going to be coming out very soon. There are reasons I did what I did when I first got to Hollywood. I was desperate and I was scared, and I hurt a lot of very nice, good people. I've apologized to Kenneth, and I'm here to apologize to you."

Kayla stared, wordless and slack jawed, at Danny.

"I'm gonna go find a good forever home for Harry, otherwise I'm gonna end up taking him home myself," he said, already retreating. "You're a really good person, Kayla, and I hope that some day you can find it in your heart to forgive me."

Kayla's smile was genuine. "I'll think about it."

Danny nodded.

"And I'm glad you're okay," she added thoughtfully. "After what happened in Philadelphia."

*　*　*　*　*

Phyllis Moyt confidently entered the pristine whitewashed dining room of Spago in Beverly Hills. Her friend and colleague Amy Price stood and greeted her with a hug when she reached their table.

People watchers at the iconic eatery would likely not recognize either of the women. They were, however, closely and reverentially observed by Hollywood insiders who were lunching in the restaurant. Amy was one of the highest grossing women in Hollywood, and Phyllis was well known for having built a multi-million dollar erotic empire. The two women occupied opposite poles of the entertainment industry and couldn't be more different from one another. The sight of them embracing warmly and taking lunch together caused eyebrows to raise and prompted manicured hands to reach for their cell phones.

"The deal is done," Phyllis said after both women had taken their seats. "Danny and I have sold all of our interest in Temple One Productions to NerdVision."

Amy studied her carefully. "That happened quickly."

Phyllis shrugged. "It was already in the making. Once Danny told me he wanted out, that he wanted to pursue a legitimate career, I decided to do the same thing and take you up on your offer. We sold to NerdVision. They've actually been eager to grab our slice of the cake for a while now."

"Not surprised," Amy knowingly intoned. "They control over ninety percent of internet porn content. The demand for that shit just keeps growing."

Amy caught the attention of a passing waiter with a simple glance in his direction. She ordered a bottle of Prosecco. It materialized within moments. The cork was popped and crystal flutes were proffered and filled.

"A toast to our new venture, then." The ladies exchanged triumphant glances before clinking their glasses and taking diminutive sips.

"A movie studio owned and run by women, and women only," Amy said.

"Here, here," Phyllis said. "From now on, men will no longer control this industry. We will pay actresses what they deserve. We'll give preference to women directors. We won't discriminate against actresses of a certain age. We will burn the casting couch."

Amy's next sip wasn't as dainty as the first. Her eyes misted over. "This has been a dream of mine for so long. I've had my ideas and my projects stolen by powerful male movie executives, who had no problem taking full credit for all of my work. I had to claw my way to the top at Mammoth Studios. I was turned down for promotions time and time again over men who weren't nearly as smart or as talented. I had to be twice as tenacious and work six times harder to become a studio head in this town. Still, it took decades."

Phyllis nodded knowingly. "When I first landed in LA, I couldn't even get a job at the studios, or at the any of the agencies," she commiserated. "I had to start my own business, a third rate

West Hollywood talent house where my highest earning clients were porn stars."

"But we both made it." Amy looked around the restaurant. "The industry is watching us and wondering what the hell could we possibly have as common ground," she told Phyllis. "The fact is that we are two very hard working women who clawed our way up from nothing."

Phyllis smiled wickedly. "And now we're going to open a studio that can turn the whole tide in this town. Women in this industry will no longer be subordinate to men. Women at every level of this business will have respect, equality, and opportunity."

Amy sat back in her chair. "This is the first time since I've gotten to Hollywood that I've actually felt content. Happy even."

Phyllis looked around the restaurant and took in the agents, the producers, the stars and the socialites. For the first time in her life, she felt equal to them. She finally felt that she belonged here.

Amy lifted her glass. "Here's to Hollywood. A town where anything can happen."

* * * * *

SIMON LAFLEUR sat at the dining room table in the apartment he shared with his mother. He was clean-shaven and clean cut. The beard that he had grown to disguise himself came off with a disposable razor in a truck stop just outside of Pennsylvania. The hoodie, baseball cap, sneakers and jeans that he wore on the day of the attack had been washed in the laundry room of a cheap motel. He deposited them, piece by piece, in clothing donation bins in states that stretched from Ohio to Arizona. All evidence tying him to the attack had been systematically erased.

He was not worried about having been tracked by street cameras in Philadelphia. Stupidly, most cities made the locations of these cameras known to the public. In order to avoid them, Simon had done a simple online search, determined the exact locations of the cameras, and planned a route from the bookstore to the parking garage where no electronic street surveillance would have captured him

From what he had gleaned from television reports, and there had been many, Simon, whom the media had dubbed Smoke, had vanished without a trace or a lead. Like a puff of smoke. Or a smoke bomb.

Simon was now glued to the news channel Q24, which had been teasing an exclusive interview with Danny on the subject of the attack in Philadelphia.

Simon bristled as Danny appeared on screen with the news anchor. *A few inches. Just a few inches and that handsome face would have been burned into oblivion*, Simon thought angrily. He controlled his rage. He wanted to focus on the interview.

"This has actually been classified as a terror attack," the interviewer began. "But you have been quoted as saying that this was in fact a very personal act against *you*. What leads you to believe that?"

Danny cleared his throat. His expression was one of concern and solemnity. "They are calling this a terrorist attack because of the nature of the crime. It was in a public place, there was a bomb, and it caused mass hysteria. But police have concluded that the attacker was specifically targeting me, and I can tell you that I am terrified to even think of what might have happened it I hadn't jumped when that smoke bomb went off."

"One of your fans was badly burned in the attack," the interviewer added. "How do you know it was you, and not him, that was the target?"

"When the smoke alarm went off, he stumbled in front of me and blocked me. Unfortunately for him, he stepped right into the line of fire. But the police have concluded that the acid was clearly intended to hit me."

"How does that make you feel?" The reporter asked.

"I can't even begin to think of enough words for how miserable this makes me feel," Danny answered honestly. "On so many levels. It makes me scared, angry, frustrated, sad, terrified … you name it. I can't even sleep at night, and generally I'm a pretty good sleeper. I have nightmares about that poor guy and his family. I have nightmares about smoke bombs and acid attacks."

As Simon watched the interview a smile played on his lips. Perhaps his attack had not been in vain after all.

"Aside from the nightmares, how has this experience changed you," the interviewer asked.

"I feel more vulnerable than I ever felt in my life. I would never have expected something like this to happen, but now I'm always looking over my shoulder. Appearing in public worries me, in fact it downright scares me."

"Yet you appeared in public at a pet adoption event in Canyon Dog Park just this weekend. How was that experience for you?"

"It wasn't publicized that I would be there," Danny answered. "My appearance was a surprise so that anyone who might be planning to hurt me wouldn't know that I was there. It's not a good way to live, though. Obviously I have to get over this and move on."

"And will you be able to get over it?" The reporter asked.

"Yes and no," Danny answered thoughtfully. "I'm sure my current level of heightened paranoia will subside, but I think I will always have a sense that something bad could happen at any given time, that anyone could be waiting in the wings to do harm. To some degree, I will always have my guard up moving forward. I definitely have lost a sense of security, and that's one of those things that you don't appreciate until it's gone"

"So, while your physical injury was relatively minor and is healing," the reporter summarized, "you suffered a permanent loss of your own sense of safety and security?"

"Yes," Danny nodded. "That would be accurate."

Simon pointed the remote at the TV screen and turned it off with a satisfied smile. He had done tremendous damage after all! The pretty boy would never forget what had been done to him, and would forever live in fear. Simon was filled with a sense of self-importance and power.

"Boy!" his mother exclaimed. She had just come out of the kitchen, where she was making cheeseburgers. "That's the first time I've seen a smile on your face since you got back from your camping trip."

Simon leaned back on the couch with a self-satisfied grin filling his face.

"That Ben Daniels or Danny Smash has sure had a lot of trouble in his young life," his mother observed. "Since he left here he's been to Hollywood, he's been to prison, he's been in porn movies, and now he was the target of a terror attack."

"He sure was." Simon smiled widely.

"I wonder why this happened to him," his mother pondered. "It seems like someone was getting revenge."

"He deserved what he got," Simon said without emotion. "He killed my gramps."

His mother nodded slowly, and knowingly. It was too much of a coincidence that Simon had gone AWOL at the exact time of the Philadelphia terror attack. She had never told Simon that she had received an anonymous and generous gift of cash soon after Simon's grandfather had died. While she had no proof, she strongly suspected that the money was from Ben. Or Danny; whatever he called himself now, she had already forgiven him. She said a silent prayer of thanks that he was okay, and she was grateful that Simon had somehow managed to get away with what he had done. But her heart still bled for the poor innocent boy who had been badly burned because of her son's actions. She said a silent prayer for the boy and his mother, wiped her hands on a dishrag, and returned to the kitchen to finish cooking the cheeseburgers.

* * * * *

STEVE HYTOWER turned the key and locked the door to his Center City, Philadelphia apartment for the last and final time. The two-bedroom unit had been emptied of its furniture, and his possessions had been moved to his new digs in New York City's Chelsea district. He would be right at home in the very gay friendly neighborhood, but was still overcome by bittersweet emotions as he headed from Philadelphia to follow his dreams of media stardom in the Big Apple.

His cell phone trilled. The screen indicated that Phil Simmons was calling. Phil was an assistant producer on *Lights, Camera, Action*, or *LCA*, an early prime time entertainment network news program that was widely watched throughout the US and in Canada. Steve had recently signed on as co-anchor.

"You'll be in New York tomorrow night?" Phil asked.

"Yes," Steve affirmed. "On my way right now." His voice was filled with excitement, but he felt a twinge of sadness as his Brian bounded up the stairs and into the hall.

"Okay, Phil told him. "A town car will pick you up at eight on Monday morning."

"I'll be waiting," Steve told him and ended the call.

"Well it's happening!" Brian said, slapping Steve on the back. "I hope you've got a big couch in that New York City apartment, because I will come up a lot."

Steve fondly pictured his new one bedroom apartment in a luxury building with a dream kitchen, marble bathroom, and rooftop deck with stunning views of the Hudson River, New Jersey, and part of Manhattan.

"Not only do I have a big couch, but I'll have a constant supply of hand sanitizer all ready for you," Steve told his friend.

"It won't be the same," Brian said wistfully. "But at least now I'll have two cities to hang out in."

"And so will I," Steve said. "Don't forget, I'll be back to visit all the time."

"I don't know about that," Brian answered. "Now that you'll be a big celebrity entertainment reporter, this may start to seem like too small of a pond for you."

Steve's exclusive coverage of the baffling attack on Daniel Smash had, in fact, shot him to instant celebrity status. The crime, in which the perpetrator had slipped away with nary a trace, now seemed destined for the pages of Hollywood's *Unsolved Mysteries*.

"I'm sure I'll still want to come back to Philly," he reassured Brian. "This is my comfort zone."

Brian jangled the keys. "The rental van is packed to capacity, and it's parked illegally out front. We'd better get going. I have to be back here for work on Monday morning, and *I'm* not getting picked up by a town car.

Steve smiled and followed Brian down the hall. "You might not have a town car to pick you up on Monday morning but at least you have that sexy new boyfriend waiting for you."

"I guess I was at the right place at the right time, too, huh?" Brian observed.

"You were!" Steve exclaimed as he left his Philadelphia apartment building for the very last time. "And if it weren't for me convincing you to go to the Rainbow Ball, you two would never have met."

They got into the van, which was packed to capacity.

"When you're right, you're right!" Brian agreed with a happy nod. With that, they began the two-hour drive that would take them to New York City.

*   *   *   *   *

ZAHARA SHELBY took in the sights of yet another new place. The Salt Lake City University campus light rail, originally built for the 2002 Winter Olympics, rocked gently past a beautiful 19th century cathedral. In the seat beside her sat a very relaxed Dr. David Bachman.

David pointed in the direction of the picturesque campus, which nestled into a flat valley surrounded by snowcapped mountains.

"Can you believe we're even here?" he asked Zee with a broad smile. "This book tour started out with five cities, and as of now we've been to twelve."

They had just left Santa Fe, New Mexico. Salt Lake City was their final stop in a successful lecture circuit that had grown beyond its original scope and taken them out of the major cities and into smaller ones where they never dreamt they'd find a substantive audience for a book about gay marriage. A book that had currently sold close to one million copies worldwide, and counting.

"When this whole thing started, I could never have imagined that we'd be winding it up in Salt Lake City, Utah," Zee said with a mix of wonder and enthusiasm in her voice. "Although I guess I shouldn't be surprised that there is an audience for this book almost everywhere."

David was leaning back in his seat, legs crossed easily before him. "You're right, I guess, but who would have thought that Salt Lake City had the seventh highest LGBT population in the entire country? Honestly, I thought it was just all Mormons out here."

"And you don't think Mormons can be gay?" Zee chided with him in a teasing voice.

"I don't know, they all seem so straight laced," he joked back.

"I can remember a time when you were pretty straight laced, yourself," she told him with a warm, knowing smile. "You were a pretty uptight guy before Philadelphia."

"I was also lonely and terribly unhappy with myself," he said introspectively.

"It's interesting how sometimes life sends angels to rescue us," she said.

Bachman smiled. He had been dating Ted McPherson, the writer from *DishMiss* magazine in Philadelphia, since shortly after Ted had interviewed him.

"As you know, Ted and I have been emailing back and forth with letters and pictures since I left Philly," he said. "And of course, he stayed with me when we were in New York. Trust me, he's no angel!"

Zee laughed. It was good to see David's sense of humor emerge. "I was actually talking about Darryl from the book signing in Philly. He gave you a shot of much needed self-worth, and you've essentially been changed ever since."

"I hear from Darryl all the time," Bachman nodded in agreement, and grinned. "He sends me pictures of his latest nail creations, and they always make me smile."

The light rail rocked to a stop. Zee and David stood to exit. "Whenever you put your good energy into the universe," Zee said, "like you did when you put out this book, it comes back to you in many brilliant and unexpected ways."

Dr. David Bachman, PhD, had never before believed in the non-scientific. He had never believed in "the universe" as a benevolent entity. As he stepped from the train, he believed it with all his heart.

* * * * *

DARRYL's manicured hand flew over the keys of his cash register. Business was booming at Glamour Nails, his tiny new storefront salon on a quiet side street just beyond the trendy Center City gayborhood. The nail stations were all filled. Darryl's personally trained staff was busily at work creating manicure magic. Florence, a newly trained manicurist, was proudly showing the collection of available colors to a customer. Pepe, the salon assistant, was restocking bottles of nail appliques on the shelf. The cappuccino machine was chugging away with free hot beverages for the many customers.

"Honey put some sparkles into those nails," he instructed Tony, another manicurist who was working on a pudgy Hispanic woman. "This is Glamour Nails, and we want Juanita here to walk out of this shop and dazzle the neighborhood."

He walked over to another nail station and examined the hands of a pale skinned, skinny teenage girl. "That magenta looks fabulous on your hands," he told her, eliciting a shy smile. "It goes well with your pretty blue eyes."

" Oh I didn't pick out the color," she admitted holding out her hands and admiring her nails. "The credit for that goes to Chloe, but she really nailed it ... pardon the pun."

"She *nailed* it! I love the pun!" Darryl exclaimed. "My workers are truly amazing, aren't they? I am going to get them all tee shirts that say *I nailed it*. What a fabulous idea you have given me! For that, your next manicure will be free!"

The bell on the door tingled and Jamar Lucius entered the shop.

"Hey baby, I was in the neighborhood checking out some space for a new restaurant," he told Darryl. He surveyed the busy little nail shop. "This place is looking good, looking busy," he said admiringly.

"Well I wouldn't even have this salon without your help," Darryl said. "And I work hard every day to make you proud of this business."

"I *am* proud and you've done a great job here," Jamar said sincerely. "But that's not why I stopped by. I just wanted to tell you in person that I booked the Moshulu for your birthday on the 19th."

"The Moshulu!" Darryl exclaimed, his hand flying dramatically to his chest. That fancy restaurant on the big tall sailing ship down on Delaware Avenue! I have always wanted to go there!"

Jamar smiled, showing perfect white teeth. "I know," he said. "I remember you telling me when we took that walk along the river on our third date." Jamar winked and tapped an index finger to his temple. "I remember every minute that we spend together."

Darryl tenderly took Jamar's hand. "You not only have perfect hands," he said mistily, "but you have a perfect heart. You treat me with such kindness it fills me with smiles. You make me feel so special."

"You are special," Jamar said. "You are more special than you'll ever know."

*　*　*　*　*

Darlene was watching her two children riding their big wheels in the street in front of her tiny, tidy, ranch style home. The house was yellow and cheerful looking. The front yard was neatly tended with stone ground cover and was landscaped with well-tended succulent plants.

"Logan, be careful not to cut in front of Emma," she called. "She's just learning how to ride that thing."

"Okay mom," Logan called back. "Can we go to the lake and go swimming after lunch?"

Darlene was about to answer when an expensive black SUV slowly rounded the corner. She yelled to the kids to get out of the street when, to her surprise, the vehicle came to a slow stop in front of the house. *Probably someone whose lost and needs directions to the golf resort*, she thought as she herded the kids into the driveway.

There wasn't much through traffic in this small neighborhood in Page, Arizona.

Danny watched her through the tinted window of the SUV. She wore a pair of simple cut off jeans, sandals, and a light pink blouse. Her hair was pulled back in a ponytail. He hadn't expected her to be outside. And he certainly wasn't prepared for the sight of his son. The little blond boy was a carbon copy of himself, and a lump formed in Danny's throat. He pulled open the door of the SUV and stepped out.

Darlene's expression froze as Danny walked around the vehicle and approached her. Her hands went to her hips and her posture became instantly defensive as she stared him down warily.

"Hi Darlene," he said. His approach was warm and direct.

"What are you doing here?" she demanded. The children, recognizing that they had a visitor, came up behind Darlene on their big wheels and stared with shy curiosity at Danny, whose eyes were glued on the little boy.

"Logan, take your sister and go play Legos on the porch," she instructed. "You guys need to get out of the sun for a little bit. Then I'll take you to the lake later."

That got a big smile out of Logan. The children turned and raced their big wheels the short distance to the porch. Danny's eyes followed his son. He felt a painful mixture of sadness, yearning and regret as he watched the tiny boy help his sister up the steps.

"What are you doing here?" Darlene again charged, this time through a clenched jaw. "Our last discussion was final. We had an agreement. I kept my end of the deal. Even though the payments stopped for a while when you went to prison, I still kept my end of the deal."

Danny looked her dead in the eyes. "I have a right to know my son. I have a right to be in his life."

Darlene shook her head violently. "You do not have a right to be in his life. I raised him, not you. He's a happy, well-adjusted little boy and he loves my husband, who is the only father he's ever known. Are you going to tell me now that you are going to try to step in an screw my little boy's head up?"

Danny looked away, turning to stare down the hot asphalt street. He felt as barren and desolate as the northern Arizona desert."

"We can work this out, Darlene," he said beseechingly. "He's my son."

"You were the sperm donor", she spat. "You were never his father."

"I wasn't present, but I supported him and I supported you," he answered, intently watching little Logan at play on the porch. "You've done a great job with him. I can tell that he's happy and well adjusted. But I can't just walk away from him again. I won't."

"You stole money from me," she said. "You left me pregnant and alone. You stole from a bunch of vulnerable old people and you went to prison for it. Then you got involved in pornography. Do you really think a judge is going to consider you a good role model?"

"I think a judge will consider the fact that I have always supported that boy," Danny said. "And that I am his biological father. And that I've made mistakes that I've paid for. And that I've learned and I've grown and now I want to be a good father to my child."

"If you want to be a good father you will stay. The hell. Out of his life!" Darlene fumed.

"I can't do that Darlene."

"What are your real intentions?" she demanded. "Why do you suddenly want to be in Logan's life? I know what a manipulative bastard you are, so why don't you tell me what you're angling for here?"

Danny looked down at the ground. "I am not that person any more, Darlene. I don't mean to hurt you and I don't want to hurt my son."

Darlene rolled her eyes angrily.

"I had to escape from that compound I was living on," he told her. "Horrible things were happening there and I couldn't drag you or anybody else into it."

Darlene folded her arms tightly over her chest. "So you wanted to escape, just not with me? That's supposed to make me understand this?"

"We were young, Darlene. We were kids. And besides, it was *you* who showed up and informed me about my baby. If you hadn't come demanding my support, I would never even know that Logan ever existed. But it's all water under the bridge at this point because now we have a son and we need to agree to some terms here."

"Oh, *we* have a son," she said sarcastically.

He exhaled out a frustrated breath. "Darlene, we are getting nowhere here. I will do whatever you want to make this as easy on you and your new husband and Logan and his sister. I will hire a child psychologist to teach us the best way to integrate me into the child's life. I will do whatever it takes and I will do it right."

Darlene's face was tight with rage. "Hire a fucking psychologist? Are you fucking kidding me? You will never get near my little boy! Leave now or I'm calling the police."

Danny turned away. "I'll leave now, Darlene. But I'm calling my lawyer. If necessary, I will see you in court. I'm sorry that you're choosing to do this the hard way."

As Danny walked back to the car, he stole a final glance at his son. The little boy waved goodbye.

*   *   *   *   *

The black Range Rover came to a slow halt at the gates of the Painted Desert farm. Danny had just left one traumatic encounter and braced himself to experience one that threatened to be far worse. The dust settled around the vehicle's wheels, and then there was nothing but heat and stillness. From the inside of the SUV's air-cooled cab, Danny stared at the gates. He remembered arriving here with his mother when his name was Danny Briggs. He remembered that she had held his hand when they first arrived here. It was the only memory he had of any physical affection from her. Lucille Briggs had been a vacant, distant woman who never hugged him, never tasseled his hair, never kissed him, and never offered comfort when he got a scrape on his knee. Had this made him cool and aloof? Right now he didn't have the luxury of self-analysis. He glanced around at the scrubby desert surroundings. He could not recall whether anything had changed since that summer evening seven years ago when he fled the compound, never looking back.

He swung the door open and diffidently exited the vehicle. The dry desert air, once familiar, now seemed foreign. Danny thudded the car door closed and, hands in pockets, approached the gate. He hesitated and forced himself to focus on the one thing he had been running from his entire adult life. He took a deep breath, pulled open the gate, then returned to the car and drove through. Time stood still as he negotiated along the packed dirt driveway. Cactus, scrubby plant growth, and rocky outcrops, once familiar as his childhood playground, were now a surreal landscape that seemed to pass his peripheral vision in slow motion.

He could see the cluster of buildings in the distance. The housing compound seemed much smaller to him than he remembered from his childhood, the tiny pueblos of his youth shabby and run down. His old house, Malchus' house and the largest, was in the center of the compound. A handful of people milling slowly along the packed dirt passageways in the ninety-degree heat watched with peaked interest as Danny parked the shiny new SUV next to a rusted and battered pickup truck.

Memories came flooding into his mind. The good battled with the bad. Happy childhood memories of endless summer skies, running free and shirtless in the desert with his arms in the air, climbing fences in the farm to play with the chickens and the baby goats, eating ice cream and pie and homemade cookies with Ellie in the main dining room. But then hellish memories darkly consumed his mind. The death of his mother. The abuse. The violation. The betrayal of trust. The rape of youth and innocence.

Danny grabbed his cell phone and pushed the door of the car open as long pent up rage and anguish mixed with fear and filled him with steely resolve. He proceeded to the front door of the house, oblivious to the curious stares from a small but growing crowd of onlookers. With each step that took him closer to the sun bleached and weathered front door, time seemed to slow down. He paused momentarily and tried turning the knob. The door gave, and he peered inside. The house was as still as a crypt.

"Hello," he called. "Hello ... "

When there was no answer, he pushed the door further open and stepped inside. The air was still, stale, and cloying. Malchus still lived here. His hat remained hanging on a peg on the wall just as Danny remembered it.

The ceramic tile floor was covered in a film of dirt and dust. A television was playing at low volume in the back of the house. Danny followed the short hallway past the bedroom, willing himself not to look inside and recall past horrors. He reached the tiny kitchen, which in his memory was clean and well kept. Now it was a chaotic and filthy mess of plates, dirty dishtowels, un-eaten food, overflowing garbage bags, empty frozen food containers, rotten fruits. Danny almost choked. The smell was disgusting.

Emotions left him. He felt as though he had stepped directly into a dream. He followed the sound of the television into the sunroom in the very rear of the house. He stood at the doorway. Inside, an older woman fussed in front of a tray of food that was placed on a table before an old man in a wheelchair.

Malchus.

"Can I cut your food for you?" the asked him.

Danny's eyes widened, his mouth dropped, and his heart raced.

Malchus, the man, the monster, whom Danny remembered as powerful, predatory, and tirelessly dictatorial was now a feeble, emaciated invalid hunched in a wheelchair. Danny's fear evaporated at the sight of the decrepit man with long stringy hair, gray, sagging skin, and eyes sunken into a skeletal head. Malchus' wheelchair had back and side supports to keep him in an upright position and his clothes hung limply from an atrophied body.

The terror that held his heart captive for so long was gone. He felt strength and a peace he'd never known before as he pulled his cell phone from his pocket.

The old woman was cutting Malchus' food when she looked up and saw Danny watching her. Cutlery dropped with a clatter onto the tray.

Danny stepped into the room and calmly held up his hand. He was holding a cell phone, already on video mode and recording.

"It's okay, Maya," he told the woman, entering the room and moving toward Malchus. "I won't hurt you. I mean no harm. Do you remember me? My name is Danny. I used to live in this house. Malchus here used to call me his son."

She stared at him as if she were seeing a ghost. She nodded slowly.

Danny pointed the camera at Malchus, who looked up with dull eyes that held more than a glimmer of recognition. The old woman stepped back, her fear now replaced by an expression of curiosity

Danny scratched a barely visible scar on his arm. It was all that was left from the acid burn, which had been repaired by a plastic surgeon. "I know you remember me Malchus. It's Danny. I was the innocent little boy who trusted you and looked up to you. I'm not innocent anymore, Malchus, because you stole that innocence from me a long time ago."

Malchus shrunk into the wheelchair.

"It took me years to even begin to face what you did to me, Malchus." Danny hissed the man's name with venomous hatred. "I will never forgive you for it, Malchus. But I'm ready for my close-up, now. When I was a little boy, you made sick, perverse movies of me. Now we are going to make a movie about *you*."

Danny moved the camera in so that Malchus' face filled the tiny screen. "Meet Malchus," he said. "The man who raped me repeatedly from the day I turned thirteen. The man who damaged me almost beyond repair or recognition. The sweet, innocent little boy that I used to be was completely gone by the time I was a week into my teenage years. Meet the monster who stole my innocence and almost got my soul."

Danny forced his hardened features to soften. He turned the camera back on himself. His expression was wounded and vulnerable as he addressed what he knew would become a viral audience.

"I was once a little boy named Danny Briggs. I am now known as Danny Smash. But as well known as I have publicly become, and in spite of how harshly the public has judged me, no one ever really knew me. I'm not excusing any of my actions. I take full ownership. But the public also needs to know that from when I was a young boy until I escaped from here, from this place, at the age of 16, I was sexually abused and violated, on a daily basis, by this man."

Danny turned the camera back on Malchus, whose body shook with Parkinsonian tremors as he struggled to turn his face from the camera. Spittle drooled from his mouth. The old lady stood like a statue, watching, transfixed.

"His name is Malchus and he is a child molestor," Danny continued. "A child rapist. A monster of the worst kind. When he sexually abused me, he videotaped every single assault."

Danny pulled a tiny postage stamp sized video card from his breast pocket. He pointed his camera at the tape, then fixed it back on Malchus.

"And I have the proof. Malchus here resides at a commune in northern Arizona called the Painted Desert Farm. I used to live here too. So you see, I've been in front of the camera for many years. More than anyone ever knew. As an adult, I've been in the public eye and I am known for my career, but the public has only known me for my image. And now I'm telling *my* real story. I am going to be the voice for the countless other kids who are victims of sexual abuse who don't have a voice, or who live every day in fear and terror like I did."

The old woman watched transfixed as Danny's words were live-streamed over social media. Her expression was a mixture of grief and disbelief. Danny turned the camera back on himself.

"I came to live at this place with my mother when I was a little child. She died shortly after we got here, and Malchus, who was the leader of the commune, took care of me. All I had was Malchus, and he was like a father to me until the abuse started when I was thirteen. On my thirteenth birthday, in fact. There were no other kids living on the compound. I had no one but Malchus to take care of me. I lived in his house. Before he started raping me, I loved and trusted him."

Tears ran down Danny's cheeks, and for the first time in his life it was not an act. I remember it being my birthday. Malchus came into my bedroom, and I thought he had a special surprise for me. A present."

Danny paused and reflected deeply. "That is the last memory I have of ever feeling happiness." He took a deep, emotional breath, turned the camera back on Malchus and continued. "He had a surprise for me, all right."

Danny held up the videotape. "Here's a little souvenir from the man who dared to call himself my 'father' on my 13th birthday."

Tears were spilling down the old woman's face and now she regarded Malchus with a look of pure revulsion.

"I will be presenting this tape to the local police department here in Bitter Springs Arizona, and they will be able to confirm that every word I have shared today has been true and accurate.

If the reaction of the old woman in the room, now crying hysterically, was any indication, Danny's words, now streaming live to millions of Twitter, Instagram and Facebook followers, were having the intended effect. He shut off the camera and regarded Malchus directly.

"I know you can hear me. I know you understand. I will never forgive you for what you did to me. You are toxic. You touched me and you made me toxic. But I will move on. I will survive. I will heal. You, *Malchus*, will sit and rot in that wheelchair and everyone will know what a monster you are. You've gotten exactly what you deserve."

With that, Danny turned and left the house. He wiped the tears from his face. Finally he was able to mourn the loss of his mother, his innocence, his childhood, and his ability to trust. He felt nothing but peace. As he walked to his car, the sound that could be heard above the gravel crunching under his boot heels was his phone blowing up. He watched the screen intently, letting all calls go to voicemail except for one. It was Kenneth Shapiro.

"That was an incredibly brave thing you did. I'm proud of you," Kenneth said in a choked up voice. "Now get back to Hollywood. It's time for you to come home."

ABOUT THE AUTHORS

Gregory Mantore

Greg has master's degrees in Education and Counseling. He has worked extensively with adolescents for over thirty years as a teacher and a school counselor. In his free time, he likes to travel and enjoys living a gluten free lifestyle. When he is not cooking, cleaning or keeping tabs on the latest Celiac disease information, he is watching horror movies and enjoying time with his family and friends. Greg lives with his partner in New Jersey. This is his first novel.

Tony Sawicki

Tony Sawicki is a former television correspondent who has extensively reported on the entertainment industry and conducted interviews with a wide range of film, television, music and theatre luminaries. He produced, directed and wrote two educational television series, *Under the Pink Carpet* and *Urban Animals*, which were broadcast on PBS affiliated TV stations across the United States. He currently plays the lead character of Lucius Zajack in the television series *City and the Beast*, a screwball comedy that he also produces and directs.

Sawicki was awarded the Harry Wieder Passion Fruit Award for outstanding service to the artistic community in New York, and was also awarded by the New York Pet Fashion show for his contributions to animal education. His work has been praised in Philadelphia City Paper, Philadelphia Daily News, Out in New Jersey, Hamptons Magazine, Get Out Magazine, and the North Bergenite. He holds a master's degree from Rutgers University and a Bachelor of Science from Fairleigh Dickinson University in New Jersey.

He previously resided in Philadelphia and now lives just outside New York City. This is his first novel.